PHANTOM'S
BLADE

BOOKS BY JAKE TYSON

JAKE TYSON

THE VINDICATORS BOOK FOUR

PHANTOM'S BLADE

THE SICARAN WAR

Ambassador International
GREENVILLE, SOUTH CAROLINA & BELFAST, NORTHERN IRELAND

www.ambassador-international.com

Phantom's Blade

Hardcover ISBN: 978-1-64960-646-4
Paperback ISBN: 978-1-64960-507-8
eISBN: 978-1-64960-550-4

Cover design by Hannah Linder Designs
Interior Typesetting by Dentelle Design
Edited by Maggie Platt

AMBASSADOR INTERNATIONAL
Emerald House
411 University Ridge, Suite B14
Greenville, SC 29601
United States
www.ambassador-international.com

AMBASSADOR BOOKS
The Mount
2 Woodstock Link
Belfast, BT6 8DD
Northern Ireland, United Kingdom
www.ambassadormedia.co.uk

The colophon is a trademark of Ambassador, a Christian publishing company.

For Emma Darling
I hope everything I do makes you proud that I'm your dad.

ACKNOWLEDGMENTS

Jessica, my wife, for always being there for me, listening to me, encouraging me, and being one of my first readers and my number one fan forever. Thank you for falling in love with my characters as much as I have and for wanting the world to love them, too. And Emma, my baby girl, because her mere existence drives me to work harder.

My family—Dad, Mom, Zac, Hunter, and MaKayla—as well as my in-laws and my extended family, for always being supportive of my desire to write, encouraging me to do so, giving me feedback on my writing, letting me bounce ideas off them, asking questions about the writing process, and upselling *The Vindicators* series to anyone who'll listen!

All the members of the Realm Makers Consortium who helped me figure out things like character names, superpowers, motivation, costume design, and on and on. Specifically, to Daniel Slusser for "Ravener," the best villain name to possibly fit this character.

Ambassador International, for believing in the world of *The Vindicators* I'm creating and for continuing to publish my stories! Thanks also to the editors and cover designers who have helped make these books the best they can be.

Thank you to all the readers of the first three *Vindicators* books. I'm so glad that there are readers enjoying this world I've crafted. Here's to many more (books *and* readers)!

Most importantly, I couldn't have done this without the desire and the ability to write given to me by my Heavenly Father, and I couldn't have written anything honoring Him if He had not saved me through Christ. Thank you, God, for leading me to this opportunity and for giving me the ideas for Gideon and his friends!

TEAM ROSTERS

The Vindicators:

Carter Jonson/The Crusader—Son of Wyatt Jonson, the first Crusader, nineteen-year-old Carter has taken up his father's mantle and his mission to protect the Brooks.

Gideon Turner/The Seraph (retired)—The hero who started it all, Gideon Turner became the Seraph after his captivity in Venezuela, where Dr. Jeremiah Ashcroft gave him light powers. In the aftermath of Ashcroft's defeat, Gideon lost his powers and retired as the Seraph.

Jolie Turner (honorary)—Jolie is Gideon's wife and a detective for Sojourn P.D. at the twelfth precinct in the Brooks.

Raina Watts (honorary)—Carter's girlfriend, Raina serves as Carter's backup/tech support. She uses her uncle's police monitor to report crimes to the Crusader.

Silas Rockwell (honorary)—A good friend of Carter's, Silas provides intel from the streets.

The Thieves:

Joanie Sellers—A tech whiz extraordinaire, Joanie uses her hacking skills to assist in breaking into the thieves' targets.

Ned Burns—He is one of the members of Ty Vickers' thieving team.

Richie Stanton—He is one of the members of Ty Vickers' thieving team.

Ty Vickers/Lurk—A mysterious thief from Japan, Ty has the power to phase his body through any material.

Others:

Katrina Monahan/Lancet—Monahan is a deadly assassin who was responsible for the death of Wyatt Jonson, the first Crusader.

Maddox Odell—One of Dean Sterling's best friends, Maddox is one half of the duo that helps the Vindicators with any tech issues they run into.

Ravener—He is a deadly swordsman haunting the Brooks.

CHAPTER 1

The coarse brick wall pressed against the skintight black fabric of Ty Vickers' jacket. Shifting to his right or left caused the rough material to scratch against his damp skin. A deep breath in, another one out, and his trembling body stilled. He had the discipline necessary to remain unmoving as long as necessary, but sweat beaded on his upper lip as he waited for the security camera above him to blink off.

Come on, Joanie; don't let me down. He had made it too far to back off. Getting inside Sojourn City Bank was a feat most considered impossible. If Joanie couldn't get that camera off in five seconds, Ty would be forced to backtrack. Otherwise, he risked the guard on patrol running right into him.

If only I could turn invisible . . .

Ty had been blessed with an extraordinary gift after a rampaging monster nearly killed him several months before. He wasn't sure how it had happened, and he didn't really care. All he knew was that he had gone to sleep that night in his bed and awakened on the floor, the tip of his nose centimeters under the bed frame. His panic had been so great that he somehow fell through the floor and into his basement. Thankfully, the mysterious phenomenon stopped before Ty continued downward into the foundation.

If anyone from Ty's past knew how he used his gift, they would be ashamed of him. There was so much good he could do with the ability to phase through solid matter, but Ty's life was hard. He didn't have the luxury of being a hero. He needed cash—and his newfound power gave him a foolproof way to get it.

The camera stopped swiveling. Ty tensed, ready to spring into action.

"You're clear," Joanie said.

Ty rushed through the crisscrossing hallway and ducked behind a stone pillar on the other side. He peered around the edge, straining to see in the dim, golden light. There was no sign of the guard. He pressed himself against the pillar and waited. A few moments later, footsteps clacked on the stone floor. Ty's fingers drifted to his belt, past his array of throwing knives and to his collapsible baton. He wasn't in this game to hurt anyone, so the knives were a last resort. He would rather incapacitate a guard with a quick strike from his baton than wound or kill someone.

The footsteps receded. Ty exhaled. The vault sat on the other side of a huge antechamber. The enormous round door was impossible to open, with anything short of heavy explosives. Lucky for Ty and his gang, he didn't need to open it. He stepped toward the door and extended his right hand. He felt air pass through his fingers as his flesh became intangible. He had never quite adjusted to that sensation. He brushed the door with his fingertips. They phased through.

"I'm going in."

"Hurry," Joanie replied. "You've got approximately thirty seconds before the cameras boot up again. Shutting them down a second time will definitely tip off the guards."

Ty pushed the rest of his body through the vault door. He wondered what would happen if he lost concentration and stopped phasing in the middle of a solid object. He hoped he never found out. It was sure to be . . . unpleasant.

He grabbed the sack looped through his belt, opened it, and shoveled stacks of cash inside. His chest tightened as he did. *This is someone's hard-earned money, you selfish freeloader.*

Ty squashed the pang of guilt and continued to fill the sack. It wasn't like he was doing this for purely selfish reasons. He had to survive, and he had tried to do it the right way. No one wanted to keep him around. His home address and his family name branded him as untrustworthy.

"Ten seconds," Joanie hissed. "Get moving!"

Ty knotted the bag and hoisted it over his shoulder. He wished he wasn't the only one of his friends with powers. He, Joanie Sellers, and their friends—Ned Burns and Richie Stanton—had been pulling small jobs together for nearly a year; but since he had developed his powers, Ty did most of the work. Joanie hacked the cameras and monitored him, but Ned and Richie practically sat on their hands and waited to profit from Ty's actions.

He shoved his irritation aside, phased back through the vault door, and rushed across the hallway.

"Ty, wait—" Joanie started.

"Hey, you!"

Ty spun. The guard had returned. The aging man reached for the sidearm in his belt. Instinct and training urged Ty to pull one of his knives, but he couldn't bring himself to risk killing the guard. He yanked his collapsible baton free and hurled it at him. The baton spiraled through the air and struck the man's wrist. The guard recoiled, dropping his pistol to the floor. Ty rushed toward the nearest window and phased through.

He grunted as his knees smacked into the wet grass, dampening his black jeans. Raindrops pattered against his black hood and ski mask. He pushed off with his right foot, no doubt leaving a print in the mud; but he didn't have time to worry about that. Muffled by the window, an alarm sounded inside the bank. Ty ran through the small yard outside the bank, phased through the iron fence around it, and hopped into the back of the waiting van.

"You did it!" Ned whooped. "You'd think they'd start making these places amp-proof or something."

"Drive, you idiot." Ty yanked off his mask. "A little warning about the guard would have been nice, *Motherboard*."

Joanie rolled her eyes. "If you moved a little slower, you might have heard me before it was too late."

"You were the one who was on me about getting out of there in time. Anyway, it doesn't matter. I made it out, and the guard didn't see my face. With any luck, we'll be well away from the bank by the time the police arrive. You blacked out the traffic cams, right?"

Joanie nodded. "They shouldn't be able to spot the van."

"Good job."

Provided Ty had not left behind any trace evidence, they had escaped scot-free. *I hope I didn't leave fingerprints on the baton.* He was wearing gloves; but if he had touched the baton handle earlier that day and forgotten to wipe it clean, the police would have a piece of evidence that would lead right to him.

Ned and Richie—the former pale and verging on the edge of overweight, the latter dark-skinned and athletic—joked and bounced in the front seats.

Ty gritted his teeth and ignored them, but it took all the restraint he had to keep from yelling, *You didn't do anything, you idiots, so why do you deserve a cut of the profits?* He had to find some way for the two of them to become useful again—either that or cut them out of the loop entirely. They needed cash, too, albeit not as desperately as he did. They had fallen into thievery together to eke out a better living. He did not want to take that from them. Not yet.

"Will you two shut up?" he growled.

Richie blinked. "Sorry, man. What's got you?"

Ty inhaled slowly and counted to five. They were greedier than he was, always focused on the next big score, every moment of the day spent daydreaming about scoring big off their escapades—off Ty's powers. They wanted to be filthy rich. He wanted to get by.

"Nothing," Ty said. "The guard shook me up. That's closer than we've come in a long time."

"Well, you're good, man. He didn't get you." Richie grinned. "We did it again."

"Hey, Joanie," Ned called, "why don't you make yourself useful and start counting that loot, huh?"

Ty glanced at Joanie. She scowled at the back of Ned's seat and clenched and unclenched her fists. Joanie—her skin a few shades lighter than Richie's, hair perpetually woven into complex dreadlocks—was the youngest member of their group. The other two treated her like hired help. But not Ty. Joanie was like a little sister to him. He kept her from making stupid mistakes, like she did for him; and he protected her from the likes of Ned, Richie, and worse personalities in the Brooks. That didn't make her a slouch. Joanie had grown up in Sojourn City's slums. She knew how to survive.

Ty put a hand on her shoulder. Joanie's expression softened, but she made no move to pick up the bag of cash. Ty was perfectly fine with that. Joanie didn't owe them anything—her computer expertise was more than enough. If Ned and Richie couldn't see that, they were dumber than Ty thought.

Ned patted the steering wheel. "We did it, lady and gentlemen. No cops, no vigilantes—we're home free."

Ty rested his head against the van's inside wall and held his tongue. They'd made it this time. How long would it be until their lucky streak ran out? How long before he had to choose between a score and someone's life? If Ned or Richie had been inside that bank tonight, he was sure they would've killed the guard. That wasn't him. He had seen enough death in his lifetime.

CHAPTER 2

When the Romanian crime lord Luca Serban had reigned supreme in the Brooks, the warehouse district had been one of the hottest centers of his operation. Dozens of the huge abandoned or illegally procured buildings had served as staging points for his criminal operations or storehouses for his armaments. Since his defeat, some of those warehouses had returned to their proper owners, while others had been condemned and demolished. The latter blocks of property had been repurposed for affordable housing that were under construction in an effort to further clean up the Brooks. Still other warehouses, however, had fallen into the hands of Sojourn City's surviving criminal elements.

The warehouse on the corner of Washington and DeVry was filled to the brim with members of the Red Dogs gang, all of them packing serious heat. Since Detective Jolie Anderson had killed Serban at the end of the previous year, the Red Dogs had rekindled their turf war with the Tyrants, the other prominent gang in the Brooks. Dozens of people had been injured in the crossfire. From the looks of things in the warehouse, the Red Dogs were strapping up for something big. That would not happen if the Crusader had anything to say about it.

Clad in a red-and-black Kevlar-lined suit with a gray cross emblazoned on the chest, armed with a *jo* staff and an array of technological devices, the vigilante knelt in the rafters above the gang. He had been keeping an eye on the Red Dogs for weeks. This was the first time he had been able to follow one of them to an arms cache. He watched as they loaded their weapons into SUVs.

The Crusader reached into his utility belt and withdrew a Crybaby—a sonic grenade with the *oomph* to make ears bleed. Detonating one of them would provide him plenty of time to get down into the middle of the Red Dogs and engage them hand-to-hand before they could open fire on him. All he needed was the right opportunity.

A pair of Dogs hoisted a crate of arms into the back of one of the SUVs and slammed the door shut. They walked back toward the middle of the room, closer to the Crusader. He had counted ten of the gangsters when he entered the warehouse, all armed with fully-automatic rifles. Five of them were below him, and with the two approaching, there were seven of them close enough for him to take out quickly. The other three could present more of a problem. One was in the driver's seat of the leftmost SUV. The other two patrolled the perimeter of the warehouse.

The Crusader couldn't wait any longer. If they left the warehouse with those weapons, it could mean a bloodbath on the streets. Activating the sound-dampening buds pressed into his ears, he armed the Crybaby and dropped it in the midst of the seven gangsters below. The metallic sphere hit the ground with a *thunk* and bounced once. The gangsters looked down at it and then up toward its source.

The Crybaby went off before their guns came up. As the gangsters cried out and clutched at their ears, the Crusader dropped from the rafters, landing amid the gangsters, and lashed out with his staff. The strike caught the closest man in the gut. The Crusader twirled and arced the staff toward the next man, striking him across the cheek. One of the Red Dogs had the presence of mind to stomp on the Crybaby, but the Crusader dropped another of his comrades.

Three down. Seven to go.

With the screaming Crybaby silenced, the gangsters reoriented themselves. The Crusader looped his arms around the closest man's dominant hand. He leveraged him forward, hurtling the gangster into a front flip that splayed him out on his back. The Crusader dropped his knee into the man's chest and rolled forward as two of the other Red Dogs opened fire on him. He came up in a crouch between them and thrust his staff out horizontally. The short polearm caught both men in the knees. The Crusader activated the electrified ends of his staff and jabbed each of them in the gut, zapping them into unconsciousness.

Four to go.

The last of the men in the cluster charged, swinging the butt of his rifle like a bludgeon. The Crusader rolled under the blow, came up behind the Dog, and kicked him in the back. The gangster stumbled and sprayed a wild sheet of gunfire in the Crusader's direction. The vigilante threw himself behind a steel support column. The automatic gunfire pinged furiously off the metal.

Think fast. The SUV driver would soon join the shooter, and the other two Red Dogs could be anywhere in the warehouse. If they came around, they could catch him in a crossfire. He looked around. *I need to get out of this situation fast.* There was a stack of crates to his left. If he could get to them, he wouldn't be pinned down, at least.

He threw himself out from behind the column in a forward roll, came up in a crouch, and pushed off with his back foot. It took a moment for the shooter to swivel and track the Crusader. By then, the

Crusader was behind the crates. A few bullets grazed the edge of the crate near his shoulder. He took a breath.

The crates were stacked three high, and the topmost would put him almost directly over the shooter. The Crusader grabbed the lip of the first crate and hoisted himself up, aware that if the shooter was prepared for his tactic, cresting the top of the stack would bring the Crusader into his line of fire. But he didn't have time to freeze and think through every possibility. He had to move. He came up on top of the third crate and didn't pause to get his bearings. He leaped off, coming down at the gunman.

The Red Dog didn't swivel toward the Crusader until it was too late. The vigilante came down on top of him and drove his fist into the Dog's face, knocking him flat. But the SUV driver had joined the fight, and the Crusader sprinted for cover as the driver opened fire with a pistol. One of the shots grazed the Crusader's shoulder but did not puncture his armored uniform. He changed the angle of his run and came straight at the driver. He hurled his staff like a spear. The shooter ducked back behind the SUV, giving the Crusader enough time to round the vehicle, grab the man's head, and slam it into the side of the car. The gangster struggled; and the Crusader repeated the move, slamming the man's head into the black vehicle again. This time, the driver crumpled.

Only the two patrollers remained. The Crusader picked up his staff. The remaining Red Dogs opened fire, and the Crusader ducked behind the SUV. The two gangsters stood amidst their unconscious comrades, too far for the Crusader to reach while avoiding both their fields of fire. He clenched his jaw. This had started off well enough. If he did not play his next move right, it might not end so well.

"Come out, little vigilante," one of the Dogs said.

"Playtime's over," the other growled.

The Crusader split his staff into two smaller truncheons. They were too far away for him to throw an adhesive bead or shock bead with any accuracy. If he could draw them in, get them to engage him closer, he might be able to take them out. As long as they stayed where they were, he was stuck.

Footsteps clacked on the warehouse's concrete floor. The Crusader tensed, ready to move as soon as they got close enough.

"Sojourn P.D.!" a hard voice yelled. "Freeze!"

Gunfire erupted again—and stopped seconds later. Cautiously, the Crusader peeked his head around the corner of the SUV. Both gunmen lay sprawled on the ground, and a squad of police officers approached. The Crusader recognized the man leading them, Officer Paul Jordan. Dark-skinned, gray-haired Paul was one of the more pro-vigilante officers on the force, although he was nearing retirement. The policeman glanced up at the Crusader and nodded.

"Thanks for the assist." The Crusader sheathed his truncheons and ran the back of his hand along his forehead. "You probably saved my butt."

"Don't sweat it." Jordan tilted his head toward the door. "Get out of here. We can handle bagging and tagging these guys."

The Crusader rushed out the warehouse door and fired his grappling hook at a roof across the street. Reeling the line in, he soared toward the rooftop and vanished into the night.

CHAPTER 3

Detective Jolie Turner, née Anderson, rubbed the sleep from her eyes as she ducked under the crime scene tape. A dozen officers and CSIs milled about Sojourn City Bank, along with a throng of reporters crowded around outside the yellow tape. The media representatives snapped pictures and shouted questions at Jolie and the other cops. She ignored them and hurried up the stone steps to the bank.

An ordinary bank robbery wouldn't rate this level of response, but this was no ordinary bank. It was the biggest bank in the city, and it was right in the middle of the government district. While the neighborhood was hardly crime-free, it was safer than the Brooks and better patrolled. It should have been all but impossible for anyone to rob SCB and get away with it—which was why her superiors had dragged Jolie out of bed earlier than usual and assigned her to the case.

It was an honor to be the detective chosen for it, but she would have preferred if they chose her after she'd hit the snooze button a few times. She would much rather be in bed, cuddling with her husband, Gideon.

Officer Rosita Rojas gestured her over. "Detective."

Jolie looked around the lobby. "What do we have?"

"Looks like it was an amp." Rojas pointed at a guard sitting nearby. "He was on duty last night when the robbery took place. He said the thief knocked his gun out of his hand and jumped through the window

. . . while the window was closed. The thief passed through unharmed, leaving the window completely untouched."

"Great. I'll talk to him."

Superhuman sightings were rare in Sojourn City but not unheard of. Last year, a mad scientist named Jeremiah Ashcroft had tried to unleash a superhuman serum. He had failed on a worldwide scale, thanks to the efforts of Gideon and his team of superheroes, but reports of new superhumans were still trickling in from Dallas, Chicago, Juncture City, Washington, D.C., and other cities. The media had taken to calling them amplified individuals—or amps, for short.

This was the first new amp Jolie had heard of in Sojourn City. Somehow, she doubted they would be the last.

Maybe Gideon could shed some light on the case. Jolie crinkled her nose at the thought, grateful she hadn't expressed the sentiment aloud. Her husband's former superpower was light projection, but he had lost that ability about five months before. She would have to remember to phrase the request differently if she actually asked for his help.

"Is there any footage of the break-in?" she asked.

Rojas shook her head. "Looks like the security cameras were hacked."

"How about traffic cams?"

"Same deal. These guys are professionals."

"Okay, thanks."

She stepped past Rojas and toward the guard who had witnessed the crime. He was in his mid-fifties, with a bushy gray mustache and a strong brow. He massaged one hand as if it were aching.

"Excuse me, sir?" she said.

The guard stood from a soft, leather chair. "Hudson, ma'am."

"Mr. Hudson." Jolie shook his hand. "I'm Detective Turner. Is there anything you can tell me about what you saw last night? Any specific details you might have left out of your initial report?"

"I don't think so, ma'am." Hudson scratched his chin. "I was making my rounds when this guy, dressed all in black—down to a ski mask— ran out of the vault antechamber carrying a full sack. I shouted at him and reached for my gun, and he hurled a baton at me. Knocked the gun right out of my hand."

"How far away would you say he was?"

"Probably a couple dozen feet, at least. It was some throw. I've never seen anything like it."

If the guard was not exaggerating, a throw like that was impressive. Batons were not weighted for long-distance throws. Tossing one for accuracy at any distance was a feat worth noting. Jolie wondered if that was part of the thief's power set or if his targeting skills were naturally honed. If it was the latter, she might have something to work with. People with skills like that usually had a reputation.

"What happened next?"

"He ran for the window, and he . . . jumped through. The window didn't shatter or move at all. It was like he passed through without touching it. After I recovered from my shock, I sounded the alarm. But that's all I can tell you."

"All right. Thank you, Mr. Hudson."

"My pleasure, ma'am." As Jolie stepped away, Hudson snapped his fingers. "Wait. There was one more thing. I think I saw some knives on the guy's belt. Don't know why he threw the baton and not a knife." Hudson shrugged. "Glad he didn't. Thought you might like to know."

"Thank you."

Jolie was puzzled at the last bit of information. The reported skill of the thief, combined with the knives he carried, alluded to the mysterious attacker's training. With the accuracy he had thrown the baton, he would have been deadly with the knives. He could have killed Hudson on the spot. Instead, he had chosen to use a nonlethal means of escape. That could mean that the perp was not a career criminal. More likely, he was someone down on his luck who had decided to use his powers to get the income he felt he could not receive anywhere else. In Jolie's experience, desperate people who were willing to go as far as robbing banks often weren't prepared to take lives while doing it, unlike seasoned gangsters or repeat offenders. On the other hand, an average guy who had lost his job and needed quick cash usually did not have expert knife-throwing skills.

Figuring all that out would come later. She had to question the bank manager about how much was taken, see if the CSIs could get DNA or prints off the baton, and search the perimeter for evidence. She needed a coffee. It was going to be a long day.

CHAPTER 4

After a year of working security, Carter Jonson still wasn't used to wearing a gun on his belt. For all the time he had operated as the Crusader, the guys with guns had usually been the bad guys. Carter himself had stuck with his *jo* staff and tech, such as his grappling hook, the Crybabies, adhesive beads, and concussion gauntlets. But a gun? That had never been Carter's style because it hadn't been his dad's style—or Gideon's.

But this was for a legit job, and his boss required him to carry the sidearm. So he did. He rested his right hand on the butt of the Glock and looked around the Sterling Enterprises lobby. His days usually passed in boredom. Ever since Luca Serban had taken this very lobby hostage five months ago, security had been much tighter. As a result, they never saw anything interesting. It was better than working at a grocery store, but Carter wasn't getting any thrills from sitting behind a desk and checking people in, watching security cameras, and patrolling the halls of the upper levels.

Maybe that was for the best. Carter spent his nights running around the Brooks as the Crusader. If both his day job and his vigilante activities were equally dangerous, he was sure his mother would throw a fit. Carter was twenty years old, but she had lost her husband. She wouldn't be able to handle losing him, too. Ever since Jolie had killed Serban, crime had gone down—way down. The city's criminals were afraid, but hard cases like the Red Dogs and the Tyrants kept him on his toes. The previous night's encounter had been too close a call. If not for Officer Jordan . . .

The lobby doors parted, and Alistair Wheaton, the company's new CFO, sauntered through. Carter doubted he would ever get used to seeing Wheaton come in instead of Dean Sterling, the CEO and one of Carter's former allies on the Vindicators. Dean had moved to Washington, D.C., not long after Serban's incursion. He was brokering a deal between Sterling Enterprises and the U.S. government; and over the past few months, Dean had started a life there. It didn't seem like he would be returning soon.

"Mr. Jonson." Wheaton raised his chin in greeting. "Good morning."

"Morning, sir."

Carter held out a bin for Wheaton's watch, keys, and phone. The CFO placed the items inside with a sniff and an eye roll. Wheaton stepped through the x-ray machine and extended a hand for his belongings. Carter handed him the bin. It wasn't that Wheaton was a total blockhead, but . . . well, he really was. He acted like he was the most important person in the world no matter where he went. It got on Carter's nerves. His gelled-back black hair and ax-nosed, clean-shaven face didn't help much.

The CFO nodded and gave Carter a tight-lipped smile, adjusted his watch, and strutted toward the elevator. Carter tried not to glare at the man's back. He supposed if he were the CFO of a Fortune 500 company, he would have a hard time not getting a big head, too.

Carter's phone buzzed. He stepped away from his station, slipping his phone from the pocket of his black trousers. One of the other guards stepped in to take his place. Carter smiled at the caller ID. It was Raina, his girlfriend. He answered the phone.

"Hello?"

"Hey, handsome. Anything exciting going on in the big world of corporate security?"

"Is there ever?"

"Nope. That's why I knew it was okay to call." Raina laughed. "You'll probably hear about it soon enough, anyway, but I was listening in on my uncle's police scanner. It sounds like there's a new amp in the city."

"What?"

"Sojourn City Bank got hit last night. The vault wasn't opened, but there was still cash missing. One of the guards reported seeing a man phase through a window."

Not any ordinary superhuman—a supervillain. What a time for all of Carter's friends to be away. The Vindicators could have handled one amplified criminal as a team. When Carter had narrowed the focus of his vigilante activities to local crime, he had not expected to deal with amps anymore.

"Did you get any other information?" Carter asked.

"Nope. The security footage was wiped, so all the police have to go on is the guard's description—which isn't much, from what I can tell."

"Well, I'm sure they'll strike again. Probably soon. If they do, I'll be out there waiting for them this time."

"I knew you would be."

Carter hadn't waited long to tell Raina that he was the Crusader. A secret like that would only hurt a relationship. The two had been friends and coworkers at an old grocery store in the Brooks. Carter's friend Patrick had suggested they turn that friendship into something more, and Carter was glad he had listened to the redheaded speedster. She was one of the best things that had ever happened to him. Raina was intelligent, poetic, and beautiful. The fact that her uncle was a retired cop and still had a police scanner was only a bonus.

"I've got to get back to work, but thanks for letting me know. I'll check in with you after I get off."

Carter retook his position from the other guard. One thing was for sure. If Carter was going to deal with a superhuman, he needed all the tech he could get his hands on to level the playing field. He had never taken an amp down by himself before. He hoped he was up to the challenge.

CHAPTER 5

Hands tucked in his pockets, Carter stepped out the back door and into the alley behind Sterling Enterprises. It was the same alley where he had chased Luca Serban five months ago. He had sprinted after the criminal, unarmed but determined not to let the crime lord get away again, knowing fully well that Serban had a gun and could easily kill him. It had been a stupid decision. Carter should, by all accounts, be dead; but he had survived. And Serban had been killed. It was hard to believe that someone who'd had such a profound effect on Carter's life and the lives of almost everyone he knew was gone for good. If not for Serban, Carter's dad would probably be alive.

Carter wound his way toward the parking garage across the street, zipping up his leather jacket and pulling up the hood to shield him from the icy, late-winter rain. A few droplets slipped past and stung Carter's face with their chill. If he could change anything about Sojourn City—besides the crime, of course—it would be the weather. Crime-fighting was a lot less exciting when he had to stand on rooftops in below-freezing temperatures for hours.

If the superhuman thief was going to strike again, Carter had to be out there to stop him. So, elements or not, even on a chilly February night, Carter would go out and do his job. But first, he needed to go home and check on his mother and siblings. His mom, Joanna, insisted that she was more than capable of handling things on her own, but she shouldn't have to. Carter set aside much of his paychecks to provide for his mom, Ellis, and Rhonda.

Carter was at the point in his life when he could strike out on his own. He could get an apartment, experience adult life, maybe think about college. But he was the man of his household. He had to be responsible for them first. He had to—for his father.

Carter palmed his key fob and unlocked his car, a black Ford Focus. Dean had offered to buy him whatever car he wanted. Billionaires could do that kind of thing. At first, Carter had fantasized about a Camaro or a Mustang or a Corvette, but he didn't need to draw attention to his family. Someone of their social status owning a car like that was sure to stand out. He had gone for a more practical choice instead, though it had been a painful decision. Impressed with Carter's maturity, Dean had also paid for a motorcycle that the Crusader could use to patrol the streets.

Carter climbed into the Focus, started the car, and pulled out of the parking garage. Rain pattered against his windshield. Carter blinked against the sleepiness that threatened to wrap around him like a warm blanket. The cold, dreary weather always made him want a nap, but today wasn't the day for that. He made a mental note to stop for coffee on the way home. He would need it.

The car's automatic headlights flashed on. Carter pulled onto the bridge and drove away from the Platform. In the distance, the lights of the Sterling Maglev zipped across the lake toward the city. The winter night, combined with the overcast sky, tinged the air with an ominous warning. Carter hoped it was simply foreboding weather and not a sign of things to come. He had never been a superstitious person, but some part of his mind warned him that everything was not as it should be.

* * *

Jolie would have killed for the slightest breakthrough in the bank case. Unfortunately, a full day of investigation had led nowhere. She huffed in frustration and pushed her apartment door open, stuffing her keys back into her jacket pocket as she did. The heavenly aroma and tempting sizzle of bacon on the grill wafted across the apartment to greet her. Her stomach rumbled. Jolie pressed her hand against it and shut the door behind her.

Gideon stood in the small kitchen. Clad in a light gray shirt, dark blue jeans, and brown boots, he darted back and forth between several different pans. Jolie took off her jacket, placed it on the back of their recliner, and stepped into the kitchen. Gideon looked up and grinned at her from behind the short scruff of his beard.

"Hey, you." He wrapped an arm around her shoulder and kissed her. "How was your day?"

Jolie smiled and kissed him back. "Better now."

"That bad, huh?" Gideon stepped away from her to check on the food. "Well, breakfast for dinner always cheers you up. I mostly made it because of the weather, but I had a feeling you might need this."

"And without superpowers." Jolie pretend-gasped. "How do you do it?"

Gideon winked. "Husbandly intuition."

"Is that a thing?" Jolie nuzzled against him and kissed the corner of his jaw. "I'm not sure that's a thing."

"It's definitely a thing." Gideon kissed the top of her head. They stood there for a moment, pressed against each other until he stepped back and gestured to the dining table. "Sit down and relax. Dinner's almost ready. Tell me all about what's bothering you."

Four months into their marriage, they were still in the honeymoon phase. Jolie shook her head as she dropped into one of the wooden chairs around their table. He had set silverware and a glass out for her. She hoped he still did things like this when they had been married for a year, or ten, or twenty-five. Her stomach let out a ferocious growl, and she giggled. Hopefully, he hadn't heard that over the popping and sizzling of the bacon.

"There was a robbery at Sojourn City Bank," Jolie said. "Trouble is, whoever did it had a skilled hacker watching their back. There's no footage on the security cameras or any of the traffic cams in the area. But the real kicker is that the thief was amplified. The guard said he phased through a window, and the vault was still closed and locked. So, it's a safe bet that he phased into and out of the vault, too."

Gideon looked up at her. "We had to figure amp criminals would show up eventually. We stopped that rampaging nephiloid pretty quickly, but we always knew there was a possibility that it bit someone."

Jolie shuddered at the memory. She had not been present when the gray-furred beast tore through Lakeside, but she had seen the footage from their armor cams. It was terrifying. The monster, an abominable creation of Jeremiah Ashcroft, had venomous fangs that passed on Nephilim DNA to anyone it bit, imbuing them with superpowers. The Vindicators' battle with the beast had only lasted a few minutes, but Gideon was right. There was a possibility that early in its escape, the nephiloid had transformed at least one victim.

"I wish it had bitten someone who used their powers for good."

"Me, too." Gideon shoveled eggs and bacon onto a plate. "Phasing, huh? We haven't seen that power yet. Wonder if he's got anything else."

"It could be unrelated, but he threw a baton at the guard with crazy accuracy. That could've been natural skill and training."

If he was former military or some kind of ninja, she might need Gideon's help. He was the best fighter she knew. Without his powers, Gideon was still a force to be reckoned with, but the last thing she wanted was to drag him back into the vigilante life.

Gideon set the plate down in front of her. "Could be. I take it there hasn't been much progress in tracking down the thief—or thieves?"

"No progress at all. None of my informants have ever heard of this guy, or at least they won't say if they have. And no matter how many traffic cams we check, we can't find anything unusual within blocks of the bank."

Gideon grabbed a carton of orange juice, filled her glass and then his, and walked back into the kitchen to prepare his own plate.

"Something will turn up." He returned to the table with his food. "If you need my help, I'm in. I may not be a superhero anymore, but I spent enough time fighting crime in the Brooks to know a thing or two. I'll see what I can track down if you want me to."

"Thanks, babe. For now, all I want is this food." She leaned across the table and kissed him. "Let's pray and dig in."

Gideon nodded, bowed his head, and began to pray. As he did, Jolie smiled and said a prayer of her own. *Lord, thank You for this amazing life You've given me. I pray that I'll always be grateful for Your abundant blessings. Protect my fellow officers and help us to catch this guy. Amen.*

CHAPTER 6

Visualization was everything. The key to mastering anything was to picture doing it, imagine each step, and follow through. It was true for martial arts, and it was true for using superpowers, too. Ty had learned that from experience.

He closed his eyes, took a deep breath, and tightened his grip on the short sword in his right hand. Ty's father, Shiro, had been a martial arts master. He had trained Ty since Ty was old enough to handle a sword without falling on its edge and throw a knife without cutting his fingers. Everything good Ty had, he owed to his father.

Almost everything, anyway.

Picturing imaginary foes around him, Ty opened his eyes and slashed through a series of katas. His blade flashed right and left, the dim light of Ty's garage glimmering off the polished metal. *Block high, slash low, spin, crosscut, parry.* Ty jumped back, grabbed a throwing knife from his belt, and hurled it at a target across the room, spinning as he threw to block an imaginary blow from behind.

He danced and spun through the garage for the next five minutes, never breaking form except to end one kata and begin another. He spun on his heel, reached behind him, and grabbed a second sword from the table. Spinning the twin blades in tight arcs, Ty weaved through an array of invisible opponents. Finally, his shirt drenched in sweat,

Ty stopped and placed the swords back on the table. He stepped over to his target and removed the throwing knife from the bull's-eye.

These were lethal weapons, meant to be used with lethal intent. For all the crimes he'd committed, Ty had never taken a life; and he never intended to. So, why did he still train with these weapons? His time would be better served practicing with his batons—or his powers. But something, whether tradition or nostalgia or a misplaced desire to please his long-dead father, made him stick with his blades.

Ty grabbed a towel and dried his sweat as best he could. He ran the towel over his thick, dark hair and looked around the garage. It was a far cry from the two-story home he had grown up in, with its beautiful courtyard on a grassy oceanside cliff in Japan. Everything about his adult life was different. His friends, his home . . . his name. Ty Vickers certainly was not the name given him at birth, but it was the one that kept him safe.

The sound of popping static jerked Ty from his thoughts. A soft whimper carried over the airwaves of the baby monitor resting on the table. Tossing the towel aside, he pushed his way through the garage door and into the home. He walked through the kitchen to his infant daughter's bedroom. The cry of her complaints intensified at the sound of the door opening. Ty stepped over and reached down into her crib. Emi whimpered softly as Ty rested her against his shoulder.

"It's okay, baby," he whispered. "Daddy's got you."

* * *

There were some things that Carter could not do, and math homework was one of them. He'd barely passed math in high school, and Ellis was dealing with the same problems. Rhonda, on the other hand, was a virtual math prodigy, but she was a year behind Ellis. She hadn't yet learned what he was struggling with, meaning she couldn't help, either.

Carter looked up helplessly at his mother as Ellis jabbed his finger furiously at his calculator. Carter would have given almost anything to have Dean back. That guy was an all-around genius; Carter was pretty sure he could've handled a little math homework. Carter studied the gibberish of numbers and letters mashed together on the page.

"You need a tutor," he finally said with a groan.

Ellis held his head in his hands. "I'm sorry."

"Hey, don't apologize. I was in the same boat you are. I wish I could do more to help." He put a hand on Ellis's shoulder. "Hang in there."

He stood and walked away from the kitchen table. It wasn't that he didn't want to help anymore. If he kept trying, he was going to get mad; and yelling wasn't going to help anyone. But he was good and angry at math, so it was a good time to go out and beat up some criminals.

His mom followed him into the hallway. Was she going to ask him to stay a little longer? Thank him for his help? Cry into his shoulder in overwhelmed exhaustion?

Instead, she smiled softly. "Be careful tonight."

"I will." Carter nodded. "You good here?"

"Of course." She chuckled. "Unless you want to help Rhonda with her boy problems."

"No way. I think a mother's touch is needed on that one." Carter kissed her on the cheek. "I'll be back."

Carter stepped into his bedroom, closed the door behind him, and removed from his closet the chest that held his Crusader uniform and gear. He took off his plainclothes and pulled on the red and gray costume. He buckled the boots and heavy gauntlets, slid the mask over his eyes, and pulled on his utility belt.

He did a quick equipment check—grappling hook, shock and adhesive beads, Crybabies, *jo* staff . . . that was everything. Carter reached into the chest and pulled out a short blade. Given to him by Gideon, the blade had once belonged to the assassin Katrina Monahan. Gideon had broken it off her gauntlet and given it to Carter after Monahan tried to kill him. Carter had kept it ever since and had attached a short hilt to the blade so he could use it as a knife in an emergency.

Tucking the knife into the sheath on his belt, Carter walked toward his window and looked out at the city. His heart rate accelerated, as it always did as he prepared to go out and become the Crusader again. It was partially thrill, partially fear. Carter took a deep, steadying breath and opened the window. With any luck, tonight, he would catch the superhuman criminal, provided he showed his face. Carter dropped into the alley behind the house, mounted his motorcycle, and sped off into the night.

CHAPTER 7

Crouched on the corner of a rooftop, body tucked into a ball to conserve body heat, the Crusader watched over the Brooks. His *jo* staff rested on his knees, balancing there as he rubbed his gloved hands together. He was thankful for the thermal layer beneath his suit, which Dean had installed before he left the city. Carter was glad the tech genius had the foreknowledge to realize that Carter would need it. How had Carter's dad done this? Wyatt Jonson had not had special uniforms or stitched thermal layering. He had gone out in a sweatshirt and a leather jacket, no matter the elements. Carter's dad had been a different breed, that was for sure. Carter had been on the streets for less than an hour, and he was ready to give up and go home before he caught hypothermia.

Raina laughed. "I can hear your teeth clacking."

The Crusader clenched his jaw. "Why don't you come out here, sit on a rooftop for half an hour, and tell me how you feel?"

"Yikes, snippy. It was a joke."

"Sorry."

Raina's borrowed police scanner had gone a long way toward helping the Crusader fight crime more efficiently. After Dean had left and the old Vindicators lair at Lakeside Central Tower had been shut down, the Crusader had been forced to search for crime at random. It had been difficult, and most nights he returned home frustrated at his lack of success. Crimes had slipped by under his nose, and people had been injured. But with Raina's police scanner, they could at least find out where crimes were taking place and get a jump on the cops. It wasn't a perfect system—there were dozens of crimes that were too late to stop by the time they were reported, from rapes to muggings to homicides—but it was a start.

The Crusader stood and backed away from the edge. He couldn't sit there forever. Maybe a little movement would help him stay warm. And if he was lucky, maybe he would run into a crime in progress and be able to stop it. He took a deep breath, bounced up and down on the balls of his feet, and dropped into the alley below. Mounting his motorcycle, he peeled off into the street.

"What's that sound?" Raina asked. "Are you moving?"

"Got tired of waiting."

"What if a crime gets reported in the opposite direction?"

"I'll turn around."

Wyatt had never had the luxury of a motorcycle. If he used transportation at all, it was the family car; but he had always preferred to avoid that. He had told Carter once that if a criminal ever saw the Crusader get into a car and followed him home, Wyatt would have led them right to his family. That was the last thing he had wanted. Unfortunately, Carter's lamebrained attempt to mimic his father's heroics had led to the assassin Katrina Monahan discovering the Jonson household, anyway.

That had been before Gideon's training. Carter was much better equipped than he had been in those days. He knew how to spot and shake a tail, but having separate vehicles for personal use and patrolling was a bonus that Carter was grateful for. The motorcycle was faster and more agile than his car.

"Shots fired on Teller!" Raina said.

Carter's blood pounded. "On it."

He bore left at the next intersection. Traffic was minimal at this time of night, but he had to weave around a few slow-moving sedans as he sped toward the crime scene.

The Crusader tightened his grip on the handlebars as he approached the next intersection. "Where on Teller?"

"Near the intersection with Fifth."

That's two blocks from here. Every second he wasted was a chance someone else would die. He hurtled down the street, coaxing more speed out of his bike.

He skidded to a stop at the corner of Fifth and Teller and dismounted his motorcycle. Staff at the ready, he scanned the street around him. The street was eerily silent. No gunshots echoed through the air; no screams or police sirens drifted to meet his ears. He clenched his fist around his staff and furrowed his brow.

"I don't see anything. I wish Dean was here. He could access the traffic cameras or something. Do you have any kind of eyes on the area?"

"Carter, honey, I'm an athlete-slash-poet, not a hacker." Raina paused for a moment. "Okay, the report mentioned an apartment. Do you see any apartment buildings around you?"

The Crusader pursed his lips and looked up at the six-story building on the corner of Teller and Fifth. It looked like an apartment complex, all right.

The front door was smashed, and the office windows had been shattered. The Crusader stepped over the fallen door, scanning the room beyond, ready to make a move. A fluorescent bulb flickered above him. He walked further into the room and flitted his eyes back and forth, watching for any sign of a threat.

Someone whimpered nearby. He lowered his staff and stepped toward the sound. A desk was overturned in the back corner of the office. A head peeked over the desk and ducked back down with a yelp. The Crusader split the staff into its two halves and sheathed them. When dealing with civilians and victims, he had found that it was best to be as non-threatening as possible.

"Are you all right?" he asked.

"F-fourth floor," a voice said.

The Crusader stepped around the desk. A thin, blond man huddled behind it. He wore gray coveralls and had a large keyring on his belt. *Janitor.*

"What's on the fourth floor?" he asked.

"M-Markos. Aren't you here for him, too?"

"Too?"

"Is he talking about Markos Howell?" Raina asked. "He's one of the city's biggest drug dealers; he was arrested last year and got out on a technicality."

"What apartment?" the Crusader asked.

"Four twelve."

The Crusader rushed for the stairs. He wondered if the janitor's statement implied that the police were there for Howell, or if a rival drug lord had come looking for him. *Is Howell the shooter . . . or the victim?* Carter bounded up the stairs. He rushed up to the fourth floor, stopped at the doorway, and peered out into the hall. There was no sign of movement, no telltale shadows of a lurking perpetrator.

He edged his way into the hall and peered through the dim lighting at the door numbers. Was this apartment building always so dark? Glass crunched under his feet. A quick glance up revealed that the lights had been shot out. Two bodies lay sprawled out in the hallway, guns resting near their hands. The Crusader knelt next to their bodies. Both were already dead. No bullet wounds—their injuries had come from a blade. He drew his staff and raised it defensively. No telling if there was still potential danger—*418, 416, 414* . . . the door to 412 hung wide open. The Crusader's heart hammered in his chest.

"Oh, boy."

"What is it?" Raina asked.

"Door's open." The Crusader stepped forward. "I'm going in."

He kept his head on a swivel as he entered, in case the attacker was still active. His gaze fell on a smear of red that stained the kitchen counter. Bullet holes riddled the far wall, and the living room window was shattered. A chill breeze wailed through the broken glass, sending a chill through Carter's bones. He suppressed a shiver. So, the apartment had been the source of the gunshots. Carter wondered where the bladed weapon that had killed the men outside came into play.

He rounded the kitchen counter. A man lay in the middle of the tile floor next to a gun. Slash marks criss-crossed his chest, and blood stained his t-shirt and the flannel shirt he wore over it. The man coughed and clutched at the bleeding wounds. The Crusader dropped to his knees, pressed his fingers to Howell's neck, and found a pulse.

"I need an ambulance!"

"Already on the way," Raina said.

Carter patted the man's face. "Are you Markos Howell?"

The man nodded. "Y-y . . ."

"Stay still." It wouldn't be safe to move Howell in this condition. On the other hand, if the Crusader left him there, Howell would probably bleed out. "Who did this?"

"M-masked." Howell's eyes widened, and his breaths became short and choppy. "Can't escape . . . him."

"Who was he?"

"Asked about . . . Liang."

"Who's Liang?"

No response. Howell's eyes went vacant, and his head slumped back against the bloodstained tile. The Crusader eased him down and searched for a pulse again. Nothing.

"He's dead." Carter slammed his fist against the wall. *If I had arrived a few minutes sooner . . .* "I'll check for any other evidence."

He walked back into the living room and scanned the floors. The attacker hadn't left much to go on. He was smart, whoever he was. A bladed weapon didn't leave behind spent brass. But maybe the janitor had seen something more. If he was still downstairs, maybe he could tell the Crusader something.

"Raina, have you heard of Liang?" Carter stepped over Howell's body and hurried back the way he had come. "The name doesn't sound familiar."

"Not to me, either. I'll do some digging."

He double-timed it down the stairs. By the time the Crusader reached the office again, he could hear sirens in the distance. Ignoring them, he walked around the corner and looked behind the desk. The janitor was gone. That left him with no further evidence on the killer.

In addition to an amplified thief, Carter had a murderous masked swordsman running around the Brooks.

"Hey, there's a car accident three blocks from you," Raina said. "If you hurry, you might make it in time to help."

"What about the killer?"

"We've got nothing on him. The victims of that accident might still survive. Which one would you rather deal with?"

She was right. With a sigh, the Crusader ran from the apartment building. The attacker would have to wait.

* * *

Carter slumped down on the couch and let out a long, loud groan. The comfortable upholstery seemed to suck him in and wrap itself around him, tempting him with the sweet embrace of a long sleep. At that moment, Carter could not imagine wanting anything more. But from experience, he knew that if he fell asleep in his Crusader gear, he would wake up with a terrible crick in his neck. Dean was a genius, but he hadn't had leisure in mind when he designed the armor.

"Good job tonight," Raina said.

Carter opened his eyes as she half-skipped into the living room. Dressed down in baggy, gray basketball shorts and a forest-green tank top with the words "I woke up like this" in white, she wore her curly dark hair with blonde streaks tied in a messy bun atop her head. She was beautiful. Carter shifted slightly to allow her to sit down on the couch, and he rested his head on her lap. She reached down and removed his domino mask.

"Thanks," Carter muttered. "Doesn't feel too good."

"You pulled those people out of a burning car. You stopped a mugging. I call that a success."

"Yeah. But there was no sign of the amplified thief, and there's a killer on the loose."

"Can't win 'em all." She played with the short curls of his hair. "Don't worry. You'll find both of them, sooner or later. It's a big city but not that big. They'll turn up."

"Anything on Liang?"

"A few names popped up in connection with Sojourn City but none directly relating to Howell. I'm not sure which of them, if any, the killer might be after. Don't worry. You will get him."

She was right. Carter did his best imitation of a nod, closed his eyes, and enjoyed the rest. He would have to go home soon if he wanted to get any real sleep before work in the morning, but he wanted to be with Raina and unwind with her first. Between his job, her college classes and search for a job, and his crime fighting, it seemed like they had less and less time together by the day. He would take whatever he could get.

But try as he might, he couldn't take his mind off the attacker. The sight of Howell's bloody form lying in the kitchen haunted him. Whoever had done it had been brutal. There had been no efficiency to the kill—it had been torture. The two men in the hallway, on the other hand, had been efficiently executed. Not Howell. Whoever this guy was, he wanted to send a message. But to whom? Liang? If so, who was Liang?

There was one person Carter knew who might be able to shed some light on this—his old coworker, Silas Rockwell. Silas ran an after-school program for underprivileged or struggling boys, and he was familiar with the ins and outs of the drug trade in the Brooks. Before turning his life around, Silas had actually been a gangster. More recently, Carter had caught him and a friend smuggling a drug called Shine—not to sell it, but so Silas could destroy it. He might have intel about Howell that could lead Carter to the attacker. He would try to meet up with Silas after work the next day.

Content for the moment that he had the beginnings of a solution, Carter finally forced the thoughts of the mysterious swordsman from his mind and tried to relax. However, the images of Howell's bloody body remained.

CHAPTER 8

Gideon Turner rolled over in bed and draped his arm over his wife's midsection. Gently, so as not to wake her, he traced his fingers across her soft flesh. He had never thought he could love her more than he did when he proposed, but marriage had proved him wrong. Every day, he loved Jolie more than he ever had. If he could have, he would've chosen to remain with her all day. Unfortunately, that was not possible.

The sun peeked through the window. Gideon squeezed his eyes shut against it and buried his face in his pillow, but hiding from the sun would not make it go away. He had places to be. He had to get up. Slowly, he raised his head and gazed at Jolie. Her dark hair was pooled everywhere, her face half-hidden and smooshed by her pillow. *She's too cute.*

Chuckling softly, he stretched out to kiss Jolie on the cheek and slipped out of bed, leaving her to sleep. She had been so exhausted when she came home from work last night. He figured she could do with a little extra rest.

He shuffled across the carpet and into their bathroom, closed the door behind him, and turned on the shower. He stepped in and let the warm water wash away most of the drowsiness that clung to him. Gideon was grateful to his best friend, Dean, for getting him a job at Sterling Labs. It had come during a time of Gideon's life when he hadn't been sure what to do. He had taken lives, broken the Hippocratic Oath, and so felt unprepared to return to a career as a surgeon. Dean had offered him the job as a way for him to use his medical training in a laboratory setting. It wasn't exciting work, but Gideon had been content with it.

At least, he had been while he was a superhero. After losing his powers last year, he had hung up the proverbial cape. His job in the lab became more and more dreary by the day. He found himself staring at the clock, waiting for the day to end so he could go home and wait for Jolie to get off work—making a difference in the city. He was proud of her and the work she had done as a detective; but as hard as it was for him to admit, he was a bit jealous. He missed stopping crime and saving lives. He and Carter met often so Gideon could train the younger man, but it wasn't the same.

God took my powers away for a reason. He knew that for a fact. God had a purpose for his life; and apparently, it wasn't for him to be a superhero anymore. The best way to discover it was through prayer and meditation. It would come. He had to trust God's timing.

It could be that the time had come for Gideon to return to the medical field. The pain of taking lives, even in self defense, was not gone completely; but it had waned. Gideon understood that taking those lives did not detract from the good he had done as a doctor. He was not so black and white, so extreme, anymore. He was not sure if he ever wanted to be a surgeon again, but it was something to consider.

He shut off the shower and wrapped a towel around his waist. Wiping the fog from the mirror, he examined his reflection. His blue eyes stared back at him accusingly. Could he really see himself working in a laboratory for the rest of his life? Running tests, mixing cocktails, watching simulations . . . It was not the life he would've picked for himself. There was something else out there for him. But until he found it, he would do this job to the best of his ability. At least, he wasn't doing it alone. Jolie would be beside him every step of the way—and most importantly, God would be right next to him, too.

He dressed in khaki twill pants, brown shoes, and a navy-blue button-down shirt. He ran his hands through his wavy blond hair, somewhat taming it and tousling it the way he liked it. Satisfied, he stepped back into the bedroom. Jolie was still passed out on the bed. Gideon smiled and stepped over to her side. He knelt, resting his left elbow on her bedside table, and ran his right hand lightly through her hair.

"I love you," he whispered.

Gideon kissed Jolie on the top of her head, backed out of the room, and carefully closed the door behind him. His Bible rested on the table in the kitchen; while his coffee brewed, he crossed the apartment to grab it. There had been a time when he hadn't needed coffee. Somehow, his powers had energized and rejuvenated him each morning. But it had become a mainstay in his life since they had gone away. Unlike Jolie, however, he liked it simple: strong and black as it could be.

He carried his Bible over to the kitchen table and read a passage from Proverbs 16 while he ate his cereal. He stopped at verse nine, which said, "A man's heart deviseth his way: but the Lord directeth his steps."

Gideon ate breakfast and finished his devotionals. He prayed over Jolie and her cases, his own career and choices, and Carter's safety in defending the Brooks. With a cup of coffee steaming in his mug, he headed out the door to face another day.

CHAPTER 9

It would've been nearly impossible to make it to the Brooks and back to Sterling Enterprises on Carter's lunchbreak—by car, anyway. But because of the Sterling maglev, Carter figured he should have enough time to hop on, eat during the trip, talk to Silas, and ride the maglev back to the Platform before his break ended.

God bless Dean for building that stupid train, he thought wryly. He hadn't loved the maglev so much when he had to help save it from crashing.

Bundled up in his jacket, a pair of gloves, and a beanie, Carter ducked out the back door and rushed for the maglev. There was a train scheduled to depart for the Brooks in ten minutes. He could make it if he booked it. If only he had superspeed, like Patrick. There was a useful superpower. But God had not smiled on him that way, so Carter ran past the parking garage and down the sidewalk, forced to move at a normal, human pace.

Hopefully, it would not be a wasted trip. Silas had to have some nugget of information that would explain why a murderous madman had gone after Markos Howell. Carter had nothing to go on, so any tip would be beneficial.

What would Dad make of this killer?

Wyatt would have done everything in his power to hunt down Howell's murderer and give him the justice he deserved. Carter's father had not been a killer. He had taken down drug dealers like Howell dozens of times; but to Carter's knowledge, he always left them alive. In his opinion, murdering the criminals would've made him like them. Carter agreed.

Carter skidded to a halt at the back of a short line of people waiting to board the maglev. When he reached the ticket booth, he put a five-dollar bill in, accepted his ticket, and ducked aboard the train.

He considered his plan while he ate lunch. The amplified thief would have to wait. He had not yet taken any lives. The masked killer, on the other hand, had already brutally murdered someone. Carter wasn't willing to bet that it was a one-time event. His focus had to be on the attacker. Jolie and the cops could handle the superhuman thief.

Superhuman thief. Masked bladesman. Carter needed to come up with better nicknames for them until he found out who they were.

Opening the Vindicators' group text, he sent out a message: *Got some new baddies in need of nicknames. Amp thief with phasing powers and unpowered murderer with a penchant for blades.*

He followed with a second text: *Ideas?*

When the train finally pulled to a stop in the Brooks, Carter stuffed his trash in a receptacle on the way out. Silas had told Carter that he would be at Pop's Gym during his lunchbreak. That was only a few blocks from the station. Carter checked his watch. He still had over half an hour before he had to be back to work. That should be plenty of time.

He jogged down the street toward Pop's Gym. The old building had been a boxing arena at one point, but its owner had fallen on hard times and sold it. It was still used for boxing, but it had become a training gym for anyone who could pay the fee, rather than an arena for famous fighters. Silas, an army veteran, had been training at Pop's Gym for years. Carter had never seen him fight; but between his army training and his boxing skills, he had to be formidable. Silas had been a tough customer in his younger days, too. The former gangbanger had ominous tattoos to show for it, not to mention a couple scars marring his dark brown skin and shaven head.

Carter stepped into the gym and walked through the hallway to the dimly lit boxing ring. Silas stood off to the side, throwing punches at a bag chained to the ceiling in the corner. Carter approached him and waited for him to finish. Silas jabbed and crosscut, hitting the bag from opposite angles and rocking it. The sound of the heavy gloves smacking into the bag echoed through the mostly empty gym. After a few more blows, Silas lowered his hands and pulled at the Velcro straps around his wrists. He grinned at Carter and walked over. Sweat soaked the armpits and collar of his gray t-shirt.

"What's up, man?" Silas popped Carter on the shoulder. "Life treating you well?"

"Well as can be. What about you?"

"Doing fine. But you didn't come here to catch up, did you?" Silas gestured to a bench against the wall. "Take a seat. Tell me what's going on."

Carter dropped onto the bench and leaned back against the wall. Silas tossed his boxing gloves to the floor, removed the sweat-stained shirt, and pulled a towel and a replacement shirt from a duffel bag. Carter clasped his hands in front of him, resting his elbows on his knees while Silas dried sweat from his face. Carter noticed the older man's broad shoulders and huge muscles. Combined with the scars, he cut an imposing figure. *I hope I never have to go after someone that big.*

"There was a pretty brutal attack last night," Carter said. "By the time I got there, the killer had already gone; and the victims died before help arrived."

"I'm sorry to hear that." Silas slipped on a long-sleeved white shirt. "What does it have to do with me?"

"The victim was Markos Howell, the drug dealer. Since you're aware of the ins and outs of the drug trade in the Brooks, I was wondering if you have any idea who wanted to pop Howell."

Silas put his hands on his hips and chewed on his lower lip. "I could list dozens who wanted him dead, but it's hard to believe someone went through with it."

"Why?"

"Howell had dirt on everybody. He made sure that if he 'disappeared,' that dirt would come to light. Whoever killed him either hated him more than they feared what he could leak, or he didn't have dirt on them at all." Silas furrowed his brow. "If it's the latter, that means the killer probably wasn't a member of any organized crime group in the Brooks."

"Great. We're either looking at a freelancer or someone who's new to the game."

"Or someone who's not scared of him," Silas added. "When Luca Serban solidified his rule over the Brooks, Howell was one of the top drug lords in Serban's empire. Maybe he threatened the wrong guy, and one of Serban's lieutenants is out for payback."

"Whoever he was, he asked Howell about someone named Liang before he killed him."

"Liang?" Silas frowned. "I'm not familiar with that name. I'll do some digging."

"I was hoping you would. Raina looked into it, but no one of note popped out. If they exist, they're under the radar. And one more thing—the killer used some kind of bladed weapon. That might narrow the search."

"That is interesting." Silas pressed his lips into a thin line. "I'll reach out if I hear something."

Carter could avoid wasting his time investigating gangs like the Red Dogs and the Tyrants along with drug rings, outside of Howell's. Even if Howell didn't have dirt on them, swords weren't really their style. If Carter was looking for a freelancer, the killer was a needle in the very large haystack of the Brooks. Assuming he lived in the Brooks. And if he was looking for a former member of Serban's organization, that would be harder. The police were still figuring out how far that man's reach had stretched.

"Well, it's a start." Carter stood. "Keep an ear out. I need to stop this guy before he decides to go on a murder spree."

"Will do. Stay safe, kid."

"You, too."

Carter shook Silas' hand and headed back for the exit. The visit had not been nearly as helpful as he hoped; but at least, it had narrowed his search down somewhat. With a killer on the loose, he would take what he could get.

* * *

Balancing Emi on his shoulder, Ty paced back and forth in his small, shag-carpeted living room as Joanie, Ned, and Richie filed in. Joanie flopped into a recliner and pulled out a tablet. Ned and Richie took the couch. Both men had the cocky air they always seemed to carry with them. Joanie, on the other hand, was completely nonchalant.

Ty had been on track for a great life outside the Brooks, where he could live peacefully with his daughter and do some good for the world. Because of someone else's boneheaded mistake, he had become a common criminal, living in a run-down rented home with his daughter, stealing to ensure that they survived. His life had been ruined because of someone else's actions. He would never forget that.

"How did we do?" he asked.

Joanie held up her tablet. "Got away with a clean 17,500. Divided between the four of us, that's $4,375 apiece."

That should be enough to get him and Emi by for the next month or so. Hitting somewhere as large as the Sojourn City Bank had probably drawn more attention to them than they wanted to deal with, especially if that guard had seen him use his powers to escape. They needed to lie low for a while. He hoped that by the time this money ran out, the heat on them would diminish enough to chance making another hit.

"What about the cost of laundering?" Ned asked.

Ty and his crew were in the habit of exchanging their stolen cash for nonsequential bills via an underworld loan shark of sorts. Unfortunately, anyone who would provide a laundering service also took a significant cut.

Joanie started typing on her tablet. "Based on previous rates, they'd probably set us back thirty-five hundred. Leaves us with fourteen thousand total—or thirty-five hundred each."

Thirty-five hundred would more than cover the rent and utilities for Ty's house, plus groceries and other necessities; but it would not leave much wiggle room. He had hoped to store up some of that cash in savings. If he could build a safety net, he could stop stealing. Thirty-five hundred did not provide the extra funds to do that. Their next job would have to happen sooner than he expected.

"Not bad, not bad." Richie nodded eagerly. "But I think we can do better."

"Better?" Ty pursed his lips and composed himself. He didn't need to get worked up with Emi in his arms. He did not want her sensing his anger. "Maybe you should phase through the walls of the bank while the security cameras are down next time, huh? Can you do that, Richie?"

Richie held up his hands. "Hey, easy, man. I didn't mean anything by it. You did great. You always do. But we need a big score. Something that'll have us sitting pretty for years."

"I don't care about 'sitting pretty,' Richie." Ty shook his head. "This isn't about making it big; it's about survival. I've got to take care of myself and my kid. I'm not interested in lining your pockets with cash. If we go too big too fast, it'll draw more heat. Maybe we've already gone too far. You've all seen the news. The cops are looking for us. Where can we hit that won't raise their attention?"

"Come on, man!" Ned hoisted himself off the couch. "If you're rich, you and Em are set! You won't have to worry about taking care of her week to week. One big score, and you can take her and leave Sojourn City, set up somewhere nice."

Ty clamped his jaw shut. As much as he hated to admit it, that part made sense. He knew Ned had only said it out of greed and a desire to get Ty to play along. It was as transparently manipulative as could be. Unfortunately, he was right. If Ty landed a big score, he could get out of Sojourn City. He could say goodbye to the Brooks and to the past that haunted him. Emi could grow up somewhere other than one of the most dangerous neighborhoods in the country.

Ty glanced at Joanie. She peered over her tablet and gave a noncommittal shrug. She would back his call. She always did. Joanie was a team player; but she was loyal to Ty, not Ned and Richie.

Ty pointed to Richie, then Ned. "Bring me options. Viable ones. Scope out the areas, tell me where the weak points are and when they're least guarded. Figure out how you can be useful because if we do this, I'm not going in alone. You two are going to pull your weight for once. You want a score? You'll have to work for it."

The two men exchanged looks, communicating silently. They'd go for it. They were too greedy to turn down a chance to get rich, no matter how risky. But he wasn't going to sign off on this until he was sure it was a feasible venture. He wouldn't risk getting caught and thrown in prison, leaving Emi virtually orphaned. If Ned and Richie thought they could succeed and made off with enough to leave Sojourn, that was fine with Ty. But he would leave both his friends in the lurch before he was caught himself. Nothing would come between him and keeping his daughter safe.

CHAPTER 10

Jolie rested her head in her hands and stared down at her desk. There was no trace of this wall-phasing, baton-throwing thief. It was as if when he vanished through that window, he had also vanished from the face of the earth.

She had tried searching for records of expert knife-throwers who might fit the bill. She found there was no such convenient list in any of the major databases, and she gave up on that tactic. She knew she wouldn't have enough evidence to pursue charges, anyway. It would be like bringing in every one-armed person in the city if their only lead was that the criminal was missing an arm. It wouldn't work. Her investigation would be shut down in a heartbeat.

For the first time in a long time, she felt completely stumped. She hadn't run into a wall this hard since she tried to track down Katrina Monahan. But she had powered through that case, and she could do the same with the amp thief. They could try to track the bills' serial numbers, but there were launderers in the Brooks. And she had at least had a physical description for Monahan. Without a security camera's view of the thief's face, she had no idea who she was looking for, other than that the suspect was male.

Wait.

Jolie's head shot up. She jumped from her desk and wound her way through the precinct toward the crime lab. Nate Walker, the head CSI, glanced up as she entered.

"Detective, what brings you down to my lowly lair?"

"The Sojourn City Bank case." Jolie leaned against his desk. "There's got to be a way to track whoever hacked the security cameras, right?"

"Hypothetically, yes, they'd leave a digital footprint. Or if the access was direct—as in, the thief hacked in from within the bank—you might be able to track him based on past activities. He would've had to find an access point for the cameras, for example."

"If he hacked from inside, he would've been caught on camera at some point when he cased the bank."

"And if he didn't, and it was a remote hack, we may be able to back trace it."

"Great!" She grinned. "Finally, some good news. Can you get on that for me?"

"Will do, Detective."

"You're the best, Nate."

While Nate worked on that, she could comb over files from past crimes that involved knives or knife-throwing tactics from the thief. If this thief brought his knives with him to Sojourn City Bank, it was because he expected to use them, which meant he may have done so in the past. She smiled and strode more confidently down the hall. With her mental block knocked down, she could make inroads and get to the bottom of things. Maybe the case wasn't as unsolvable as she had feared.

* * *

Carter snapped out a kick toward Gideon, which the older man blocked with both forearms. As Carter pulled his foot back, Gideon stepped forward and lunged toward Carter's head, his right arm snaking around to grab Carter in a chokehold. Carter ducked under the grab and chopped at Gideon's lower back with a straightened hand. The blow landed—firmly, but not too hard—and Gideon stumbled forward a step and punched high with his left hand. Carter brought his right arm up to block the blow.

Gideon pulled back at the last second, instead lashing out with his right leg. Carter tried to jump out of the way, but it was too late. Gideon's leg struck the back of Carter's knee, buckling the joint. Carter grimaced as he dropped to the mat. Gideon completed the chokehold he had attempted earlier, wrapping his right arm around Carter's neck and bracing it with his left hand. Carter gritted his teeth. From a kneeling position, he was at a serious disadvantage. Unless . . .

He grabbed Gideon's right forearm with both hands and threw the full weight of his body forward, gracelessly flopping face-first toward the mat. The momentum of the movement hurled Gideon forward. Carter's mentor flipped and landed on his back in front of Carter. Massaging his throat, Carter stumbled to his feet and dropped back into a ready stance.

"Impressive." Gideon jumped back to his feet and faced Carter. "I didn't see that one coming."

"Probably wouldn't work too well on the bad guys, considering it would require me probably going headfirst into the pavement."

Gideon circled Carter. "True, but you're thinking tactically. That will save you."

"Thanks." Carter paused to catch his breath. "Have you trained with swords?"

Gideon lunged. Carter caught his arm and deflected it to the side, spun so his back was facing Gideon, and brought up his left elbow to strike Gideon's jaw. Gideon grabbed Carter's elbow and shoved it aside.

"I'm not a master swordfighter by any means, but I've practiced *kendo* in my martial arts training. I could teach you a few things."

"I mainly want to defend against one." Carter shrugged. "Feels like I'm at a bit of a disadvantage."

Gideon stepped off the mat, signaling an end to their bout. "Next time we train, I'll bring practice swords. We'll work through a few drills, and I'll show you the strengths and weaknesses of a sword. The key to defeating someone with a weapon is to be intimately familiar with that weapon yourself."

"Works for me."

Carter checked the Vindicators' group chat. The other heroes had thrown out a few ideas on what to call his suspects. He smirked at a few of them: Hannah's dry suggestion of *Knife Guy* and *Ninja;* Jarrett's predictably quippy idea of calling them *Smoke* and *Mirror;* Patrick's TV references of *Casper* and *Leonardo.*

He's not a TURTLE ninja, Carter responded.

Audrey sent a trio of laughing emojis.

Jarrett followed with a single facepalm emoji.

Hannah said she was silencing her phone because she was about to go fight a gang of traffickers.

Dean corrected him: *Ninja Turtle, not Turtle Ninja.*

Gideon laughed. "This is getting you nowhere."

"I kinda like Smoke and Mirror, even though as far as I can tell, the two cases aren't related."

Carter knelt and folded the mat. Since they didn't have their lair at the Lakeside Central Tower anymore, they trained in Carter's garage. It was the *only place private enough to do it without an audience, although Ellis and Rhonda liked to watch sometimes—especially Ellis, but Carter didn't want him getting any ideas. No way his younger brother was going to join him out in the field.*

That's probably how Dad felt about me.

"I'd better get going," Gideon said. "If you ever need anything . . . "

"I'll let you know." Carter pulled Gideon into a backslapping hug. "Love you, bro."

For the first time in a long time, Carter was reluctant to suit up. He wanted to stay in with Raina and watch a movie. He would like to do something relaxing, something normal. With the blade-wielding killer on the loose, he was . . . Scared.

Dad was probably scared, too. Lots of times. That hadn't stopped Wyatt from going out and fighting, anyway. Carter wondered why this particular threat scared him so much. Maybe because his father had been killed with a sword. Carter shuddered and shut the thought out of his mind. He wouldn't meet the same end that his father had. He would stop the swordsman, so no one else ended up dead, either. It was his duty.

* * *

Raina Watts stared down at the small journal in front of her and ran her hand over the tanned-hide cover. The journal was a graduation gift from her father. It had become one of her most treasured possessions. One day, she hoped the poems that she scribbled out on these pages would be as world-famous as those of Robert Frost or Emily Dickinson or Maya Angelou. Poetry had fallen by the wayside in a world of graphic novels, movies, and binge-worthy TV series; but

Raina was determined to restore the art to its rightful place. The only problem was, every page in the journal was empty.

Raina's heart was with her poetry, but her mind seemed determined to evade her every attempt to put anything down on paper. She had dealt with writer's block before, but it had never been this severe. Despite her best efforts, not a single line had found its way onto the pages. Maybe it was her brain reminding her that she should be working on college homework or practicing her archery, instead of creative writing.

A pair of strong hands came down gently on her shoulders and began massaging, the thumbs digging down into her flesh and rubbing away the tension that had formed there. She closed her eyes, smiled, and leaned back in her chair to enjoy the sensation.

"You okay?" Carter asked.

"A bit frustrated." Raina groaned as he hit a particularly tense spot. "This helps."

"Good. Maybe this will help, too."

Something paper crinkled as it touched the desk in front of her. Raina opened her eyes to find a McDonald's to-go bag resting next to her journal. Raina looked over her shoulder at Carter and smiled.

"That might do the trick."

She reached into the bag and pulled out a chicken sandwich. She unwrapped the food, the delicious smell of the cooked poultry wafting through the air. Raina closed her eyes again as her stomach rumbled.

"I probably shouldn't eat this. If I ever want to make it to the Olympics . . ."

"Raina, you take archery." Carter laughed. "I don't think a fast food meal is going to detract from your aim."

"Okay." Raina looked down at the tempting sandwich. "You win."

"Want to talk about whatever's bothering you?" Carter asked.

"It's nothing I haven't said before. I don't know what to write about—nothing's coming to me. My muse has run dry."

"Aw, come on. No, it hasn't." Carter snagged a fry from the red carton, popped it in his mouth, and frowned. "Well . . . maybe it has."

"Gee, thanks."

"No, hear me out. When a plant is dry, what do you do to it? You water it, right? You give it what it needs. Maybe your muse is dry because you haven't been watering it. When was the last time you read or watched something new and challenging?"

Raina's eyes popped open. That was a surprisingly astute observation. It wasn't that Carter wasn't smart—she wouldn't have dated him if she thought he was a dummy—but his intelligence rested more in the material realm than the creative. It was one area where they were vastly different, and she had come to accept that. But maybe he was right. She had mostly been reading the same poems and short stories her whole life, the ones that inspired her and had become her favorites. But though they would always be special to her, how could she come across new ideas when she was filtering them through the same handful of pieces? Maybe she needed to branch out.

"Thanks," she said. "That . . . helps."

"The massaging, the meal, or the metaphor?"

"The metaphor." Raina smiled and took a bite of the sandwich. "But the massaging is nice, too. So is the alliteration, for that matter."

"Didn't mean to do that."

"You're a poet, and you didn't know it." Raina smirked. "So, what brings you here? Besides delivering a surprise meal, I mean."

"I wanted to check in on you. And let you know not to worry too much because I'm working with Gideon to make sure I'm ready for this blade-crazy killer when I track him down."

"I always worry." Raina put her hand on top of one of Carter's. "But you can take care of yourself."

"Thanks." Carter kissed the top of her head. "I'll contact you once I'm out in the field. Shout if you hear anything on the scanner."

"I will. Good luck."

"Thanks. You, too. On the poetry, I mean."

Carter stepped away. Raina spun around in her rolling chair to say goodbye, but he was already gone.

CHAPTER 11

Emi cooed and wiggled happily in the middle of the floor, clutching at her favorite blanket. It was more of a swatch of cloth, really, but she clung to it like a lifeline. Ty couldn't bear to take it from her, even to give her something better. That little blanket was one of the last ties Emi had to her mother. She could keep it until it was tattered into little strips.

Ty sat on the couch and sharpened one of his knives as he watched her play. Ned and Richie hadn't contacted him with a prospective target yet, but Ty knew it would only be a matter of time. Their deep, insatiable greed ensured that. Dozens of times over the past day, Ty had considered grabbing Emi, jumping in the car, and driving as far from Sojourn City as their meager funds could take them.

But he stayed. Maybe it was for Joanie. He knew she could take care of herself. More than that, the girl would probably slit Ned and Richie's throats before they could touch her. She was no fighter, but she wasn't a slouch, either. But she would hate him for leaving. He was her only family, and she was his. They looked out for each other. Ty would continue to do so until she told him she didn't need him anymore. He had no doubt she would do the same for him.

Ty examined the razor edge of his knife. Satisfied with its sharpness, he tucked it into its sheath and set it on the couch next to him. Emi had rolled over onto her belly and wobbled her way toward the couch.

Ty grinned and slid onto the floor. Tantalized by her father's closeness, Emi opened her mouth in a toothless smile and bounced toward him.

"Hey, baby." He scooped her up. "Dada loves you. *Oton* loves you."

Ty rarely spoke Japanese, but he wanted his daughter to be able to call him *Dad* in his mother tongue. If she never learned another word in the language, she would know that one.

Emi looked into his eyes with complete seriousness and babbled back at him. Ty kissed her forehead. Their life would've been completely different, if not for Ty's godfather. Ty's birth father was a noble and shining example of parenthood. On the other hand, the adoptive father who had taken Ty after his parents' deaths seemed to be the source of everything wrong in Ty's life. Somehow, Ty could never escape the man's clutches. It was repulsive, the thing Ty hated most about himself. He wished he could cut away all memory of his godfather and start fresh.

He glanced at his watch. The teenage girl who babysat Emi was due to arrive at any moment. Ty lay Emi in her playpen. He had a job interview—a legitimate one. Using his assumed name of Ty Vickers, he might escape the background check that would connect him to his godfather. That connection had doomed every job Ty had tried so hard to attain so far. After the interview, Ned and Richie wanted to meet, but he was uncomfortable having them in his home again. This was his refuge, the place he could pretend he wasn't a criminal, that his life hadn't gone to waste the way it had. Having them here ruined that.

The doorbell rang. As Ty rose, he scooped up the sheathed knife on the couch and hid it in his belt at the small of his back. He opened the door. The girl outside had dark skin and hair braided down the back of her neck.

"Hi, Mr. Vickers!" she said. "Sorry I'm a little late."

"Don't worry about it, Rhonda." Ty smiled. "You're right on time."

* * *

Jolie focused on the target across the shooting gallery, steadied her aim, and pulled the trigger. A shell casing clinked to the floor beside her. She fired again. *Clink.* Again. *Clink.* With each shot, she pulled the trigger faster and faster. Finally, the slide locked in place as the last round flew from the barrel. Jolie ejected the magazine, slammed another into place, and continued to fire.

Shooting at something seemed like the only way to relieve her frustration. Tracking the serial numbers on the cash stolen had proven a bust. Somehow, the thieves had already exchanged it. One of the stolen bills had been used at a gas station in the Brooks, but the culprit had been completely unaware that the cash was stolen. His alibi checked out. Nate's attempts to track the hack had also been less than successful. The hacker had used some kind of spoof to throw off his or her digital trail. Nate said he might be able to track them if they struck again; but with only one hack to go on, it was more difficult. And combing over the security footage from the days before the heist had yet to produce any results, although Jolie wasn't ready to give up on that avenue of investigation yet.

She glanced down at her watch. She had not realized how late it was getting. She hoped Gideon hadn't prepared dinner again, or it would be cold by the time she got home. She picked up the spent shell casings, dumped them in a bin by the door, and headed out. As she walked, she took her phone from her pocket and texted her husband.

Jolie walked out of the police station to where her old Camry was parked. The car had served her faithfully for years, but it was starting to show its age. It wouldn't hold up in a high-speed pursuit, that was for sure.

She reached down to unlock the door, and something thumped against the pavement behind her. She scrambled for her gun and spun around. Her weapon was half-raised when she recognized the red-armored figure. Exhaling in relief, Jolie holstered her gun and stepped toward the Crusader.

"Everything okay?" she asked.

Carter crossed his arms. "I'm trying to track down Markos Howell's killer."

"Sergeant Pulaski's taking point on that case; but from what I've seen, you need to be careful. That guy, whoever he is, is deranged. He butchered those men."

"I know. I was there. The killer had already fled the scene, but I managed to talk to Howell before he died."

"What did he say?"

"The killer asked about someone named Liang. I talked to my contact, and he said that name didn't ring any bells."

"Doesn't sound familiar to me, either. I'll pass it along to Pulaski, and he can run with it. I've got my own case to deal with—the superhuman thief. I assume you've heard?"

"I have. I was out looking for him when the killer struck Howell. My focus has to be on this killer; but if you find out anything about the superhuman, I'll be glad to lend a hand." Carter chuckled. "Jarrett thinks we should call them Smoke and Mirror, but I'm not sold yet."

"Sounds like something he'd say. Thanks for the tip on the killer. I'll reach out if I hear anything about our amp."

"My pleasure, Detective." The Crusader backed away. "Good night."

He extended his left arm, and a grappling hook fired out from the small gun in his hand, striking the building above them. The Crusader sailed through the air as the line drew him toward the rooftop. Jolie opened her car door and climbed in. Between this new thief, the trouble between the Red Dogs and the Tyrants, and the killer, Jolie didn't like the way things were going in the Brooks. It reminded her all too much of Serban's reign.

* * *

"P-please, leave us alone," the man said.

Three red-jacketed thugs stepped further into the small diner. One shut the door behind them. From his vantage point on the rooftop across the street, the Crusader could see that all of them were armed. They were Red Dogs, probably there to collect protection money from the diner's owner. In their part of town, every small business owner paid them or suffered retribution.

Not this time.

The Crusader rappelled down from the rooftop. The diner was narrow and packed with tables. Fighting in those confines would be tight, and it would be harder to maneuver his staff inside. He split his staff into separate truncheons and crossed the street in a crouch. The Dogs were visible through the window, approaching the restaurant's owner.

The Crusader hit the front door with the full weight of his body, knocking it open and striking the closest gangster. As he fell, the Crusader battered him across the face with one of his batons. The other two Red Dogs spun toward him, and the owner ducked behind the counter. Each of the thugs got off a shot, but both missed and hit the far wall. The Crusader hurled one of his batons at the farther of the two thugs, striking his gun hand. At the same time, he leaped at the closer of the Dogs, grappling him and dragging him to the ground. He drove his fist into the back of the man's head.

The last Red Dog had picked up the Crusader's hurled baton. He wielded it in his left hand, twirling it and activating the electrified tip. The Crusader dropped into a fighting stance as the Red Dog rushed forward.

The restaurant's lights died.

"What in the—?" the Dog started.

The front window crashed inward, raining millions of glass shards on the interior. A shadowy figure sailed through the opening. Before the Crusader could react, the figure surged toward the Red Dog, drew a sword, and slashed the thug's left arm off at the elbow. The Dog screamed and dropped to the ground, clutching the stump.

The Crusader lunged toward the swordsman. The dark figure raised his sword as the Crusader's baton descended. The blade sliced cleanly through the weapon. The Crusader continued his forward motion, stumbling past the swordsman. As he did, the attacker's elbow came down on his back. The Crusader smashed into a table.

The impact jarred through his body. His muscles tensed and locked up, and he worked to force himself into motion.

With a groan, he managed to roll over. His body responded but not quickly enough to mount a defense. Despite the Crusader's vulnerability, the attacker didn't come for him. Instead, he knelt next to one of the thugs—the one Carter had hit with the door—and placed the edge of his sword near the man's throat. The Red Dog whimpered and tried to slide away.

"Where is Liang?" the swordsman asked.

"H-who?"

"You worked for Serban!" the swordsman shouted. "Where's Liang?"

"I—I don't—"

The attacker raised his sword. The Red Dog squealed and covered his face. Before the blow could land, the Crusader hefted the remains of his baton and hurled it through the air. The projectile struck the sword's blade. It didn't knock the weapon free from the swordsman's hand, but it drew his attention. With a low rumble, the assailant whirled on the Crusader.

"Stay out of this!" the dark warrior growled.

In the dim illumination provided by the streetlights outside the shattered window, the Crusader got a better look at his attacker. His mask was like a ski mask, but more ornate. *A ninja?* The rest of his outfit was likewise black, other than a silver tabard crossing his chest. The Crusader reached into his belt, pulled out an adhesive bead, squeezed, and pulled back his hand to throw it.

A throwing star buried itself in his forearm. The Crusader cried out at the piercing wound and clutched his wrist. The attacker shook his head, turned away from the Crusader, and lowered his sword. Two of the Red Dogs were nowhere to be seen. The one-armed Dog remained near the counter, clutching his stump and whimpering. The swordsman stepped over to the maimed gangster and knelt.

"Tell Liang I'm coming for him," the swordsman rumbled.

He rose and leaped out of the window. The Crusader stumbled to his feet. Two steps were enough to tell him that he was in no condition to pursue. Fury heated Carter's face and neck. The sword-wielding assailant had eluded him again. As adrenaline flushed from his body, he realized how much pain he was in. His legs loosened, wobbling like noodles. His anger drained away, replaced by a hollow exhaustion.

There was no time to rest. If he didn't stop the injured Red Dog's bleeding fast, the gangster would die. Carter knelt next to him and placed the adhesive bead he still clutched against the wounded man's stump. When he released the bead, blue-green goo spread across the wound and crept upward until it covered the thug's whole arm. He wondered if Dean had ever imagined using the adhesive gel to stop a bleeding wound. He liked to think the tech genius would have been proud of his innovation.

The Crusader dropped the bead and tapped his earbud. "Raina, I need an ambulance at my location."

"On it," she replied. "What's going on?"

"I've got a wounded subject. Our swordsman came back. I think he's a renegade vigilante."

He remained with the Red Dog and the restaurant owner until sirens wailed in the distance. Deciding it was best that he was not present when the authorities showed up, he clambered out of the shattered window, crossed the street, and used his grappling hook to ascend to the rooftop. It was a slow climb, his muscles protesting as his feet padded against the brick facade of the building, but he finally crested the roof and eased down to sit on the edge.

Carter removed his mask and watched as police cruisers and ambulances swarmed the restaurant. In moments, the ambulance sped away from the diner, taking the injured Red Dog with it. Carter hadn't started fighting crime with the intention of helping criminals, but he couldn't have let the guy die. The restaurant owner might have disagreed with him on that, but Carter wasn't a killer. Standing aside while someone bled out was almost the same as doing the killing himself.

His staff was ruined. The baton that had been cut in half was damaged beyond repair. He needed a replacement. Maybe Gideon still had a backup from his days as the Seraph. If not, it might be worth a call to Dean to get a new one. Carter's fingertips brushed the makeshift knife at his belt, the one made from Katrina Monahan's blade. If only he'd had the presence of mind to throw that at the swordsman instead. The knife would've stopped him for sure, and it probably would not have broken against the sword.

His phone chirped, alerting him to a new text. It was Dean. Was he psychic, in addition to his technological prowess?

But the text had nothing to do with Carter's staff. Instead, he had finally come through with a codename. *For the swordsman, how about Ravener?*

Ravener. That sounded suitably ominous.

Whoever the swordsman was, he had it out for Liang; but it seemed like he was willing to go after anyone from Serban's organization. That wouldn't have been a bad thing in Carter's book, but the assailant seemed intent on killing them. If Carter hadn't been there, Ravener would have murdered all three Red Dogs. He had been willing to injure Carter, too. If Ravener was a vigilante, he was intent on fighting crime in the most violent and destructive way possible.

The damage to the restaurant was a shame. The shattered window probably cost more than however much the Red Dogs had been shaking the owner down for.

If only there had been time for Carter to tag Ravener with a tracking device. Regardless, he would catch the swordsman eventually. Carter replaced his mask, rappelled down his grappling hook line to his motorcycle, and drove toward home.

CHAPTER 12

Gideon settled on the couch with Jolie and leaned in for a kiss when someone knocked at the door. He glanced at Jolie, who frowned and shrugged. Neither of them was expecting anyone, and it was unusually late for someone to show up unannounced. Gideon muted the TV, stood, and walked toward the door. With his formerly secret identity now public, it would not be hard for a vengeful criminal to find his address. There were no weapons within easy reach; and without his powers, he would have to rely on hand-to-hand combat if the visitor was hostile. Clenching one fist, he rested the other on the doorknob.

He peered out the peephole. Carter stood outside the apartment with his girlfriend, Raina. Relief washed through Gideon, loosening the tension in his body. He opened the door and stepped aside.

"Hey, guys. What's wrong?"

"Can we come in?" Carter asked.

At Gideon's nod, Carter and Raina stepped inside; and Gideon closed the door behind them. Carter had a bandage around his right wrist, and he was carrying a backpack in his left hand. Jolie stood from the couch and approached them.

Carter scratched the back of his head. "We need help. It's the swordsman I told you both about. I would say I fought him tonight, but that would imply there was any competition. He kicked my butt."

Carter extended his right arm. A small, red spot stained the white bandage. Gideon unraveled the cloth—which, judging by the unprofessional wrapping job, had been applied by either Raina or Carter himself. A small cut marked Carter's wrist—deep, but not dangerously so. If this was the only wound Carter had taken from this swordsman, he had handled himself well. Gideon mouthed "first aid kit" to Jolie, who hurried off to the other room. Gideon, Carter, and Raina took seats at the small dining room table next to the door.

"Looks like you got lucky. Fighting an opponent with a blade usually ends with injuries a lot worse than this, even if you win."

"Like I said, it wasn't much of a fight. I tried to stop him, but he knocked me into a table and hit me with a throwing star when I tried to use an adhesive bead. But otherwise, he didn't seem interested in me."

Jolie returned with the first aid kit. Gideon accepted it from her and set about treating Carter's wound. "Why not?"

"He was interrogating the Red Dogs I was fighting." Carter sucked in a breath as Gideon applied rubbing alcohol to the wound. "He cut one of their arms off and almost killed another guy before I distracted him. He was asking about Liang again, like he did with Markos Howell. The only thing I can figure is this guy is a vigilante, like me, and he's got a grudge against this Liang guy."

Gideon clenched his jaw. He could not shake the feeling that he should be on the streets with Carter. Gideon could have helped Carter fight the swordsman. The two of them might have been able to take him down or at least fight him off. Carter didn't have powers, and he more than held his own with years' less training and experience than Gideon had. Carter's father had managed to strike fear into the hearts of the city's criminals with nothing more than a ski mask and his fists.

Maybe Gideon had given up his life as the Seraph too soon. His powers were gone, but did that mean he had to give up fighting to help others?

"Sergeant Pulaski will make every effort to find this swordsman," Jolie said. "Don't worry. He won't be out there long."

Carter gritted his teeth. "I'm not sure the police can take him. He moved so fast. It reminded me of Katrina Monahan's fighting style."

A ghostly tremor snaked up Gideon's spine. Monahan had come closer than almost anyone else to killing Gideon when he had been the Seraph. During a fight on a rooftop, she shot him three times and threw him off the building, damaging his spine. If it hadn't been for his armor and landing in a snowbank, he likely would've died. It had taken him months to recover. Monahan had also killed Carter's father. If this guy was anything like her . . .

"So, why'd you come here tonight?" Gideon asked. "No offense—we don't mind you being here—but your wound looks fine, and there's nothing we can do to find the swordsman tonight."

Carter set his backpack down on their kitchen table and unzipped it. He pulled out three lengths of metal. One was recognizable as a truncheon, half of the *jo* staff Carter used to fight. Gideon had once used it himself before handing it off to Carter. It took Gideon a moment to realize that the other two pieces were the remains of the other truncheon. The swordsman must have cut the weapon clean in half.

"I need a new weapon. I was wondering if you might be able to give me a hand."

Gideon nodded. "I'll see what I can do. All my own weapons are for practice, not field use, so they wouldn't do much good against a trained swordsman. Equipping for a fight was a lot easier when Dean, Arianna, and Maddox were at Sterling Labs, but I'll figure something out."

"Thanks."

Gideon glanced at Raina. "You haven't said much. You okay?"

She nodded and nudged Carter's shoulder with her own. "I'm worried about him."

"I can sympathize," Jolie said. "Don't worry. Carter will be fine."

Raina abruptly looked up at Gideon. "Can you teach me to fight, too? I don't ever want to be caught off guard."

Gideon blinked. Evidently, she was concerned about more than Carter. Maybe it was fear that someone would trace Carter back to her. In that event, it might save her life if she could defend herself. When he was the Seraph, Gideon had taught Jolie some tricks beyond her police training. If Raina wanted to learn how to fight, he would be glad to accommodate her.

"Next time Carter and I meet, you can come, too."

"Thank you."

Carter glanced at his phone. "We'd better get going. My sister's babysitting tonight, and she needs a ride home. I'll see you guys later, but . . . thanks. For letting us talk."

"You're welcome." Gideon grasped Carter's shoulder. "You're doing good work. Don't get discouraged."

"I'll try." Carter smiled. "Thank you both. I couldn't do this without either of you."

Jolie leaned against Gideon's shoulder. "If you need anything else, we'll be here."

Carter and Raina left, and Gideon closed the door behind them. He picked up the remains of the truncheons and shook his head. This guy—Ravener, as Dean had named him in the group chat—could've killed Carter. And while it would have had nothing to do with Gideon, he still would have felt guilty. He had trained Carter and let him become a vigilante. He was at least partially responsible for whatever happened to the young man.

"Swordsmen and superpowered thieves." Jolie sighed. "I think the city's starting to go crazy again."

Because I stepped down as the Seraph. Gideon struggled to get the feeling under control. He had not chosen to give up his powers; they had been taken from him, and he knew God had a reason for that. He had to trust that. But part of him wanted to pull the Seraph suit out of the box it was stored in and go help Carter take Ravener down, powers or no. If he still had them, it would've been a breeze.

"Hey, don't," Jolie warned.

"What?"

"I can see it all over your face." She put a hand on his chest. "None of this is your fault. You've been doing a great job of accepting that you don't have your powers anymore. Don't let doubts creep in."

It was astounding how easily she could peer into his mind. Not long ago, Gideon had the ability to sense trace emotions. Jolie did it so easily without a hint of superhuman DNA.

"I shouldn't second guess how things happened," he said, "but I wonder sometimes why God had to take them. I could help so many people as the Seraph."

"Clearly, He wants something else from you."

"But what?" Gideon looked down at her. "Working in a lab isn't cutting it, Jolie. I don't feel like I'm making a difference."

She stretched up to kiss him. "When it's time to move on to the next thing, you'll know."

"You're right. Come on, let's relax and take our minds off this. Tomorrow, I'll see what I can do about getting Carter a new weapon. Maybe I'll call Dean and see what he suggests."

"That sounds like a good idea."

They settled back down on the couch, and Gideon wrapped his arms around Jolie as she selected a show to watch. But try as he might, Gideon couldn't shake the idea that he could still be doing more—and should be.

* * *

Ty liked to think he was open-minded. As a criminal, he had to be. He had to reconsider options most people would reject out of hand. If he shut down every absurd idea, he would never accomplish anything. But Ned and Richie had brought him a new plan, and he was close to denying it before he heard any details.

He stared at them, aware that his eyes were probably bugging out of his head but not particularly caring. It was the most ridiculous idea he had ever heard. The two of them shuffled awkwardly on their couch and waited for his response.

"Are you insane?" he demanded. "You want to steal an armored car?"

"It's coming into town this weekend," Ned said, "bringing in a fresh influx of cash. Why wait 'til the money's in the bank? Let's nab it on the way!"

Ty drew his lips into a thin line and stared at the moron he, for some reason, called a friend. Ned's bushy eyebrows were raised in anticipation and excitement. Clearly, he thought it was a fantastic idea. Ty swiveled to look at Richie, who bobbed his head up and down in agreement.

"Do you have any idea how well-guarded that truck will be? They're bringing in that cash to replace what we stole." Ty looked at Joanie. "Please, tell me you understand why this is insane."

She pressed her lips together. "Oh, one hundred percent."

"Come on!" Richie groaned. "The guards won't be a problem; we've got you! You can phase in and out of that truck, take your time loading up, and get out before the truck gets to the bank. It's foolproof!"

"Don't you think they'll be expecting that? They know I have powers. I used them at the bank. There are bound to be guards inside the truck; and as soon as I take them out, the driver or anyone else on security duty is going to call for backup."

"Not if their communications are jammed." Ned pointed to Joanie. "She can do that, right?"

Ty rubbed his forehead. They really were a special kind of stupid. Joanie nodded rapidly, her dreadlocks bouncing in time with her head, while Ned and Richie stared at him with disappointed frowns.

Ty stood, planted his hands on his hips, and stared at the floor. "Maybe if we were a professional team, we could pull this off. But we're amateurs, and our only saving grace is that I have superpowers. For an armored car job, that might not be enough. You're thinking big; but for a big score, you have to have a big plan. If you come up with something more concrete than a half-baked idea, we'll talk. Otherwise, it's off the table. I'm not going to prison."

He yanked open the door, stormed outside, and hopped in his car. Hopefully, that little tirade would knock some sense into them. They had approached a high-stakes job with the flippancy of a drug store robbery. Their suggestion was impossible. Unfortunately, his job application had been rejected. He would have to steal again to survive.

Maybe that was why his emotions threatened to boil over. If one thing could go right, maybe his life wouldn't seem so completely ridiculous.

A stoplight ahead turned red. Ty slammed his palm against the steering wheel. It felt good, so he did it again. He pounded the wheel over and over and let out a primal scream. By the time the light switched to green, the tide of negative emotions had washed over him, leaving his fingers trembling but his mind calm. Maybe Ned and Richie's idea, suicidal as it was, was the only glimmer of hope left in Ty's broken drudgery of a life.

Finally, he pulled into his driveway. An unfamiliar new-model Ford Focus was parked on the curbside. Ty climbed out of his car. With his left hand, he reached for the knife tucked at the small of his back. He doubted the owners of the vehicle were a threat, but his father—his real father—had taught him to keep a constant vigil. He unlocked the front door, tucked the keys into his pocket, and pulled the door open, keeping his other hand wrapped around the knife hilt.

Rhonda sat on the couch with another girl and a boy, both sharing her dark skin tone. Ty guessed they were in their late teens or early twenties. Rhonda looked up as Ty entered, a smile wide on her face.

"Hey, Mr. Vickers! This is my brother Carter, and his girlfriend Raina. They came to pick me up. I didn't realize you'd be this late."

"Oh." Ty took his hand away from the knife. "Sorry, that's my fault. My appointment didn't go quite as planned."

"I'm sorry to hear that. But Emi was a perfect angel."

Ty studied the floor. "She always is."

Ty stepped toward Rhonda, took out his wallet, and counted out bills. With each one, he cringed internally. He was throwing all this money away on a babysitter when it could be going toward food or clothes, things Emi really needed. *I should've been here.* And if Emi's mother was still around, none of this would've been a problem.

Out of the corner of his eye, Ty sized up Carter, purely out of habit. He was of average height, but he had a muscular frame. Something about the way he sat gave Ty the impression that he was a fighter. It took a moment to pin it down, but Ty finally realized that Carter sat with his back perfectly straight and his head on a swivel, always watching. Someone had taught Carter lessons similar to the ones Ty's father had given him all those years ago.

He handed Rhonda her payment. "Fifty bucks. The extra is for staying later. Sorry again, kid."

"Thank you, Mr. Vickers." Rhonda took the money. "Emi's fast asleep in her crib."

Carter and Raina rose and followed Rhonda toward the door. Ty swiveled as they walked to prevent them from seeing the knife tucked in his waistband. The three young adults filed out the door. Ty closed it and locked it behind them. He slumped down on the couch. He was stretched so thin he had nearly drawn a knife on a couple of teenagers because he didn't recognize their car. Vigilance was good, but paranoia was dangerous. Maybe a good night's sleep would wash away the terrible day.

That was unlikely. It never had before.

* * *

"That was odd." Carter pulled open his car door. "That guy—Mr. Vickers? He seemed really tense, like he was expecting trouble. Did you see how he had his hand behind his back?"

He realized that Rhonda probably hadn't noticed. She hadn't been trained to observe body language and watch for threats. But Carter had seen as soon as Vickers had walked through the door that the man was a fighter. His muscles were taut, and the way he held his left arm hinted at a weapon hidden behind his back. Whoever Vickers was, he had seen his share of trouble. But who in the Brooks hadn't?

Rhonda shrugged. "He's protective of Emi."

"I can see why." Raina beamed. "She's such a cutie."

Carter started the car and pulled away from Vickers' house. He was sure they were right; the man probably wanted to protect his daughter. He remembered more than once seeing his father clench his fists and half-rise from the couch when someone knocked on the door. Living in the neighborhoods in the Brooks bred excessive caution.

Yet there was something odd about Vickers. He looked East Asian, while his name sounded English. To Carter, that set off the warning signals of a pseudonym. It was possible that he had simply been adopted or changed his name for any number of reasons, so Carter decided to downplay his suspicions for Rhonda's sake.

He glanced over his shoulder at his sister. "That's a pretty sweet haul. You wanna share some of that loot?"

Rhonda clasped the bills protectively. "You've got a job, dummy."

"Oh, yeah. I guess I do." Carter chuckled. "Wish my job was taking care of cute babies. I have to take care of ugly adult babies in business suits."

Raina and Rhonda laughed. Carter grinned and rounded the corner toward Raina's house. He would drop her off first and go home with Rhonda.

"Hey, what happened to your wrist?" Rhonda asked.

Carter pulled his jacket sleeve farther over the bandage. "Uh, nothing."

"Don't give me that." Rhonda leaned forward between Carter and Raina's seats. "You got hurt tonight, didn't you?"

"A little bit." Carter reached over and playfully shoved her head. "Nothing too serious, and nothing I can't handle."

If only that were true. Carter stared out the windshield at the road ahead. He would never tell Rhonda—or Raina or anyone else—but he was pretty sure Ravener was so far out of his league that no amount of training with Gideon would make up for it. Still, he had to try. His father and Gideon had legitimized the reputation of vigilantes in the Brooks. Carter wasn't going to let a murderous swordsman tarnish that.

CHAPTER 13

It had been two days since Carter's confrontation with Ravener. The cut on his wrist was healing nicely. Unfortunately, his pride wasn't as cooperative. He couldn't wait to get out on the streets and track Ravener down. He wanted to take the ninja down a peg—both to stop him from killing anyone else and to show him that no one messed with the Crusader. But until Gideon got back to him with a new weapon, it didn't seem wise to push his luck.

His lack of weaponry didn't prevent him from protecting the Brooks from other threats in the meantime. Carter was a skilled hand-to-hand fighter. He could take down stray thugs easily enough, and the amplified thief—who Dean had coined the Phantom—was still on the loose. But if he met Ravener again, the mysterious vigilante might not be as merciful as last time.

Carter snapped back to reality as the lobby doors opened and Mr. Wheaton strode in, dressed in his usual pressed, gray business suit. Carter tightened his jaw as the CFO approached. It never got easier to see his smug face.

"Good morning, Connor."

Carter crinkled his nose. "Carter, sir."

"Right. Carter."

Wheaton handed over his briefcase and put his other items into a bin. Carter watched as the thirty-something CFO stepped through the x-ray machine. He wondered why Wheaton had tried to call him by his first name, rather than the usual "Mr. Jonson." Trying to be more personable with his employees? If so, he needed to learn their names before he tried that. Carter stepped to the other side of the x-ray and handed the briefcase back to Wheaton.

"Have a good day, sir."

"Thank you." Wheaton took the case and his belongings. "Enjoy your morning."

"Blowhard," one of the other guards grumbled.

Carter grinned. None of the guards who worked for Sterling Enterprises liked Wheaton. Carter doubted any of the other employees did, either. They all missed Dean. He was a boss who cared about the people who worked under him. Carter wished he would hurry up and come home from D.C., but Dean seemed happy there.

"At least he was in the right ballpark." Carter shrugged. "He could've called me 'Joe' or 'Billy.' Honestly, I don't expect much from him anymore."

Carter dropped into the seat behind the security desk. While he killed time, he planned out his evening. He would check in with Silas before training with Gideon and Raina. He had been as surprised as anyone when she asked Gideon to train her, but he was glad she was doing it. He would feel better if she could protect herself, and it meant he could spend more time with her. That was a big plus in his book.

* * *

Jolie looked up at the pawn shop and scanned the area around it. There was an alley exit, which meant if things got ugly, someone could run out the back. A security camera was mounted over the front door.

That might give her a clue if she got a warrant to see the footage. She stepped inside, a little bell ringing above her as she did, and looked around the interior.

Items of varying value cluttered the shelves. The shop owner stood behind the glass counter, leaning against it and watching her. Jolie was glad it was glass. She could see underneath and keep an eye on the man's hands. As far as she could tell, there was no gun that the owner could reach for. She didn't see a door that matched up to the alley exit, but there was a door directly behind the owner that led to a back room. The alley door was most likely back there.

"How can I help you?" the owner asked.

He was a man of average height and build, dressed in blue jeans and a maroon polo shirt. A tattoo of a compass marked his wrist, and a short, scruffy beard lined his jaw. He didn't look like a threat, but appearances could be deceiving. Jolie kept her guard up.

"I'm looking for Andreas Hall."

One of her criminal informants had told her that Andreas Hall ran a laundering business out of his pawn shop. If that was true, the amplified thief might have come to Hall to exchange the stolen bills for clean, nonsequential ones. The story lined up with what the man who spent the stolen bill had told her. She had called him to follow up and ask if he had visited a pawn shop recently. His confirmation was all the evidence Jolie needed to check out Andreas Hall's shop.

A quick search at the precinct confirmed priors for Hall— racketeering, illegal gambling, theft, and more. And based on the mugshot she'd seen, the man behind the counter was Andreas Hall himself. But it would probably be better if she didn't clue him in that she knew that.

"What for?" he asked. "And who's askin'?"

Jolie moved her jacket aside, revealing the badge clipped to her belt and, subtly, the gun next to it. Hall glanced down at her waist, and his casual half-smile straightened. He looked up at her with a frown.

"What do the cops want with Andreas?"

"I need to ask him a few questions." Jolie leaned against the glass counter with one hand.

Andreas backed toward the door. "I'll see if I can find him."

"Don't move." Jolie's hand dropped to her Glock. "Stop playing games, Hall. Do you want to talk to me here, or would you prefer to go down to the police station? Either way, we are having this conversation."

"You don't have anything on me. Otherwise you would've come in here with a warrant."

Hall took another step backward toward the swinging door. Jolie stepped forward—and a meaty arm shot from behind one of the shelves and wrapped around her throat. Jolie cried out as Hall pushed through the back door. Jolie gasped for air, but the arm tightened around her. She raised her feet, placed them against the shelf opposite her, and shoved. She tumbled back into the shelf behind her, knocking it flat on top of her assailant. Jolie groaned as she came down on top of the shelves, each one digging into her back. But the muscular arm let go.

Jolie rolled to her feet and rushed through the swinging door. The back room of the pawn shop was set up like a little crime den— gambling tables, metal cases opened to reveal stacks of cash, a few stray guns. To her left, the door to the alley hung wide open. Jolie bolted through it, drawing her gun as she ran. There was no sign of Andreas in the alley, but the only way out was back onto the street, where Jolie's car was parked. She hurried in that direction and looked both ways. To her left, a brown-haired figure in a red polo shoved his way through the heavy mid-afternoon crowd.

Jolie pounded after him. She pumped her arms and weaved between pedestrians. She had no idea if Hall was armed, but it was a safe bet that he was, especially considering the weapons that had been sitting in the back of the pawn shop. He would have been stupid not to grab one. Jolie darted around a couple walking hand-in-hand and kept her eyes on the red polo. Hall reached an intersection and turned left. Jolie came to the same turn three seconds later and rounded it.

She found herself staring into the barrel of a black pistol. Her heart skipped, and she froze. There was no way she would get her own gun up in time to stop him from shooting.

A fist came down on Hall's forearms, and the gun clattered to the ground. Another blow struck him in the jaw, knocking him flat on his back. Her rescuer was a bald, dark-skinned man wearing a blue button-down shirt tucked into black slacks, and he was muscular enough that his sleeves were tight against his biceps. She thought she recognized him from somewhere but couldn't quite place him.

"Thank you. I thought I was dead for a second." Jolie knelt and pulled a pair of handcuffs from her belt. "Have we met?"

"Silas Rockwell. I was coming out of the gym when I saw this guy pull his gun. I couldn't stand by and let someone get hurt."

Jolie recognized the name. Silas had helped take down the Shine drug trade. Jolie and Silas had met briefly after the drug dealer Vince Powers burned his apartment building to the ground in an effort to kill him.

"Thanks, Silas." Jolie finished cuffing Hall and pulled him to his feet. "You probably saved my life."

"No problem, Detective . . . Anderson?"

"Turner, actually. Anderson was my maiden name. You have a good memory."

"Right." Silas backed away. "I'll leave you to it. If you need any more help, I'm always down to smack around a few bad guys. And tell your husband I said hello and that we miss seeing him around these parts."

As Silas blended into the crowd, Jolie picked up Hall's gun and pushed her suspect down the street toward her car. Hall growled at her, and Jolie tapped the small of his back with the barrel of her gun. He quieted down.

"That's what I thought. Let's get you and your friend down to the station, Mr. Hall. I have a feeling you've got a lot to tell us."

CHAPTER 14

Ned and Richie had not made a peep about the armored car heist in two days. Maybe that was for the best. The transport was set to arrive in Sojourn City in two more days, and they were nowhere near prepared to hit it. If they brought it up with so little time to plan the theft, Ty's concern for their sanity would be confirmed.

But unfortunately, they had to do something. Ty still had several weeks' worth of cash, if he used it right, but they couldn't wait until he was broke to plan their next job. And since the career market consistently failed Ty, another robbery was his only option. *The world has made me truly desperate.* It hadn't been that way, not so long ago. He'd had a wife, a line on a great job . . . He had been set.

Until someone in authority connected the dots between Ty and his godfather. In a single day, all his hopes had drained away. Ty could not find it within himself to be angry. He understood why no one would hire him. Who would trust the son of a man who had done the things Ty's godfather had? They hadn't bothered trying to trust him, so he hadn't bothered trying to earn their trust. They feared he was like the man who had helped raise him, so that was exactly what he would become.

Someone knocked on the door. Ty grabbed his knife, held it reverse-grip in his left hand, and approached the door. He peered out the peephole. Joanie stood on his porch, looking around nervously.

Ty pulled the door open and slid his knife back into its sheath. She stepped inside and grabbed his arm.

"The cops grabbed Hall."

Ty frowned. "What?"

"Hall—the guy who launders our money." Joanie shut the door behind her. "Some detective came to his pawn shop earlier this afternoon and arrested him."

Ty's stomach knotted. "Can the money be traced back to you . . . to us?"

"Possibly. I met with Hall myself, but I didn't tell him my name. He charged extra for that, by the way. He's seen my face, and he could give the cops a description. But it's not like I'm the only mixed girl with dreadlocks in the Brooks, so maybe it'll be okay? But the cops are getting way too close for comfort and—"

"Easy." Ty put a hand on her shoulder. "Take a breath. You're right. They are getting close. Let me think for a minute."

Ty wasn't as worried about Hall giving the cops a description of Joanie as he was that the money exchanger might have a video recording of her entering his store or of the exchange itself taking place. If that was the case, the authorities would soon have Joanie's picture. It was a short jump from her to Ty; and if that happened, all of them would be in trouble.

"Have you told Ned or Richie yet?"

"No."

"Good." Ty rushed toward the garage, and Joanie fell in behind him. "We need to get to Hall's store and erase any footage he might have of your visit. That's going to be the cops' number one piece of evidence. If we can do that, we should buy ourselves enough time to take another haul and get out of Sojourn City."

He opened the garage door and walked to the cabinet that held his gear. It was almost nightfall. If he left immediately, it would be dark by the time he reached Hall's place. He could sneak inside, erase the footage, and sneak back out before anyone knew.

"What about Emi?" Joanie asked.

"You stay here with Emi." Ty began pulling on his black suit. "I can delete a video file. If I need help, I'll call. This shouldn't take more than an hour."

"Don't you need a lookout? What if the cops show up while you're inside?"

Ty paused for a moment. He could phase out of the room if the cops showed up, but if that happened while he was in the middle of deleting the files, he might not finish the job. They might find some footage he failed to erase. If Joanie was there to warn him, he might be able to finish up in time or at least come up with a backup plan.

"I'll call the babysitter. Go start the van."

Joanie sprinted out of the garage. Ty finished putting on his suit, gloves, and utility belt. He tucked his mask into his belt for the time being, along with his knives, and closed the cabinet. He went inside to his bedroom, grabbed a knee-length black coat, and pulled it on. Once he was dressed, he picked up his phone and dialed Rhonda.

"Hello?"

"Hey, kid, it's Mr. Vickers. Something came up last minute, and I really need someone to watch Emi tonight. Do you think you could be here in fifteen minutes?"

There was a brief pause. "My mom says she can bring me. I'll be there in ten."

"Thanks, kid."

Ty hung up, stuffed the phone in his coat pocket, and walked out to the living room. With the police potentially on their tail, every minute counted.

Ten minutes passed like a decade. Ty paced across the living room floor, continually reaching down to the hilt of one of the knives on his belt. He half-expected to hear sirens as the police bore down on his house, ready to take him away from his daughter and throw him in a cell. He took a deep breath and held it, like his father—his real father, the one he loved and desperately missed—had taught him. He let the air out through his nose and felt some of the stress leave with it.

Finally, there was a knock at the door. Ty pulled it open and ushered Rhonda inside. She opened her mouth to speak, but Ty put a hand on her shoulder.

"Thank you for being here on such short notice. I really have to go, but I won't be gone for more than an hour—hopefully."

"O—okay."

Ty stepped outside without another word, closed the door behind him, and hopped into the idling white van sitting on the curbside. Joanie put the van in drive and peeled away from Ty's house. He could not help but notice that when it came down to the wire, Ned and Richie were not present. Part of him knew it was because Joanie had only brought the problem to him, but that told him enough. They did not have one gang. They were two duos, allied out of convenience. Ty and Joanie. Ned and Richie. At least, he knew whom he could trust the most.

As the van trundled down the street toward Hall's shop, Ty removed his overcoat and pulled on his mask. He hoped he didn't encounter any cops because he hadn't had a chance to replace the baton he lost at the bank. His only weapons were throwing knives. If it came down to a fight, the odds were good that he would have to kill someone; and that was the last thing he wanted.

"Here we are," Joanie said. "Computer should be in the back room. Access the stored files from the security cameras and delete them. You may want to delete a few more than the ones I'm in. Pick them randomly. It'll make it harder for the cops to figure out which one we were after."

"Good thinking." Ty looked out at the pawn shop. "I'll be back."

He phased through the van door and crept toward the pawn shop. There was a camera above the front door. It would be better to take the alley entrance. Ty wove around the building and phased through the metal door. The back room was dark. Ty pulled a flashlight from his belt and shone it around the room. An old computer sat in one corner. Ty pushed past a gambling table and sat down in a rusty folding chair in front of the computer.

The monitor flared to life, its bright blue screen lighting up the room. Ty set his flashlight down and focused on the computer. The blue loading screen was replaced by a login request—and it required a password. Of course. Why hadn't he thought of that? Ty hissed between his teeth and slammed a fist down into the desk. He could get Joanie in here to hack into the computer, but there was no telling how long that would take. The cops could show up while she was working. He'd have to go with a cruder solution.

He pushed the monitor aside, grabbed the computer itself, and phased his hand inside. He tore through the hard drive and pulled his hand out. The monitor blinked out, and the console spat sparks. Satisfied, Ty rushed back out the door and onto the street. He jumped into the van and buckled in.

Joanie's eyebrows shot up. "That was fast."

"I took a more direct route. I phased into the computer and destroyed the hard drive."

"Well . . . whatever works."

Ty glanced at his watch. "I told Rhonda I'd be gone for an hour. We've still got time. Let's go to Ned and Richie's place. There are things we need to discuss."

* * *

The Crusader dropped from the rooftop, grabbed the lip of the porch's awning, and used it to swing onto the porch, landing in a crouch. Silas, leaning against one of the pillars supporting the awning, turned at the sound of the Crusader's boots touching the ground. A small smile played over Silas' face.

"You have to be that dramatic?"

"Part of the charm." Carter smirked. "Have anything for me?"

"I've looked everywhere for any information on someone named Liang, but no dice. Whoever it is, they're covering their tracks pretty well."

"Must be. Well . . . thanks for looking. Call if you hear anything else."

"Will do. Hey, are you helping Detective Turner on her case?"

"The superhuman thief?" Carter shook his head. "I've been more focused on this swordsman. Why?"

Silas pressed his lips together in a grim line. "She almost got shot today. You might want to keep an eye out for her."

"Jolie can take care of herself. Trust me on that. Thanks for looking out for her, but be careful. I'd hate to lose you, and your family needs you." Those words sounded all too familiar, and strange coming from Carter's own mouth, especially directed at a man who was over a decade older than him. "I say that from experience."

"Sure, but Detective Turner's family needs her, too."

The Crusader nodded. "Watch your back, Silas."

"Thought that was your job." Silas grinned. "I'll watch your back; you watch mine; and we'll all be a whole lot safer."

Carter dropped his hand to the wound on his wrist, memories of his battle with Ravener coming back to him. "Don't trust me to watch your back. I can barely get my own."

"That's why we work together. I could help you fight if you need a hand."

"Maybe." The Crusader's job had been easier when the Seraph and the other Vindicators were with him, that was for sure. "But not against this guy. He's fast, and he's deadly. I'm not willing to risk your life to stop him."

"It's mine to risk. Anyway, offer's on the table. You ever want a hand, I'm there. Otherwise, I'll keep digging."

"Thank you."

The Crusader fired his grappling hook and zipped away from Silas' house. He was all out of leads. But he was sure it wouldn't be long before Ravener showed his face again. He wasn't ready for that. He hoped his new gear was ready soon, or the bloodbath in the Brooks was going to get a lot messier.

CHAPTER 15

Ty pushed his way through the door to Ned's home. Both Ned and Richie were already there, watching TV and eating popcorn. The TV was an expensive seventy-five-inch flatscreen, and the red leather couch looked like it cost as much as the television. A burst of anger welled in Ty's chest at the sight. With one smooth motion, he drew one of his throwing knives and hurled it across the room, burying it in the wall between the two men. They jumped, spilling their popcorn over the living room floor.

"What is wrong with you?" Richie exclaimed.

"Are you nuts?" Ned shouted.

"Shut up!" Ty glanced over his shoulder as Joanie entered and closed the door. "We need to talk."

"You didn't have to almost skewer us." Richie pulled the knife from the wall. "We're good to talk anytime."

Ty took his blade back. "I need you to understand how serious I am."

"Consider it understood." Richie scowled. "What's going on?"

"We almost got caught tonight. The guy who laundered our cash got busted by the cops, and he had footage of Joanie meeting with him. I destroyed the footage before the cops could get it, but it was too close. You were right. We need to get out of Sojourn City." Ty glared at them. "Which is why it bothered me when I came in here and found you munching on popcorn, sitting on a thousand-dollar couch, and watching sports on a ludicrous TV instead of planning the truck heist."

Ned and Richie exchanged glances, and their eyes lit up. It was clear that they had not been doing their due diligence. They only had two days to plan the heist, and there were a lot of obstacles to overcome. It was the kind of hit that pro thieves spent weeks planning.

"Actually, we have been. We were taking a break." Ned jumped up from the couch, spilling more popcorn that had been resting on his stomach. "Here. Look."

He crossed the room, picked up a stack of papers from the kitchen counter, and handed them to Ty. The papers were crumpled and covered in grease stains, but they were legible. Ty unrolled them and skimmed the pages. There were blueprints for the truck, schedules, and a roster of guards. All in all, it was impressively detailed. There were a few pages at the bottom of the pile that looked like blueprints for some kind of technology.

"What are these?" he asked.

"You wanted us to be useful." Richie tapped those blueprints. "That's how. Those are high-tech weapons made by Sterling Labs. If we get those, we can do more than sit in the van."

Ty frowned. "How are we going to get them?"

"We can break into Sterling Labs tomorrow night—"

"Two jobs in two nights? Are you insane?" Ty seemed to be asking them that question all too often. He was beginning to think the answer was obvious and that he was equally insane to listen to them. "There's no way we can pull it off."

"No, listen." Ned raised his hands in front of him. "The guy we got all this info from has a friend who works security at Sterling

Labs. He'll conveniently step out for a smoke tomorrow night, and we're in."

"Uh-huh. And what's in it for the guard?"

There was a pause. "A tenth of the profit we make off the truck heist."

Ty ground his jaw. A tenth was a big part of their score. They might not walk away with as much as he hoped. But if things went off smoothly, he might still get enough to leave the city with Emi and never come back. As insane as it was, it sounded like their only option. Anything else wouldn't win them the funds he needed.

"Okay. I've got to get back to my daughter before the sitter gets suspicious, but we'll hit Sterling Labs tomorrow night and hash out the details of the truck heist on Saturday."

"We're actually doing this?" Richie asked, grinning.

"We're doing this." Ty backed toward the door. "But only because we don't have any other choice. And after this, I'm out. For good."

He opened the door and left without waiting for their response. Joanie's soft footsteps pattered on the sidewalk behind him. Ty jumped into the van and waited for her to get in. As she did, he studied her expression. Her eyebrows were furrowed, and her dark eyes were wide and locked on his face. Maybe this plan was too risky for her.

He cut her off before she could protest. "It's the only way."

"The cops are onto us." Joanie stared at him. "If we screw this up, we'll all go to jail for a long time."

"I'm aware." His shoulders tensed and he spoke in a clipped tone he rarely took with Joanie. "Start the van; let's get going."

"Whatever you say, boss."

* * *

The wooden rod *whooshed* through the air over Raina's head as she hurled herself backward into the foam mat to avoid being struck. She let out a shrill yelp and rolled to the side as the rod came down toward her. She came up in a crouch and somersaulted as the rod swung toward her a third time.

Raina grunted as the rod smacked into her thigh. Stinging pain spread throughout her right leg, and she grimaced and clutched at the injured spot. Seeing that she had stopped, Gideon lowered his weapon and chuckled.

"You're fast and agile, but you've got to fight back at some point. You'll wear yourself out, and your attacker will catch up to you."

Raina panted. "Fair . . . point."

She much preferred archery. Why couldn't she use that to defend herself? She had been shooting her whole high school career and was good enough to make the college team, too. And while Gideon was right about her dodging, that was another area she felt comfortable in. She had participated in track and field, and she was used to moving quickly.

Gideon twirled his weapon. He said it was called a *bokken*. It was shaped and weighted roughly like a sword. He had brought a pair of them to Carter's garage, so Carter could get experience fighting with a sword and against someone who used one. But Raina had asked to go first, since she didn't have any martial arts experience. She thought her athletic experience would at least prepare her for the exertion the training would require.

That had been a mistake.

"Need a break?" Gideon asked.

Raina smiled sheepishly. "Maybe for a minute?"

"Okay." Gideon gestured with the *bokken*. "Carter?"

Raina stepped off the mat as Carter stepped on. She grabbed a water bottle from a table set up in the corner and hopped up to sit on the table. Carter walked into the center of the mat, his feet pressing down into the blue foam, and twirled his own *bokken*. It looked heavier than the truncheons he usually used. Raina sipped at the water as Gideon stepped up to face Carter.

"Ready?" Gideon asked.

"Go."

Gideon stepped forward, swinging his sword down vertically toward Carter's head. Carter raised his weapon horizontally, blocking Gideon's strike. He smacked Gideon's weapon aside and swung diagonally for Gideon's neck. Gideon stepped back and parried.

The wooden blades clacked loudly in the garage as the two men stepped up their duel. They danced across the mat, swords flying at lightning speeds. Raina was impressed. Carter picked up on swordplay fast—not perfectly, of course. More than once, he had to throw himself into a shoulder roll or backflip to avoid being struck by Gideon's *bokken*; and too often for Raina's liking, the older man's weapon found purchase on Carter's body. Gideon tried to pull his blows whenever he struck, but they still sounded painful. Her boyfriend stubbornly refused to give up, and he fought until his gray t-shirt was soaked with sweat.

Wonder what it's like to have a normal boyfriend. Not that she would trade Carter for anyone, but sometimes, she wished he spent his nights taking her on dates or cuddling up and watching a movie rather than beating the snot out of criminals. She was proud of him, and she'd been a big fan of the Crusader long before she knew he was Carter Jonson. It was hard sometimes, but she had to be strong for him. She knew he felt God had a purpose for the Crusader, and she wouldn't argue with that.

She picked up her pocket notebook, which she carried with her everywhere, and scribbled the word *purpose* in it. She still hadn't managed to create a new poem, but Carter's words about new experiences had stuck with her. It was another part of the reason she wanted to learn how to fight.

Gideon broke away from a lock with Carter. "Let's take a break. You should rest."

"Nah." Carter raised his sword. "Let's keep going."

Raina rolled her eyes but smiled anyway. His stubbornness was both frustrating and endearing. She was glad they hadn't argued much. She was as stubborn as he was.

"You can't master swordsmanship in one night." Gideon rested his weapon across his shoulders. "You need rest and time to think about what you've learned. Practice it on your own, but don't overdo it."

"Fine."

"You both did well." Gideon took Carter's *bokken*. "I'm going to try to have new gear ready for you soon. Until then, stay careful. You don't want to run into Ravener while you're unarmed."

"Thanks, Gideon."

Raina hopped up from the table. "Yeah, thanks. Hopefully, I'll do better with practice."

"You will. Good night, guys."

Gideon left the garage, and Raina wrapped her arm around Carter's waist. She knew he was itching to find Ravener; she could read it in the taut lines drawn across his face. But Gideon's advice was sound. Taking on that swordsman while unarmed would be a death sentence.

"I'm going to go take a shower," Raina said. "I suggest you do the same."

Carter glanced down at his shirt. "What? You don't like the sweat?"

"Don't like the smell." Raina crinkled her nose and laughed. "I'll see you tomorrow."

"Okay." Carter kissed Raina's forehead. "Good night."

"Night."

Raina picked up her jacket, bundled up, and walked out the same door Gideon had. She climbed onto her moped and looked back at Carter's house for a moment before she started the little electric scooter and headed home.

CHAPTER 16

Gideon padded down the sidewalk toward Sterling Labs, assuring himself that this wouldn't be another tired day of monotony. He had to make the most of the job he had, at least until he found some clarity on what he should do next. Pushing the dread and looming boredom from his mind, he stepped into the courtyard that decorated the lab's front lawn.

Silas Rockwell's message, delivered through Jolie yesterday, hadn't helped his spirits. *We miss seeing him around these parts.* He could tell she had been reluctant to mention it. She told him that she hoped it would remind him of the difference he had made in the city. It had, but that only made him wish he could do it again.

As he walked, he pulled out his phone and dialed Dean's cell phone. If he could not fight crime directly, he could help those who were. Carter needed new gear if he was going to defeat Ravener, and Gideon wasn't technically proficient enough to build it himself. Dean was. Dean could help whether he was present in Sojourn City or far off in Washington, D.C.

"Dean Sterling's phone, this is Dean Sterling speaking. How may I help you?"

Gideon laughed. "Hey, Dean."

"Hey, Gid." Gideon heard the grin in his best friend's voice. "What's going on?"

"It's about Carter. He needs new gear if he's going to handle Ravener. He cut up Carter's staff and did a number on him."

"He broke my staff?" Dean growled. "This means war."

Dean had designed the truncheons for Gideon and had later installed the clasp that bound them together into a staff. He had also invented the adhesive beads, grappling hook, and the suit of armor Carter wore. Everything Gideon had used, and everything Carter used in his wake, was a product of Dean's mind.

"Well, lucky for you, I might be able to help out," Dean said. "Not directly—but Maddox is heading back to Sojourn City to pick up some things for me. I'll send along some design ideas and let Maddox put them together for Carter there."

Maddox Odell was half of the science duo that had helped Dean with the designs on many of the devices Gideon and Carter used. Maddox and his partner Arianna Serafin were certifiable geniuses who had joined Dean in D.C. If Maddox was going to be in town, it would be easier than asking Dean to work on new gear from D.C. Relief washed over Gideon. Carter wouldn't have to do without equipment for much longer.

"Tell Maddox about any upgrades you want to Carter's tech or suit. He'll be there tonight; his flight leaves in a few hours."

"He could be here in half the time if he brought the Raptor." Gideon chuckled. "Flying coach seems so understated."

The Raptor was the supersonic jet that Sterling Labs had upgraded for the Vindicators' use. It had allowed the team to break into groups and simultaneously save Chicago and Washington, D.C., from Jeremiah Ashcroft's nephiloids. Gideon wondered what Dean had done with the plane since the superhero team was fractured.

"Nah, we might need the Raptor here. I'll have Maddox give you a call when he lands. And don't worry, Audrey and I will visit Sojourn soon. Love you, bro."

"Love you, too."

Gideon stuffed his phone in his pocket and shook his head. He and Dean had been friends for almost longer than Gideon could remember. Before they were superheroes together, they had *played* superheroes as kids, wearing towels as capes and bandanas as masks. Dean's prolonged absence left an unwelcome hollowness for Gideon. Dean and Audrey liked their lives in D.C. Gideon didn't begrudge them that, but he would've given almost anything to have his best friend back in Sojourn City.

He shifted his thoughts back to Carter's gear. They should take full advantage of Maddox's presence. There were a few more upgrades Carter might need. On his lunch break, Gideon would swing by Carter's house, pick up the Crusader suit, and have Maddox work his magic on it. It would be a nice surprise for Carter, and it would help him bring down Ravener, too.

* * *

Carter stepped out of the Sterling Enterprises lobby, hands tucked in his pocket, and whistled. It was unusually sunny for a late-winter afternoon in northern Michigan. The air was still a little too chilly for comfort, but the distant warmth of the sun balanced it out. With his lunch bag tucked under his arm, Carter walked around the corner toward the park behind Sterling Enterprises.

He wasn't the only one taking advantage of the beautiful day. Several picnic tables around the park were filled with people. He recognized some from Sterling Enterprises. Others were likely from the other corporate buildings that surrounded the park. As Carter walked toward an empty table, he looked out at the lake. There on the boardwalk, he had stood with Gideon and watched Jolie shoot and kill Luca Serban. It had only been five months ago, but it seemed like a lifetime.

He sat down and opened his lunch sack. He removed his roast beef and cheddar sandwich when his phone vibrated in his pocket. Rolling his eyes, Carter replaced the sandwich in its Ziploc bag and pulled out his phone. It was Raina. Irritation fading away, Carter answered the phone and pressed it to his ear.

"Hey, what's up?"

"We've got an armed robbery," she said. "Jewelry store at the edge of the Brooks, Twelfth Street. It looks like they're taking hostages."

Carter rose. Lunch would have to wait. "On my way."

He darted through the park toward the parking garage. He didn't have the Crusader suit or any of his tech with him, but he had to do something. He ran up to the parking garage's second floor, slid into his car, and peeled out of the garage.

"Is it the Phantom?" he asked.

"Not sure. The police chatter hasn't mentioned powers yet, but it's possible."

If the amplified thief had struck again, Carter was woefully unprepared to face down the criminal. Some of Dean's tech helped give Carter an edge when he fought amps; but without that gear, all Carter had to rely on was his hand-to-hand combat skill. An amp with the ability to phase through solid mass would be almost impossible to touch. Still, Carter had to try.

As he weaved through traffic toward the Brooks, he reached over and opened his glove compartment. His father's old Crusader mask was in there for such an event. He took the mask out, closed the glove compartment, and pulled the mask over his face. He zipped his black leather jacket over his security uniform, all the while steering with his knee. It hit him how much he looked like his father—the black leather and ski mask had been Wyatt's exact ensemble. And Wyatt had used his fists rather than technology or weapons to stop crime. Carter could do it, too.

He brought the phone back to his ear. "Any update?"

"The police have surrounded the jewelry store, but the robbers barricaded themselves inside with the hostages."

"Multiple robbers?" Carter tightened his jaw. "Maybe the amp has a gang, or maybe this is someone else. Do we have any more clues to who they are?"

"Police think they're members of the Tyrants."

"I'll be there in five."

He pulled off the interstate and into the Brooks, parking a block from the jewelry store on Twelfth. He could try to go in the back, but it would be better for him to coordinate with the police first so they didn't shoot him accidentally. He didn't look like the Crusader usually did. He probably looked more like a robber.

As the Crusader approached the police cars that created a semicircle around the store, he looked for Paul Jordan. He spotted the aging cop halfway down the lineup and jogged toward him. Several officers saw him and raised their guns. The Crusader froze and lifted his hands.

"Easy! It's me—the Crusader."

Paul spotted him and approached. "Stand down, boys. Keep an eye on the store while I talk to our vigilante friend."

Most of the cops returned their sights—and their guns—to the storefront, but a couple others kept a wary eye on Carter. Paul circled around one of the cruisers and approached the Crusader.

"Going old school today?" Paul asked.

"Didn't have time to get my gear." The Crusader glanced at the jewelry store. It occupied the first floor of a five-story building. "I have the basics: robbery-turned-hostage situation. What are the details? How many guys? How many guns? How many hostages?"

"We count five suspects, all armed with handguns. Several customers managed to escape the store when they saw the robbers enter, but two customers and the clerk are trapped inside."

"Do any of the perps have superpowers?"

"Not as far as we can tell, no."

Carter suspected the Phantom was not among the thieves, given that information. If he was there, he probably would have phased out and escaped already. It was more likely that Carter was looking at a run-of-the-mill, but still dangerous, gang heist.

"Is there a back entrance?"

"No—otherwise they would've already been out of there." Paul pointed at the store. "But there may be a way to get down into the store from one of the upper floors."

"I'll check it out." Carter backed away. "Be ready to move in when I engage."

CHAPTER 17

The Crusader edged into the alley behind the jewelry store. Halfway down, a rickety stairwell led to a rusty door on the building's second floor. He ascended the stairs and tried the knob. It was unlocked. As the door opcned, he glanced down at the gun holstered at his hip. He had forgotten to remove the gun from his uniform before leaving work. Immediately, he rejected the idea of drawing it. If the gangsters saw the weapon, they were bound to start a shootout; and the hostages could get caught in the crossfire.

The door opened to a stairway leading to the building's upper floors. The Crusader crept up the stairs. There had to be a reason the Tyrants hadn't come out that way. When the police had shown up, they would have searched for alternate exits. At the top of the stairs, he crept in the direction of the jewelry store.

He came to a heavy steel door that blocked off the rest of the hallway. It was locked from the Crusader's side. He reached for the latch and unlocked it. *No wonder they didn't come through here.* The door was too thick for them to break down if it was locked. Cautiously, in case there were any extra Tyrants waiting on the other side, the Crusader opened the door.

The room on the other side was empty, save for some dusty furniture. Two windows on the far wall overlooked the street where the police were assembled. On the left side of the room, another doorway opened to a stairway descending to the jewelry store. The Crusader peered around the corner into the stairway. His path was clear. He descended the stairs slowly, listening for any hint of the Tyrants approaching.

"What're we gonna do?" The voice was high-pitched, nervous. "There's no way out!"

"Shut up! Let me think."

"Let's use the hostages," a third voice said. "We walk out of here holding 'em in front of us, and we say we'll blow their brains out unless the cops let us walk."

The Crusader reached the bottom of the stairs and looked into the jewelry store. The three hostages knelt in the middle of the store, hands on their heads. Two of the robbers stood behind them, guns trained on them, while the remaining three huddled at the back of the store near the Crusader. The one closest to him had a crown tattoo on the side of his neck, the mark borne by all of the Tyrants.

The scene before him reinforced his suspicion that the Phantom was not among the thieves. None of them carried throwing knives or batons; and if the Phantom had been among them, he could have easily phased through the steel door upstairs to escape. Carter fought to quell a rising disappointment. It would have been encouraging to catch one of the two most dangerous villains plaguing the city.

Whimpery Voice bobbed his head eagerly. "That might work. We can put 'em in the car with us and dump 'em a few blocks away."

"What good will that do?" the second voice growled. "The cops will see our plates. They'll follow us; and once we dump the hostages, they'll swoop in and arrest us. No, that won't work."

The first speaker was smaller and slimmer than the other two—probably the youngest of the group. He wore a heavy brown coat and kept his pistol pressed against his leg. He tapped the trigger guard restlessly. The second speaker, who seemed to be the leader of the group, sounded older and was more heavily built. His gun was tucked into his waistband at the small of his back.

"Are you kidding? They've probably found the car. If they have, they've already got the plates." The third speaker, the logical one, gestured to the stairway. "Let's check upstairs again."

Similar in size to the second speaker, Captain Logic had removed his jacket and tied it around his waist. Judging by the way the back of his neck glistened with sweat under the store lights, he was nervous. The Crusader couldn't see his gun from this angle, but he did see another crown tattoo, this one on the man's left wrist.

"That door's unbreakable," Whimpery Voice groaned. "We'll never get through."

The Crusader weighed his options. The two Tyrants near the hostage were his immediate concern. Unfortunately, they were farther away, and the three men discussing their plan were between them and Carter. If only he could get the hostages out. But to do that, he would have to create a distraction. If he had his equipment with him, he could do that easily enough; but with a nightstick, a gun he wouldn't use, and a taser, his options were limited.

"Let's go look at it," Captain Logic muttered.

The Crusader crept back up the stairs. If he could ambush the men upstairs, that would leave their two companions alone downstairs. He could work with that. He walked back through the heavy door and closed it. Footsteps thumped up the stairs. The Crusader leaned against the door and waited. The footsteps grew closer. A fist pounded on the door.

The Crusader rushed the slab of steel and rammed into it with his full weight, knocking it open and sending the man on the other side stumbling back. The Crusader leaped over him and swung his nightstick at the next closest man, Captain Logic, striking him across the face, grabbing his wrist, and twisting. The man's gun fell to the floor. The gangster punched the Crusader on the side of his head. His ears rang, and he grimaced and smashed his nightstick into the Tyrant's head again—and again. This time, the man crumpled. He hurled the weapon at the man he'd hit with the door—Whimpery Voice—who was starting to rise. The nightstick hit him in the forehead, knocking him out.

The third man—the leader of the group—fired at the Crusader. As the bullet fired, the vigilante flipped through the air and planted a foot on the wall. He pushed off and leaped toward the shooter. The Tyrant fired again, and the bullet narrowly missed the Crusader. The Crusader slammed into him, knocking him flat. He slugged him across the jaw again for good measure.

Panic burned through Carter like acid. The gunshots had not been silenced. There was no way the two remaining Tyrants had not heard the ruckus. He hoped they didn't do anything stupid. Crossing the room, Carter retrieved his nightstick and jogged quietly down the stairs. The two men were speaking in sharp whispers. The one with the tattoo on the back of his neck gestured toward the stairs with his gun.

"Let's take our chances," he growled. "Shoot one of the hostages and walk out of here with the other two."

"No way! If we kill someone, they'll never let us go."

"Did you hear that shooting up there? Something's going down. If we don't move, we're toast."

The Crusader threw his nightstick at Neck Tattoo's extended gun hand. The weapon found its mark; and the man yelped and recoiled, dropping the gun. The Crusader vaulted over the glass counter and slammed both feet into the man. As the gangster fell, he wrapped his arms around the Crusader's waist, dragging him down. The Crusader brought his knee down on the man's chest. The Tyrant's grip loosened, and the Crusader elbowed him in the jaw. Neck Tattoo went limp.

"S-stop!" the last gangster said. "I-I'll shoot!"

The Tyrant had his gun pressed against one of the hostages' heads. He was desperate. There was no way he could escape, but he had said he wouldn't kill anybody. The Crusader took a step toward the man. If he could talk the gangster down, the robbery could still end without bloodshed.

The gangster's voice jumped an octave. "I said stop!"

The gangster swiveled his gun up from the hostage to point it at the Crusader. Before he could fire, a bullet tore through the glass storefront and into the Tyrant. Police officers stormed the building, and the hostages scrambled away from the bodies of the two gangsters.

The Crusader looked down at the Tyrant. The man was obviously dead. Blood pooled below his masked head.

"Good work." Paul kept his gun trained on the downed gangster as he glanced at Carter. "It might not have worked out this way if you weren't here."

The Crusader looked up at the cop and nodded numbly. He searched for a response and came up empty. He wished the cops hadn't fired. He could have taken the Tyrant out once his gun was pointed away from the hostages. They hadn't given him time. Because of that, a man was dead. Criminal or not, the Tyrant didn't deserve to die.

"I have to go."

Carter tucked his nightstick into his belt and stormed out of the store. *Someone died because I wasn't fast enough.* They weren't superhumans. They weren't ninjas. They were two-bit thugs. Stopping criminals like them without loss of life was his job. If he couldn't do that, why was he the Crusader?

As he climbed back into his car, he pulled his mask off and shook his head. The hostages were safe, and that was what mattered most. But the victory was entirely too hollow for his liking.

CHAPTER 18

"What do you mean, you can't get anything off it?" Jolie exclaimed. "That's our only lead to the thieves. You've got to find something!"

Nate blinked and took a half-step back from her. Jolie took a deep breath. There was no reason to take her frustrations out on the head CSI. Nate was the best in the business; so if he said he couldn't get anything off the hard drive, no one could. Jolie knew her frustration should be directed at her target, not at him.

Maybe Dean could get something from it . . .

She raised her hands palms outward. "I'm sorry. It seems like every time we get a lead, it vanishes."

"I understand. Sergeant Pulaski is feeling the same about the sword killer. I don't seem to be of much use to anybody around here lately."

"Don't say that, Nate." She put a hand on his shoulder. "You're doing the best you can."

"The bad guys are better."

"They're not better. They're careful. Sooner or later, they'll slip up. They always do."

Andreas Hall had confessed to trading the thieves' stolen bills for nonsequential ones, and he had given a vague description of a young, dark-haired girl with dreadlocks. He also claimed to have a recording of her entering his shop. That would have put Jolie's investigation over the top. If they had a picture of one of the suspects, the process would flow much easier. Jolie had returned to the pawn shop to retrieve his computer, only to find its hard drive destroyed. The thieves must have heard about Hall's arrest and taken precautions.

"There is something else, Detective. I found some . . . unique . . . energy signatures on the computer."

"What kind of energy?"

"I can't be sure, but it was similar to an energy signature we detected at the bank, specifically near the window and the vault, where the thief phased through."

"Are you telling me this guy leaves an energy trail when he uses his powers?"

"I think so. And if he does, maybe someone can track that energy signature. It's beyond anything the precinct has the tech to do, but you've got friends at Sterling Labs, right? I bet a few of their high-tech scanners could register the energy signature."

"That's brilliant!" Jolie grinned. "You're the best, Nate. Maybe this guy finally slipped up. I'll see what Sterling Labs has for us."

"No problem, Detective. I should probably get back to Sergeant Pulaski's case. This swordsman is still on the loose. When you get a scanner, we'll see what we can do."

"Will do. Good luck."

Finally, she had something the thief couldn't cover up. They could get rid of stolen bills and delete video footage; but if he emitted a unique energy signature when he phased and didn't realize it, it was only a matter of time until he used his power again. When he did, Jolie would be there.

* * *

The cold steel of Monahan's blade turned softly between Carter's fingers. He stared down at the short dagger, seeing past it and visualizing the jewelry store. He hadn't pictured much else since he left. The body of the dead Tyrant haunted him. It could have easily been his body or one of the hostages'. That, more than anything else, gave Carter pause.

Other gangsters had died since Carter became the Crusader. Barely a week ago, the cops had killed two Red Dogs in the warehouse raid. Like at the jewelry store, they had done so to save Carter's life. But that had been in the middle of a pitched battle, and he hadn't watched them die. This time, he had looked right at the Tyrant as the bullet hit him. He watched a human being fall and breathe his last. He had been powerless to stop it. That Tyrant, Markos Howell, the Red Dogs . . . Too many people were dying around him lately.

He shook himself. He needed to do something so he would stop moping. Normally, Carter would gear up to go out at that time of night, but Gideon had taken all his equipment. The knife Carter held was the only thing he had left. The suit and all his tech were gone while Maddox reworked it. For one night, Carter was as good as grounded.

A knock sounded at his bedroom door. Carter looked up at it and debated whether to open it. He wanted to be alone to ponder this situation and its ramifications. Maybe if he stayed quiet, whoever was on the other side of the door would go away.

Knock-knock. He rubbed the bridge of his nose. Maybe they wouldn't.

"What?"

"It's Ellis." His brother's voice was soft, subdued. "Mom asked me to check on you."

"Come in."

The doorknob rattled; the door creaked; and Ellis peeked into the room. Carter smiled and gestured for his brother to enter. Ellis walked in, closed the door behind him, and sat on the bed next to Carter. He looked down at the dagger in Carter's hand. Carter held it up and extended it hilt-first. Cautiously, Ellis took it.

"This is the one the Seraph gave you, isn't it?"

"It is. He got it from the assassin who attacked us here the night he and Dad saved us."

"Cool." Ellis studied the dagger for a moment and looked at Carter. "Are you all right? You've hardly said a word all day."

"I'm good, El." Carter stood and walked to the window. "I had to stop a robbery today. Someone died in the process. He was one of the bad guys; but he still died, and there was nothing I could do to stop it."

"Oh. That's rough . . . But things like that are going to happen, aren't they? I mean, nobody's perfect. I'm sure people died on Dad's watch. The Seraph's, too."

"Yeah, probably. It's different when you watch it happen."

Carter knew Ellis was right. Surely, Wyatt and Gideon hadn't been able to save everyone they set out to. But it sure seemed like it sometimes. Trying to live up to their legacies was exhausting. He was barely twenty, a young man fighting gangsters and criminals and assassins who were years older than him. Those years carried experience. Gideon had been twenty-five when he first put on the Seraph suit. The weight of his responsibility as the Crusader rose around him, threatening to drown him beneath its black waves.

"I want to make them proud."

"You already have." Ellis handed him the knife back. "You've saved a ton of people and put a bunch of bad guys behind bars, and you've done it all while working to provide for Mom and me and Rhonda. Dad would be so proud of you. I bet the Seraph is, too."

Carter didn't respond for a moment. He wondered if the reason the Tyrant's death was bothering him so much was because of how recently he had watched Markos Howell die. It reminded him that Ravener was still somewhere in the city on a murder spree. If Carter didn't stop him, more people were going to die. Maybe a lot more. But Carter hadn't been able to stop a few robbers without someone dying. How was he supposed to stop Ravener?

He had been hunting the ninja for less than a week. It had taken Gideon months to track down Monahan and Serban and nearly a year to find and defeat Ashcroft. No superhero was perfect.

"Thanks, El." Carter patted him on the shoulder. "You can tell Mom I'm going to be all right."

"You bet."

Ellis stood, smiled at Carter, and walked out of the room, closing the door behind him. Carter turned the dagger over in his fingers again. If he could take down this swordsman—if he could stop him from killing anyone else—maybe he would feel like he had honored his father's legacy. Maybe . . . But he still had a long way to go before he achieved that.

* * *

Gideon stayed after hours at Sterling Labs, waiting for his chance to talk to Maddox, who had been attending to other business since he arrived earlier in the day.

The sun was well below the horizon when the smiling scientist stepped out of the elevator and into the lobby. Maddox's hair, once shaved nearly to his dark skull, was knotted in tight cornrows. Gideon grinned, hopped out of his seat, and crossed the room. He and Maddox hugged tightly and laughed.

"Good to see you, Gideon. Dean tells me our friend Carter is in need of an upgrade." Maddox held up a tablet. "I have some designs we've been working on; but first, why don't you show me what we're working with?"

Gideon picked up the case containing Carter's gear. "There's a killer in town who's a bit out of Carter's league. He destroyed his staff—"

Maddox winced. "No."

"Sadly, yes. Carter needs a serious overhaul if he's going to take this killer."

"Lucky for him, a serious overhaul is exactly what Dean had in mind. You didn't think he had given up designing superhero tech because the Vindicators split, did you?" Maddox gestured to the elevator. "Come on up to my lab. I should be able to put most of this together in a few hours. Tell me more about the killer."

Gideon followed Maddox toward the elevator. "He's a master swordsman, and his weapon must be extremely sharp to cut through Carter's staff the way it did. Dean made that staff before the company discovered aionium, but it was reinforced steel. Any blade that can cut through that is something to be worried about."

"I can work around that." Maddox scratched his chin. "While we're at it, Dean wants me to streamline a lot of the Crusader's gear. We've been doing some work on Dean's gear as practice, so we can integrate the tech more efficiently."

Ten minutes later, the two men had the Crusader's gear laid out on a workbench. Maddox took the utility belt and examined it in silence. Gideon leaned back against the wall and watched him work. This was far from his area of expertise, but he had the benefit of field experience. If Maddox needed an opinion on how a piece of equipment should work ideally, Gideon wanted to be there for him.

It occurred to him that the process could take hours. They could be burning the midnight oil by the time they finished. He pulled out his phone and dialed. Jolie answered on the third ring.

"Hello?"

"Hey, babe. Listen, I'm helping Maddox with some things for Carter tonight, so I might be home late. I didn't want you to worry."

"Okay. Actually, if you're still at Sterling Labs, there's a piece of equipment I need for this investigation. I might come see if Maddox can recommend something."

Jolie sounded excited, or at least hopeful, for the first time since she had started investigating the bank robbery. He hoped that whatever new angle she was working would finally lead her to the superhuman thief.

"Sure. I'll come down to the lobby to open the door when you get here." He said goodbye, hung up, and glanced over at Maddox. "Jolie is coming. She needs to borrow some equipment for an investigation."

"Fine by me." Maddox picked up one of Carter's gauntlets. "There's a mold I need over in that cabinet. Can you get it for me?"

Gideon crossed the room to the cabinet. When they were done with this, he hoped Carter would be more than a match for Ravener.

CHAPTER 19

Kneeling in the back of the van, Ty pulled on each piece of equipment he needed for the Sterling Labs infiltration. Provided the guard that they paid off stayed quiet, all the pieces were in place for the job to go off without a hitch. Ty could phase into the building and unlock the door for the others. Together, they would take the elevator up to the lab on the top floor and steal the gear Ned and Richie had chosen. Hopefully, this tech would make Ty's would-be friends useful.

The security cameras at Sterling Labs were state-of-the-art, but Joanie insisted she was up to the task. She typed furiously at her tablet. Until she gave the signal, he couldn't go in. While she worked, he pulled his sleeve aside to glance at his watch. With any luck, they would be home before Rhonda grew suspicious. She was a good kid, and Ty couldn't risk her learning anything about his late night activities.

"And . . . we're . . . in." Joanie looked up from her tablet. "The camera feeds are looping."

Ty glanced out the rear doors and into the parking lot. There were still four cars parked there. One likely belonged to the security officer, but there was no way to predict who else was inside. He checked to make sure his knives were in place. He didn't want to kill anyone, but he could not let them stop him, either.

Joanie tilted her head toward the door. "Go."

Ty jumped out of the van and crept toward Sterling Labs. His boots scraped softly against the sidewalk as he wound through the courtyard to the front doors. The lights in the lobby were off, save for a few dim wall fixtures, and he didn't see anyone. He approached the glass double doors, took a breath, and made his body permeable. He took a step forward and phased through the glass.

He studied the interior lock. With time, he probably could've picked it, leaving no evidence behind that anyone had entered the building, but he did not want to take the time necessary to attempt that. The longer they took, the higher the likelihood that they would be caught. He phased his hand through the lock, shattering it. He pushed the glass door open and waved toward the van.

The doors popped open. Ned and Richie rushed for the lab, while Joanie remained in the van. Ty hoped she would be all right in there. Of the four of them, she deserved to be caught least of all. As Ned and Richie entered the lobby, Ty glanced back at the van one last time, closed the door, and followed his companions toward the elevator.

Ned was clad in a blue jacket with tan sleeves, and Richie wore a bright red bomber jacket. Each had a pistol tucked into his pants at the small of his back.

Richie called the elevator. Ty swept his gaze over the lobby and the hallways that joined it. There was no sign of any guards, so this probably wasn't an elaborate ruse to trap them. He turned back to the elevator as the doors slid open. Ned and Richie rushed in, and Ty walked in after them. Ned tapped his foot against the floor, while Richie popped his knuckles.

Ty pinched the bridge of his nose. "You two are way too jittery. Calm down."

Ned hit the fourth-floor button. Neither man responded to Ty's criticism, but they did stand still. *Thank goodness.* Ty wasn't going to get caught because his teammates had the jitters. He would've been glad to do this job alone. Unfortunately, one man could not carry the equipment they needed alone.

The elevator doors slid open, revealing a dark hallway with doors lining both sides, leading to different laboratories. Ty stepped out of the elevator, brushing the hilt of a knife with his right hand, and glanced back at Ned and Richie.

"Where to?"

"We want the applied sciences lab," Ned said. "Should be the third door on the left."

Ty nodded and led the two men down the hallway. He approached the indicated door and froze. Across the hall from the applied sciences lab, a light shone from underneath a different door. Ty crept to it and pressed his ear to the surface. Soft murmuring echoed from inside. The plaque on the wall to the right of the door read "Research and Development." He clenched his jaw. They would have to be doubly quiet to make sure no one in that lab heard them.

He backed away from the door. Richie had drawn his gun. He looked at the research and development lab questioningly, hefting his weapon. Ty shook his head. *Idiot.* This was a heist. If Richie went in there and started blasting, it would turn into a murder; and the cops would be all over them. He motioned furiously at the applied sciences lab. Richie lowered his gun with a shrug. Ned opened the lab door and flicked on the light.

"Okay." Ned rubbed his palms together. "Let's do this. We're looking for shock rifles, concussion gauntlets, and something called a 'mag-gun.'"

"Five minutes." Ty watched the door. "Then we go."

* * *

Jolie leaned against an empty workbench and watched as Gideon and Maddox pieced together Carter's new and improved Crusader gear. Gideon shot her a helpless *I-don't-know-what-I'm-doing* glance, eyebrows raised and mouth quirked to the side. Jolie hid a chuckle behind her hand.

The work was boring to watch, but it was better than sitting at home and waiting for Gideon to finish. And this way, she got the tech she needed to track the thief, too. Win-win.

"Almost done," Maddox said. "The metal in the sword and shield molds should be cooled. Close that panel, please."

Gideon snapped the panel together. "Sword and shield molds?"

"That's right." Maddox chuckled wryly. "In Dean's words, if Carter's going to call himself the Crusader, his equipment should match the name. I made a backup staff in case Carter prefers using that, but Dean thought a sword might be a more useful tool against another sword. I infused a dose of aionium into the weapons, as well as the new breastplate, greaves, and vambraces on the Crusader suit."

Aionium was a near-invulnerable metal. Dean had used it to build Gideon's second Seraph suit, as well as the twin shields that Dean used in combat. Bullets and explosions didn't so much as dent the metal; so there was no way a sword, no matter how sharp, could pierce or cut it.

"And these gauntlet upgrades?" Gideon asked.

"Streamlining the tech." Maddox grinned. "Forget scrounging through the utility belt; all the gadgets Carter needs will literally be at his fingertips. Shock beads, adhesive beads, grappling hook . . . And we miniaturized the Crybabies into what we're calling 'sonic beads.' All he'll need the belt for is storing reloads. And . . . we're done."

He backed away from the suit and walked over to the mold where the metal truncheons were cooling. He pulled the mold casings open one at a time. First, he revealed a broadsword the length of a yardstick. The center groove on the blade glowed a soft blue; and when Maddox pressed a button on the hilt, the groove crackled to life with electricity. Next, he removed a deep red, curved shield with two points on the upper half tapering into one on the lower. An electric blue cross emblazoned the shield. Finally, he removed a pair of truncheons. He flourished them and struck one against the wall. Nodding in satisfaction, he set the truncheons down next to the Crusader suit.

"Thank you, Maddox. Carter will appreciate it."

"My pleasure. And how can I help you, Jolie?"

"There's a superhuman thief in town that can phase his body through matter," Jolie said. "But we recently discovered that doing so leaves behind a unique energy signature. I hoped you might have some tech that could track that kind of signature."

"I may have something." Maddox jerked a finger at the door. "Let's check the applied sciences lab."

Gideon packed the Crusader gear into a duffel bag and picked it up. For a moment, it looked like he was tempted to break out each of the weapons and try them out himself. Maddox flipped off the lights and walked out into the hallway. Jolie joined him—and stopped. The light in the applied sciences lab was already on, shining through the gap at the bottom of the door.

"Who's here?" Gideon whispered.

"No idea." Maddox went stiff. "We should be alone. The light in that lab was off when I came in."

Gideon set the duffel bag on the floor and withdrew the sword. Jolie's heart pounded as she reached for her sidearm. Gideon hadn't been in a fight in a year, and he didn't have his powers. He could die as easily as she or Maddox. But she knew he wouldn't wait out here if she told him to. They were a team.

"Stay here, Maddox," Jolie hissed.

Exchanging glances with Gideon, Jolie flicked her eyes toward the door. He crept toward it and reached for the doorknob with his free hand, while Jolie kept her gun trained on the door. Gideon turned the knob.

Jolie rushed in with her gun raised. A pair of men, dressed in colorful jackets and ski masks, were pulling equipment from shelves on the left side of the room. She saw guns tucked at the smalls of their backs. In the center of the room was a third man, dressed all in black with a similar mask. A pair of knives were sheathed at his belt. She raised her gun.

"Sojourn P.D.!" she shouted. "Freeze!"

The three men swiveled almost in unison. The two men to her left reached behind them for their guns. Jolie twitched to her left and fired at the floor. They froze. The man in black, however, did not. His hand flicked forward, and a silvery shape shot through the air. Jolie backed up—and Gideon's hand shot out, catching the thrown knife by the hilt and stopping it just shy of Jolie's shoulder.

"That's my wife." Gideon twirled the knife. "You really shouldn't have done that."

He rushed toward the black-clad man, sword in one hand and knife in the other. Jolie faced the other two, who had thrown themselves to the ground behind a row of shelves. She ducked behind a table as they opened fire on her. She poked her head and arm up and squeezed off a shot.

She ducked again as the thieves fired another volley. A stack of papers fluttered through the air, ripped apart by the bullets. Jolie leaned around the table to her left. She tracked movement and adjusted her position to get a better view. The two thieves were making their way to the door. Jolie fired low. Her shot ripped through the Achilles tendon of the heavy-set man in the blue jacket. He screamed and stumbled into his partner.

Jolie jumped up—and dropped down again as the uninjured man trained his gun on her and fired. The gunshots stopped a moment later. Jolie scrambled to her feet. The men were not in the lab anymore. Jolie ran into the hall. Maddox lay on the floor, his body twitching slightly. He grimaced and looked up at her.

"They got a shock rifle!" he said.

Jolie glanced down the hall. The elevator doors were already sliding closed. There was no use in trying to catch them. But the third thief was still in the applied sciences lab. She could help Gideon take him down, and he could lead them to his partners. She rushed back into the lab.

* * *

Gunshots echoed through the lab, but he trusted Jolie to handle the other two thieves. Gideon kept his focus on the man in front of him. As he neared the thief, he swung his sword in a downward strike at the thief's head. Lightning crackled off the edge of the blade. The masked man leaned back, allowing the sword to swing past harmlessly, and stabbed his remaining knife at Gideon. Gideon blocked with his own knife and thrust the sword toward the thief's legs. His opponent danced behind Gideon's swing and slashed Gideon's forearm. The blade cut through his sleeve and bit into skin. Gideon jerked his arm back. Droplets of blood soaked into the navy blue fabric of his shirt.

Gideon spun and kicked at his opponent's head. The thief ducked under Gideon's leg and stabbed his knife upward, toward Gideon's sternum. Gideon knocked the blade aside and slashed with his knife, and the blade passed through the thief's forearm without leaving so much as a mark. *The Phantom!* Gideon brought his sword up to block the thief's knife as it came back in toward his shoulder. He stepped inward and swung the flat of the blade at the thief's head. Again, the weapon passed through his opponent.

The thief lunged at Gideon—and was gone. Gideon shuddered as his body tingled. He spun around and saw the thief rushing for the door. There was no sign of Jolie or the two men she had followed. *Did he phase through me?* Gideon raised the knife in his left hand, aimed it at the thief's back, and threw it. The blade flew across the room, through the thief's permeable body, and lodged in the wall.

Jolie barged back into the room. The Phantom froze. Before Jolie could speak, the black-clad man dropped through the floor. Gideon shook his head in disbelief. Even as a former superhero himself, it was still hard to believe when he witnessed another's amplified powers. He lowered his sword and walked over to Jolie.

"You okay?"

"No." Jolie stomped her foot on the spot where the thief had vanished and growled. "They got away again."

CHAPTER 20

"Who *was* that guy?" Richie gasped.

Ty threw himself into the back of the van. Ned clutched their stolen gear to his chest and dropped into the passenger seat with a pained howl. Ty leaned up between the seats to check on him. His white sock was stained deep red where the detective had shot him. Richie sucked in a breath; but when Ty shot him a look, he spun around and slammed on the gas. As the van screeched out of the parking lot, Ty dropped down next to Joanie, removed his mask, and took a deep breath. That had been too close.

A series of slow inhales and exhales brought Ty's heart rate down to a steady rhythm. Able to process logically again, he grabbed onto Richie's question and finally processed it.

"You didn't recognize him?" Ty asked. "That was Gideon Turner—the Seraph."

"The Seraph?" Richie groaned. "Aw, man! I thought he was history!"

It was a cruel irony. Not too long before, Ty had looked up to the Seraph. The hero had been a symbol of hope, a tantalizing promise that the Brooks could get better and that Ty's life, and his family's, might improve. But despite the Seraph's presence in the city, Ty's wife, Rachel, had been gunned down. Despite the presence of the rest of the Vindicators on the street several months ago, that radioactive monster had still mangled Ty and cursed him with powers.

It was his own actions that had brought him into conflict with the Seraph. It was hard to believe he had fallen so far.

"He may not be a superhero anymore, but he can fight." It wasn't often that Ty met an opponent who matched him nearly blow for blow. "He was almost as good as me. If not for my powers, I'm not sure I would've escaped."

"How did the cops find us?" Ned asked.

"I don't think they did. I think they were in the lab across the hall. It was bad luck they came over while we were still inside." Ty grabbed the first aid kit from the back of the van and withdrew a roll of gauze. "Sit still, Ned. I'm going to patch you up."

"I need painkillers." Ned reached up to wipe tears from his cheeks and succeeded only in smearing blood across them. "Aw, man. Aw, man. It hurts so bad. Am I gonna bleed out?"

"No, Ned." Ty shoved a bottle of aspirin into Ned's hands. "Take some of those and pipe down. You're not going to be running anytime soon, but I'll do my best to bandage you up."

"Should w-we go to the hospital?"

Ty shook his head. "They'll be looking for victims of gunshot wounds to the ankle in all the hospitals in the city. Sorry, you're going to have to do without."

Ty had heard rumors of a few underworld doctors who would pay house calls to fix up wounds like this. They were expensive; and judging by the luxuries in Ned and Richie's apartment, they had blown all their cash. Ty would probably have to give up the rest of his earnings from the Sojourn City Bank job to get Ned fixed up. Unfortunately, it didn't look like he had any other options. Ned was an important part of their plan to rob the armored car the next night.

"Good thing we were wearing masks," Richie said. "You don't think they'll be able to track us, do you?"

"My loop should have wiped any footage of the van that the security cameras in the parking lot might have picked up," Joanie said. "Unfortunately, if any traffic cameras get us, they might be able to track us from those."

"Man, can't you hack those?" Richie swiveled around to look at her. "Why do we keep you around if you can't cover our tracks?"

"Hey!" Ty jabbed a finger at Richie. "Shut up. She's more useful than either of you losers. Keep your eyes on the road."

Richie grumbled but did as instructed. Ty returned his attention to wrapping gauze around Ned's ankle.

"Besides, do you want to park the van long enough for me to get a connection?" Joanie asked. "Or do you want to get out of here?"

"Keep moving," Ty said. "We don't have time for this."

When he finished wrapping Ned's wound, he studied the haul of items that Ned and Richie had managed to grab. They had one shock rifle, the mag-gun—whatever that was—and one pair of the concussion gauntlets. It would've been nice to get more than one of each item, but they would make do.

Ned looked over his shoulder. "I think we should ditch the van. I can hook us up with some new wheels, but it's too risky to—"

"No. We don't have time to get a new vehicle and plan the truck heist. Besides, it's a cost we can't afford if I'm going to pay for a doctor to look at your leg. We'll have to hide the van until we're ready to move. We can worry about transportation after we've got the loot. Get us back to the Brooks, Richie."

Ty looked down at his knife. When he threw his other blade at the cop, he'd aimed for her shoulder; but one wrong move and it could've killed her. For all his conviction about not wanting anyone to die, when the chips were down, he had been willing to take the risk.

No wonder Turner had attacked him so ferociously. Ty had attacked his wife, after all. That fight had been too close. Ty had only used his powers to phase through walls, never to defend himself in a fight. It had been an instinctive move, and it had taken a lot out of him. Ty seldom feared being outmatched by an opponent, but someone of Turner's skill was worrisome. The former superhero was aware of Ty's existence, and he might not stop until he caught him.

He wondered how his father would have handled Turner. Ty had been a child when Shiro died. It was not so hard to predict how his godfather would have handled it. Shiro had been a man of honor; but Ty's godfather, a former business partner and friend of Shiro's, had been a member of the Chinese triads. A mobster. A villain. He would have left the lab and immediately searched for Turner's loved ones to leverage them over the hero.

Shiro never would have done that. Ty would not, either. If he had to face Turner again, he would defeat the hero with honor and nobility; or he would retreat as he had in their first duel.

"Hey, we made it." Richie was still out of breath, but there was a note of enthusiasm in his voice. "We got the stuff. We're going to do this thing!"

Ned did his best impression of pumping his fist. "Yeah, we are."

Ty eased back in his seat across from Joanie. "Don't celebrate too soon. None of this is going to matter if the cops pick us up before we leave the Platform."

* * *

Carter sat in his car outside Vickers's house, waiting for the man to return home so Rhonda could leave. What was Vickers doing out so late? In the Brooks, it could be anything. Carter didn't want to judge without knowing the man's circumstances, but leaving his daughter with a babysitter into the wee hours every night didn't earn him any marks in Carter's book.

It was possible Vickers went out searching for odd jobs, hoping to find income to support himself and his kid. But something about him made Carter wary. The way he had entered his house so defensively when Carter was there last time still bothered him. There was more to Vickers than a first glance showed.

A clunky van trundled up the driveway, and the side door opened. Vickers hopped out, clad in a black overcoat like he had been the last time Carter had seen him. An arm reached out from inside the van and pulled the door closed, and the vehicle backed down the driveway. Carter exited his car and pursued the man up to the front door.

"Mr. Vickers!" he called.

Vickers spun, and his hand dropped to his belt. "What—Oh. You're Rhonda's brother, right?"

"That's right. I'm here to pick her up."

"I'm sorry it's so late." Vickers unlocked the door. "Come on in."

Vickers stepped inside; and Carter followed him, letting the screen door swing closed behind him. Rhonda looked up as they entered and smiled. Vickers walked over to her. As they talked, Carter scanned the living room. There was no sign that this was anything other than an old but serviceable home owned, or more likely rented, by a man scraping to get by. Nothing sinister stood out. On the other hand, Vickers had been strangely spooked by Carter's approach.

Carter jerked his thumb toward the door. "Come on, Rhonda. Let's get home."

He led her out the door and to his car. In the future, he intended to keep an eye on Vickers until he was sure of the man's intentions and activities. He didn't want his sister babysitting for someone dangerous. Whether he was a criminal or not, Vickers was obviously paranoid about something and ready to fight over it. Carter had seen his kind before; and more often than not, they ended up dead. He hoped Vickers would be the exception to that rule, if only for the sake of his infant daughter. The Brooks had created enough orphans already.

* * *

After giving Maddox a once-over to ensure no permanent damage had been done, Jolie went down to the security office to see how the guards on duty had missed a trio of robbers breaking into the building. What she found explained the anomaly but created a new one: the guard post was empty. The security cameras were on, but the footage was looped.

It was definitely the same crew that hit the bank. If seeing the black-clad thief phase through the floor hadn't confirmed it already, the technological prowess of the hack reaffirmed Jolie's suspicion. There was something oddly unprofessional about the accomplices. Their gunshots had been wild and inaccurate, and they were dressed in garish colors. There was no sign of a woman with them, either. Andreas Hall had identified a dark-skinned woman with dreadlocks. Perhaps she was their getaway driver.

"Any luck?"

Gideon stood at the entrance to the guard room, leaning against the doorjamb. He held himself loosely, his brow furrowed in concentration and no trace of fear behind his eyes. Jolie had witnessed only a few brief seconds of his fight with the Phantom, but Gideon had looked more energized than she had seen him in weeks. She suspected that despite the danger, some part of him had enjoyed trading blows with an equal. It had been months since he hung up the Seraph's hood. The duel must have felt oddly nostalgic.

She decided not to bring that up. Gideon was struggling with his new role. She would let him enjoy the adrenaline of the fight while she focused on her investigation.

"Nothing," she said. "They looped the camera feed. And they must have bribed a guard, too, because there's no one here."

"Is there any footage of their vehicle pulling in on the exterior cameras?" Gideon walked into the room. "Maybe they weren't able to hack the feed until they were already parked."

Normally, Jolie would have disregarded the idea. A cunning thief would park at a distance and approach on foot to hack the camera feed, but the sloppiness in the two men she fought indicated it was possible they would slip up.

"Let's see."

She rewound the footage. The loop broke, and a white van briefly flitted across the screen. She paused the rewind and let the footage play forward. When the van appeared on the screen, she paused it again.

Gideon leaned in close. "Looks like a van for a utility company. But the markings have been scraped off."

"I could be stolen, or it may belong to one of the thieves. I'll see if there are any BOLOs out for stolen white vans. If not, I'll put one out." She peered closer at the screen. "I can't make out the license plate. I'll have CSI comb this footage, see if they can get anything. There might be forensic evidence in the lab, too. I think I hit one of them, so he might have left a blood trail." Jolie put a hand on Gideon's chest. "Thank you for your help tonight."

"You're welcome. Truth is, it was good to be back in action."

"I figured as much." It would be a lie to say that didn't concern her. Jolie smiled softly and backed out of the room. "Come on. Let's wrap things up here so we can go home."

CHAPTER 21

Carter seldom had the good fortune to sleep in. His work week was jam-packed, and he had to leave the house early to get across town to the Platform. On Sundays, he got up early so that he could usher Ellis and Rhonda into getting ready for church. Saturday mornings were a rare and precious gift.

Exhausted from a week of hunting a superhuman thief and a murderous swordsman and watching a criminal bleed out, Carter kept his head buried under his pillow long after sunlight spilled through the window of his bedroom, allowing the peaceful sensation of half-sleep to ease him toward consciousness.

Did Gideon ever have days like this? The Seraph had always seemed so . . . intense. Sometimes, Carter thought Gideon's sole motivation in life was to be a hero and fight crime. Carter had become the Crusader to honor his father first and foremost. Protecting the innocent was gratifying on its own merits, but the burden of carrying his father's legacy weighed heavily on him. People depended on him to protect them the way Carter's dad had. It was a burden he chose for himself, and one he would continue to carry with honor, regardless of its weight.

The burden he *hadn't* chosen was the unexpected guilt he carried over the death of the Tyrant in the jewelry store. No matter how many ways he tried to rationalize the situation, the guilt remained.

He had fallen asleep hoping that a night of rest would eliminate the relentless feeling, but the closer he grew to consciousness, the more keenly he felt it.

He couldn't shake it alone. His father had been a faithful Christian, as was Gideon. Their relationship with God rooted them in the certainty of their mission and comforted them when they failed. Carter believed in God as much as they did and had a spiritual relationship with Him; but sometimes, he felt like that part of his life was resting on the backburner. He tried to shunt the fault to his youth and inexperience, but that was no excuse. Patrick Omer, who was a year younger than Carter, was one of the most passionate Christians Carter had ever met, and he was a superhero, too.

Beyond his own spiritual well-being, he had to be a good example for others, too. Ellis and Rhonda looked up to him. His mother needed his help. Raina was his girlfriend and looked to him for companionship. How could he provide those things if his own spiritual life was in tatters? He resolved that he and Raina would be in church the next morning, along with his family, and that he would soak up everything he could from the service.

Realizing that sleep would not return, Carter tossed his pillow onto the floor and sat up. It was time to start his day. After showering, Carter dressed in a pair of black jeans, a red and gray t-shirt, and a pair of black sneakers. He settled onto his bed, opened his father's worn Bible, and scanned the pages. *He giveth power to the faint; and to them that have no might he increaseth strength.* That passage in Isaiah 40:29 was appropriate for the struggle Carter faced.

"Carter!" his mother called. "Raina's here!"

Carter checked his phone. He and Raina had a lunch date planned. The screen warned him that it was nearly noon. Closing the Bible reverently, he placed it on his nightstand. He picked up his phone, keys, and wallet. On his way out, he grabbed his denim jacket and shrugged it on.

Raina stood next to the front door and smiled as her eyes fell on Carter. Her blonde-streaked brown hair tumbled over her shoulders in wavy tresses. Raina was dressed in sparkling black jeans, a black leather jacket over a dazzle-pattern blue and silver top, and a pair of black wedge heels. He clenched his jaw to keep from gaping. Sometimes, he wondered how he was lucky enough to win the heart of such a beautiful woman.

"You look . . . " A thousand words bounced around his skull, but he picked carefully. His mother was in the next room. "Beautiful. If I knew you were going all out, I would've dressed up a little more. Maybe a button-down shirt or something."

"Don't be silly. You look good."

"Thanks." Carter glanced at his mother. "See you later, Mom! Do you need me to grab anything while I'm out?"

"No, baby." His mom smiled. "Have fun!"

Carter nodded and followed Raina out the door. Her moped was parked on the sidewalk next to the porch. He crinkled his nose in amusement as he passed it. They walked to his car, and Carter opened his door for her.

"What a gentleman." Raina winked. "Thank you."

He closed the door and circled around to the driver's seat. He dropped in, started the car, and pulled out onto the street. Raina reached over and grabbed his right hand.

"Do you have any Crusader-y plans today?" she asked.

"That depends on whether Gideon has my suit ready or not. That jewelry store thing yesterday almost went south because I didn't have it. I'm not going to risk a repeat of that."

"That's not the way I heard it." Raina held up her phone. "Every local news story about the robbery says you saved the hostages' lives. You did fine without the gear. But I don't blame you for not wanting to take on Ravener without it."

The lives he had saved had almost flown under the radar. The guilt he felt over the Tyrant's death had consumed him so much that he had forgotten the men and women who were alive because he had taken down their captors. He resolved to focus on the ones he had been able to save, not the one he had failed.

Raina was right about Ravener. "That gear could be the difference between stopping Ravener and getting myself killed. That and Gideon's training, of course. We'll meet up with him tonight for another session."

"He's a good teacher, and you're a quick learner." Raina patted the back of Carter's hand. "You'll beat Ravener."

I hope so. As much as Carter could use a day off, that would have to wait until Ravener was out of the picture. As long as the serial killer was out there, Carter couldn't relax in good conscience. But for Raina's sake, he pushed it out of his mind. At least until lunch was over, he had bigger priorities.

* * *

Near the old railroad tracks in the Brooks, a series of abandoned steel warehouses were positioned far enough from residential areas that unusually loud noises often went unnoticed. It was the ideal location to test the technology from the Sterling Labs heist. In Ty's estimation, Ned and Richie were having entirely too much fun with their new toys.

Ned shot a steel drum with the mag-gun, lifting the cylinder into the air inside a rippling energy field. He cackled in delight, waved the floating cylinder around, and reversed the polarity on the gun. The drum flew across the room to smash into the wall. Ned whooped.

Ty rolled his eyes. "Very exciting."

"Come on, man!" Ned threw his hands in the air. "We don't all have superpowers! Let us have our fun!"

Joanie looked up from her tablet. "As much as I hate to say it, Ty, it is pretty cool."

He narrowed his eyes and glowered at her. "Don't help."

"Sorry."

Richie stepped forward. "Hold that thing up again!"

Ned trained the mag-gun on the drum, lifting it back into the air. Richie shouldered the shock rifle. A blue bolt of light zapped through the air between his weapon and the drum. The impact sent electrical bolts rippling across it and to the floor, creating a web of sparks around the magnetic field.

"Whoo!" Richie looked at Ty. "We need some nicknames. You're Lurk, and Joanie's Motherboard. Ned and I need cool names."

"Of course, you do." Ty found his eyes rolling again. "Don't you think we should focus on the logistics of the heist instead of some childish nicknames?"

"Ooh, I'll call myself Shock Jock!" Richie grinned. "What about you, Ned?"

Ty clenched his fists. It was all he could do not to smack Richie. "Fine. Ignore me. When you children are done playing games, I'll be ready to talk."

Ty pulled himself up to sit next to Joanie, who was perched on a five-foot-high concrete wall that surrounded the yard outside the warehouse. He leaned over to see what was on her screen. It looked like the schematics of an armored car. He was relieved that someone had their head in the game. He never doubted that he could count on Joanie. She had been there for him ever since his wife died.

Ty's wife, Rachel, was also Joanie's sister. Joanie had come to his aid, taking care of Emi while he was in the throes of grief. When he came back to himself, he had repaid the favor by protecting her from a criminal bookie to whom she owed money. Ty was fully aware that he didn't think rationally when it came to Joanie's safety because family came first for him. It always had. His own family had been a model for compassion and protection, until he lost them. The moment he became an orphan, Ty knew that if he ever found another family, he would never let them go. Unfortunately, his godfather was Shiro's polar opposite. Ty never once believed that he had mattered to that man. He was determined to be better for those who relied on him. He had failed Rachel. He wouldn't fail Joanie or Emi.

"So, how are these toys going to help us get into the truck?" Ty asked.

"The first step is to stop the transport," Joanie said. "We have a few options for that. We can either take out the driver or physically stop the truck."

"How do we do that?"

"The driver's going to be the harder option. The windows are bulletproof, and you won't kill him, anyway. But those windows also mean we can't hit the driver with the shock rifle. The only way to take him out would be for you to phase into the truck and knock him out."

He would have to pass through the moving truck at the right height to get inside the cab. Timing was essential. "Doable, but risky."

"Stopping the truck is the easier route, but it's riskier. The only way to take the truck out is to use the concussion gauntlets. They're strong enough that a single punch to the front of the truck should stop it dead in its tracks. But it'll be noisy, which means the odds are greater that someone will notice and call the cops." Joanie looked Ty dead in the eye. "And if the person with the gauntlets mistimes their punch, the truck will barrel them over. Boom. End heist, one dead thief."

"What about the mag-gun?" he asked.

"It's strong but not strong enough to stop the truck completely." Joanie pointed at the tablet. "But we can use the mag-gun to rip the rear doors off their hinges. Richie can hit the guards with the shock rifle once they're open. All that's left is to grab the loot and haul it out of there."

Ty considered. "I'll phase inside the truck and knock out the driver. That frees Ned and Richie to open the rear doors and shock the guards. It'll be faster that way—and the faster, the better."

Joanie's brow furrowed in concern. "But more dangerous for you."

"I can handle it." Ty studied her. "Joanie, when we get the loot, I'm taking Emi, and I'm getting out of this city. I want you to come with us—if you want to, that is."

"Oh, Ty." Joanie leaned in close to him and looped her right arm under his left armpit. "Sojourn City doesn't have anything for me. It never did, other than Rachel. You're my family. Where you go, I'll go."

"Good." Ty dropped off the wall. "We'll do this, Joanie. For Rachel."

Richie and Ned approached the wall. Both were grinning, still enamored with the power of their new weapons. Neither of them had tried on the concussion gauntlets yet. That was probably for the best, considering the force those things applied. Once they saw the gauntlets' power, they might suggest killing the guards to make things simpler. As long as their attention was on the mag-gun and the shock rifle, deaths were less likely.

Ty clapped his hands. "We've got a plan. Gather 'round."

"Decide on a name?" Joanie asked Ned.

Ned hobbled closer, grinning. "G-Storm."

"G-Storm and Shock Jock." Joanie poked out her lower lip in thought. "Not bad."

"All right, let's focus," Ty said. "We've got one shot to make this work. We pull this off, and we walk away like kings. But if one of us messes up, it's all over. Let's not mess up."

CHAPTER 22

Gideon zipped his jacket and looked down at the case that held Carter's newly upgraded Crusader gear. Without seeing Ravener's skill for himself, Gideon couldn't say how much of an advantage the tech would give Carter. Technology was great, but a skilled combatant could work around it and defeat a better-equipped opponent. For that reason alone, Gideon was determined to ensure Carter—and Raina—had all the skills they needed to survive. Training would serve Carter better against Ravener than the finest gear Dean, Arianna, or Maddox could think up.

Gideon was not blind to the advantages of specialized tech. He had used lots of gear supplied by Dean when he was the Seraph. If Carter did not put too much reliance on the tech and instead used it as a buffer to enhance his skill, he would come out on top. Gideon reached for the case and stopped before his fingers brushed the handle. *I could help him.*

Gideon's newer Seraph suit, the one made of aionium, had been damaged beyond repair in battle with the supervillain Torrent, but his first suit was still in working condition. He could pull it out of storage, join Carter in the field, and fight by his side again. It was tempting to relive those days.

He knew that would be the wrong move. Carter had to learn how to be his own man. Gideon couldn't come in as a crutch every time

Carter faced a challenge. If Carter asked for help, Gideon would show up in an instant. But until he asked, Gideon had to trust Carter to handle himself.

Jolie stepped out of their bedroom and leaned against the doorframe. Clad in Nike shorts and a salmon-colored tank top, she was a tantalizing sight. He considered taking her in his arms. If Carter hadn't been waiting for him . . .

She smiled at him as he wrapped his fingers around the case's handle. Something told him she knew exactly what he had been thinking.

"Any word on the Sterling Labs break-in?" Gideon asked.

She shook her head. "We can't find any sign of the van, and we can't make out its license plate in the footage. Nate thinks they may have had something hanging over the plate to obscure it. I did find some blood, but the DNA tests were inconclusive. A fingerprint would've been more helpful, but they didn't leave any of those behind."

"Don't worry. You'll find them."

Jolie furrowed her brow. "You okay? You looked a little concerned a second ago."

"Concerned?" Gideon chuckled. "Is that how I looked?"

"Before you saw me, I mean." Jolie stepped out of the bedroom doorway and crossed the living room so her body was pressed against his. "I know what you were thinking when we made eye contact, but what was bothering you before you picked up that case?"

"I was thinking about Carter. I was actually considering pulling out my old Seraph gear for a minute. Don't worry. I decided against it."

Her fingertips traced along his collarbone. "I saw how alive you were when you fought the Phantom. If I'm being honest, I'm glad you decided not to suit up; but if you made that decision, you would be absolutely sure it was the right thing to do. That wouldn't stop me from worrying about you, though."

"Any more than I can stop worrying about you, Detective." Gideon leaned down to kiss her. "I'll be back soon. As soon as I possibly can."

Jolie's eyes lit up. "I'll be waiting."

* * *

Jolie stood in the middle of the living room for several long minutes after Gideon left the apartment. She knew Gideon missed being the Seraph; but seeing him in action last night, she knew that more than missing it, he *needed* it. Becoming the Seraph had been a critical shifting point in Gideon's life, and losing that part of himself had cast him adrift. Somehow, he had to get his old self back.

Her husband wanted to make a difference. It wasn't the glory or excitement of the action that he missed the most. It wasn't the long nights wandering the city in a cape. It was the feeling of helping people. Gideon felt the need to help others down to his bones, and it was not being sated by his work at Sterling Labs. He needed something more. She prayed he would find it.

Jolie walked back into the bedroom and pulled a pair of blue jeans and a gray button-up top from the closet. There was still a lot of work to do on the superhuman thief case. Gideon would be training Carter and Raina for a few hours, at least. That gave her the time she needed to follow up on a few leads. She had the spectrum scanner from Sterling Labs. She had a starting point from which to trace the thief's energy. The problem was catching him. Not only could he phase through solid matter, but his two companions also had state-of-the-art weapons in their possession.

Jolie pulled on her clothes; threw on a brown leather jacket; and picked up her badge, gun, and the spectrum scanner as she walked out of the bedroom. She tucked the former two into her belt, kept the scanner in her left hand, and ducked out the front door, locking it behind her as she went. She bounded down the stairs to her Camry, unlocked the vehicle, and slid into the driver's seat. As she put the key in the ignition, the car sputtered for a few seconds before it came to life with the groan of a crotchety old man.

She put the car in gear and pulled out onto the street, heading for Sterling Labs. She would scan the walls and floor the Phantom had phased through. That should allow the spectrum scanner to lock onto his energy signature. She could program it to search for the same signature around the city. With any luck, she would have a lead on him before Gideon was home from training.

CHAPTER 23

Carter threw himself to the mat to avoid the swinging *bokken*. Before Gideon could pull back and bring the weapon down toward Carter, the younger man rolled aside, came up in a crouch, and raised his *bokken* to block a sideways slash coming in at his right side. The wooden blades clashed together, creating a sharp *clack* that echoed painfully in the cramped garage. They kept their weapons pressed together for a moment, and Carter studied Gideon.

He had a tendency toward high, wide strikes. That would be useful if Carter had a smaller or lighter weapon. He could duck inside Gideon's guard and hit him while he was mid-swing. But the *bokken* was long and heavy; and by the time Carter got it in under Gideon's defenses, it would be too late. He wasn't good enough with the weapon yet to go on the offensive, so his only remaining choice was to stay on defense and wait for Gideon to wear out. However, blocking the heavy blows was wearing Carter out as quickly as landing them was wearing Gideon out. It was a quandary for which he had yet to find a solution.

Fighting the real swordsman, Carter had a variety of new advantages. The shield Maddox had built for him would provide a defense from Ravener's sword while Carter used his own blade, heavy as it was, to counterstrike. Alternatively, Carter could abandon the sword and shield in favor of the new aionium truncheons. Ravener's fluidity in combat hinted that his sword was lighter than a *bokken*, so

Carter could not count on the truncheons' lesser weight to carry the fight for him.

Carter pushed his blade harder into Gideon's, struggling to push the *bokken* aside. Gideon disengaged, allowing Carter's weapon to swing past him, and stepped forward to jab the pommel of his sword at Carter's head. The blow landed, and Carter grimaced as his temple exploded with pain. He stumbled and landed in a sitting position. Gideon stepped forward; and Carter lashed out with his leg, sweeping Gideon's legs out from under him. As Gideon fell, Carter jumped to his feet and pointed the tip of his *bokken* at Gideon's throat, kicking his mentor's weapon out of his hands as he did. Gideon blinked in surprise, held up his hands in surrender, and laughed.

"Very good."

It had been a desperate move, one made in anger. Carter didn't expect the same tactic to work on Ravener. He helped Gideon stand and handed him back his *bokken*. Raina, sitting in her usual position on the nearby table, whistled and clapped.

"Thank you, thank you." Carter mock bowed. "It was nothing."

"Caught me by surprise," Gideon said. "That counts for something. In the heat of battle, the man with the upper hand is often the one with the element of surprise."

Raina slid off the table as Gideon put both *bokkens* down on it and reached for the case that he had brought in with him.

Gideon popped the case open. "Maddox and I finished the upgrades to your suit. Come take a look."

Carter stepped up to the table as Gideon pulled the Crusader suit out of the case. He had expected it to look roughly the same as it had before. He was wrong. A single chest plate made of segmented armor replaced the lighter breastplate Carter had worn. The small silver cross had been replaced with a large, electric blue cross that lit up the chest from belt to collarbone. The bright red armor shone under the garage lights. It was made of aionium, he realized, which would make him much harder to kill. Besides the chest plate, the mask was different— the domino mask had been replaced by a cowl with a sleek blue visor. A silver cross marked the cowl's forehead.

His heart ached unexpectedly. His father's Crusader mask had borne the silver cross on the forehead.

"Maddox streamlined the suit for efficiency." Gideon handed him one of the gauntlets. "No more reaching into your belt for adhesive beads or your grappling gun—you can use them with the flick of a fingertip." He pointed at the hole in the center of the gauntlet, where the back of Carter's wrist would be. "That will fire any tool you need. Flick the switch on the forearm plate to determine what comes out."

Carter examined the gauntlet. It had four options—grappling hook, adhesive bead, shock bead, and sonic bead. Combined with the new weaponry, he had much better odds against Ravener than he had before.

"Both gauntlets have the same capabilities," Gideon added. "That way, if you need to fire shock or adhesive beads from one gauntlet while you're swinging a weapon with the other, you can. The left gauntlet also magnetizes to your shield, which is practically impenetrable. Like the sword's blade, the surface of the shield can also be electrified, in case you need to strike an enemy with its face."

Carter whistled. "I like it."

"And here's the staff, if you prefer it." Gideon pulled two truncheons from the case and locked them together. "Made of aionium, so no sword will cut it. It's weighted perfectly. So is the sword. I took that one on a test run last night."

"Whoa, you went out on the streets?" Carter frowned. "I thought you were done with that."

"No." Gideon chuckled. "I didn't go out. While we were at Sterling Labs, finishing up your suit, the Phantom broke into the lab across the hall. I fought him, but he got away. He and his friends stole some gear from Sterling."

"Oh, man. You think they're planning something with that tech?"

"They've got to be. But Jolie has a scanner that can trace the energy signature the phaser leaves behind when he uses his powers. She's hoping she'll be able to track him down before he strikes again."

"If you need any help with that, give me a call." Carter set the staff down on the table and took up the sword and shield instead. "Did you get a good look at the guy?"

Gideon shook his head. "He was wearing a mask, and so were his friends. But we saw their vehicle—a white utility van."

A white utility van sounded familiar, but he could not remember why. Carter thought back over the last couple of days, considering. He had seen so many vehicles, and they all blurred together. For the van to stick in his memory, he must have seen it at an important moment. Something about the vehicle had been notable . . . or something about the person who was in it.

That was it. Ty Vickers had been dropped off by a white van the previous night, and he had seemed tense. He was wearing all black, too. Was it possible that Vickers was the thief Jolie was looking for? It would explain why he needed a babysitter at night so often. *Has Rhonda been babysitting for a super-criminal?* The assumption seemed absurd.

He couldn't say anything until he knew for sure. His speculation was the definition of circumstantial evidence. If he ratted on Vickers and he was innocent, his life could be upended, and the real Phantom might get away. But Carter could do some looking himself; and if it panned out, he could tip off Jolie.

Raina leaned against his shoulders. "So, when are you going to take this new rig out?"

"The sooner, the better. The longer that swordsman's out there, the more likely he'll be to strike again. Next time he does, I want to be there to stop him."

"You will," Gideon said.

Someone knocked on the door that led from the garage to the house. A moment later, the door swung open; and Carter's mother stuck her head in.

"Carter, you have a visitor. Your friend Silas."

He didn't usually visit Carter's house and never unannounced. If he was there, he probably had something big. Carter nodded to her and split his staff in two, placing the separate pieces back into the case. Joanna stepped aside, allowing Silas to enter the garage.

"Hey, everybody." Silas nodded to Gideon. "Good to see you all."

Carter held out a hand, which Silas shook. "What's going on?"

"I've been doing some digging on this Liang guy, and I think I've finally come up with something that could be useful to you."

Gideon crossed the garage and grabbed four folding chairs, placing them in a circle. Carter sat in one; and Raina, Silas, and Gideon took the others. Silas leaned forward, clasping his hands together in front of him.

"It took a lot of doing, but I found out that there was a bookkeeper in Serban's mob named Chin Liang. Liang used to be a gangster in

China, apparently, but nobody can tell me more than that. He was presumed dead after the Uprising, but his body wasn't recovered."

"If he survived, do you have any idea why Ravener wants him dead?"

"No clue. Liang's past is a mystery. He lived in Sojourn City for about ten years. Up until he joined Serban's organization, he seemed like an upstanding citizen. Nobody put together his triad connections until after the fact. But he was good at what he did. They say he never let a debt slip by. If someone owed Serban, Liang made sure they paid. He wasn't only a bookkeeper; he was an enforcer—one of Serban's deadliest."

"Maybe he hurt someone who's out for revenge." Carter cupped his chin in his hand. "There have to be hundreds of people who'd love to take a piece out of Liang. How would we ever narrow it down?"

"You couldn't. And if you could, there's no guarantee this swordsman is someone from Liang's time in Sojourn City. It could be someone holding a grudge from Liang's past. An old comrade from the Chinese triads, looking to take revenge for a betrayal. Or a victim of the triads looking for retaliation."

"If Liang's not dead, who might know his location? Family? Friends?"

"When he came to Sojourn City, his only relative was a son, a Japanese boy he adopted under the Chinese name Tao Liang. No one has heard from Tao since the Uprising, and there is no record of his Japanese name. If he's alive, he may have fled the city after his father's criminal activities were discovered."

"Thanks, Silas. At least we identified our swordsman's target. It explains why he's been killing people affiliated with Serban." Carter shook Silas's hand again. "Keep your head down. I don't want you or your family in anyone's crosshairs because of this."

"No worries. See you later." Silas waved to Gideon and Raina. "Bye, guys."

As Silas exited the garage, Carter scratched his chin and pondered the situation. Liang must have been alive, and the swordsman knew it. But who was Ravener? Enough of Liang's past was shrouded in mystery that anybody could want him dead. It could even be the son, Tao, if there was bad blood between father and adoptive son.

Or since Ravener had only uttered the name "Liang," perhaps the swordsman was on the hunt for Tao, not Chin.

Carter looked at Gideon and Raina. "What do you think?"

"I never heard of Liang when I was fighting Serban's organization, but that doesn't mean he doesn't exist," Gideon said. "Serban's plot had wheels within wheels. Many of them were probably hidden from the others. It's possible that only the people who had direct contact with Liang knew he existed."

"Would've made it really easy to disappear," Raina murmured.

Carter ran a hand over his hair. "This doesn't narrow down Ravener's identity. We've got a lot of work to do."

CHAPTER 24

Before Carter hit the field that night, he had to take Rhonda to Vickers's house. He needed a babysitter again. That opened the perfect door for Carter. He could have Rhonda do a little searching while Vickers was out. She could report anything suspicious. Meanwhile, he would be free to look for Ravener—or for Liang. The former would probably be easier to find, but the latter had to be out there somewhere, too.

"Bye, Mom!" Rhonda called. "See you tonight!"

"Bye, baby! Bye, Carter!"

"Bye, Ma." Carter pulled the door closed behind him and walked through the chilly evening air toward the car. "Hey, Rho, you wanna help me with something?"

His sister's eyes sparkled. "Is it Crusader-related?"

"Sure is." Carter climbed into his car and blasted the hot air. "While you're at Mr. Vickers's house tonight, I want you to have a look around."

"You want me to snoop?" Rhonda furrowed her brow. "Why?"

"I . . . think Mr. Vickers might be involved in something he shouldn't be." Carter pulled away from the curb. "But I'm not sure, so I don't want to tell the police or go after him yet. I want to give him the benefit of the doubt."

"Okay . . . So what would I be looking for?"

"Anything that might point to him being a criminal. A stash of money, a lockpicking kit, a black costume with a mask . . . knives. If you find anything like that, take a picture and text it to me."

"If Mr. Vickers is a criminal, what happens to Emi? He doesn't have a wife or a girlfriend, I don't think."

The question hit like a gut punch. Carter hadn't considered the baby's fate. If the child's father turned out to be a criminal and went away to jail, where would she end up? How many kids Carter's age had ended up on the streets of the Brooks because their daddies were in prison? How many of those same kids had Carter had to take down as the Crusader because they sold drugs to keep the lights on?

"I guess she'd go into foster care."

"That doesn't seem right. If Mr. Vickers is stealing, maybe he's desperate. It's still wrong; but if he's trying to be a good dad, it doesn't seem fair to take her away from him, does it?"

Carter was taken aback by the fervor in Rhonda's voice. He hadn't expected her to be so passionate about it. As much as he hated to admit it, part of him agreed with her. If Vickers was the Phantom, or involved somehow, his actions were wrong; but Emi didn't deserve to lose her only parent. But if that happened, it was on Vickers. There were other methods to provide for one's kids. Carter's dad had proven that. If there was anyone who could understand going through a hard time and trying to provide for family, it was Carter.

But that motive was speculation on Rhonda's end. How much did any of them know about Vickers? Maybe he was a good dad. But there were plenty of deadbeat dads in the Brooks, too. It was possible Ty was greedy. Carter was not prepared to assign motivation to Vickers' actions until he knew what those actions were.

And if Rhonda was regularly visiting a dangerous criminal's house, Carter needed to be sure.

"No . . . I guess it's not fair, but there's always a right way to do things. If Vickers is breaking the law and he keeps it up, he could get hurt."

Rhonda was silent for a moment. "Okay, I'll help you. But if I do find something, think about Emi, okay?"

"I will. I promise."

* * *

The program that Nate had set up to track the Phantom was constantly scanning the city for a matching signature. The CSI had based the search parameters on the readings Jolie had gathered from Sterling Labs, Sojourn City Bank, and the computer terminal the thief had destroyed. If it got a hit at any point, Nate had programmed it to send a text to Jolie with the address of the ping.

Jolie studied the equipment. "I seem to be saying this a lot lately, but you're a genius, Nate."

The CSI grinned. "Thanks, Detective. I love my work."

"What would I do without you?"

"You may find out sooner than later." Nate scratched the back of his head. "I'm transferring to Detroit. I got an offer from the FBI."

"The FBI?" Jolie whistled. "Wow. I'm . . . happy for you, Nate."

"Thanks. Don't worry. I'm sure whoever replaces me will be as much of a genius as I am, Detective."

"I doubt it." Jolie stepped toward Nate and hugged him. "I'll miss you."

"I'll miss you, too. But hey, I'm not leaving for another few weeks. I'll make sure this case—and Pulaski's sword-killer case—are all wrapped up before I step out. Wouldn't want to burden my replacement with cases in progress."

After they said goodbye, Jolie walked out of the lab and shook her head in disbelief. She had worked with Nate since her promotion to detective. It would be tough to adjust to working with a new CSI. Whoever got the job would have big shoes to fill. She hoped they had Nate's good-hearted nature and strong work ethic. He never seemed to grow tired of his job.

An idea blossomed in Jolie's mind as she walked. It was a long shot—and it would require jumping through some hoops and cutting some red tape—but she thought she had a perfect replacement. And if it worked out, it would solve a lot of people's problems all at once.

* * *

Ty sat in the rocking chair in Emi's room, cradling his little girl and staring down at the black hair that framed her dark brown face. She got her wispy hair and angular eyes from Ty, but that skin was all Rachel's. Ty ran the back of one finger along Emi's cheek, taking in the beauty of his daughter and wishing he never had to leave her again. The injustice, the cruelty of her mother's death, was that while Ty was Emi's only parent, he had less time to spend with her because he had to provide for her. In a just world, he would have inherited his godfather's wealth. Living off that fortune, he could stay home with his daughter and care for her.

But the world was not just. Ty had learned that long ago. He rued the day he first heard the name Chin Liang. Shiro had been a fool to befriend the gangster. From the time Ty's godfather had uprooted and brought Ty to Sojourn City, Ty had realized that the man did not care for him in the slightest. When Ty had tried to distance himself from Liang, his godfather's crimes had followed him and ruined his chances at a solid career. After six months of job-hopping, during which Rachel had gotten pregnant, he was penniless. Rachel's death had cemented the truth that the world had no intention of being kind to Ty. That was when Ty had chosen a life of crime.

If he was caught, Emi would grow up without either of her parents. That was a life Ty had barely avoided, as he clung to a few furtive memories of his parents. But if that happened, he hoped Joanie would be able to care for her somehow. Joanie and Rachel had grown up in foster care, never living in one home for more than a few years, at best. When things finally seemed good, Rachel had died. The world had been as hard to Joanie as it had been to Ty, yet she stayed hopeful.

A knock on the door snapped Ty from his reverie. He kissed Emi on the head, walked over to her crib, and rested her inside.

"I love you, baby."

He walked out of her room and glanced around for anything incriminating. Finding nothing, he walked over to the door and reached for the knob. Through the peephole, he saw Rhonda. He opened the door to let her inside. Rhonda smiled at him, as she always did, but there was something fake about it. Ty's shoulders tensed.

"Emi's sound asleep. I'll be back as soon as I can. Thank you for your help."

"You're welcome." Rhonda shifted from one foot to the other. "Good luck on . . . whatever you're doing."

"Thanks."

Ty picked up the duffel bag that held his throwing knives and black catsuit, shouldered it, and walked out the door. *This is the last time,*

Emi. One way or the other, he was done. His kid deserved better than this, and he was determined to give it to her. He'd learned to live in a world that was unforgiving, but he would show Emi a better world. Her mother would've wanted that.

* * *

Rhonda Jonson looked around Vickers' house with new eyes. Before, it had seemed a cozy, if outdated, home with ugly carpet but an otherwise inviting atmosphere. A little messy, but that was to be expected of a single father, wasn't it? Since her talk with Carter, all she could see was the den of a criminal. She hoped Carter was wrong about Mr. Vickers and that she would find nothing on her search, but part of her feared that he was right. With no job, what else could take Vickers out of the house so regularly?

She peeked her head into Emi's bedroom. The baby was sleeping soundly for the moment, so Rhonda turned on the baby monitor and walked back out into the living room. She had no idea where to begin. She picked up an empty fast food bag, stained with grease, and filled it with the refuse that littered the living room. Granola bar wrappers, empty water bottles and beer cans, a broken plastic fork . . . Rhonda cleaned up the mess, wadded up the burger bag, and took it into the kitchen. The trashcan was nearly full. Shaking her head, Rhonda threw away the to-go bag, pulled the plastic liner out of the trashcan, and tied it. It took a bit of doing—she had to force the trash down inside to make it all fit—but once it was done, she set the full trash bag down next to the kitchen counter.

Stop stalling. Carter needed to know if he was right about Vickers. The only way to prove that Rhonda was right about her employer was to do what Carter had asked and look for evidence. It felt wrong, like she was snooping, but it was for a good cause. She opened each of the kitchen cabinets first; but all the cabinets contained were plastic cups, a few hodgepodge dishes, and food.

She tiptoed back into the living room and opened the door to Vickers's bedroom. *Why am I sneaking? Who's going to catch me? Emi?* Rhonda shook her head and flicked on the lights. The bedroom was as dirty as the living room, covered in clothes piled on the floor and the bed, which was unmade. She rifled through his dresser drawers and peeked under the bed and inside Vickers' bedside table drawers. There was nothing incriminating. Maybe Carter was wrong.

A quick check of the bathroom also proved fruitless. The only place left to check was the garage. Rhonda peeked back into Emi's room and found her still sleeping. Steeling herself, she walked through the kitchen and out the side door into the garage. It was mostly empty, other than a workbench, a cabinet, a bicycle, and a few plastic storage totes. Rhonda crossed to the cabinet and reached for the handle.

She gasped. Inside the cabinet hung a pair of short swords, crossed at the blades, and four throwing knives. On either end of the cabinet were empty hooks where two more knives could hang. On a shelf below the swords, there was a folded outfit that looked like a martial arts uniform of some kind.

"Oh . . . " she whispered. "Oh, no."

CHAPTER 25

The Crusader's new suit fit differently. Standing on a rooftop, he stretched his arms and legs in an effort to acclimate his body to the feel. It was heavier than the old suit, mostly due to the added aionium plates and the extra weaponry. The weight was worth it. The advanced tech would give him a ton of advantages in combat. He could disable targets from a distance with the shock beads and adhesive beads that fired from his gauntlets. He didn't have to worry as much about getting hit by bullets, so he could be more aggressive, which he hoped would lead to faster takedowns. To make up for the weight difference, he planned to up his workout regiment at the gym. In a few weeks, he wouldn't notice the extra pounds.

The toys were great, but they needed a test run. It was a Saturday night. There was bound to be an uptick in criminal activity somewhere in the area. He raised the kickstand on his bike and was about to put it in gear when his phone chimed. He stopped and opened the pouch in his utility belt where he kept his phone.

It was a text from Rhonda: *Found something.*

He opened the text, which had an image attached to it—an image of a pair of swords and four throwing knives.

"Uh . . . Raina?"

Her voice came over his earbud instantly. "Yeah?"

"I think I've got something."

The knives in Vickers' house lent credence to Carter's suspicion that he was the Phantom, but there were no reports of the thief using swords. Was Vickers also connected to Ravener? Silas said it was possible that Liang's adopted son had changed his name to avoid identification with his father. And if he had discovered that Liang was still alive, it could explain his sudden murder spree across the city. Tao—or Ty Vickers, or whoever he was—might be tracking down his would-be father by cutting through the criminals Liang had worked with. Alternatively, Ravener could be Chin Liang's alter ego. Maybe the older man had fled the city after Serban's defeat and was back, looking for his adoptive son.

Either option presented a problem. If Carter's first theory was correct, Rhonda hadn't been babysitting for a mere bank robber—she'd been babysitting for a serial killer. If the second theory was more accurate, Rhonda might be sitting in the home of Ravener's target.

Or all of his ideas could be wrong. The killer could have been a living relative of Tao's Japanese family coming to reclaim him from Liang or a triad rival of Chin Liang's. The swords in Ty's house could have been a memento of his home country, nothing more. There were too many possibilities and nowhere near enough answers.

"What's wrong?" Raina asked.

"Rhonda sent me a picture from Vickers' house. He's got a stash of swords and throwing knives."

The Crusader kicked his bike into gear. There was no way he was letting his sister stay in that house. If Vickers was not the Phantom, Ravener, or both, he could be connected to either one.

"Where are you going?" Raina asked.

"Vickers' house. I can't leave Rhonda there alone."

"Whoa, big guy. Vickers isn't home, otherwise Rhonda wouldn't be there. You need to worry more about where he is, rather than where he isn't."

Carter brought the bike to a screeching halt. Behind him, a driver laid on the horn. Grimacing, Carter zipped into an alley, so he wouldn't block traffic. A young couple, kissing behind a garbage bin, jerked up in surprise at the sound of the bike. The Crusader waved distractedly as they took a picture and ran off, leaving him alone.

"So, where is he?" Carter asked. "Assuming he's both Ravener and the Phantom, he could be out doing either job."

"You said the swords are still in his house, right? So, let's assume he's not on a killing spree. He might not need those weapons for a heist. Besides, assuming he's one—let alone both—is a big jump."

He supposed she was right. The more Carter thought about it, the less sense it made that Vickers could be both his suspects. While the Phantom hadn't taken any lives so far, Ravener was leaving bodies all across the city. When the Crusader fought Ravener, the assassin never used phasing powers; but according to Gideon, the Phantom had done so during their fight at Sterling Labs. So, the odds of them being the same person were minimal. And the swords in Rhonda's photo looked different from Ravener's katana.

With a moment to breathe, Carter realized how rash he had nearly been.

"So . . . what do I do? We can't anticipate what the Phantom's crew will hit, or where, or when." He bit his lip. "Jolie. She's got that scanner, right? As soon as the Phantom uses his powers, we'll know it."

"That's right!" Raina sounded relieved. "Then you and the police can work together to take him down."

"Let's hope we can get to them in time."

* * *

Jolie stepped out of the kitchen as Carter's voice spilled from the phone speaker. Much of his explanation was speculation; but if he was correct, the Phantom and Ravener could be connected. As a worst-case scenario, they might have been the same person. That didn't sound right to Jolie because they didn't have remotely the same M.O. There was no reason other than circumstantial evidence to believe that they could be the same person. The evidence that Vickers was one suspect or the other was likely, but it didn't mean he was both.

"Carter, slow down."

"He's out there somewhere," Carter pressed. "My sister's babysitting for him while he goes and steals or kills or—or whatever!"

"Relax. Maybe he's a guy with a hobby. But in case he's not, we're going to find Vickers." She put Carter on speaker and set the phone down in front of her. "I've got the scanner running; so if the phaser uses his powers, we'll be there. I'll tip Pulaski to Vickers' address and mention we got a lead that he *might* be involved in the swordsman killer case. He'll probably want to go over and have a look, so Rhonda will be fine."

"Okay. What about me?"

"Keep your phone on you. As soon as we get a hit on the scanner, I'll tell you where; and you can help us bring the thief in. Then, we'll focus on the swordsman killer if they're two separate people."

"Thanks, Jolie."

"No problem. Stay safe out there."

Jolie hung up and rested her palms against the kitchen counter. So much for the nice dinner she'd been preparing. She took a deep breath and glanced over at the stove. The steamed broccoli and mashed potatoes were already on. If she left, they would be ruined. But maybe Gideon could finish them up.

"Hey, babe?" she called.

Gideon walked out of the bedroom and pulled on a t-shirt. "What's up?"

"I have to run. That was Carter. He thinks this Vickers guy Rhonda babysits for could be the Phantom, Ravener, or both. Either way, he thinks Vickers is going to move tonight because he's not home. If the Phantom's crew stole those weapons for a job, they're probably about to make a move. If they do, I need to be there."

"Of course. I understand."

"If you don't mind, keep an eye on dinner, all right? And don't wait up—it'll probably be a while before I'm back. Go ahead and eat, or put it in the fridge, or whatever you want to do. I'm so sorry, Gid."

She saw the disappointment in his eyes and wondered if it was because she was leaving him or because he couldn't come along and help. She was tempted to invite him along, but her superiors would frown on that.

"No problem." Gideon forced a smile. "Go get your man."

"I'll try." *I may fail if it comes down to a car chase . . .* "Hey, I hate to ask, but could I borrow the Mustang? My car's acting a little . . . cantankerous."

Gideon laughed. "What's mine is yours."

Jolie's phone beeped. She glanced down. A map of the Brooks had appeared on the screen, and a bright red dot marked Washington Avenue. The Phantom's powers were active. "Speak of the devil . . . I love you, but I've got to go."

"Love you, too."

Jolie grabbed her badge, gun, and the keys to Gideon's car and rushed out the door. She would not let her suspect escape again.

* * *

Ty knelt on the rooftop above the intersection of Washington and Fifth. In the distance, the armored car trundled toward the intersection, escorted by two SUVs. He pulled his mask on and looked down at Fifth Street. The white van sat in a parking spot, innocuous and unthreatening.

"I see the truck."

"Roger that," Joanie chirped. "Deactivating traffic cams in this vicinity in three, two . . . now."

"Shock Jock, G-Storm, be ready to move on my signal." Ty—Lurk, until the job was done—stood and flexed his fingers. "We've got to do this fast."

Lurk checked the knives on his belt. He didn't expect to have to use them on the driver or the guards. Phasing into the cabin would startle them long enough for him to knock them out with a few quick punches. If it came down to it, he would use the knives to maim them before he considered a lethal blow.

The armored truck stopped at the intersection. As soon as it crossed through, it would be right beneath Lurk. The trick would be to drop from the rooftop and phase into the cabin. He had to stop at exactly the right moment to keep from phasing too far and missing the truck or not phasing far enough and getting stuck in the roof of the truck, either of which was likely to be lethal. He had never attempted anything like this before.

As the truck pulled through the intersection, Lurk braced himself. It passed the intersection and reached the edge of the building he stood atop.

He leaped from the rooftop, making himself incorporeal as he fell. The steel roof of the truck rose to meet him. As soon as he saw the inside of the cabin, Lurk reverted his body to its natural state. With his left hand, he lashed out and struck the driver below the ear. With his right, he grabbed the rifle in the hands of the guard in the passenger's seat. He jerked the rifle upward to hit the guard in the chin. The truck swerved, and Lurk reached forward to grab the wheel. He snaked his leg between the driver's and slammed on the brakes. The truck screeched to a halt in the middle of the road.

"Move!" he shouted.

He kicked open the driver's door, climbed over the man's body, and jumped out onto the street. The two SUVs behind the armored truck stopped; but as the doors opened and cops jumped out, blue electric bolts shot through the air, striking them from behind. Shock Jock came around the corner, rifle at his shoulder, and sprayed the cops with blasts. G-Storm rushed to the back of the truck and aimed the mag-gun at the doors. Lurk leaped and phased into the back of the truck before G-Storm could rip the doors off. He emerged standing amidst four armed guards.

With his left hand, Lurk jabbed the nearest guard in the throat. No sooner had the blow landed than he swept the legs out from under the guard behind him. From the crouching position, he rose and grabbed a third guard, shoving him toward the wall and phasing through, carrying the guard out onto the street. As the guard struck pavement, Lurk punched him in the jaw, knocking him out. He leaped back into the truck and snapped out a kick to hit the final guard in the chest.

Lurk faced the doors as the air began to ripple around them, and the metal fixtures began to cave in. Seconds later, the doors flew free from their hinges and slammed into the ground between the two SUVs. Shock Jock and G-Storm clambered into the back of the truck.

Shock Jock whooped. "Nice work!"

"No time to celebrate." Lurk picked up a bag of cash. "Let's get—"

Police sirens wailed. He cursed under his breath. *Less time than I thought.* Ty grabbed another bag and jumped out of the truck. If they made it to the van, they might escape before it was too late. Ty could go home and get his daughter, and they and Joanie could get out of Dodge with the small score. Ned and Richie could do what they wanted.

A hefty shield lashed out, striking Lurk across the skull before he had time to phase through it. He reeled back, dropping the bags of cash on the ground next to him. Ty's attacker stepped forward and twirled a sword. He was clad in familiar red and black, but the glowing blue cross emblem was new. So were the sword and shield, for that matter.

"What's wrong? Did you forget your sword, Phantom?" the newcomer asked. "Stand down. Make this easier on yourself."

The Crusader.

CHAPTER 26

Tap-tap-tap-tap.

Rhonda jumped and yelped. She took a deep breath and willed her trembling hands to stop. The sound was someone knocking on the screen door. Emi whimpered in her arms, disturbed by Rhonda's reaction. Rhonda kissed the baby on her forehead and set her down in her playpen.

Taking another breath, Rhonda peered out the peephole. The man outside had dirty blond hair and was dressed in casual street clothes, but a police badge hung on a chain around his neck. Rhonda unlocked the deadbolt and pulled the door open.

"Yes?" she asked.

"I'm Sergeant Tom Pulaski. Detective Jolie Turner sent me to check out the house—said there was evidence of potential criminal activity?"

"In the garage. Through there." Rhonda pointed toward the kitchen. "There's a cabinet with swords and knives."

"You did the right thing reporting it, ma'am."

Pulaski stepped inside, and Rhonda closed the door behind him. As she waited, Rhonda wondered if she had made a mistake. Lots of guys around the world were sword aficionados. Vickers owning a couple didn't mean he was connected to the swordsman killer case. If he got arrested because of her, and he was innocent, she would never forgive herself. He might never forgive her, either.

Rhonda walked over to the playpen while Pulaski stepped around the corner through the kitchen. Emi fussed and kicked, so Rhonda leaned down and picked her up. Emi stilled and cooed contentedly. Rhonda wished Vickers getting in trouble wouldn't prevent her from seeing the precious baby anymore. She had spent a lot of time with Emi over the last few weeks, and she'd grown to love her.

Pulaski reentered from the kitchen. "Thank you for the tip, miss."

"What's going to happen?"

"We'll bring Mr. Vickers in for questioning; and if he turns out to be the man we're looking for, we'll arrest him. If not, he'll be released." Pulaski put a hand on Rhonda's shoulder. "I'll be waiting in my car outside for Vickers to return. When he does, I'll come back to speak to him. Okay?"

"Okay." Rhonda nodded. "I—"

The front door crashed in. Rhonda grabbed Emi from the crib and ducked behind the couch. Her heart pounded in her chest, and she pressed the baby to herself, protecting Emi with her body. She peered up over the edge of the couch. A man in a black and silver costume stood in the doorway, holding a sword loosely in his right hand.

"Where is Liang?" he rumbled.

Pulaski raised his gun. "Drop the sword and get on your knees!"

"This does not concern the police." The swordsman stepped inside. "Leave, and you will be spared."

Pulaski fired. Rhonda screamed. The swordsman threw himself to the side in an elegant spin, dodging the bullet. Pulaski fired twice more, but the swordsman dodged into the kitchen, taking cover around the corner. Pulaski strafed to the side with his gun trained on the entryway. Emi wailed and kicked, tears flowing down her cheeks. Rhonda shushed her softly and stroked her head.

Pulaski's mouth opened to speak, but a silver star cut through the air and embedded itself in his left hand. Pulaski gasped and stumbled back. The swordsman rushed forward, kicked Pulaski in the chest, and ran out the door. Pulaski slammed into a bookshelf. The rickety shelf toppled with the weight of the police officer and crashed down on top of him. He was down, groaning and clutching his bloody hand and trapped beneath the bookcase. Rhonda's eyes widened. After returning Emi to her playpen, she stepped toward the sergeant and knelt at his side. The bladed star protruded from the bottom of his hand, blood dripping down it.

"Are you all right?" she asked.

"I'm fine." Pulaski groaned. "You?"

"Yeah. Who was that guy?"

"I thought he was Vickers." Pulaski pulled the star from his hand and tossed it to the floor. With Rhonda's help, he slid out from under the bookcase. "Considering that would mean he broke into his own house, I guess I was wrong."

* * *

The Crusader swung the flat of his sword at the Phantom. The thief pulled his shoulder back to the right, avoiding the attack, and stepped forward. He rammed his palm into the Crusader's chest. The Crusader stumbled back, caught himself, and raised his shield in a block as the Phantom punched at him. The Phantom's arm phased through the shield and rematerialized in time to strike the Crusader in the solar plexus.

He grimaced and spun away from his opponent. How was he supposed to fight someone who couldn't be touched? Carter's first priority was getting the Phantom's mask off. He needed to prove that it was Vickers.

The Phantom reached into his belt and withdrew two throwing knives, and Carter's mind flashed to the photo Rhonda sent. Two knives had been missing from Vickers' shelf. Before the thief could throw his knives, the Crusader raised his right arm and fired an adhesive bead. The sphere passed through the Phantom and struck the sidewalk behind him, exploding harmlessly and spreading its blue-green glue on the pavement. The Phantom hurled one of his knives. The Crusader dodged, the knife passing by his left shoulder. He closed the remaining gap with two steps and swung his shield at the Phantom's head. The thief ducked under the strike and jabbed with his remaining knife. The blade bounced harmlessly off the Crusader's armor. The vigilante kicked upward, striking the distracted Phantom in the jaw.

He advanced before his opponent could recover, bringing his elbow down on the back of the man's head. As the Phantom crumpled to the ground, the Crusader raised his sword for a disabling blow.

A metallic creaking sound screeched above the din. One of the SUVs was off the ground, hovering in the air amidst a sphere of strange, rippling waves. One of the Phantom's partners stood at the foot of the armored truck, holding the SUV with some kind of gravity weapon. The police trained their guns on the man.

"Drop the weapon!" Jolie shouted.

Something slammed into the back of the Crusader's kneecaps. He cried out and dropped to his back. The Phantom jumped to his feet and looked down at the Crusader. Carter tensed, ready to move if the Phantom pressed his attack. Instead, the thief backed away. The SUV crashed into the ground, sending the cops rolling for cover. The Crusader pulled himself to his feet and glanced in the direction of the chaos. When he looked back, the Phantom and his companions were gone.

He rushed to Jolie's side. She shoved her pistol into its holster. "They can't get far. One of my officers spotted their van back there and went to secure it, so they're without transportation."

"But the Phantom can phase in and out of buildings."

Jolie held up a device the size of a lunchbox. "We can track him when he does. We'll run him to ground—it's only a matter of time."

The Crusader's phone rang. He removed it from his belt pouch and glanced at the screen. *Rhonda.* Jolie's phone rang, too. He looked at her.

"That's never a good sign," she said.

They both answered. Carter stepped away from her and held the phone to his ear.

"Hello?"

"Carter? Hey, it's me. I-I wanted to let you know I'm okay." Rhonda's voice quavered. "But there was a-an attack."

His heart stopped. "What?"

"Some guy with a sword broke into Vickers' house asking for someone named Liang. Sergeant Pulaski fought him off, so I'm fine."

There was no way the Phantom and Ravener were the same person. Carter had been fighting the thief at the same time as Ravener hit Vickers' house. Ty could be one or the other, but not both. If Ty was not either perpetrator, which Carter found less likely as the pieces fell into place, he was clearly connected to at least one of them. Was he Tao Liang? Was he associated with the Phantom? Carter would have to find Vickers and ask him.

"I'm sending Raina to get you, Rhonda. Stay there."

"Did you see Mr. Vickers?"

"I think so. He's probably a bank robber; but at least he's not a serial killer, like I was afraid of."

"That's good . . . I guess. What do you want me to do when Raina gets here? I can't leave Emi by herself."

And if she took Emi with her, Vickers was bound to track her down with a vengeance. There weren't any good options, other than to find Vickers before he made it back to his house.

"Raina will stay with you. I doubt the swordsman will come back, and I'll try to find Vickers before he gets home. Love you, Rho. You did good." Carter hung up and tapped his earbud. "Did you hear all that?"

"Yeah," Raina said. "Poor Rhonda. She must be so scared."

"You good to go watch her?"

"Sure thing. But what if Ravener does show up again? I haven't trained enough to fight him off."

"I'm sure Pulaski will stay at the house or leave some cops there until he's sure it's safe. I'll swing by as soon as I can, but first I've got to track down the Phantom and figure out what is going on here."

Carter tucked his phone into his belt pouch. Jolie spoke softly but urgently into her phone and hung up. Worry was etched in her features.

"That was Sergeant Pulaski," she said.

"Ravener?"

Jolie nodded. "You heard?"

"My sister called. She had a front-row seat to Pulaski's little duel."

"Poor girl. Looks like we're after two different suspects, after all."

"Yeah, but there's a connection. If we can find Vickers, maybe we can figure out what Ravener wants with him." He looked around. "That scanner of yours showing anything?"

"No. Wherever the Phantom went, he must not be using his powers—which means we may be doing this the old-fashioned way."

"Fantastic."

CHAPTER 27

How did they do it?

Ty ducked behind the empty restaurant's counter as the white beam of a cop's flashlight shone through the front window. There was no way they could've predicted that Ty and his friends would hit the armored truck. But they and the Crusader had been on the scene moments after he took out the driver.

If Ned had not distracted the cops with that SUV trick, they would all be in custody. They had managed to escape with two small bags of cash, but it was nowhere near the haul they'd been expecting. And they'd lost the van, too. Thankfully, Joanie had been smart enough to duck out of the vehicle and hide in an alley as soon as the cops pulled up.

"What do we do?" Ned whispered.

"Shh!" Ty hissed. "I'm thinking."

The white light disappeared. Ty sagged to the floor. They were trapped. He could phase his way through these buildings and get home; but to do that, he would have to leave Joanie, Ned, and Richie. He was pretty sure they'd insist on keeping the money with them. And if he could get the money, he wouldn't leave without Joanie.

Ned's ankle was far from healed, and he was slowing them down. From the way he was breathing, his whispered query a few minutes earlier was almost too much for him. He was exhausted, and he was in pain.

He'll never make it if we make a break for it.

"We've got to make a break for it!" Richie exclaimed.

Ty groaned.

"Are you insane?" Joanie asked. "As soon as we run, they'll see us. Some of us are bound to get caught."

Ty grabbed Richie's shoulder. "This is a team. We stick together."

Actually, he would ditch Ned and Richie in a heartbeat. Unfortunately, he did not trust them to keep quiet if they were captured. In fact, he was sure they would rat on him and Joanie. That meant he had to get them out safely, too.

It seemed the Crusader knew something already. That question about leaving his swords behind . . . *How does he know I have swords?*

If the Crusader knew who he was, it wouldn't be long before the police did, too. On the other hand, the vigilante had called Ty "Phantom," rather than by name. He did not know Ty's identity with enough certainty to call him out.

He peered over the counter. There was no sign of the police outside anymore, but they were probably close by. Any wrong move could get them caught.

"We can't stay here forever," he said. "Ditch the guns and masks. We need to blend in."

"What?" Ned hissed. "If we walk out of here without masks, we're toast!"

"Trust me." Ty removed his mask and wrapped it around his remaining knife, which he tucked into his back pocket. "I'll phase us one at a time through this building and into the next one over." Through the walls, he heard the staccato beat of pulse-pounding music. "It's a nightclub. We'll blend into the crowd for a while and duck out when a big group leaves."

"All right, not bad." Richie bobbed his head eagerly. "But what about the guns? Won't the dudes who own this restaurant find them when they open in the morning?"

There was nothing on the guns that would lead the cops back to Ned and Richie, but it would be a shame to lose the tech. Still, it was better than dying. But what about the money? They couldn't carry two huge bags of cash into the club. They would have to stash it with the guns, somewhere it wouldn't be discovered. Somewhere like inside a wall.

"I can phase the guns and money into the drywall. I'll come back tomorrow, sneak in, and grab them."

Ned and Richie exchanged glances, but Joanie had already removed her mask and unzipped her black jacket, which she tied around her waist. She shook out her long dreadlocks and loosened her blouse, making her look more like a party-going college student. Ned and Richie were slightly too old for the nightclub's crowd, but they would have to work with it. Ty watched them intently, waiting for them to decide.

"Okay," Richie said. "But you've gotta come back for that loot ASAP."

Ty removed his own jacket, underneath which he wore only a black t-shirt. Not exactly clubwear, but it would have to do. Ty was only in his mid-twenties, so no one would be too suspicious of him. Ned and Richie's more riotous colors would help them blend in a bit more, hopefully offsetting their ages. Ty took their weapons and the bags of money from them and walked toward the wall that sat between the restaurant and the club.

He phased his hands and head inside. There looked to be enough empty space to store it all. One at a time, he placed the shock rifle, mag-gun, and bags of money inside the wall, along with their masks and jackets. Satisfied that they would not be discovered, he walked back to the front of the restaurant.

"All right. Let's go."

Ned, Richie, and Joanie crept to the back wall. Ty grabbed Joanie's shoulders, took a breath, and rushed the wall. He pushed through and came out in the middle of a throng of young people, all dancing, shouting, and laughing. He patted Joanie on the shoulder and phased back into the restaurant.

"Who's next?"

Ned stepped forward. His forehead looked clammy with sweat, and his eyes were heavy. He wasn't doing well. Ty grabbed his shoulder and tensed as a flashlight swept across the front of the store again.

Why would they come back to a store they already checked?

The cops had passed the restaurant five minutes ago. And there was no sign of them doubling back until Ty phased into the nightclub.

And they hadn't shown up at the crime scene until after Ty phased into the truck.

They are tracking my powers.

The possibility washed over him like a bucket of cold water. That was the best explanation for how they showed up to the crime scene so quickly and why they came back to the restaurant a second time. Tracking powers might not be possible, but he had to take it as a certainty until he knew otherwise. He only had a few seconds left. He would never be able to make two trips. With his free hand, he grabbed Richie.

"We're all going together. Hold on!"

He had never phased himself and two others at the same time, but they didn't have another option. He clenched his jaw, closed his eyes, and stepped toward the wall, pushing both men with him. He felt his body straining as their molecules mingled into the wall—and they were through. He sighed in combined relief and exhaustion.

It wasn't over yet. The police would check the club next.

"We need to get out," he shouted over the pounding music.

Joanie sat on a stool nearby, looking disinterested as a man about Ty's age flirted with her, gesturing grandiosely with one hand and clutching a drink in the other. Ty weaved his way toward her and gave her unwelcome suitor a hard glare. The inebriated man did not spare him a glance. Instead, he continued his advances. Ty stepped up to him.

"The lady isn't interested."

"Who're you?" The man slurred his words. "Her bodyguard?"

"Try brother-in-law." Ty grabbed the man's wrist. "Leave. There's no reason for this to get unpleasant."

He applied a little more pressure than necessary to the joint, and the punk winced and cried out. Ty shoved him away. Sullen, the man sulked away to find someone else to flirt with. Ty glanced at Joanie.

"The cops might be tracking my phasing. We need to go."

CHAPTER 28

Jolie swept her light through the empty restaurant's lobby as four of her fellow officers moved into the kitchen. The scanner indicated that Vickers had used his powers there, but there was no sign of him.

"Paul, what's adjacent to this restaurant?"

Her old partner glanced up at her. "A nightclub, I think."

"He's right!" Officer Rojas called from the kitchen. "I can hear the bass thumping from here."

"That must be where they went." Jolie spun for the door. "They'll blend in with the crowd in the nightclub and try to slip out."

She sprinted down the sidewalk toward the club's front door. Carter, who had been waiting outside in the shadows, matched her step for step. Around the corner, a line of twenty-somethings blocked the sidewalk—patrons waiting for their shot to get into the club, no doubt. Jolie stepped out onto the street and walked past the line. As she approached the club door, a bouncer held up his hand to stop her; and she gestured to her badge. The bouncer nodded and froze as Carter, decked out in his Crusader gear, pushed forward. Several of the partygoers waiting in line pulled out cell phones to snap pictures of the vigilante, leaning in for selfies. Others rushed away from the club, no doubt expecting trouble and not wanting any part of it. Jolie followed Carter inside the club.

The pounding music combined with the strobing lights—predominantly blue and purple—gave Jolie an instant headache. She grimaced and looked around for the DJ. Their best bet was to shut everything down and go through the club one person at a time. With the rest of the officers still outside, waiting to catch any runners, there was little chance of Vickers or his friends escaping.

She took a step toward the dance floor, and a gunshot echoed over the music. She reached for her own sidearm, and the gun fired twice more. Jolie drew her weapon and scanned the club for the shooter. Patrons screamed and flocked for the door, creating a tidal wave of frantic, sweaty partiers. Carter held up his hands to calm them, but they shoved past the Crusader and Jolie. She pressed herself against a pillar to avoid being trampled.

In moments, the club was empty except for the two of them, the music still thumping loudly. Jolie stepped away from the pillar. A gun rested in the middle of the dance floor, along with three spent casings. No one was wounded, and there was no sign of blood. Jolie removed a latex glove from her pocket and used it to scoop up the weapon.

Blood rushed to Jolie's face. *A diversion.* No one had ever been in danger at all. Firing the gun had been a clever ploy to empty the club.

She stomped her foot. "They got away."

* * *

"What was that?" Ty exclaimed.

"A distraction!" Richie shouted the response from several yards behind as he struggled to help Ned hobble along. "You're welcome."

Ty and his companions hurried down the street away from the club as the cops sought to control the panicked crowd. When Richie had pulled the gun from his waistband, Ty had feared he would start shooting at random. Instead, he'd fired three shots straight up, dropped the gun, and joined the screaming crowd. Ty had quickly motioned for Joanie to do the same, and they met Ned and Richie outside.

"Someone could've gotten hurt!"

"But no one did," Richie protested. "We're home free."

Ty clenched his jaw to keep from snapping back. "What about fingerprints?"

"Relax, man." Richie held up a gloved hand. "I'm good. And I got that gun at a pawn shop and filed off the serial number. We're clean."

As much as he hated to admit it, Ty was impressed with Richie's resourcefulness. It had been a bold move, but one that paid off without anyone getting hurt. And it had probably saved all their skins. The cops had been closing in; and with officers watching the exits, Ty and his friends never would have made it out of the club if not for the mass exodus. For once, Richie had proven his usefulness.

Ty started walking home. Without the van, it would be a long trip.

"We'll come back for the money tomorrow night," he said. "Until then, lay low. The last thing we need is to draw attention to ourselves. It's already late—Rhonda has to be wondering where I've been. Ned, you keep off that leg as much as possible." Ty looked at Joanie. "Let me know when you make it home."

The four of them split off, heading for their own homes. The walk was tense and nerve-wracking. More than once, Ty had to duck behind cover as a police cruiser drove by. But as long as he kept from using his powers, he had no reason to believe they'd be able to track him. They had never seen his face, and he was alone. They were looking for a gang of robbers, not one man out for a walk.

He finally rounded the corner to his street. As his home came into view, his heart dropped. Two police cars were parked out front. Ty froze and dropped back, hiding behind a neighbor's car. Ty's instincts urged him to rush in and check on his daughter. If Rhonda had called the police, something bad must have happened. Or they were there waiting for him. The Crusader had seemed to know who Ty was, or at least have some suspicion. If the police had discovered his identity and were waiting for him to get home, rushing in there would only get him arrested. But if he left, his chances of ever seeing Emi again evaporated.

What do I do?

He racked his brain, desperate for answers. He could phase inside, find Emi, and go on the run with her. If the cops were tracking his powers, they might detect him instantly. It would be impossible to escape while lugging around an infant. They would never make it. He had to learn whether the cops were there for him or not. There had to be some way to listen in . . .

Listen in. That was the answer. Joanie had downloaded an app onto his phone that could patch into Emi's baby monitor. He dropped down on his haunches, opened the app, and pressed the phone to his ear. He was immediately met by cooing. Relief washed over him. Emi was okay.

"I know, baby." That was Rhonda's voice. "You miss your daddy, huh?"

Everything seemed all right, which made it more likely that the police were waiting there for him. He wondered where he could have slipped up. He had been so careful not to leave clues behind.

"I don't know when Daddy will be back, Emi," the girl continued. "I think he might be in a lot of trouble. But don't worry. Rhonda's going to take good care of you."

Ty's chest tightened, and his stomach twisted. Dropping to his hands and knees, he vomited onto the street. Tears stung at the corners of his eyes. His worst nightmare had come true. In trying to provide for Emi, he had sealed her fate to grow up as parentless as he had. Rhonda was a good caretaker, but she was a child. Odds were good that Emi would go into the system. She would grow up in foster care. Based on Joanie's stories of growing up, that was not the fate Ty wanted for his daughter. He stood, wiped his mouth, and tucked his phone in his pocket.

"I'll find my way back to you," he whispered.

Without looking back, Ty rushed away from his home and toward a future all too uncertain.

CHAPTER 29

Three weeks had passed since the night of the truck heist, and there had been no sign of Vickers. He hadn't returned to his house, and Jolie's scanner hadn't detected a use of the Phantom's powers since that night. Perhaps he had not used them, or perhaps he was so far away that the scanner couldn't register the energy signature. The owners of the restaurant adjacent to the nightclub called the police two nights after the robbery, reporting that their walls had been vandalized in the night. The working theory was that the vandalism and the Phantom's crew's disappearance were related. Carter and Jolie theorized that the thieves had hidden something in the wall, but there was no way to be certain. If they had, why had they broken it down rather than having the Phantom phase inside to retrieve them? Given the lack of activity on the scanner, Carter suspected the Phantom was on to them. If the thief was half as intelligent as he seemed, perhaps he had figured out that they were tracing his powers.

Of course, it was entirely possible that Carter and Jolie were completely off the mark. There were no fingerprints in the restaurant, and no trace of anything pointing to the Phantom and his crew being there other than the scanner pinpointing that location after the robbery. It was all too circumstantial.

Jolie had confirmed that the throwing knife recovered from the scene of Carter and the Phantom's fight matched those still inside

Vickers' garage. The knife, combined with Vickers' sudden absence, was enough for the police to name him as their primary suspect.

Still, as long as he was hiding, there was little they could do.

In contrast to the Phantom, Ravener had been quite active. His hits were escalating, becoming quicker and deadlier. They were always against former members of Serban's mob. Carter could not understand the assassin's motives. Ravener had attacked Vickers's house and asked for Liang, which led Carter to believe that Vickers was Tao Liang. But if Ravener had learned the identity of his target, why was he still striking other targets? There was another piece of the puzzle Carter was missing. Once he saw it, maybe it would lead him to the final solution.

Rhonda was shaken up from her encounter with Ravener; but more than that, she wasn't taking Vickers' disappearance well. Her main grievance was that baby Emi had been surrendered to state custody until Vickers or one of his relatives showed up. There was little information on Vickers' family; and those relatives, if they existed, seemed reluctant to reveal themselves. Jolie had found a record of Vickers' wife—Rachel Vickers, née Sellers—who had died in a gang-related shootout less than a year ago. Rachel had grown up in foster care, with only a biological sister named Joanie to call family. Joanie Sellers, who matched the description of an associate of the Phantom's, was proving as hard to find as Ty Vickers.

Now Emi, like her mother, was in the foster system. She had been placed in a temporary foster family on an emergency basis until a more permanent situation could be secured. Jolie's boss had assigned a police detail to monitor the foster home, in case Vickers showed up to take her. Using some Sterling Labs tech, Carter was watching the family, as well. With Vickers' powers, there was always the chance he would risk discovery to phase in and retake his daughter.

In the meantime, Carter and Raina continued their sword training with Gideon. Raina was picking up a few tricks and had lasted nearly a minute on the mat before Gideon landed a blow on her. By his own estimation, Carter's skills were improving, too. He was eager to track Ravener down and face him again. The fight would be far less one-sided this time.

Carter picked up his old high school letterman jacket and slipped it on over his t-shirt as he headed for the door. The last vestiges of winter were receding, but it was still chilly enough to need the light jacket. He bounded down the stairs and into the living room, where his mother and siblings were already preparing for church.

Carter waved as he passed them. "See you at church!"

Carter drove to Raina's apartment and parked at the curb. Moments later, she came down the steps, dressed in a pretty yellow top, blue jeans, and a black denim jacket. She slid into the passenger's seat and leaned over to kiss Carter on the cheek. He smiled as he pulled away from the curb and drove toward church.

"No word on Vickers yet?" she asked.

"Nothing. Guy hasn't made a peep."

"It's like he vanished. You don't think he left the city, do you?"

"I don't know Vickers well, but Rhonda insists that he loves Emi too much to leave. As long as his daughter's here, he's here."

"Yeah, but where?" Raina reached for the knob to lower the intensity of the heat. "The piddly amount of money he and his goons stole on that truck heist must be stretched thin. How are they surviving?"

"It would help if we knew who Vickers' accomplices are. His sister-in-law is a safe bet; but she's gone off the radar, too, and we've got no way to find her."

"They'll turn up."

"I hope so." Carter stared out the windshield. "I'm not sure Vickers is actually a bad guy. Ravener, on the other hand? He's a serious threat. If he finds Vickers first . . . well, I really don't want Emi to become an orphan."

* * *

Three weeks.

It had been three weeks since Ty had seen his daughter, since he had held her in his arms and kissed her. Three weeks since he had cradled her as she cried, threw her up in the air, and tickled her as she giggled. His arms ached with the desire to hold her, his heart with the knowledge that it was his fault.

He had spent the last three weeks trying to figure out where they might have taken her. He knew she was in state custody but could not learn more than that. His list of friends was thin. At the moment, it included only the people in the room with him. He had no contacts in the government or criminals with an inside source to give him a tip. Joanie might have been able to get something from a police or government computer if she could get close enough to hack it, but going anywhere near a municipal building would be suicide. Joanie's face was plastered on wanted posters, along with Ty's. Emi's location would remain a mystery for the foreseeable future, it seemed.

You never deserved her. She was the best part of you, the part you rejected. He tried to ignore the incessant voice that whispered to him in the night when he couldn't sleep. But he couldn't because the voice was right. The voice, he realized, belonged to his father.

If Ty had chosen a different path, a better path, he would still have Emi. Rachel would've been ashamed of the decisions he had made. Ty's parents would have been, too. He could've found a job—some manual labor or janitorial job. Nothing fancy, but something to pay the bills. His bitterness at his godfather had driven him to anger. That anger had led to crime, and he had embraced it.

I'm sorry, Oton. I'm sorry, Okan. He was almost relieved that his parents were gone, so they did not have to see the ruins Ty had made of his life.

Unfortunately, circumstances were unlikely to improve anytime soon. He and Joanie had been squatting at Ned and Richie's place for three weeks. During that time, the two men had grown increasingly agitated. Ned was healing, but he had taken to using his injury as an excuse for any complaint the others raised against him. Richie was irritable and snappy. Whenever Ty asked about it, Richie said he'd tell him later.

"Later" seemed to have come. Richie stood in the apartment's tiny living room, pacing back and forth. Ty had a sneaking suspicion that his nervousness had to do with the source of his information for the truck job. They still hadn't paid the security guard from Sterling Labs, and they hadn't paid the source of the tip, either.

"I'm pretty deep in debt to some heavy hitters," Richie said. "I told them that I'd have their money if I could find a mark. They pointed me at the truck, and they set up the deal with the Sterling Labs guard, too. They're saying my time's up."

"Did we make enough on the truck heist to pay them off?" Ty asked.

"Not by half." Richie shook his head. "I'm in trouble; and because you're associated with me, you are, too."

"Who exactly do you owe, Richie? Where did you get the information on the truck?"

Richie put his hands behind his head. "It was the Red Dogs, man."

Ty's face warmed. He clenched his fists and shot to his feet, struggling to contain the rage that built up inside him.

"You got in debt to the Red Dogs? And you dragged me *into it?*"

"I'm sorry, man—"

"No. No apologies. You know my policy about gangs, and the Red Dogs are the worst of the lot." He traded looks with Joanie, who lowered her eyes. Finally, she nodded. "Rich, there's a reason I don't work with gangs."

"Why?"

Ty got in his friend's face. Richie's breaths were short and shallow, blowing hot air into Ty's face; but he ignored it. He needed Richie to realize how serious he was about this—and why he was so angry.

"My wife died because she got in the crossfire of a gang shootout—a shootout between the Red Dogs and the Tyrants. It was a Red Dog who killed her. You want me to help you out of a jam with the same gangsters who *murdered my wife?*"

Richie backed away. "I—I'm sorry. I didn't know that!"

"No, but you knew I hated gangs, and you went behind my back and made me a part of this. You betrayed me, Richie. You, too, Ned!"

He shoved his way through the apartment door before Richie could protest, slamming it behind him. It was risky showing his face outside, but he couldn't stay in there. It was all he could do not to draw his last throwing knife and skewer both of his so-called friends. Once he cleared his head, he would return. And he would have a long talk with Richie about what he'd done. He had no choice but to help clear Richie's debt with the Red Dogs because the Dogs more than likely knew Ty was involved already. They would hold him accountable for Richie's debt.

After that, he was done with Ned and Richie. They had burned him for the last time.

* * *

Carter shifted in his seat as Pastor Jeff preached. Pastor Jeff was a compelling speaker; and he had been a youth pastor before he took a leadership role at the church in the Brooks, so he knew how to keep the attention of people Carter's age. Despite that, Carter had trouble thinking of anything other than Ravener prowling the Brooks, looking for more criminals to murder.

"God pursues us relentlessly," Pastor Jeff said. "He feels a love for us that none of us can imagine. His desire is for all of us to abandon our broken lives and live fully in His grace and mercy. As a shepherd who leaves ninety-nine sheep to rescue one, He pursues those He loves so that He may call them His children. God doesn't pursue us to tackle us to the ground. He pursues us to bring us back into the fold, to embrace us and comfort us."

Carter concealed a smirk at the mental image. He had tackled more than his share of perpetrators. It had never been out of love. With everything that had been going on lately, Carter wondered if his attention had been so far off from God that He was chasing Carter down, trying to regain his focus.

One thing was for sure: he couldn't hunt Ravener with tenderness and love, but he could be relentless. And until the swordsman was caught, the Crusader would prove how relentless he could be.

* * *

Jolie watched Gideon as he stared down at the thick application packet sitting on the kitchen counter in front of him. He studied the bold lettering on the front page in silence, no doubt processing everything before choosing how to respond. In the past few weeks, Jolie had made some inquiries; and after returning home from church that afternoon, she handed Gideon the packet—an application to become a CSI.

"You want me to do what?" Gideon finally asked.

"Hear me out." She rested a hand on his bicep. "You miss crime fighting. I see it every time you talk to me or Carter about one of our cases, and I saw it more clearly when you were fighting Vickers at Sterling Labs. But without your powers, you don't feel like you can be the Seraph anymore. So, don't be. There are other ways to fight crime. Nate's leaving to join the FBI, so we need a new CSI. You've got a bachelor's degree in biology, not to mention your doctorate. Medically, you're more than qualified for the job."

"I haven't studied forensics, and I'm not the best with computers." The corners of Gideon's mouth curved downward. "Dean always did that kind of thing."

"Well, you'd have to go to the police academy first." Jolie pictured her husband in a form-hugging navy blue uniform t-shirt. *Maybe there's more than one reason this is a good idea.* "If you sign up, I can almost guarantee you'll get in. Your name pulls a lot of weight in the department. The police really respect what you did as the Seraph—most of them, anyway, and they're the ones who matter."

Gideon stared at her for a moment, looked down at the packet, and shook his head. But she saw the frown he had worn start to curve upward. He liked the idea; she could tell. It was better than working at Sterling Labs. At least, he could feel like he was making a difference in the world. She could almost see all those thoughts running through his mind as he pulled open the packet and scanned the pages.

"If I do this, I'd probably take a big pay cut compared to what I make at Sterling Labs."

"Is it about the money?"

He looked up at her. "Not in the slightest."

Between the two of them, they already made more than enough to live comfortably. Gideon had made big money during his career as a surgeon; and since he had lived with a billionaire until the wedding, he had years of savings stored away. They would be more than stable if he took a pay cut.

"Let me pray about it first, but I'll consider it."

Jolie grinned. "I'm glad."

She rounded the counter, kissed his cheek, and rested her head on his shoulder. Gideon wrapped an arm around her waist. She was thankful to have something good happen for a change. Between Vickers' escape and the revelation that Ravener was a different individual, who also seemed to be hunting Vickers, the past few weeks had been exhausting. This moment, however small, was one that Jolie had desperately needed.

CHAPTER 30

A harsh pounding rattled the door. Ty shot up from his reclining position on the couch to grab his sheathed knife off the side table. Richie held up a calming hand and stepped toward the door, reaching behind him with one hand to grip the gun tucked at the small of his back. Ned dropped a bag of potato chips and placed his own gun on the kitchen counter, training the barrel on the door and keeping his finger on the trigger guard. Joanie, sitting to Ty's left, dropped to the floor, crouching between the couch and the coffee table.

Richie leaned forward to look through the peephole. With his left hand, he reached for the doorknob; but he didn't remove his right hand from his gun. Ty stood, ready to draw his knife at a second's notice. Richie pulled the door open. A pale man in dark blue jeans, brown boots, a white V-neck shirt, and a navy blue leather jacket with red piping on the biceps stepped into the room. He wore a smug smirk under a thick black beard, marred by a scar that rose from his chin to cross his lips and meet the right side of his nose.

"Richie, my boy." He opened his arms and pulled Richie into a hug. "Is that any way to greet your pal Shank?"

Ty lowered his knife but kept it in hand. He flicked his eyes over to Ned and saw that his hand was still resting on the butt of his gun. Richie, however, took his hand away from his gun, hugged Shank back, and stepped away from the gangster. Ty looked down at Joanie and gestured with his chin for her to stand up. He stepped around the coffee table, positioning himself so he was between her and Shank.

"So, this is the crew, eh?" Shank looked at Ned. "You can put the piece away, Hoss. I'm not here to pop anyone."

Ned narrowed his eyes; and for a moment, Ty thought he'd keep the gun where it was. But finally, he pulled the gun off the counter and tucked it at the small of his back. Ty put his knife in his belt where he could reach it easily.

Shank scanned the room. "I think introductions are in order, aren't they?"

Richie stepped aside. "Right. Come on in."

As Richie shut the door, Shank dropped into the recliner sitting by the front door—a seat that allowed him to watch the whole room. Ty tucked his thumbs in his pockets so his left hand was resting right beside the hilt of his knife. Richie stepped back into the living room and stood between Ty and Ned.

"Well, Shank, this is Ned, Ty, and Joanie," Richie said. "Guys, this is Shank—the Red Dog I was telling you about."

"The guy who was nice enough to share information about that armored truck," Shank added. "Don't forget that part. Or the part where you owe me a neat ten thou."

Ten thousand? Richie hadn't mentioned his debt was that deep. Ty glared at him, but Richie kept his gaze firmly on Shank, ignoring Ty's look.

"Yeah, how could I forget?" Richie laughed nervously. "Look, I'm sorry the truck job went bad. I don't know how the cops knew we'd be there or—"

"Water under the bridge." Shank clasped his hands in front of him, leaned back in the recliner, and rested his hands on his slightly protruding gut. "You can repay your debt to me in other ways."

"What . . . what other ways?"

"The boss saw your new toys in action through traffic cam footage. Those pieces could be quite useful to the Dogs. Matter of fact, the boss is setting up a job that they'd be perfect for."

"So . . . what? We give you the guns, and we're square?"

"Ha!" Shank slapped his thigh. "I do love your sense of humor, Richie boy. No, we don't want the guns. We want you. Your gang—because you all can do things." He looked at Ty. "Can't you?"

Ty scowled. "Wait a minute—"

In an instant, Shank was sitting forward, and a massive .50 caliber Desert Eagle pistol was in his hand, trained on Joanie. Ty froze.

"Do I have your attention?" Shank asked. "I know what you can do, boy, and who you are. I've done my research. If you so much as think about phasing out of here, this poor girl will be a stain on that wall."

You don't know everything I can do. Ty thought about throwing his knife and knocking the gun out of Shank's hand before the gangster could squeeze the trigger, but he couldn't gamble with Joanie's life like that.

"The boss wants to hit the federal reserve. Between your new toy guns, this girl's computer skills, and the phasing powers of Mr. *Vickers* here, we might pull it off."

Ty noted the emphasis Shank put on his last name. How much information did he have? As a member of the city's criminal underworld, it was certainly possible that he was aware of everything.

"You do that," Shank said, "you get us our money, and we're square."

Ty shook his head. "We can't. The police have some way of tracking my phasing powers. If I use them in the federal reserve, it'll alert the cops right away."

"Let us worry about that." Shank's gun hadn't wavered a centimeter. "Do we have a deal? I really don't want to shoot her."

Ty ground his jaw. What other choice did they have? They would do the job; and when he saw an opening, he would bury his knife between Shank's shoulder blades.

"We're in."

"Good." Shank stood and lowered his gun. "I'll text Richie an address for you to meet us at. We'll go over the details there."

The gangster left without another word. As the door clicked shut, Ty felt his face burning. He knew Richie would be able to see the anger there. He didn't care. It was all he could do to keep from strangling his friend.

"We are done." Ty jabbed a finger at Richie's chest. "We'll do this job. We have to because if we don't, we're all going to die. Once this is done, I'm leaving; and I never want to see your face again. You hear me?"

Richie hung his head. "I hear you."

"Good." Ty stormed out of the living room. "Should probably go get some sleep. We've got a federal reserve to rob."

CHAPTER 31

"A CSI, huh?"

From his usual position on a rooftop overlooking the Brooks, Carter listened as Gideon laid out his conversation with Jolie the day before. During training earlier that evening, Gideon had asked if he could listen in on comms while Carter was in the field that night, so the Crusader had both Raina and Gideon in his ear.

"That's right," Gideon said. "And as crazy as it sounds, I'm considering it."

"That's not crazy." The Crusader sat on the edge of the roof, balancing his staff across his knees. "Your passion is helping people by stopping criminals, and you're a genius. Dean gets all the credit in that area, but you're almost as smart as he is. You were a surgeon at twenty-four. Without your powers, being a CSI is the perfect way to live out your passion."

A loud crack sounded over the comms—probably Raina popping her bubblegum. "He's right. I don't know you nearly as well as Carter does, but I can tell when you train us that you're in your element."

"I guess that's true. I would love to help her with her cases."

"So go for it, man." Carter chuckled. "You're under thirty. It's not too late to learn some new tricks."

"Hey, we've got reports of gunfire on Doppler Avenue," Raina said.

Carter's pulse pounded. "On my way."

The Crusader dropped from the rooftop, sheathed his staff, and mounted his bike. There was no way to determine whether the gunfire was gang-related, a domestic dispute turned violent, or another appearance of Ravener. He peeled out onto the street anyway.

Five minutes later, he pulled his bike to a stop in the middle of Doppler Avenue. The street was completely abandoned, but a dilapidated house to the Crusader's left had its porch lights on. The interior lights flickered through busted windows. He clenched his fist around the hilt of his sword and stepped toward the front door.

Bang. Bang.

More gunshots. That meant the fight was ongoing. If it had lasted five minutes, that meant there was a significant number of participants. The Crusader pushed through the front door, his boots squeaking on the wooden porch, and stepped into the house. The living room was dark, the fluorescent lights of the adjoining kitchen providing the only illumination and casting an eerie ambience around the already creepy home. A pair of bodies lay in the middle of the room—both marked with crisscrossing cuts across their chests.

"Ravener's here."

"Be careful." Gideon's voice was tense. "You've trained for this."

The Crusader tightened his gloved fist around his sword. With his other hand, he unslung his shield from the harness across his back. The aionium armor around his vitals would render most weapons useless, and his upgraded weapons should be able to resist the razor edge of the sword that had cut through his previous staff like butter. He knelt and examined the bodies in front of him. One had a crown tattoo on his left wrist.

Bang.

"Someone's still in here with us." The Crusader stood and walked toward the hallway at the right side of the living room. "They're Tyrants."

He shuddered. The bodies reminded him of the horrific sight of the Tyrant in the jewelry store being gunned down in front of him. He halted, frozen in place by the memory. He had not been able to save that gangster from a police officer. Could he save anyone from a deadly assassin like Ravener?

He had to. No one else was going to die on his account. Stiffly, he resumed his stride toward the hallway, keeping his sword ready in his right hand and training his shielded left arm at the entrance, ready to fire a shock bead. He stepped into the hallway.

It was empty. The bedroom door at the far left of the hall hung ajar, and light spilled from it. The Crusader crept toward it, keeping his gauntlet and sword at the ready. The gunshots had stopped; so, either Ravener had already killed everyone, or he had disabled the last of the shooters and was interrogating them—in which case, they probably wouldn't be alive much longer, anyway. Ravener didn't tend to leave witnesses.

The Crusader pushed the door the rest of the way open and stepped into the room. It was empty of furniture but full of stacks of thick white packages.

Against the far wall was a man with a crown tattooed on his neck, whimpering and holding up his hands. His left hand was bloody and missing a finger. The black-and-silver-clad warrior stood between the Crusader and the gangster, his sword hanging loosely at his side.

"You've got nine more fingers," Ravener rumbled. "If you don't want to lose them, start talking."

"I—I've never met anyone named Liang! I swear!"

The Crusader squeezed his left fist, and a shock bead shot from his gauntlet. The bead exploded, and the warrior dropped to his knees as blue arcs of electricity coursed over his armor. The Tyrant, caught in the current, spasmed and slumped to the floor.

"Stay down, Ravener."

The swordsman chuckled. "Ravener? That's what you're calling me? It's not bad."

"Do you have another preference?" The Crusader flourished his sword. "Maybe a real name?"

"Not one I want to hear from your mouth."

Electricity crackled over his form, but Ravener did not drop his sword. The Crusader tensed and prepared to fight if the swordsman tried to attack him.

"This is the second time you've interfered in my mission, Crusader."

"Your mission is getting a lot of people killed." The Crusader circled around so he stood in front of his opponent. "It's my mission to stop people like you."

"The only people I'm killing are people who deserve to die—people you'd fight yourself, if not for me. Only, you wouldn't do what's necessary and take them off the streets for good. Your brand of justice would see these animals back out on the streets, killing and stealing again. It's inefficient."

"It's moral. Murdering isn't."

"What we do is the *only* morality in this depraved world."

"Don't compare us." The Crusader pointed the end of his sword at Ravener's chin. "We're nothing alike. I save lives. All you do is hurt people. For what? A personal vendetta? What do you want with Chin and Tao Liang?"

"What do you know about them?"

"He's stalling, Carter," Gideon interrupted. "Take him down."

The Crusader lowered his left hand and reached down to his utility belt for handcuffs. His fingers brushed them, and Ravener's blade came up, slapping the Crusader's sword aside. The warrior kicked the Crusader in the chest, backflipped, and came to his feet in the middle of the room, holding his sword in a ready stance. The Crusader dropped into a ready stance, his shield in front and his sword back and high, ready to strike.

"You will not interfere a third time," Ravener growled.

He lunged forward, leading with his sword and angling it for the Crusader's throat. The Crusader raised his shield, batted the blade aside, and spun, jabbing his sword toward Ravener's chest. The swordsman swiveled aside and grabbed the shield with his free hand, at the same time driving his shoulder into the Crusader's back. The Crusader stumbled forward, but he kept a grip on his shield and jerked it away from his opponent. He tucked himself into a roll and came up in a crouch, toppling over a stack of drug packages.

No sooner had he come up than Ravener was on top of him. The Crusader rolled to the left. A cloud of white powder filled the air as the swordsman's blade slashed through the drugs. The Crusader whipped his sword forward. Ravener parried and stepped in, swiping his blade at the Crusader's neck. Ducking under the sword, the Crusader struck his opponent's left knee with the face of his shield. The joint buckled, and Ravener dropped into a crouch. The Crusader drove his left fist into the warrior's mask, and the black-clad man fell back. Ravener rolled backward over his shoulder, coming back to his feet across the room and raising his sword with both hands, the hilt near his right ear, the blade pointed forward at the Crusader.

The Crusader twirled his sword in a tight arc and held it diagonally across his chest, keeping his left flank angled slightly toward his opponent. He kept his breaths short and shallow, trying to keep from inhaling any of the powder that had permeated the air. The Crusader clamped his jaw shut and pressed his thumb against the activator on the sword hilt, ready to bring its electrified blade to life.

Ravener tilted his head. "Your skills have improved. You've had training. You have better weapons. Impressive."

"I don't care how impressed you are. You're coming with me."

"No. I'm not."

The Crusader stepped forward, swinging the flat of his blade downward toward Ravener's head. The swordsman brought his sword up, blocking the strike. As the weapons connected, jolts of electricity crackled down Ravener's blade and dissipated at the crossguard. The Crusader broke off and swung the opposite direction. His blade found its mark on Ravener's left hip, cutting a furrow in the black cloth and the skin underneath. Ravener hissed between his teeth, lowering his weapon and staggering back in response to the wound.

Abruptly, he lunged forward, spinning and swinging his blade high. The Crusader raised his left arm and blocked with his shield. More lightning crackled through the room as Ravener's sword activated the shield's electrified cross symbol. Ravener moved quickly and dropped to his haunches, spinning as he did. The Crusader interposed his sword in front of the blade, but he was blocking one-handed. Ravener knocked the Crusader's blade aside. Ravener angled his weapon as it swept in, and he struck the Crusader on the hip with the pommel. The blow knocked the Crusader back a step.

Ravener was on top of him, raining down blows with his blade. The Crusader raised his shield to block, but Ravener knocked it aside. The shield dislodged from the Crusader's arm and struck the far wall. He stumbled back as Ravener advanced, relentlessly slamming his sword down on the Crusader's armored gauntlets. Carter's lungs ached with the need for air, but he ignored the urge. *Too much cocaine in the air still.*

The swordsman raised his blade for another strike, and the Crusader thrust both of his forearms upward in a scissor block. He grabbed Ravener by the wrists as the assassin brought his weapon downward. The Crusader planted his feet and gritted his teeth as he pushed back against his opponent.

"What . . . do you . . . want?" the Crusader asked.

"Justice." Ravener pushed harder. "And you will not stand in the way."

Abruptly, Ravener pulled back, dragging the Crusader with him. He brought his knee up, striking the Crusader's jaw. Pain exploded in his head, and stars floated in front of his eyes. His mind clawed through a fog to stay conscious.

Ravener backed away. "You fought well. You've earned your life. But don't come after me again. I won't be so merciful next time."

The Crusader staggered to his feet, leaning on the wall for support. His vision faded in and out for a few moments. When it finally returned, Ravener was gone. The sound of sirens split the air, and red and blue lights flashed from outside the open window. The Crusader picked up his sword, sheathed it across his back, and placed the shield over it. Rearmed, he leapt out the window. He hit a bush outside ungracefully, grunted as he rolled to the ground, and came up in an unsteady crouch.

"Carter?" Gideon urged. "Are you there?"

"Yeah, I'm . . . I'm here." He leaned against a tree and took in a deep breath of sweet air. "He got away again."

"Are you all right?" Raina asked.

"A little bruised, but I'll live. Hopefully, I didn't breathe in enough coke to get high." The Crusader pushed off from the tree and walked away from the house. A fresh wave of pain pierced his head like a spike. "Get some ibuprofen ready. I'll still need something to numb this pain."

CHAPTER 32

Raina sat on the couch next to Carter and dabbed at his lip with a handkerchief. Blood stained the white fabric. Carter grimaced and sucked in a breath as she touched him, and she saw him struggle not to recoil. She dabbed the cut more gently. Gideon stepped into the room from the kitchen and handed Carter an ice pack.

"Thanks." Carter started to press it to his face, but Raina eased it aside and kept cleaning. "Okay, okay. I'm letting you."

"You're welcome." Gideon sat down on the coffee table, facing Carter. "You did good. From what I could see in your suit cam, you held your own against him. Your cowl probably saved you from a concussion."

Raina shuddered at the memory of watching the fight through the tiny camera installed in the breastplate of the Crusader's armor. She had been unable to see what Carter was doing, only how Ravener reacted. Each blow had caused her to worry more. Seeing her boyfriend fight for his life and being unable to do anything to help was terrifying.

Carter shook his head. "I can't keep playing catch up. We've got to figure out where this guy's going to hit next and get there before he does. He's dropped enough bodies. I have to stop him before he drops more."

"Anticipating his next move would be good," Gideon agreed. "Finding out who he is would be better. We've been operating under the assumption that Ty Vickers is Tao Liang. If that's the case, Ravener could be Chin Liang, hunting his own son; but that's not a given. He was at Vickers' house, but he never returned. There may be something else in play here, something from Liang's past that we haven't learned."

"Vickers doesn't have any obvious gang connections," Raina added. "So far, Ravener's only gone after gang members. If he's looking for his son, he's doing a pretty terrible job of it."

"Chin Liang had gang connections," Carter said. "Ravener must be a third party, looking to get to Liang through his son and operating on the same assumptions we are."

Gideon pressed his lips together. "I'll check with Jolie about Vickers, but the swordsman isn't her case. It's Sergeant Pulaski's. For tonight, get some rest. Even superheroes need it."

As Gideon left, Raina finished cleaning Carter's injury and pulled her hand away so he could rest the ice pack against his lip. He was obviously angry at himself for letting Ravener slip away again. She put a hand on his shoulder and rubbed it gently.

Carter grumbled and leaned back on the couch. Raina leaned against him, resting her head on his shoulder. She wished she could solve the case for him and take away the burden he was under. But since she couldn't, she would stick by his side until the end.

* * *

Carter's body screamed in protest with every step he took toward the lobby of Sterling Enterprises. He hadn't taken too many hits from Ravener, but each one had left bruises that ached despite the ointments and medicines he had applied. Gideon was right—his cowl had probably saved him from a concussion. He pursed his lips and attempted to mask his pain as he approached the front desk. There was no need for his coworkers to see the pain he was in and wonder what had happened.

The only external sign of his injuries was the cut on his lip, and he could come up with an excuse for that on the fly if he had to.

The lobby doors parted, and Alistair Wheaton entered. Carter cringed instinctively at the sight of the CFO. *How will he misremember my name today?* Wheaton stepped toward the x-ray machine, and Carter noticed a hitch in his step. It was subtle, but Wheaton was limping. Judging by the tension in Wheaton's face, the man was definitely nursing an injury of some kind.

"Are you all right, sir?" Carter asked.

Wheaton stepped through the x-ray machine. "Fine. I sprained my hip working out."

Wheaton took his belongings and sidled toward the elevators without another word. Carter watched him go. Wheaton was doing his best to conceal his limp. Why? Another guard leaned in close to Carter.

"Working out, my butt." The guard snorted. "More like dancing the night away with a bunch of models in a club."

"Really? I wouldn't have taken him for a partier."

"Oh, he's a total party boy. He acts all snooty and refined here, but he's a player outside the office. At least, that's what I've heard. Gossip magazines and all."

"You shouldn't listen to all the gossip you hear." Carter chuckled. "Or any of it. Those rags don't publish anything halfway true. But either way, Wheaton's injury isn't any of our business."

"Hey, you were the one who brought it up, kid."

"Right." Carter blushed and lowered his head. "Sorry."

He watched intently as the elevator door slid open and Wheaton stepped inside. Wheaton was favoring his right hip, the spot where Carter had cut Ravener the night before. *It couldn't be . . .*

What was it that Ravener had said when Carter had asked what he preferred to be called? *Not one I want to hear from your mouth?* That sounded like something arrogant and smarmy enough for Wheaton to say.

"I need to step away for a second. I forgot I have an important phone call to make."

The other guard tossed him a thumbs-up. "Sure thing, kid. Everything all right?"

"Yeah. I need to call my girl . . . see if she can run an errand for me."

* * *

Her mouth full of half-chewed Fruit Loops, Raina tugged her phone from her pocket as it vibrated. *Carter.* Chewing as quickly as she could, Raina answered the phone and brought it to her ear. She swallowed the slightly too large chunk of cereal, gulped loudly, and cleared her throat. *Smooth.*

"Hey, babe. What's up?"

"Hey, could you do me a favor?" Carter paused. "Find Silas and ask him to look into Alistair Wheaton. He's the CFO of Sterling Enterprises. Specifically, see if Wheaton has any connections to Liang."

"What, you think Wheaton is the swordsman?"

"He was limping when he came into work today, and he was favoring the hip that I hit Ravener on last night. It might turn out to be a coincidence, but I'd like to be sure."

"Will do." Raina checked her watch. "I've got class in half an hour; but as soon as it lets out, I'll track down Silas and see what he can tell us."

"Thanks, babe."

The line clicked off. Raina tucked her phone in her pocket, jumped out of her chair, and placed her empty bowl in the kitchen sink. She needed to get moving if she wanted to make it to class on time. Finding Silas would be more interesting, but she had always been a dutiful student. She had to keep her grades up if she wanted to stay on the archery team and push for that Olympic career.

Class, then Silas. Raina pulled on her jacket, slung her backpack over her shoulder, and headed out the door.

CHAPTER 33

Jolie sat down across the desk from Sergeant Pulaski. She still wasn't sure how Ravener overlapped with Vickers, but they had to be related somehow. Pulaski had been there himself when Ravener broke into Vickers' home. Since both of them were struggling for leads, Pulaski had been more than eager to partner up and look at the cases together.

Pulaski leaned back in his rolling chair and crossed his legs. "So, Turner, any idea why my swordsman has it out for your lead suspect?"

"Nothing concrete. Vickers and his sister-in-law have gone to ground. This obviously would be easier if we could bring them in and ask them; but based on tips from a confidential informant, I've got some theories. The swordsman is looking for Chin Liang, right?"

Pulaski nodded. "Right . . . "

"Liang adopted a son, Tao. He should be about Vickers' age. What if Vickers and Tao Liang knew each other? Or what if they're one and the same?"

"You think your suspect is the son of my suspect's target?"

"Possibly." Jolie shrugged. "Our file on Ty Vickers is limited. Before last year, it's like he didn't exist. Is there any way I can get a look at Liang's file?"

"Okay. My perp got away again last night after murdering two more people and maiming a third. I'll do anything to put him behind bars;

so if working with you on this brings it to an end sooner, I'm all for it. I'll let you see the files, but on one condition: you have to clue me in to whatever you're going to do, so I can be there."

"Deal."

Pulaski picked up a stack of papers from his desk and thumbed through them. He came to a manila folder, opened it, and nodded. She reached for it and skimmed the opening pages.

Chin Liang's file was about as thin as Ty Vickers'. They had a file photo: an aging Chinese man with hard, craggy features and thin lips pinched into a scowl. He was wanted in connection to Luca Serban's mob, based only on the confession of a few low-ranking members of the gang. Aside from that, there was virtually nothing. No aliases. No family connections. Not a passing mention of the adopted son.

"This is . . . worthless," she said.

"You're telling me." Pulaski massaged his scalp below his hairline. "This guy's as much a ghost as the swordsman."

"What about the son?"

"Well, as you can see, there's no record of any son." Pulaski waved his hand toward the holding cells. "I've questioned a few members of Serban's mob. Either they don't know about Liang's son, or they're buttoned up and won't say anything about him."

"Great. Another dead end." Jolie leaned back in the uncomfortable chair. "Tao was Japanese. Maybe he didn't go by his adopted name. If he doesn't have a good relationship with Liang, maybe he reverted back to his birth name or took on an alias."

An alias like Ty Vickers? But aside from Ty's Japanese heritage, there was little concrete evidence in that direction. She needed proof, not speculation.

"Hey, Detective." Officer Rojas crossed the bullpen with a file in hand. "I got the results back on that facial rec you asked me to run for Vickers. We got something. Two things, actually. We got Vickers' driver's license, which is only a few years old, and nothing before. Not under that name. But check this out."

Jolie accepted the manila envelope and opened it. It was a file on a man named Taro Watanabe.

Pulaski lurched forward. "Wait, I recognize that name. He was in the police academy with me. He dropped out, and none of us ever really knew why."

Jolie thumbed through the file. "Here's why. There's a note on Watanabe's file. It came out that he was connected to someone in the mob. His superiors were eyeballing him for an undercover job, but it looks like Taro left the academy when he was confronted."

"I can't say I blame him." Rojas's lips drooped. "If his fellow trainees found out about his mob connections, they never would've trusted him. When did this happen?"

Pulaski tilted his head. "I graduated not long before Serban showed up, so . . . a few years ago—back when the city was at its worst."

"Which would be around the same time that Ty Vickers showed up . . . " Jolie thumbed to the next page. "It's him."

A photograph was paperclipped to the second page of Taro Watanabe's file, a photograph that portrayed the visage of Ty Vickers.

Pulaski leaned across the desk to look at the file. "You're kidding."

Vickers had been in the police academy until a connection to the mafia shook loose. After that, he had changed his name and become a thief. The last pieces clicked into place. According to the information from Silas, Tao Liang was Japanese, not Chinese, and had been adopted by Chin Liang, who had worked for Serban. Watanabe was a Japanese name. Watanabe, Liang, Vickers . . . They were all one and the same. Two questions remained. What had become of Chin Liang? And what did Ravener want with them?

Jolie pulled the photo free and held it up for Pulaski and Rojas to see. "Our bank robber suspect must be Chin Liang's adopted son. Either our swordsman is hunting him in hopes of finding his father, or there's some other connection to Liang's—or Watanabe's—past life we're not seeing yet. Either way, Vickers is the key to both our cases."

"We need to find him," Pulaski said.

Jolie nodded. "Before the swordsman finds him and sends him to an early grave."

* * *

Raina ducked into Pop's Gym, the startling warmth hitting her like a truck after the chilly, rainy weather outside. She unzipped her jacket as she walked down the hallway to the gym's main room. On the other side of the boxing ring that took up most of the room, Silas pounded on a punching bag.

Quietly, so as not to disturb him, Raina weaved her way around the ring and stood behind him, waiting for him to finish his exercises. Each punch caused a loud *thump* that echoed through the empty room and sent the bag hurtling away from Silas. The guy was strong. Several times, it looked like the bag would snap clean off its chain and fly across the room. After a few more punches, Silas lowered his hands and turned around.

"Raina?" He frowned. "Is everything okay? Can I help you with something?"

"Yeah. Carter sent me to talk to you. He asked if you could look into Alistair Wheaton, Sterling Enterprises' CFO. I guess Carter thinks he might have something to do with Ravener."

"Why would Carter think that?" Silas removed his boxing gloves. "Isn't Wheaton his boss?"

"Wheaton came into work today favoring a wound that Carter thinks may have been inflicted by the Crusader. It sounds like a long shot to me, but Carter wanted to make sure. He asked me to check with you."

"Okay. I'll do some checking into Wheaton. Tell Carter—"

The sound of heavy swinging doors cut Silas off. The muscular man put a hand on Raina's shoulder and stepped past her, his brow furrowed in concern. Raina watched as he approached the hallway that she had entered through. Two men clad in navy blue jackets with red stripes across the biceps stepped inside the gym.

"Silas Rockwell?" one said. "We hear you've been asking questions about Liang."

The second man reached around to the small of his back, and Silas burst into action. Raina shrieked and ducked behind the boxing ring as Silas stepped forward. His left hand shot out to pin the man's arm to his side, and his right hand punched him across the jaw. Silas reversed the blow, bringing his right elbow backward into the back of the man's skull. As the jacketed man fell, his accomplice lashed out with a long knife.

Silas smacked the knife aside with his left hand and dropped back into a ready position, his hands raised defensively, his legs bent at the knees. The knife wielder brandished his weapon and feinted a stab. Silas jumped back a half-step. His head bobbed up and down. Raina realized he was watching both the knife and the attacker's eyes.

The attacker snapped his hand forward, this time going in for a real attack. Silas slapped his hand aside and stepped inside his opponent's guard, twisting his knife hand and angling it away from him. He continued his forward motion, spinning as he stepped, so his back was pressed against the attacker's chest and he was holding his opponent's knife hand with both arms. Silas bucked with his hips and threw his shoulders forward, and the knife-wielder flew over his head and slammed into the floor. Not yet releasing his wrist, Silas stepped around the man until he was standing directly on top of him, twisting the limb until the attacker dropped the knife. He leaned down and slammed the attacker's face into the concrete floor. The man went still.

Raina stood. "Wow, that—"

Cool metal touched her throat, and she froze. A firm hand grasped her shoulder. She glanced down and saw the edge of a knife resting beneath her chin.

"Don't move!" a voice behind her growled. "So much as twitch, and this girl will be bleeding out in front of you."

Raina's heart pounded. Gideon had been teaching her to defend herself. She knew how to get out of situations like this, but it was hard to think with the adrenaline pumping through her. She took a deep breath through her nose and tried to still her trembling hands.

The knife was not pressed firmly against her throat. It was still there, but her captor was no longer applying force to it. He was focused on his conversation with Silas, no doubt confident that his captive would be unable to escape. Raina closed her eyes and recalled the moves Gideon had taught her.

"Hands up, Rockwell! Do it, or—"

Raina's right hand shot up, catching the man's knife hand by the wrist. She ducked out from under his grip and pulled his knife hand along with her, driving it down into his thigh. The man screamed as the blade pierced flesh. Raina punched him across the cheek, and he dropped to the floor. Silas rushed to her side and inserted himself between her and her captor. She massaged her knuckles. Punching someone in the face hurt more than she realized.

"You all right?" Silas asked.

"Yeah. Ow . . . I think I broke something."

"Good move. Watch out for those cheekbones." Silas looked down at the man, who was still writhing in pain. "Come on, we need to get out of here. There could be more of them. I'll get your hand bandaged up, and we'll see about your boyfriend's request."

"You won't escape him for long," the man growled through gritted teeth.

Silas stepped forward and kicked the man in his face. He slumped to the floor, out cold. Raina studied the still form. He was wearing the same navy blue jacket with twin red stripes on the biceps.

"Who are they?" she asked.

"Red Dogs. I recognized one of them, but these uniforms are new."

"What does that mean?"

"I'm not sure. There's clearly more going on here than we're aware of. Come on. We need to get you home."

Raina nodded eagerly. Silas put his hand on her back and ushered her toward the door. As they passed the two men, he knelt and pulled a gun from one man's waistband.

He checked the gun's magazine. "Let's go."

CHAPTER 34

Jolie pulled up to the curb outside Silas's house. Raina had called her in a panic, urging her to get to Silas' place as quickly as possible. She hadn't explained why, but Jolie knew the girl wasn't prone to exaggeration. The Camry creaked in protest as Jolie slammed on the breaks. Crinkling her nose in disgust at her vehicle's age, Jolie put the car in park, hopped out, and ran up the sidewalk toward the house. As she approached the porch, the front door opened; and Silas and Raina walked out.

"What happened?" Jolie asked.

Silas looked out at the street, his expression grim. "The Red Dogs attacked me for looking into Liang. Raina should be safe at her apartment. I don't think any of them got a good look at her, but my family can't stay here. The Dogs know me, and they'll be coming after us."

"Okay. We'll get you to safety. Raina, get in the car. Silas, get the rest of your family and follow me. I'll lead you somewhere safe."

The man nodded and rushed back into the house. A few moments later, he came out with his wife and three children—including a baby—in tow. Jolie walked back around her car and climbed into the driver's seat as the Rockwell family piled into their own vehicle. As soon as their doors shut, Jolie pulled out onto the street.

As she drove, she looked over at Raina. "Give me the whole story."

"Carter sent me to talk to Silas, but I don't think the Red Dogs' attack was related. They came in and said that he had to stop looking into Liang, and then they attacked. Silas took them all out—he's a really good fighter—but one guy said he wouldn't escape for long."

"Liang must still be in Sojourn City somewhere. Everyone assumed he died or left after the Uprising; but if the Red Dogs are targeting people who are looking for him and Ravener's targeting Red Dogs to find him, he must still have a presence here." She pressed her lips together. "He was an officer in Serban's regime. Maybe when the mob fractured, Liang took a chunk of the command structure."

"Silas said the Red Dogs are wearing new uniforms," Raina said.

That tracked with the increase in Red Dog activity in the Brooks. If Chin Liang had solidified a leading position in the gang, he could be using his experience from the Chinese triads to turn the shoddy street gang into a militant crime family.

Ravener could be a former triad member, hunting Liang for leaving China. If he had knowledge of Liang's past life, that might explain why he had targeted Vickers. He probably thought the young thief knew where his adoptive father was. If that was the case, they had to find either Vickers or Liang fast—before Ravener struck again.

"Where are you going to take Silas and his family?" Raina asked.

"A safehouse. There's a place outside the Brooks that used to belong to Serban. After he died, the government seized it—and we're going to use it to protect someone from the very organization that used to own it."

"Ironic."

"Poetic justice, really. Are you sure you want me to drop you off at your apartment?"

Raina folded her hands in her lap. Jolie knew the girl was trying to hide it, but she was scared. Her hands trembled, so she squeezed them tightly together.

"Maybe I could stay with you." Raina swallowed. "Until Carter gets off work."

Jolie offered her a soft smile. "Of course."

The rest of the drive passed in tense silence. Jolie kept glancing in the rearview mirror to make sure Silas was still behind them—and that no one was behind Silas.

* * *

This is my fault.

Carter rushed up the sidewalk to the peaceful-looking suburban home. He had gone straight to the safehouse after clocking out. From the outside, there was no hint that the residents were hiding from a gang of murderers out to make them their next victims. If Carter had kept Silas out of this, he and his family—and Raina—wouldn't have to be there.

As he approached the front door, it swung open; and Jolie peeked her head out. Carter nodded to her. She pulled the door open the rest of the way to allow him to enter. Raina hurried up to him, and he pulled her into a crushing hug.

"I'm okay," she whispered.

"Good." Carter swallowed. "If they'd hurt you . . ."

Leaving the rest of the sentence unsaid, he grabbed Raina's hand and walked into the living room. Silas sat on the couch, bouncing his youngest child on his knee.

Silas smiled grimly. "Hey, Carter."

"I'm so sorry, man. I should've never asked you to look into this. It almost got you killed. I wasn't thinking, and—"

"It's cool, man. I'm doing some good for my city. There are always going to be people out to stop that from happening. If we give up every time there's a hint of danger, we would never get anything done. Besides, I'm used to danger. I was in the army, remember? I'll do whatever it takes to protect my family."

Carter puffed out a breath. "Yeah, I guess so."

"Don't worry, man. We'll be fine. And I'm still going to do some checking on this guy Wheaton. It'll be discreet."

"Silas, no. You should be with your family."

"What did I say? I need to help you. It's the right thing to do. Don't worry, I won't put myself in any unnecessary danger. But you need to stop this swordsman's killing spree, so I'm going to do whatever I can to help. I've been doing this a long time, Carter. I'll be fine."

Carter hoped that was true. If Wheaton really was Ravener, his access to Sterling Enterprises provided him with virtually unlimited resources in addition to his deadly skills. If he found out Silas was looking into him, he would make him pay.

"Don't worry." Jolie put a hand on Carter's shoulder. "I'll stay with them as much as I can; and when I can't, I'll have another officer I trust sit with them. Nobody's going to get in here without a fight. And this safehouse is off books, anyway. Silas and his family are going to be fine."

"Thank you." Carter glanced at her. "Anything on Vickers?"

"Yes, actually. Vickers' real name—his birth name—is Taro Watanabe. When he became an adult, he went back to using that name and applied to the police academy. He was still in the academy when his adoptive father's ties to the mob were revealed. He left the academy in shame and changed his name again."

Carter whistled. "That explains Ravener showing up at his house."

"My thoughts exactly. Sergeant Pulaski and everyone else the department can spare are looking for Vickers."

"That's good. I'll do the same. Between us, maybe we can find Vickers before Ravener does. We'll sit on him until he shows up, at which point we can spring a trap."

"The problem is actually finding Vickers."

"He'll turn up." Carter nodded to Silas and walked for the door. "Sooner or later, these guys always show themselves. And when he does, I'm going to be there."

* * *

Ty clenched and unclenched his fists as Shank, another man, and a woman—all three in Red Dogs jackets—ushered him and his friends through a pair of swinging doors and into a cramped kitchen. Shank had shown up at Richie's place that morning and taken them into a black van, which had brought them to the Bronze Dragon, a swanky Chinese restaurant near the edge of the Brooks, a part of the neighborhood that had been ostensibly cleaned up after the Uprising.

Despite the cleaner streets and decreasing random crime, the gangs still had a firm grip on the Brooks. The rich fools on the Platform truly believed that their money had gentrified the area, but all they had really done was pour more cash into the pockets of the most dangerous gangsters in town.

Apparently, the Red Dogs were no exception. From their new navy blue and red jackets to the surplus of state-of-the-art weaponry on display in the kitchen, it was evident that the gang was not hurting financially. What would it take to bring them down? Seeing the gang that had killed his wife prospering turned Ty's stomach. It was a good thing Shank had taken his knife. Ty wasn't sure he could have restrained himself from drawing both and cutting a swath through the kitchen.

Shank, who had been walking in front of the group, stopped and faced them. Ty stopped, and Richie bumped into him from behind. Ty glared back at his friend. Richie's dark eyes widened; and he backed up, holding up both hands apologetically. Joanie stepped up next to Ty and clutched his left arm with both hands. Ty gave her a reassuring nod and looked back at Shank.

"Why are we stopping?" he asked.

"The boss wants to see you. Alone."

Richie took a half-step forward. "Uh, shouldn't it be me? I'm the one who owes the debt, and I—"

"You are not the leader of this group." Shank rolled his eyes. "That much is obvious. We will talk to Mr. Vickers here first and loop the rest of you in once the details are smoothed out. Consider yourself lucky, Rich. The boss isn't favorable toward those who have shirked their debts to us."

Richie clamped his jaw shut and stepped back next to Ned. Ty looked back at them and shook his head. He put his hand on Joanie's shoulder and gently pushed her back toward the other two. The fear in her eyes was evident, but she nodded and stepped away.

"Lead the way," Ty said.

As Shank wove through the kitchen, Ty eyed each occupant in turn. The two "chefs" had M9 pistols tucked into their waistbands, and the five uniformed Red Dogs—three men and two women—were armed with AR-15s, as were the man and woman who remained behind with Ned, Richie, and Joanie. If a fight broke out, Ty and his friends were as good as dead. Shank pushed his way into an office attached to the back of the kitchen and motioned for Ty to stay where he was. The burly gangster spoke a few words to someone inside the office and looked back at Ty.

"Come on in."

Ty stepped past Shank and into the office. Immediately, his hope of a reasonable conversation evaporated. He stopped in his tracks, his heart sinking to his stomach, and gaped at the man who sat behind a desk against the far wall—a man he had thought dead for over a year.

Ty opened and closed his mouth, finally croaking out two short words. "Hello, Godfather."

"Hello, son." Chin Liang leaned against the desk and smiled. "It is good to see you."

CHAPTER 35

"I thought you were dead."

Ty stormed across the small office toward Liang. Two Red Dogs, stationed on either side of the room, stepped forward and raised their automatic rifles, training the barrels on Ty. He was tempted to keep moving and phase through whatever bullets they fired; but if the police were still tracking him through use of his powers, he would bring the cops down on all of them. So instead, he stopped and glared at Liang.

The old man's expression hadn't flickered. There was no trace of fear, amusement, or compassion. He was the same as he had ever been, an emotionless statue. Ty couldn't remember Liang ever showing any kind of response to anything Ty had done, other than disapproval. Cheating death didn't seem to have improved Liang's demeanor.

"Are you going to sit there, or are you going to explain how you're here and not six feet under?" Ty clenched his fists. "Because after everything that's happened, I think I'm owed an explanation. Don't you?"

Liang rested his palms on his desk, stared at Ty for a moment, and pushed himself to his feet. With one hand, he motioned to his bodyguards, who lowered their weapons. There he stood, dressed in a blue business suit and acting like he ruled the world. And he was in charge of the gang that was responsible for the death of Ty's wife. The rage in Ty's breast threatened to explode out through his fists. He dug his fingernails into his palms.

His godfather crossed the room, right hand tucked casually in his pocket, and extended his left hand to Ty. Biting his tongue, Ty studied Liang's hand and pondered whether to take it. He didn't owe this man anything. Liang had ruined Ty's life, and he had been relieved when the man had disappeared. Having him back was a nightmare.

Ty kept his hands clenched at his sides, and he nodded to Liang. The old man, seeming to understand, lowered his hand and gestured to a door on the other side of the office. Ty followed Liang toward the door. Neither of the Red Dog guards, nor Shank, made any move to follow them. Liang opened the door and motioned for Ty to exit into the alley first.

"Do you talk at all anymore?" Ty asked. "I guess you do because you spoke up to acknowledge my presence. What changed? You used to never shut up."

"It used to be like pulling teeth to get you to say anything," Liang replied. "Now it is you who won't shut up."

Ty recoiled, the words almost physically stinging. As a young man, Ty had been a quiet boy, reluctant to speak even when spoken to. Who could blame him? He had lost his parents, his whole life undone in a day. He was taken away from his home and every friend he had, and his name was changed from Taro Watanabe to Tao Liang. He had never felt safe opening up and had feared that every word would be rewarded by a harsh strike from the back of Liang's hand.

When Ty had reached adulthood, he never looked back. He had known that the rift between him and Liang would widen. He hadn't expected the older man to disappear entirely, as if dead.

"What happened, *Dad?*" Ty spat the last word. "Where did you go?"

Liang stepped onto the sidewalk. Ty glanced around nervously. There could be cops in the area. They might not recognize Liang as a wanted criminal, but they were actively hunting Ty. He pulled the hood of his jacket up around his face, lowered his head, and walked after his godfather.

"When the police came after the people on Serban's payroll, I knew it wouldn't be long until one of them pointed me out," Liang said. "Not many people liked me. I kept records of who owed Serban favors or money, and I made sure they paid up. I decided to cut my losses and run. But as I was heading home to get my wife and hurry to the airport . . . well, the Tyrants had already reached that part of town. I found her bleeding out in our driveway."

Ty swallowed the lump in his throat. He had never heard the details of his adoptive mother's death. She, at least, had been somewhat gentle to him. She was distant when he was a boy, but she never struck him. Learning that it was the Tyrants who killed her gave Ty reason to hate both prominent gangs in the Brooks. He kept his hands tucked in his pockets so Liang wouldn't see his clenched fists.

"What happened then?"

"I wanted to come for you, but I knew you were in the police academy. I didn't want to ruin your chances. I may not have approved of your career choice, but I admired your decision to pursue something respectable." Liang smiled softly. "Your father, unlike me, would have approved."

"It didn't matter. Once they found out who I was, I had to drop out."

It wasn't entirely true. The academy superiors had actually hoped that Ty would go undercover and help bring down his godfather and the mob, even before Serban had been named as the organization's leader. But he knew that would never have worked. Liang never would have trusted Ty completely; and when Ty returned to the police force, his loyalty would have always been in question.

"I wish I could've saved you the trouble."

"You could've, if you'd turned yourself in." Ty stopped in his tracks and glared at his godfather. "If you had given yourself up and testified that I had no part in Serban's criminal empire—and that I was unaware that you were involved—maybe it wouldn't have come to this."

"Do you understand how briefly I would've survived in prison?" Liang shook his head. "Serban may have looked out for me, but there would've been plenty of prisoners who wanted to kill me. I would've died in there."

Ty bit back the urge to say *good riddance*. Liang saw how angry he was. He didn't want to escalate their confrontation further.

"So, what? You decided to fake your death instead?"

Liang nodded. "Dozens of Serban's lieutenants were dying, and I figured that the cleanup would be difficult. The police might not notice that I wasn't among the dead, especially if I kept my activities to a minimum."

"At what point did you hook up with the Red Dogs?"

"About three months after the Uprising." Liang resumed walking. "I wanted revenge on the Tyrants for your mother's death, so I allied myself with the group I knew had the best chance of bringing them down."

Ty's stomach knotted. That meant Liang had been in charge of the Red Dogs when Rachel had been killed. In fact, considering she'd been shot during a skirmish between the Dogs and the Tyrants, it could have been Liang who had ordered the Dogs to that location. It was possible that Ty's godfather was responsible for Rachel's death.

"Did you know Richie was my friend when you decided to collect on his debt? Did you do all this to get to me?"

"I do my research on all who owe myself or the Red Dogs a debt. It was my job in Serban's organization, and I saw fit to continue. I had to do something to occupy my time. When I found out that one of your associates owed us a debt, I could not pass up the opportunity."

"You passed us the information on that armored truck and the Sterling Labs job." Ty stopped in his tracks. "All that so you could see me again."

"Of course. You are my son."

No, I'm not. "And what do you want from me?"

"Your help." Liang stopped to face Ty. During their conversation, they had circled the block and were once again in front of the restaurant. "But while Richie owes a debt, you don't. I am aware that Shank threatened your sister-in-law to ensure your cooperation, but I would not let him hurt her."

"Really?" Ty glared at him. "Because your people were responsible for my wife's death."

"I know, and I am truly sorry. I want to show you my good intentions." Liang put a hand on Ty's shoulder. "I will not force you—or Joanie—to help in this job. Richie and Ned can stay, and you two can go. I think you should consider staying and helping, however, because if you do, I will help you with something."

Ty stared at the hand resting on his shoulder, tempted to shrug it off. He wanted to leave, take Joanie, and go. But the way Liang worded his proposition suggested that he had something specific in mind. Something more than money.

"What could I possibly want that you can give me?"

"Your daughter. If you will see this job through to the end, I will ensure that Emi is returned to you."

Ty did not hesitate. "When do we start?"

* * *

The Crusader watched as a trio of Red Dogs, two men and a woman, exited the Broken Glass bar, talking and laughing uproariously. One of the men bobbed as he walked. That would make this easier than Carter had expected. He couldn't tell how drunk the other two were, but it didn't matter. Either way, he would make short work of them.

He extended his wrist and fired a grappling hook into the building across the street. Once the line was taut, the Crusader jumped from the roof, swinging directly toward the three gangsters. He extended his feet as he swung, and he struck the drunken man in the chest with both feet, knocking him back into an alley. The Crusader disconnected his grappling line, fired an adhesive bead from his wrist, and pinned the drunken man to the ground.

"What was that?" the woman exclaimed.

She reached around to the small of her back. The Crusader stepped in and snapped out a kick, catching her in the gut. He spun toward the other man and swung an elbow, striking him on the jaw. He reverse-kicked, hitting the woman's shoulder, and continued his spin and brought his fist down on the back of her head. As she fell, he fired an adhesive bead at her. Stepping forward, he grabbed the last man's collar, shoved him into the alley, and pinned him against the wall.

"Why did your people attack Silas Rockwell?" Carter rumbled.

The man breathed heavily. "I—I don't—I don't . . . "

"Don't lie to me!" The Crusader pulled the man forward and slammed him into the wall again. "Tell me who wants to hurt Silas Rockwell."

"I—I can't." The gangster shook his head. "He'll kill me."

"Who? The swordsman?"

"No! Th-the boss! The boss would kill me if I told a vigilante anything!"

The Crusader pressed his forearm into the man's throat. "The men who attacked Rockwell said that he had been asking questions about someone named Liang. Who is he?"

"I can't say!"

"Try the fishing line tactic," Raina suggested.

The Crusader pulled away from the man, fired his grappling hook into the air, and tightened his grip on the man's collar. He used the line to hoist them both into the air, clambered onto the roof, and threw the man to the rooftop at his feet. He reeled in his grappling hook and fired it again, this time winding it around the man's ankles. He grabbed the gangster and hurled him off the roof. The Red Dog screamed as he fell. Halfway to the ground, the Crusader stopped the line, pulling it taut, and reeled it back up.

"S-stop!" the Red Dog screamed. "Please, stop!"

"Tell me what I need to know!"

The Crusader released the line again, sending the Red Dog plummeting toward the alley. Once again, he stopped the man's fall halfway down and pulled him back up.

"Ready to talk yet?"

"Okay! Okay!" the Red Dog exclaimed. "The boss wanted Rockwell roughed up because he was getting too close to a plan the boss has going down."

"What plan?"

"I can't—*aaaaahhhh!*"

This time, the Crusader let him get much closer to the ground before he stopped. He kept the gangster dangling in midair for a moment before pulling him back up to the rooftop.

"Last chance."

"Okay! All right, don't drop me again. The boss is planning a heist that involves the Watanabe kid—the one with the powers. Boss didn't want Rockwell finding out who the kid was and pointing him out."

"Thank you."

"So, you'll let me g—*aaaaahhhh!*"

The Crusader ejected his grappling hook from his gauntlet and tied it to a nearby chimney, leaving the Red Dog dangling over the alley. When the cops discovered his two companions, pinned to the ground with adhesive goo, they would also discover him.

"Raina, tell Jolie there are some gangsters waiting for pickup outside the Broken Glass."

"Will do." Raina giggled. "Did you hear the way he screamed?"

The Crusader grinned. "Like a little girl."

* * *

Peter Hayes—Pippy, to the other Red Dogs—tugged at the line wrapped around his ankles. He should have let the vigilante drop him; he'd been stupid to talk. Buck and Callie were lucky. The Crusader had knocked them out. Pippy wasn't sure why the Crusader had chosen him to interrogate, but it was typical rotten luck.

He scrambled for his jeans pocket. He had a knife tucked in there. If he could get to it, he should be able to cut himself loose. He wasn't sure if he would be able to free Buck or Callie from that goo the Crusader had stuck them with; but at least, he could get away before the cops showed up.

A shadow fell across the alley. Pippy looked up. A dark figure, a sword sheathed across its back, stepped into the alley. Pippy's stomach turned to lead.

"W-what do you want?" he asked.

"Where is Liang?" The shadowy figure's voice was a low rumble, more menacing than the Crusader's. Pippy sensed lethal intent in the man's voice.

"I-I can't talk about that. He-he'd kill me."

"And what do you think I'll do? I'm not like the Crusader."

"P-please . . . please . . . "

"Talk." The black-clad figure drew his sword. "This is your last chance."

Pippy didn't want to die, but he was in a no-win situation. If he told the shadowy guy where his boss was, the boss was sure to kill him. But if he didn't, the swordsman would put a quick end to his life right there in the alley. Maybe if Pippy told him and got away, he could at least get out of Sojourn City before the boss found out.

"The Bronze Dragon. That's where the boss works sometimes. He—"

"Thank you."

The swordsman flicked his wrist, and a bladed star flew through the air and stuck in Pippy's chest. He gasped and coughed, his vision quickly fading. Pippy's pocketknife slid past his fingers and clattered to the ground. Pippy blinked rapidly one last time, and everything went dark.

CHAPTER 36

Gideon flipped through the application, mind reeling with the enormity of the task before him. It had been years since he had done anything remotely school-related. Going to the police academy would be a challenge. All the beatings he had given to criminals wouldn't prepare him for the kind of work he would have to do as a CSI. He wouldn't be out in the streets on a normal basis, except to gather evidence. But it would be a job that would allow him to fight crime with his mind, a series of complex computer programs, and the evidence he gathered, rather than with his fists and superpowers.

Was it really what he wanted? Examining dead bodies? Looking over crime scenes? He would only see the evidence of crimes he could have stopped from happening in the first place if he had still been the Seraph. He would have to look at all the bodies with the awareness that he might have been able to save them.

Gideon looked up at the sound of a clicking lock and set the application down on the coffee table. Jolie stepped in through the door, her dark hair ruffled and her eyes bloodshot. She shut the door behind her and removed her black overcoat. Gideon rose and crossed the apartment to pull her into a hug.

"Long day?" he asked.

"Carter called in a group of gangsters he'd captured in an alley. When the officers got there, one of them had a *shuriken* buried in his chest."

241

"Ravener."

"He must have interrogated the guy after Carter left, which means he may or may not have a leg up on us. Again."

"Don't worry." Gideon kissed Jolie's forehead. "You're going to catch him."

"On the plus side, Carter did get something. Apparently, the Red Dogs are trying to recruit Vickers for some big heist. That's why they tried to kill Silas. His line of questioning was getting too close for comfort."

"But we still don't have a location?"

"Nope."

Gideon rubbed his wife's back. The muscles there were knotted, tense. He remembered how tense he had been while trying to track down Serban. It had been a stressful time, and he had nearly died more than once. He had become consumed with his mission, focused on nothing more than bringing the gangster down. He didn't want Carter or Jolie to make the same mistake with Vickers or Ravener.

Easing in close, Gideon kissed her on the cheek and neck. Jolie's posture softened, her tension draining as she leaned into him. Gideon ran his fingers between her shoulder blades.

"It's okay. You're going to find them." He kissed her ear. "You need to take your mind off the case for a while."

"Yeah. I think I do."

Jolie wrapped her arms around Gideon's waist. Her fingers traced his lower back, and he smiled and kissed her again. Taking his wife's hand in his own, Gideon led her to their room.

* * *

Carter shook his head as he studied the images of the Red Dog's body, hanging limply from the line Carter had hung him by. The fall hadn't killed him—the *shuriken* protruding from his chest was evidence enough of that—but Carter couldn't help feeling responsible for the man's death. If he hadn't left him strung up like that, Ravener wouldn't have killed him.

One more death on my conscience. The image of the Tyrant dropping to the ground in front of Carter in the jewelry store flashed through his mind again. That hadn't been entirely his fault. In the alley, he could have prevented it.

"I can see you blaming yourself," Raina said. "Don't do that."

"Why not?" Carter looked up from the images, staring into her dark eyes. "This one's on me."

"Maybe. Or maybe Ravener was already nearby, and he would've jumped in and killed the guy as soon as you let him go. But whether that's true or not, one thing is: this isn't your fault because you didn't kill him. The only person guilty is Ravener himself."

Her words made sense. Ravener had made the choice to end that man's life. But Carter had been irresponsible. It was a decision he knew would haunt him, but he could use that to drive him to catch Ravener.

Carter stood and looked around Raina's apartment. "If Ravener is Wheaton, we need to know. If he's not, we need to find out who he really is. It will be the key to finding him. And understanding his connection to Liang would help, too."

"Let's go to Silas'. Maybe he's learned something."

"It's been one day. I doubt he's been able to track down anything on Wheaton, especially since he's spent most of that time settling his family into a safehouse."

"What happened to Silas yesterday can have a way of motivating a guy." Raina shrugged. "Maybe he's put in the work."

"Maybe. I still feel like we're missing something. It's all so jumbled." Carter threw his hands in the air. "It started with one amplified thief and a guy with a sword and a grudge. Then, we find ties to Serban's mob, and it turns out the thief is related to the guy the swordsman is hunting. And Alistair Wheaton might be the swordsman, or his injury may be a coincidence. And the Red Dogs are involved, too. How does it all connect?"

"I'm willing to bet that whatever is going on, Chin Liang is at the middle of it all."

"If only we knew where he is—or if he's still alive."

"Right. But let's start with what we do know. Or at least what we can safely assume." Raina rose and wrapped her arms around Carter's shoulders from behind. "You think Wheaton might be Ravener. Silas might not be able to check him out. Maybe you should do it yourself. Maybe the Crusader needs to pay a little visit to Wheaton's penthouse and shake him down."

Carter considered. Gideon had once told him that back when he had suspected that Edgar Sterling, the then-CEO of Sterling Enterprises, was involved in Serban's mob, he had crashed into Sterling's office and asked him to his face. Office security had buffed up since then, but Carter could visit Wheaton's home. If the CFO wasn't there when he arrived, Carter could have a look around. If Wheaton was the swordsman, there might be a clue in the penthouse.

"You're right. I've asked enough of Silas. He's risked his life, not to mention his family's, enough. It's time for me to do some old-fashioned sleuthing."

Raina grinned. "Go get 'em."

CHAPTER 37

The Crusader balanced on the precipice outside Alistair Wheaton's high-rise apartment. He could fire a grappling hook from his gauntlets at a moment's notice, but the sheer height of the building sent a shiver up his spine. From the look of things, Wheaton wasn't home. Maybe the rumors were true. Maybe Wheaton was a party boy, and he was out on the town, living it up with a bunch of supermodels.

Once he was over Wheaton's terrace, the Crusader took a deep breath and dropped from his perch to safer ground. He looked out over the city. Lakeside Central Tower, where the Vindicators' base had been located, was only a few blocks away. The Crusader could see the building's glimmering lights. Those days seemed so long ago.

Switching his gauntlet-launcher to shoot shock beads, the Crusader trained his right arm on the door where the latch met the doorjamb and fired. The bead struck and exploded, and blue sparks danced across the doorframe and dissipated after a moment. The Crusader stepped toward the door and reached for the knob.

"I'm going in," he whispered.

"Good luck," Raina replied.

The latch opened without protest. The Crusader stepped inside the penthouse. The lights were off. He scanned the wall for a switch, located it, and flipped it on.

The penthouse was decorated lavishly, but not to the extent he had expected. He had no doubt the gray leather couches cost more than he could make in a year. The marble table that sat in the middle of a fluffy carpet was priceless, and the television was bigger than Carter's and Raina's combined. But there were no grand portraits of Wheaton's face hanging on the walls, no gaudy paintings at all. For a rich person's home, it was nearly spartan.

"Where should I start?"

"Where do you think Wheaton would keep evidence that he's the swordsman?"

The Crusader scratched his chin. "Not the living room. Bedroom, maybe? Or more likely, behind some sort of secret door."

"Isn't that kind of cliché?"

"Yeah, I guess it's too much to hope for something like that. Vickers kept his stuff in a cabinet in his garage. Maybe Wheaton has a cabinet like that? Somewhere that no one would stumble on it by mistake."

The kitchen was to the Crusader's left. Between the kitchen and the front door was a stairway that led to the penthouse's second floor. He glanced around the living room again and headed for the stairs.

The Crusader made it to the top of the stairs and looked out over the living room from the second-floor balcony that wrapped around the back half of the room. From above, he didn't see anything out of the ordinary. He walked across the balcony and into the hallway that led to the bedroom and the penthouse's remaining rooms. A picture hung on the wall between two of the rooms. The Crusader stopped to look at it. The photo showed Wheaton with a woman about his age, who was holding a toddler.

"Hey, Raina? I don't think our Mr. Wheaton is as much of a party boy as everyone thinks. He's got a wife and son." The Crusader took out his phone and snapped an image. "He must keep his personal life very personal. I'm sending this picture to you. See if you can find out who the wife might be. Hopefully, she and the kid aren't here."

Tucking his phone back into his pocket, the Crusader resumed his walk down the hallway. The lights in each bedroom were off and the doors closed, but that didn't mean the rooms were empty. It was late. If Wheaton's wife and son were home, they could be asleep. Keeping his hands carefully away from his weapons, the Crusader opened the nearest bedroom door. It was the nursery—the nursery of a millionaire kid, but a nursery. The Crusader doubted anyone would keep evidence in there. He closed the door quietly.

He crept to the next room and opened it, revealing a bathroom. He flicked on the lights, shut the door behind him, and rifled through the cabinets. There was nothing within, except a bunch of overpriced cosmetic products. The Crusader shut off the lights and backed out of the bathroom. His stomach squirmed at what he was doing. If he had been patrolling the Brooks and seen someone else breaking and entering, he would have knocked them out. Yet somehow, he was justifying it because he was searching for the bad guy.

Am I as different from Vickers as I think I am?

There was one major difference: he wasn't stealing anything. While breaking and entering was a crime, so was vigilantism, technically. The city recognized superheroes, but much of what Carter did was a gray area. Perhaps he was doing the wrong thing by infiltrating Wheaton's apartment. But if so, he at least wasn't hurting anyone. He would be out without a trace in a few minutes, and he would wrestle with his conscience once a murderer was locked up.

He was moving for the next door when a latch clicked. His eyes widened.

"I think someone's home," he whispered.

If it was Wheaton alone, he could interrogate the man. If the whole family was present, he needed to get out.

The Crusader crept back toward the balcony overlooking the living room and pressed his body against the wall, peering down into the room below. Wheaton and his wife stood in the middle of the room, the latter cradling a sleeping toddler. Wheaton wrapped an arm around his wife's shoulder.

"I'll get Nathaniel to bed," she said softly.

"All right." Wheaton kissed her forehead. "I'll be down here waiting. Did you leave the lights on?"

The wife frowned. "No . . . perhaps the maid did."

The Crusader backed away from the balcony. He couldn't get back out to the terrace from the apartment's second floor; but if he tried to get downstairs, they were sure to see him. There was, however, a couch on the balcony. Keeping himself low so he wouldn't create a shadow, he rushed to the couch and flattened himself on the floor behind it.

Heels clicked on the stairway. The Crusader held his breath as the footsteps reached the top of the steps and crossed the balcony toward him and past him into the hallway. The steps receded, and one of the hallway doors opened. Blowing out a breath of relief, the Crusader pushed himself into a crouch and crept toward the stairs. He had to get past Wheaton himself. That would be a challenge if the man was Ravener.

"Found her," Raina said. "Wheaton's wife is Courtney Wheaton, formerly Courtney Armitage. Looks like they keep their relationship so private because Courtney's father, Will Armitage, was convicted of corporate espionage at Garvin Technologies."

That wouldn't look good for the CFO of one of Garvin Technologies' biggest competitors. No wonder Wheaton was keeping his family life on the downlow.

The Crusader reached the bottom of the stairs and peered into the living room. Wheaton wasn't there; he must've moved into the kitchen. To get to the terrace, Carter had to walk directly past the kitchen. There was no way he could do that without Wheaton seeing him.

What other choice do I have? Putting one hand on the wall, the Crusader rounded the base of the stairway. The kitchen was immediately ahead and to his right, while the door to the terrace was across the room to the left. *If only the lights were off.*

The sound of heels clicking returned to the balcony. He pushed himself off the wall and walked as quietly as he could toward the terrace door. As he did, he glanced over his shoulder. Wheaton was indeed in the kitchen, but he was facing away from the Crusader, busying himself with a bottle. The Crusader took another step, and Wheaton turned, a gun seeming to manifest in his hand from nowhere.

"Courtney!" he called. "Darling, why don't you go on up to bed? I'll meet you up there."

"Are you sure?" Courtney replied from the top of the steps.

"Absolutely. I'll be right up."

"All right, dear."

Courtney's footsteps receded again. The Crusader clenched his jaw and stared at Wheaton. His reaction time had been incredibly fast, but he had drawn a gun, not a blade or a *shuriken*. He stared at the Crusader for a moment and stepped out of the kitchen toward him, never lowering his gun.

"I knew it wasn't the maid." Wheaton frowned. "You're not who I expected, but you are intruding in my home. What are you doing here? Isn't Lakeside a little outside your jurisdiction?"

"I don't actually have jurisdiction. I'm a vigilante—"

"I was being facetious." Wheaton rolled his eyes. "You obviously aren't here to do any harm to me or my family. So, what are you doing in my home? And talk fast—before I decide to call the police."

"I was investigating you. I . . . thought you might have been the swordsman that has been killing people in the Brooks."

"And whatever would make you say that?"

"Your injury." The Crusader nodded to Wheaton's side. "When I fought the swordsman, I cut him on his hip. It's the same hip you've been favoring since that night."

Too late, Carter realized that by saying that, he implied that he had been close enough to Wheaton to notice the injury. He hoped the CFO didn't notice.

Wheaton lowered his gun. "Sorry to disappoint you, but I'm no swordsman."

"And I'm supposed to believe you?"

Wheaton glanced at the front door and the terrace. "I'm not him. I can tell you about him, but you have to protect us."

The Crusader furrowed his brow. "Protect you? From who?"

"From the very man you're looking for." Wheaton set the gun down on a side table. "A few nights ago—presumably the night on which you fought this swordsman—I was at the office, working late.

When I left, a man in black appeared and assaulted me. He cut me there, on the hip. When I fell, he pointed his blade at my neck; and I was afraid he would kill me. Instead, he told me that if I called the police, he would return and kill me, as well as my wife and son. And then . . . he left. No demands, no questions. A cut on the hip, a threat, and he was gone."

The dread in Wheaton's voice, the rapid darting of his eyes as he watched every entrance, were too genuine to be an act. Wheaton truly was scared of something.

The Crusader bit his tongue. "He set you up."

"Indeed." Wheaton spread his hands. "And as you can see, it appears to have worked."

The Crusader clenched his fists. He had played right into Ravener's hands. The assassin must have wanted free reign of the Brooks for a night or to keep the Crusader off his trail. And he had succeeded on both counts.

But he had also revealed a card in Ravener's hand, one that filled Carter with dread.

"Did he tell you anything?" Carter asked. "Anything that might help me find him?"

"I'm afraid not. I've told you everything he said."

"Okay." The Crusader stepped forward and extended his hand. "I'm sorry that I broke into your home, Mr. Wheaton. You've been a great help by telling me this. Don't worry; I'll make sure you and your family are safe."

"Thank you. Please leave before my wife gets suspicious."

"I'm going." The Crusader reached into his belt and grabbed a small signaling device, which he handed to Wheaton. "This device will send out an alert directly to my phone if you activate it. If you're ever in danger, signal me. I'll get here as soon as I can."

Wheaton nodded. The Crusader backed away, walked onto the terrace, and looked out over the city. He could see the Brooks in the distance, nestled in the middle of the city. He fired his grappling hook at the top of the high-rise.

"Did you get all that?" he asked.

"Every word," Raina said. "Ravener's smart."

"There's something else." The Crusader pulled himself onto the rooftop and opened the door to the stairwell. As he did, the horrible truth that had settled on him earlier returned in force. If he was right, everyone around him was in danger. "For this plan to work, Ravener had to have predicted that I would encounter Wheaton at some point—and closely enough to notice his limp. Which means he may know I'm Carter Jonson."

CHAPTER 38

The cramped office in the Bronze Dragon seemed smaller with Richie, Ned, and Joanie crammed inside with Ty, Liang, Shank, and the Red Dog bodyguards. Ty grimaced as they squeezed around a table, his shoulders constantly brushing against Richie's or Joanie's. On the table before them lay the schematics for the federal reserve, which had been thoroughly looked over and highlighted.

"Joanie here will shut down the security system from the outside," Liang said. "We've got a clean van for you to hide out in, one the police won't be looking for. Once she's got the system down, Ty's team will move in through the front doors. Shank, you and your boys will be waiting in the back. Richie and Ned will move through the building and let you in, while Ty moves on the computer room."

Liang's plan was far more complex than Ty had expected. He had formulated a virus that could be inserted into the federal reserve's computer systems, which would open it to an external hack. Once Ty inserted the virus, Joanie could hack into the reserve and download bank account information, social security numbers . . . It was a virtual treasure trove. Near-unlimited wealth.

"There's one problem," Ty said. "I still can't use my powers. The police can track the energy signature I leave behind. If I phase through the doors, they'll detect it. And if they see that I'm at the federal reserve, you can bet it won't be cops that show up. The FBI will be on us before we can blink—not to mention that vigilante."

"Don't you worry about Kid Crusader." Shank grinned wickedly. "He shows up, we'll take care of him."

"I think we've got a way to shake the police off your scent, son," Liang said. "There's a device being developed by Garvin Technologies, a portable energy conductor. If you wear it on your belt while you're using your powers, it should spoof whatever scanner the cops have. I have a contact at Garvin who can slip me the prototype."

Ty clenched his jaw. His godfather really had thought of everything, hadn't he? Truthfully, Ty was mortified by the plan. Whole families— maybe thousands of them—were going to lose everything they had. That wasn't what he wanted. His only motive was to make a living for himself and Emi. He didn't have a choice. He had to believe that Liang could deliver on his promise and get Emi back for Ty. It was the only thing he was living for.

He was still concerned about the police catching on. Liang said that the energy conductor *should* spoof the scanner. Ty was no scientist, but it sounded like a big stretch. If it didn't work, Ty would be walking into a trap. They needed to test it before the heist. If Ty used his powers somewhere with an easy escape route so that he could bolt if the police showed up, that would help them determine whether the conductor worked. If the cops showed up, they would need another plan.

"This goes down tomorrow night," Liang said. "Everyone needs to be ready. Study these plans. Memorize them. When we go in, we do it quickly and quietly. No one will ever suspect us. But there's no room for mistakes."

Ty nodded with the others; but inside, he was seething. Part of him hoped they would be caught, but a much bigger part of him knew they had to get away with this. If they didn't, he would probably never see the outside of a prison again.

The office door slammed open. "Boss!"

Liang raised his head, looking at the woman at the door. "What is it?"

"He's here."

Ty looked at his godfather, and he saw something on his face that he'd never seen there before. Fear.

Liang's skin went pale, his pupils dilating into narrow pinpricks. He reached around to the small of his back and pulled out a gun. Ty dropped his hands to his belt and drew his knife. Anything that garnered that reaction from Liang was trouble.

"Everyone, draw weapons," Liang said. "We need to get out of here."

Shank hefted his .50 cal. "Boss, out the back door. Lonnie, Vick, Spades, cover us."

Ty touched Joanie's shoulder with the hilt of his knife and gestured to the door. She nodded and backed toward the door, along with Liang and his two bodyguards. The woman who had opened the door to the kitchen closed it again. Ty waited along with Shank and his team. Ned and Richie drew their own guns.

Gunfire erupted from the kitchen. Ty felt his body tense, and he dropped into a fighter's stance, ready to move. He wished he had his short swords with him. Their length would've given him a greater advantage than his knife, but the swords had been back at the house when the police had combed it. The weapons were doubtless in lockup with the rest of Ty's knives. He wondered if Liang kept any swords here. The old man had been good enough with them when Ty was a child. There was no time to look for them, unfortunately.

Someone screamed. There was another round of gunfire followed by silence. Ty glanced at Ned and Richie. The latter moved toward the back of the room. Ty refocused on the kitchen door, his gaze sweeping past his father and Joanie as he did.

"Both of you, out." Ty swallowed. "I'll cover your retreat."

I must be an idiot. He had no idea what was about to come from that kitchen.

The door crashed inward, and a figure in black and silver swept through like a hurricane of shadow. Shank's goons opened fire, and the dark-clad figure danced and spun through the room, swinging a sword. He cut down Lonnie and Spades before they could turn their guns on him. Ty glanced back at the rear door. One of Liang's bodyguards had shoved the exit open, and the other was ushering Liang and Joanie outside. Ty looked back at their mysterious attacker, who had impaled Vick and was lunging at Shank. Ty flicked his wrist and hurled his knife. The blade slashed through the air and struck the attacker's blade.

"Watanabe," the attacker rumbled.

Ned opened fire. The attacker spun out of the way and extended a hand. A *shuriken* spun through the air and buried itself in Ned's shoulder. Taking advantage of the split-second distraction, Ty broke from his trance and lunged to retrieve his knife. He jabbed the weapon toward the man's sternum. The mysterious figure ducked out of the way and drove his elbow into Ty's back. Ty tucked himself into a roll and came up in a crouch, spinning to face the attacker as he brought his sword down toward Ty's head.

A gunshot grazed the attacker's shoulder. He spun to face the back door, where one of Liang's bodyguards had remained behind. Ty's eyes widened, and he shook his head as the attacker threw another *shuriken,* this one burying itself in the bodyguard's chest. At least, Joanie was gone; the other bodyguard must've taken her and Liang to safety. The assassin stormed toward Ty. As he approached, his head tilted.

"Your skills are impressive, Taro Watanabe."

Ty hefted his knife. His heart leaped at the sound of his birth name.

"You have no reason to remain loyal to Liang," the attacker said. "Your destiny is greater than the life of a common criminal. Let me deal with your godfather. We need not be enemies."

"Trust me, there's nothing I'd like more than to let you run that man through, but I need his help. Sorry."

"Anything he can offer, so can I."

Ty pressed his lips into a thin line. With the skills this swordsman exhibited, Ty had no doubt that he could sneak into any foster home and retrieve Emi. But Ty had no idea who this man was, and thus, no reason to trust him.

"Sorry. Better the devil I know."

"Very well."

The attacker stepped forward and raised his sword. Ty did a reverse-somersault as the blade descended. He came up and pushed off with his right foot, slamming his body into the attacker before the man could get his blade up. Ty drove his knee into the man's chest and raised his knife. The attacker brought his gauntlet up and blocked Ty's blade with it. He drove the pommel of his sword into Ty's gut, and the air whooshed from his lungs. Struggling to get a breath, Ty stumbled away and raised his knife in a feeble defense.

The blade slashed horizontally. Ty cringed, and the blade passed harmlessly through his body. He grimaced. The use of his power had been entirely involuntary, but it had saved his life. He lunged forward, taking advantage of the attacker's momentary surprise, and slashed his knife at the man's face. The blade cut through the fabric of his mask, digging a thin line into the flesh of the attacker's nose. The attacker grabbed Ty's wrist and shoved it aside. The knife clattered across the room. Abruptly, a bolt of electricity slammed into the attacker. He stumbled forward, and another bolt struck him. Ty looked past his attacker to where Richie was standing in the corner.

"Took you long enough," Ty said. "Run!"

Richie nodded, helped Ned to his feet, and scrambled toward the back door. The cops would be on their way. If no one called in to report the gunshots, the police had probably picked up Ty's phasing. Either way, they would arrive in force before long. With one last look at the attacker, Ty followed his friends out into the alley.

"Who was that guy?" Richie exclaimed.

"I have no idea." Ty pushed his friends, urging them to run faster. *What did he mean about my destiny?* "My godfather has a lot of explaining to do."

CHAPTER 39

Jolie strapped on a bulletproof vest as a squad of police officers gathered outside the Bronze Dragon. Pulaski had called her ten minutes before, telling her that Ravener had been spotted at the restaurant. As they drove there, the energy scanner had gone off and directed them to the Bronze Dragon, as well. Both her suspect and his were in the same place.

"We've had multiple reports of gunfire from inside," Pulaski said. "Keep your eyes peeled. You find that swordsman, call for backup. Do not engage alone. Let's move!"

Jolie followed Pulaski and the other officers as they rushed into the Bronze Dragon. Her gun held out in front of her, Jolie pushed through the door. The restaurant's lobby had already been evacuated. Tables were smashed, and one man in a Red Dogs jacket lay sprawled over a table. Pulaski motioned for an officer to check on him. He glanced at Jolie and pointed toward the kitchen.

Together, they walked toward the kitchen door, their guns trained on it. Jolie put her hand on the swinging door and glanced at Pulaski. He held up three fingers and counted down. When his hand formed a fist, Jolie shoved the door open; and Pulaski rushed inside. Jolie followed, her gun sweeping the room as she entered. Bodies littered the floor, blood staining the white tile.

The office door at the back of the kitchen was slightly ajar. Jolie stepped toward it, feeling her heart pounding against her ribcage. The swordsman had made short work of the Red Dogs, so she doubted there was anyone in the office who could have matched him, except maybe Vickers. She fully expected to see more carnage inside.

"Sergeant. Office."

Pulaski followed her gaze. Jolie stepped past him and reached out to push the office door open. The small room, like the kitchen, was littered with bodies. Three Red Dogs lay almost side by side in the middle of the floor; and a fourth lay in a doorway to the back alley, his body propping open the door. But there was no sign of Ravener—or of Vickers.

"This was a big job," Pulaski said. "Bigger than any place he's hit so far. He must be getting close to his target."

Jolie nodded. "Agreed."

She stepped over to a knife on the floor and knelt. It was similar to the knives they had found in Vickers' garage. *He was here.* And since his body was not there, he must have escaped—or else Ravener had taken him. She picked the knife up with a latex glove and examined the edge. A few droplets of blood clung to the silver blade.

Her heart jumped into her throat. There was plenty of blood in the room; but if Vickers was against Ravener, the throwing knife might contain their first trace of the swordsman's blood. They had to know who Vickers had cut.

She looked at Pulaski. "We need to find whatever security footage this place has."

* * *

"Carter, Jolie called. Ravener hit a restaurant called the Bronze Dragon."

The Crusader pulled his bike to a stop on Washington and Tenth. "I think it's close by. I'll swing over to check it out. What's the word?"

"He was gone by the time they got there," Raina said. "The Red Dogs owned the place. He tore through them. No official word on how many are dead. It sounds like it was a bloodbath."

The Crusader sped off in the direction of the Chinese restaurant. If he hadn't been so distracted with interrogating Wheaton at Lakeside, he might have arrived in time to stop Ravener. That had to be exactly what the swordsman had intended. Still, there was no way that Carter could have predicted that Ravener would learn his identity. He was simply grateful that the assassin had chosen not to target his mother, siblings, or Raina.

He slowed on the street outside the restaurant. Four police cruisers sat outside, lights flashing. Yellow crime scene tape crisscrossed the door. There was most likely an alley entrance into the restaurant. That would be a better entrance for a vigilante. The Crusader circled the building and walked down the alley. A door hung open, propped by a body. He grimaced at the sight and stepped over the corpse. Jolie and Sergeant Pulaski were inside a small office, along with a CSI and three more bodies.

"What're you doing here?" Pulaski asked.

"I want to help," the Crusader said. "Sorry I'm late."

Jolie looked up at him. "Did you find out anything that could be useful to us?"

"One thing. Ravener attacked Alistair Wheaton a few nights ago, specifically wounding him to match the injuries that I gave Ravener that same night. He wanted to throw me off his trail by making me look at Wheaton."

Pulaski frowned. "Why would he do that?"

"I don't know, but Ravener threatened to kill Wheaton's family if he went to the police. I'll have someone keep an eye on Wheaton."

Maybe Gideon could do that. It might help to get him out of his slump. "What happened here?"

"Looks like the Red Dogs were having a meeting," Jolie said. "Planning something, maybe. Ravener came in the front door and cut his way through the restaurant until he got to this office. There's no security camera footage for inside the office, but the lobby and kitchen feeds show that he knew where he was going."

"His target was here."

"Yes. And we think we know who." Jolie rose. "Ty Vickers was here, along with his gang. We got pictures of them from the security cameras."

Carter's gut clenched. "Did Ravener kill them?"

If Vickers was dead, Rhonda would be distraught. Carter barely knew the guy; but whether he was a criminal or not, Vickers was a father. If Carter had failed to save him from Ravener, that was one more victim that the Crusader had let down. How many more bodies would he have to add to that tally?

"No," Jolie said. "They all escaped, presumably with some of the higher-ups in the Red Dogs."

"This must've been what the guy I interrogated on the roof was talking about. Vickers' and the Red Dogs' heist. They must've been here planning it when Ravener hit."

"That swordsman has to be aiming for Red Dog leadership," Pulaski said. "He's hit the Tyrants a few times; but over the last couple weeks, his focus has been almost entirely on the Dogs. It's like he's narrowed down where his target might be located or who might know where he is."

"Do you think it's possible Chin Liang is leading the Red Dogs?" Jolie asked.

Pulaski cupped his chin in one hand. "If he is, he's keeping a low profile. I haven't heard a whisper of that name from anyone affiliated with the Dogs. But that would explain his disappearance after the Uprising, not to mention Ravener's single-minded focus on this gang."

"It also might explain why Vickers, who's always been a solo operative, is working with the Dogs." Jolie walked over to the office desk. "His adoptive father is the gang leader."

"These are great theories; but unfortunately, they're all circumstantial without proof." Pulaski gestured for a CSI to enter. "Let's get out of the way so the coroner and the rest of the crew can get their jobs done."

The Crusader nodded. "Keep me updated. I'll do the same for you if anything plays out on Wheaton's side of things."

He exited through the alley without another word.

CHAPTER 40

The house Liang took them to was not nearly as opulent as Ty expected. For all the money his godfather had swindled and stolen, he could've lived in a manor on the Platform. This house, while nicer than anything in the Brooks, was a simple two-story, three-bedroom home. Compared to Ty's house, it was a mansion; but it was surprisingly understated for Liang's tastes. The only sign of unusual wealth was the electric gate that blocked the driveway, which the surviving bodyguard opened for them.

The car pulled to a stop at the top of the driveway. Ty opened the door and exited the car ahead of his companions. He remained vigilant, ready for the swordsman to return and wishing he still had his knife. But as the others clambered out, the attacker did not show up.

"Who was that man?" Ty demanded.

"An old friend," Liang said. "The police and the media have been calling him Ravener. I'll explain everything to you inside. Come on."

Shank ushered Ned, Richie, and Joanie toward the front door. Ty remained in the driveway for another moment, watching the street. He half expected Ravener to appear on a motorcycle or out of thin air, ready for round two.

"Ty." That was Joanie's voice. "You coming?"

"Yeah."

Following his friends inside the house, Ty lamented the loss of his last weapon. It didn't matter that his prints were on it anymore, since the police were already on his tail; but he would miss the familiarity of the blade. With any luck, Liang had a few spares.

Shank closed the door behind them. The bodyguard left the living room, no doubt to ensure the rest of the house was secure. Liang motioned toward the couches in the middle of the living room.

"Make yourselves comfortable. I suppose I owe you an explanation."

"You think?" Ty made no move toward either couch. "We nearly got killed tonight! Who—"

"Sit. Down."

Ty glared at his godfather, and Liang maintained eye contact. Ty clenched his jaw, nodded, and sat next to Joanie. Her hands were trembling. Ty reached over and placed one hand on top of hers. With effort, she stilled them. Ty gave her a reassuring smile before turning back to his godfather.

"We're sitting," Ty said. "So? Talk."

"That man is an elite member of an organization called the Sicarans," Liang said. "A group of international assassins dedicated to effecting regime changes. Years ago, when you were a boy, I was a member of the Sicarans, a top-of-the-line warrior. That's where I met your parents."

Ty knew his father had belonged to some group of warriors but never who they were. It had never mattered. His father conducted himself with honor and taught Ty how to do the same. Whoever the Sicarans were, if Shiro Watanabe had been a member, they could not have been all bad.

"What happened?" Ty asked.

"The Sicarans were displeased with the manner of my departure. But I had to leave."

"Why?" Ty scowled. "To join a criminal syndicate instead? That's much better."

"Being a member of the Sicarans comes with a certain code of honor, yes, but they allow their assassins to work with criminal organizations if it furthers the order's mission. A criminal alliance can place an agent in the right place for a critical mission. However, there are some groups that . . . well, the Sicarans have made enemies, and working with those enemies is treason."

"And you joined one of them."

"On the contrary, I discovered corruption within the Sicarans that could have led to disaster. Your father agreed with me, and the two of us set out to bring that corruption to an end. For me, that meant working with the enemy."

Ty's stomach churned. He didn't like where this story was going. Still, he needed to hear it. Lacing his fingers together, he rested his elbows on his knees and leaned forward. Liang had his full attention.

"When my subterfuge was discovered, the Sicaran leadership was furious. There was a fierce battle. Because of his connection to me, your father was implicated. Your father and I barely escaped. He left to get you and your mother. We all planned to flee to America together, hoping to avoid the wrath of the Sicarans. Our new allies, the enemy of the Sicarans, refused to give us refuge." Liang exhaled shakily. "When I arrived at your home, it was already burning. It was a miracle to find you alive."

The burning home was forever imprinted in his mind's eye. Ty would never be able to shake the horror he had felt when he saw it, nor the dread as he rushed inside to search for his parents. And seeing his father's body . . .

"Knowing your father's wishes, I brought you home to my wife," Liang continued. "The three of us fled—as you well remember. After that, I did what I had to do to survive and to provide for you."

"Oh, so you became a criminal for *me*."

"Isn't that what you did for Emi?" Liang noted.

Ty's gut knotted. Liang was right. He had done the exact same thing for his daughter. It was the whole reason he was in this mess. He had always seen his godfather as a villain; but in reality, Ty was no better than he was. If his story was true at all, he and Ty's father had been heroes. Or, at least, as heroic as cult assassins could be.

"So, why are they here for you now?" Joanie asked. "Did it take them this long to locate you?"

"Running to Sojourn City bought me some time. Thanks to some of Luca Serban's contacts, I managed to evade the Sicarans and fool them into thinking I'd gone elsewhere. It was only a matter of time before they discovered the truth. I was a fool to think otherwise."

"You said Ravener is an old friend," Ty said. "Who is he?"

"The silver sash he wears denotes a high-ranking member of the Sicarans. I was not sure which member until I witnessed his fighting style tonight. He is a man named Kane McCrory. Among the Sicarans, he went by the title Mac Tíre, The Wolf. He and I trained together. He was like a brother to me and to your father. But when we revealed the corruption within the order, Kane chose loyalty to the Sicarans over his friends. I should have expected they would send him after me. He was the one who murdered your parents."

Heat rose to Ty's cheeks. *That man* . . . He killed Mother and Father? No wonder he had talked about Ty's destiny. He probably wanted to indoctrinate Ty into the Sicarans, make him a puppet, as Ty's parents had been.

If McCrory had trained alongside his father, he had to be up in age, as Liang was. Ty could use his youth as an advantage. All he needed was a sword. He knew how to use the weapon skillfully, and he was sure that he could take the assassin. But it was unfair that he had been put in this position.

"Your actions would put my father at risk," Ty said. "You did it anyway, and you didn't bother to tell me why we were moving to America. When I was an adult and had my own family to care for, you still left me in the dark, knowing this might come back to bite me one day. And the worst part is that all this time, as much as I've hated you, it's been for what? A lie."

"I'm sorry, Ty. I wanted to . . . "

"Protect me. I *know*." Ty stood. "We can't go through with the federal reserve heist. Not with McCrory out there."

"We will proceed as before," Liang said. "If Kane interferes this time, we'll be ready for him."

"Are you insane? If we do this, we're all going to die. Our attention will be divided between the heist, trying to avoid getting caught, and fighting Kane. Somehow, someone will slip up, and we'll all pay the price for it. I'm sorry. I can't do it. I'll . . . I'll fight Kane. I'll set whatever trap you want, but robbing the reserve at the same time? No, it will be too much. We'll fail."

"Ty, man—" Richie started.

"You don't get to talk." Ty glared at his friend. "You got us into this, too."

"Don't blame him, son," Liang said. "Whether you had come to work with the Red Dogs or not, Kane still would've found you eventually. He did, in fact; he went to your home the same night you were attempting to hijack the armored car."

Ty's legs wobbled. He leaned against the wall for support. That psychopath had been in the same house as Ty's daughter, and he hadn't been there to protect her. McCrory knew that Ty Vickers, Taro Watanabe, and Tao Liang were all the same person. He wouldn't stop coming for him. He would want Ty dead for Shiro's crimes or back in the Sicaran fold. Pursing his lips and inhaling through his nose, Ty nodded to his godfather.

"All right, I'm in. But I want a new deal. If we do this, not only do you help me get Emi back—you help me relocate, get somewhere that no one's ever going to find us. And when the fighting starts, I get to be the one who puts McCrory in the ground. That man took my parents from me. I'm going to make him pay."

* * *

They gathered in Carter's garage—Carter, Raina, Gideon, Jolie, and Silas. Although the Vindicators' lair in the Tower had been too far from the Brooks for Carter's purposes, meeting in the garage was cramped and less than ideal. Ellis and Rhonda or his mom could listen in. Carter didn't want to worry his mother with what they were discussing nor did he want his siblings getting any ideas.

Note to self: Find a lair.

"Ravener did a number on those Red Dogs," Jolie said. "The only one left alive was a guy we found smashed over a table in the dining area. He asked for his lawyer and hasn't said another word since we got him transferred from the hospital to a holding cell."

Silas pursed his lips. "Even with a lawyer, I doubt you'd get anything. Those gangsters are as loyal as they come. None of them are going to give up their boss."

"The one I fought in the alley did," Carter noted.

"So, where do we go from here?" Raina asked. "We've hit dead end after dead end with these guys; and if it keeps up, the Brooks are going to fall back into anarchy. Liang, or whoever the leader of the Red Dogs is, keeps them on a leash. Without him, they'll go back to the strong-armed thugs they were before."

"Ravener's identity," Gideon said. "That's the key to all this. When Dean and I were fighting Serban's mob, we tracked down Monahan by looking at international records of assassins with similar MOs. Maybe we need to do the same thing here. The level of skill this swordsman displays, he's got to be on someone's database somewhere."

"We've got a sample of Ravener's blood," Jolie said. "We'll run it against international databases. Agent Ross, a friend of mine in the FBI, can help with that."

Carter stared at the concrete floor of the garage, his mind spinning. Something Gideon said sparked an idea. *Monahan.* Jolie's blood sample might provide answers, but it wasn't a guarantee. And if it did, it could take too long. Since Monahan was an international assassin, maybe she could identify others in her line of work. It irked him that his father's killer might be the key to solving the case, but he was desperate.

He cleared his throat. "We have another problem. Alistair Wheaton. Ravener injured him to put me on the wrong trail. If he knew I'd encounter Wheaton, he might know who I am. Wheaton's life could also be in danger. Ravener told him that if he went to the cops, he'd kill Wheaton and his family. He didn't go to them; but I went to him, and he told me the truth. We need to keep an eye on him. Gideon, do you think you could manage that?"

Gideon nodded. "Since my identity as the Seraph is public, I could tell Wheaton that the Crusader sent me to watch his back."

"Thanks." Carter turned toward the door. "I think that's all we can do for tonight, so let's break. We've got a lot of work to do."

He opened the door, stepped out, and nearly bowled over Rhonda. She shrieked and backed up, looking at Carter and smiling sheepishly.

"Sorry."

Carter folded his arms. "What are you doing?"

"I wanted to find out if you have any news about Mr. Vickers . . . or Emi?"

"No news about Vickers." Carter relaxed and put his hand on her shoulder. "Don't worry, sis. Emi's still with her temporary family. By all accounts, they seem to be good people."

Silas stopped as he exited the garage. "Who's Emi?"

"Mr. Vickers' baby," Rhonda said. "Her mom's dead; so when Mr. Vickers went on the run, Emi went into the system."

"Rhonda used to babysit Emi," Carter explained.

Silas smiled. "It's sweet of you to care about that baby so much, kiddo. I'm sure Carter's right. Emi's probably being taken care of."

"I hope so."

"I can do some checking if you'd like. And I'll reach out to my own contacts about getting a list of international assassins in case Jolie's blood sample comes back empty."

"Thanks, Silas. You're the best."

Carter stepped past his sister and walked Silas and the others to the front door. Gideon, Jolie, and Silas left, while Raina stayed behind. Carter shut the door behind them, a draft of freezing night air blowing in and spreading goosebumps up his arms. He latched the door and looked at Raina.

"You've got an idea, don't you?" Raina asked.

"Yeah. Is it that obvious?"

"You've got your idea face on." Raina smirked. "You go really serious and stare off in the distance, and the corners of your nose crinkle up. The others might not have noticed, but I did. What are you thinking?"

"I'm thinking that I need to go to prison."

CHAPTER 41

Stone Gate Penitentiary was about as interesting as its name inferred. Everything was a dull shade of gray, the concrete walls marked with darker gray arrows to give directions. Escorted by a guard who was also dressed in gray, Carter kept his hands tucked in his jacket pockets as he walked toward the visiting room where he would meet with Katrina Monahan. His heart pounded in his chest, and he took a deep breath to slow it. No amount of steady breathing could calm his nerves. He was about to speak to his father's killer face to face.

The guard opened the door to the visiting room. Carter stepped in. A long row of booths bisected the room. Two other people occupied this side of the room, speaking with imprisoned friends or loved ones on the other side of the glass. Carter ignored them, walking to a booth in the middle of the room and sitting down.

On the other side of the glass, a buzzer sounded; and a door slid aside. Escorted by another guard, Monahan entered the room, dressed in bright orange. Her uniform was the only sign of color in the dreary place. Her blonde hair was tied in a severe ponytail behind her, and her hands were bound at the wrists by superpower-dampening cuffs.

As the door closed behind her, a blue-white light flickered on above the doorway, signaling the activation of the room's built-in dampeners. A guard removed the cuffs from Monahan's wrists. Monahan could fire powerful concussive lasers from her eyes. It had made her a challenge to defeat the last time Carter had faced her. The cuffs—and the dampeners in the visiting room walls—prevented her from using her powers. Without the dampeners, no prison could hold her.

With her hands free, Monahan rubbed her wrists and looked around. Her gaze fell on Carter and lit with mischief. She sashayed across the room and picked up the phone on her side of the glass. Carter grabbed his own phone and held it to his ear.

"Well, well." Monahan smirked. "Look who it is."

For a moment, Carter feared she would reveal his identity as the Crusader to everyone in the room. She could blurt it out in front of every prisoner on her side of the divider. *Why didn't I think of that?* He had been stupid to come here and stupider to believe that she would help him in any way.

"Little Jonson," Monahan said. "Never would've expected a visit from you."

"I need your help."

She barked out a laugh. "That's rich. I can't wait to hear this."

"There's a new player in town. We've been calling him Ravener. He's a swordsman who's been cutting a swath through members of Serban's old organization; but lately, he's been specifically targeting the Red Dogs. Everyone he's attacked, he has always asked about a man named Liang. We've learned that he is referring to a criminal named Chin Liang—or possibly his adopted son Taro Watanabe, aliases Tao Liang and Ty Vickers."

"And you think because I was part of Serban's organization, I'd know this Liang?" She shrugged. "The name sounds familiar, but I can't point you to him."

"That's not why I'm here. I need the identity of the swordsman."

"Ha! Honey, I could rattle off a dozen names of international assassins armed with swords, and you'd be no closer to finding out which one is terrorizing your city."

"If it helps, he wears all black with a silver sash; and he also favors *shuriken.*"

Monahan's smirk straightened, and she blinked. "Really?"

Carter leaned forward, staring at her intently. Did he detect a trace of fear in her eyes?

"If you're describing him accurately, I can hazard a guess as to what organization he belongs to, but I'd need more to go off before I could place an identity."

Carter pulled his cell phone from his pocket. He had suspected that Monahan might need more than a verbal description of Ravener, so he had downloaded footage from his armor cam onto his phone and compiled a series of clips from each of his fights with Ravener. Hopefully, the visual depiction of the man's fighting style would help Monahan narrow her suspect list.

"Check this out," he said.

He called up the footage and pressed his phone screen against the glass. Monahan's eyes dropped to focus on the screen, but Carter kept his gaze fixed firmly on her face. As the video played, Monahan's complexion grew pale. Her eyes remained locked on the screen, emotionless, but her pupils dilated ever so slightly.

"I've seen enough." Monahan looked back at Carter. "If you want his name, I want a deal."

"I'm not exactly the person to talk to about deals. Even if I had any pull around here—"

"*You* don't." Monahan looked past him. "But he might."

Carter swiveled in his seat. Silas stood leaning against the back wall. The older man's mouth was pressed in a thin line. Confusion sent a series of questions tumbling through Carter's mind.

Silas had mentioned that he would speak to a source. It was possible that the source in question was a convict, since Silas had a past as a gangster; but Monahan should not have recognized him. Silas had given up his life of crime long before Serban and Monahan's arrival in Sojourn City. And Silas certainly did not have the authority to broker a deal on Monahan's behalf. He was ex-military, sure, but that didn't mean that he had any pull in the judicial system.

He pondered which question to vocalize first. Asking Silas why he was at the prison would be redundant, since he was likely there for the same reason Carter was. But as for why Monahan had recognized him . . .

Silas stepped forward. "Hey, kid. Looks like you and I had the same idea."

"You're here to talk to Monahan, too? When you said that you had people to talk to . . . "

"They pointed me back to Monahan." Silas looked at her. "My people have been in touch?"

"They have."

"Good. Answer his questions. We'll have you transferred to a specialized facility in D.C., and we'll work out a way to reward you."

Carter looked back and forth between Silas and Monahan. He could not wrap his head around what was happening. Silas spoke like he had authority that Carter did not know about.

They would have that conversation outside the prison. For the moment, Carter had the opportunity to finally learn Ravener's identity. He picked up the phone and looked at Monahan.

"The swordsman you're looking for is Kane McCrory," Monahan said. "He's the man who trained me."

* * *

Carter didn't say a word to Silas as they left the visitor's room and walked down the hall to the parking lot. Clearly, Silas had connections that he had never leveled with Carter. If that was the case, he had been lying to him for as long as they had known each other. Carter trusted Silas and looked up to him, but he suddenly wasn't sure how much of what he knew about Silas was true.

The gate leading from the prison to the parking lot slid aside, and Carter stepped out. He bit the inside of his cheek, trying to determine whether to keep walking to his car or stop and ask Silas what was going on. Finally, he chose the latter. Stopping in his tracks, he spun to face the tall man at his side.

"What was that all about?" he demanded. "Who are you?"

"I'm the same man I've always been. There are areas of my life that are secret to everyone but my wife. There are things I legally can't disclose. I haven't lied to you, Carter. I'm still your friend."

"Who. Are. You?"

Silas pursed his lips, looked up past Carter's head, nodded, and looked back at him. "My name really is Silas Rockwell, and I really am ex-military. The part I left out is that after I left the military, I joined a government agency called CLOUD."

Carter reeled back from Silas. During the last months of the Vindicators' operations, a vigilante named Jarrett Mercer had joined the superhero team to help them hunt for Dr. Jeremiah Ashcroft. It had come to light that Jarrett was secretly a member of CLOUD, a government agency dedicated to locating and observing superhumans and other enigmas. The team had been furious at Jarrett for keeping his secret. Carter struggled to process the fact that another man that he considered a friend was part of the same clandestine organization.

"You're a government agent. Are you spying on me?"

"I've been with CLOUD for years, but I wasn't on active duty until the FBI brought Gideon home from Venezuela. One of the FBI agents who rescued him saw Gideon use his powers in the jungle. He contacted CLOUD. Since I was already living in Sojourn City, the deputy director called me and enlisted my help. I've been observing ever since. Gideon, the Vindicators . . . " Silas hung his head. "And yes, even you."

"I don't have powers, Silas. I'm a regular guy."

"We both know that's not true. You're special without powers. I watched your old man, too. I wish I could've saved him. He was a great guy. If I'd known him longer, I'd have called him a friend." Silas swallowed and reached out to put a hand on Carter's shoulder. "When he died, I knew you were probably going to take his place. I got a job at that grocery store and made sure you got a job there, too. I wanted to protect you."

Carter shrugged off the hand. "Protect me?"

"Yeah. I mean, you were a kid, and I was afraid you'd get in over your head."

"So, at the school, when Powers attacked you and Ethan—"

Carter had saved Silas and another of their coworkers from a supervillain out for revenge. He wondered if that had been necessary.

"I could've fought back," Silas said. "But I saw you there and I knew it would blow my cover with you. I was ready to intervene if things didn't go your way, but I trusted you to beat Powers. Ever since, I've been using my CLOUD resources to help your mission. They don't mind because we generally have the same goals."

Carter shook his head. For months, he had believed Silas was a regular guy. A strong, moral, well-connected guy trying to make a difference, like Carter. Like his father. And somewhere along the way, Carter had started to look at Silas as a substitute father figure. He was someone who would never let Carter down. All the while, Silas had been keeping tabs on him.

Carter fought back tears. "I thought you really wanted to help me."

"I *do*. Carter, I couldn't love you more if you were one of my own kids. You've got to believe that."

Carter stared at his friend, feeling the heat in his cheeks. The worst part was, he *did* believe Silas. He wanted to blow up at him and tell him he was a horrible person for lying for so long. But . . . he couldn't. Every word that left Silas' lips resonated with absolute conviction and honesty.

Carter swallowed. "All right. For the time being, we'll table this discussion. We've got bigger issues to deal with. You went to visit Monahan because CLOUD told you that she might give you the identity of the swordsman?"

Silas nodded. "And they gave me authorization to have her transferred to a CLOUD facility."

"For what purpose?"

"Doesn't matter. We've got what we need. Ravener's name, his reason for hunting Liang . . . everything."

That much was true. Monahan had given them more than he could have imagined. McCrory and Liang were both members of a group called the Sicarans, along with Ty's birth father, Shiro. Formed after the fall of the Roman Empire, the Sicarans had been influencing world governments for centuries. Their ultimate mission, according to Monahan, was to prevent the rise of an organization called Charybdis.

Monahan had been McCrory's student when Liang turned on the Sicarans. Allegedly, he sided with Charybdis and took a young Taro Watanabe with him. Shortly after, Monahan had also left the Sicarans, choosing a life as an independent contractor rather than devoting herself to the ancient order. Before she left, she had seen how angry McCrory was at Liang's betrayal. If anyone from the Sicarans was hunting Liang, she said it had to be him.

"I'm still mad at you," Carter said. "But you're right. We've got what we need. We should call the others and tell them what we've learned. Chin Liang has to be in Sojourn City somewhere. There's no way McCrory came all this way for Ty. This is a personal mission."

"Agreed. And from everything we've put together so far, it seems likely that Liang is either the leader of the Red Dogs or, at least, very high up in their organization."

"And he's got his amplified godson on his side. I'll meet you back at my house. Whatever's going down, I have a feeling it's going to happen very soon."

CHAPTER 42

Ty arced his sword in a tight swing intended to cleave his opponent from shoulder to hip. Clumsily, Ned threw himself aside to avoid the blade, landing on his knees. Ty rushed him, bringing his sword down for a finishing blow. Ned rolled aside. Ty's weapon struck the ground, but he immediately swept it to the side, striking Ned in the shin. Ned cried out and dropped his practice weapon.

"Careful, man!" Ned exclaimed. "That's my bad leg. Why are we doing this, anyway? It's not like I'm going to be fighting the sword guy. If he comes my way, I'll hit him with the mag-gun."

"This is for my benefit, not yours." Ty twirled his practice blade. "It's been a long time since I've fought an opponent with a sword. You are far from the skill level I need to be training against, but you'll have to suffice. Shank and Richie are doing recon at the reserve, and Joanie's cooking up the virus. That leaves you."

Ned gritted his teeth and pushed himself to his feet, picking up his weapon as he rose. Ty dropped back away from him, ready in case Ned lunged unexpectedly. The two of them had been sparring for the past half hour in Liang's basement. Ty's godfather had built an impressive dojo there. It was a dark room, lit only by a handful of blue lights in the corners. The walls were lined with all manner of bladed weaponry, from knives and swords to axes to spears and polearms. Liang was a weapon collector and had been since Ty had been a child.

"What about your dad?" Ned asked. "He's got to be skilled enough for you."

Ty's face burned at the question. "He's not my dad. He's my godfather. And you're right, but I'm not sure I'm comfortable sparring with him yet. I might 'accidentally' hurt him."

"Like you're hurting me?" Ned rubbed his shin. "Come on, Ty. I get why you've been avoiding the old man, but you've got to talk to him eventually."

"No, I don't. After the federal reserve job, I'm leaving." Ty took a breath. It was the first time he'd told anyone except Joanie. "Liang said he could help me get Emi back. Once I have her, I'm taking my share of whatever Joanie's program has managed to steal at that point, and I'm going as far away from Sojourn City as I can get."

He was surprised by the pain in Ned's face. The red-bearded man had never been one to show emotion other than rage and greed.

"I'm sorry to hear that. You're the best of us, Ty. We're going to miss you."

Ty was surprised by Ned's words. He had always figured Ned and Richie found Ty's moral code stifling. "I'd better go find Liang and see if that energy damper is in. We want to be ready for every eventuality."

Ty hung his practice sword on the rack and walked up the stairs to the main floor, where his godfather kept his office. It was where he was most likely to be. Ty stepped out into the living room and found Richie sitting on the couch.

"Hey," Ty said. "How long have you been back?"

"Couple minutes." Richie nodded down the hall. "Shank's talking to your pops."

"He's not my . . . Never mind."

Ty walked down the hallway toward his godfather's office. He doubted Liang would mind if he interrupted Shank for a moment. He approached the office door and reached for the knob. The door was slightly ajar, and softly spoken words drifted from the crack. Ty stopped for a moment to listen.

"You sure he'll go through with it?" Shank asked. "What if he finds out the truth? You know why he hates us Red Dogs so much."

"Of course, I do!" Liang snapped. "I was the one who ordered you to kill Rachel, wasn't I? If Ty finds out you're the one who pulled the trigger, he'll come for you first. That means it's in your best interests to ensure he doesn't find out."

It took everything within Ty to keep from barging into the office and strangling both men on the spot. Shank was a big man, but Ty was confident he could take him out. And Liang . . . well, skilled or not, Liang was still an aging man. Ty was certain that he could kill his godfather with minimal difficulty. But he couldn't. However much he hated Liang, Ty needed his help to get Emi back. He wondered if Liang would follow through with that promise. Liang had killed Ty's wife. Ty doubted he cared any more about Emi than he had about Rachel.

"And if he does find out?" Shank asked.

"My godson only cares about two people in this life. His daughter and his sister-in-law, Joanie. We need Joanie to complete the reserve job; but once it's done, if she were to suffer a tragic death—say, at the hands of my old friend McCrory—that would drive my godson right back into our arms."

Shank chuckled. "Consider it done."

It would be safest for Joanie if Ty killed both men. But he still needed Liang's help to find Emi. There had to be another way to save

Joanie's life, one that wouldn't sacrifice his chance at getting his daughter back.

If he's lying about this, what else could I be missing?

He backed away from the door, counted to ten, and approached, stepping a little harder than necessary to ensure that the thump of his boots would carry into the office. He knocked on the door.

"Come in," Liang called.

Ty stepped through the door, glancing briefly at Shank and looking away, lest his expression give anything away. He looked at Liang and struggled to school his features to impassivity.

"Any news on the dampener?"

"It's here!" Liang slapped his palms on his desk and rose. "Let's get it fitted to a suit for you, my boy. We've only got a few hours left until the job begins."

Ty nodded. A few hours left. And once the job was done—once Joanie was safe and McCrory was dead and Ty had Emi back in his care—he would murder his godfather and Shank where they stood. He had always kept a code of no killing, but for this . . . For this, there was no justice that would satiate him, save seeing his wife's murderers lying dead at his feet next to the man who had killed his parents.

* * *

Because of his pre-Seraph interest in martial arts, Gideon had always owned a plethora of weapons, but most of them were for training purposes and not suited for actual combat. Thanks to Dean's foresight, however, Carter had more than enough weapons for himself. Gideon took the pair of aionium truncheons, leaving Carter with his sword and shield. The truncheons would serve Gideon better than fighting Ravener—Mac Tíre—barehanded.

Carter had gathered the team after his meeting with Monahan. He had revealed Silas's allegiance to CLOUD, which Gideon was none too happy about. Jarrett Mercer had proven his trustworthiness to the Vindicators, and Silas had been a great help to Carter. Still, Gideon was skeptical of the shady government organization's purpose. If their desire to protect the world from unidentified threats was genuine, Gideon hoped Silas proved it through his actions.

Once they had agreed to table that discussion for another time, Carter explained everything Monahan had told them about Kane McCrory, alias Mac Tíre. He was a member of a group of international assassins called the Sicarans. Carter assured Gideon that it was more important than ever that he watch over Alistair Wheaton and his family. If Mac Tíre wanted to hurt Wheaton, there were very few people with the skills to stop him.

Gideon parked his Mustang outside Wheaton's high-rise and looked up at the top of the massive building. Once, he could've flown up to the terrace; but that night, he would do it the way most ordinary people did—the elevator. He picked up his truncheons, tucked them in his belt, and walked into the lobby. Beneath his dark jacket, he wore a bulletproof vest. He was not sure the vest would do any good against a sword, since McCrory could go for his neck or one of his limbs; but it was better than nothing.

He entered the elevator and rode it to the top floor. Wheaton's penthouse was the only apartment on that floor. Gideon bit his lip and spent the elevator ride clenching and unclenching his fists. In his duel with Ty Vickers, he had scarcely managed to hold his own. Carter's description of Ravener indicated that McCrory was several steps above Vickers in terms of skill. Gideon feared he might be coming against an opponent that he was unprepared to face.

The elevator stopped, and the door slid open, revealing the short hallway that ended in the door to Wheaton's apartment. Gideon stayed back away from the door when he knocked, presenting as non-threatening a figure as he could. When the door opened, Wheaton stood on the other side, a gun in his hand. He studied Gideon, frowned, and lowered his weapon.

"Dr. Turner? What is one of my lab employees doing at my penthouse?"

"You know that I'm more than a bio-analyst." Gideon stepped forward. "I may not have powers anymore, but I can still fight. The Crusader sent me to watch over you until the swordsman is taken care of."

Wheaton huffed. "Well, I'm sure you'll be better security than any private security I could hire. I'm glad to have your help."

CHAPTER 43

The plan Ty came up with was sure to break Joanie's heart. She might never trust him again, let alone talk to him. He knew as he solidified each detail that going through with it would mean sacrificing his relationship with her. It was worth it if it saved her life. He only had a few hours to come up with anything, so he had precious few resources to work with. Doing nothing ensured her death.

Unfortunately, Liang was right. They needed Joanie to complete the hack. If not for her skill set, Ty would have snuck her off before Liang knew she was missing. If she disappeared before the heist, Liang would never help Ty get Emi back. But once the hack was done, any of Liang's people with computer skills could work the program from there. All Joanie had to do was wait for Ty to insert the flash drive with the virus and complete the hack from her side. It would take less than ten minutes once the virus was in. At that point, Joanie was no longer useful to the Red Dogs. That was the most likely time for Shank to strike, but it was also the perfect time for Ty to take Joanie off the board so the Red Dog enforcer couldn't hurt her.

Ty stepped outside Liang's house into the fenced backyard and pulled his phone from his pocket. The next step was the riskiest part of his plan. If Shank or any of Liang's other people caught him while he was on the call, he was done for. Liang would cut his losses, which meant killing Ty and Joanie and probably Ned and Richie, for good measure. Crossing the yard so he was as far from the house as possible, Ty dialed.

The line clicked, and a woman answered. "Sojourn City Police Department, how can I help you?"

"There's going to be a break-in at the federal reserve tonight," Ty said. "The perpetrator will be in a black Chevy SUV outside the reserve."

"Sir, where are you getting this information?"

"It will happen at midnight," Ty said.

He left the line open for a few more seconds, pulled his phone away from his ear, and ended the call. A tip like that had to be investigated. When the police arrived at the reserve that night, they would find Joanie sitting in the SUV with incriminating evidence on her tablet. Ty and the rest of the gang would be inside, giving them time to escape. Ty would have the time he needed to end Shank's life. Joanie could testify that the Red Dogs had forced her to perpetrate the hack at gunpoint. Ty was confident that with a good lawyer and a plea bargain, she would go free with no jail time.

The most difficult part would be convincing Liang that someone else had killed Shank. Ty planned to blame it on McCrory; but if the swordsman made an appearance elsewhere in Sojourn City that night, Liang would know he was lying. It was a risky game. Ty still needed his godfather's help in getting Emi back, but it was too dangerous to leave Shank alive.

Ty shook his head. What had he become? Weeks ago, he would have recoiled at the very thought of killing anyone. That night, he was planning every detail of a man's death—or possibly three men. Once Emi was in his arms, he was not going to leave anything to chance.

Liang would have to die, too; and Ty would kill Kane McCrory to avenge his parents.

It wasn't malicious. It was about justice and self-preservation. He would do what he had to. Ty hoped his real father would have understood.

* * *

Jolie read over the transcript of the short phone call the department had received and shook her head in confusion. Voice-recognition technology confirmed that the caller was Ty Vickers, based on the recordings they had of him in the police academy. But why was Vickers calling in a crime that he was a part of?

Whatever it was, Jolie still had to be there. She had called together a task force of officers, given them the rundown of the situation, and stationed them several blocks out from the reserve. They would wait until midnight, as Vickers had said. They would move in, surround the SUV, and wait outside for whomever was inside the reserve. With any luck, they would gather the whole gang in one sweep.

"Any chance my swordsman's there?" Pulaski asked.

"Very possible." Jolie picked up a folder. "Here. A source of mine gave me this info on your suspect. Turns out the swordsman's name is Kane McCrory. He's an assassin."

Pulaski thumbed through the folder. "Who's your source?"

"A previous collar. Gave McCrory up in exchange for transfer to a somewhat cushier prison."

Jolie was glad that Monahan had talked. The blood analysis had come back without a match, even against the FBI's database. McCrory was apparently good enough that he had never left blood at the scene of a crime before the Bronze Dragon.

"Mm." Pulaski bit his lip. "Thanks for this, Turner. I haven't heard of this McCrory guy; but if he's in Sojourn, I'll find him. If it's all right with you, I'd like to go along with your task force tonight. Like you said, it seems possible he'll turn up if Vickers is going to be there."

Jolie nodded. "The more, the merrier."

* * *

Raina watched as Carter pulled on the pieces of his Crusader suit. She worried about him going out when she didn't know what he was getting himself into. That night, she did know: a heist at the federal reserve. He was running headlong into a showdown with Vickers, his crew, and the Red Dogs—and more than likely McCrory, as well. They were not good odds, even with the cops as backup. She knew he wouldn't sit this out. He had been hunting McCrory for over a month, and he wanted to get Vickers, too. This was his chance to do both.

She looked over at Silas. He was on thin ice with the rest of the team, especially Carter and Gideon. Raina was angry, too, but she still trusted Silas. He had saved her life at Pop's Gym, and he had always gone out of his way to help Carter in his mission. He didn't have to do that. It wasn't part of his assignment from CLOUD. He did it because he wanted to help and because he cared about Carter.

"If McCrory shows up tonight, be careful," Silas said. "Last time you fought, you hurt him. He won't play nice this time."

"Don't worry." Carter checked his gauntlet. "I won't, either."

Raina shook her head. As skilled as Carter had become, he was still in over his head. He hadn't been able to beat either McCrory or Vickers in a straight fight; and in the coming battle, he might encounter both. If Gideon weren't already watching over Wheaton, she would have asked him to go into the field with Carter. Her own skills were not up to par. If she went to the reserve, Carter would spend the entire night protecting her. She caught Silas' eye and tried to convey what she was thinking with her expression. He barely nodded.

"You should be able to get into the reserve with no problem," Silas said. "Vickers' team will have to disable the security system to enter. That works to your advantage, too, because they won't see you coming. Get the drop on them and take out the guys with the Sterling Labs guns first if you can."

Raina stepped up to him. "I'll be on the line the whole time."

Carter hugged her. "After tonight, this will all be over."

Raina hoped so, for Carter's sake. He had worn himself thin chasing these guys. He needed a break.

Lord, please let things take a turn in our favor tonight.

CHAPTER 44

Balancing his sword across his legs, Carter sat atop the peak of his rooftop and looked out at the city. The coming night would likely bring the end to one or more of the cases Carter had been working so hard to crack. He was ready for them to be over. Ready to return to some semblance of normalcy.

There was every chance that someone would die at the reserve. With Vickers, McCrory, and the Red Dogs all present, it would be difficult to keep all of them from shedding blood. Yet something deep within him drove Carter to try. Perhaps it was that unyielding need to match his father's reputation—to stop the bad guy at any cost but to protect all the lives involved.

"Carter, can I talk to you?"

He snapped his head up. His mother had climbed out the window and was easing across the rooftop next to him. He pressed his lips together, confused, but nodded.

"Rhonda told me about Mr. Vickers," she said. "About how you think he needs to be stopped no matter what, but you're conflicted because of his daughter."

"I'm not conflicted. Not anymore." Carter tightened his jaw. "Vickers is a criminal. He has to go down. Being a dad doesn't excuse his crimes."

"Because you feel your father would never have stooped so low?"

"He wouldn't have!" Carter turned away from his mother, his face heating. "He didn't."

Her hand rested on his shoulder. The armored pauldron of his uniform kept him from feeling her palm, but he felt the pressure of her touch.

"Your father wasn't perfect, Carter."

"No, but he sure tried to be. Vickers has no excuse—"

"You don't know everything about how your father became the Crusader, do you?"

Carter blinked at the sudden change in subject. He remembered his dad sitting down with Carter, Rhonda, and Ellis and explaining that he would become a vigilante. Carter had been all for the idea. His mom made it sound like there was more to the story.

"The first time your father fought a criminal . . . " Joanna exhaled shakily. "He killed that man. He was rescuing a mugging victim; but when the attacker told your father, 'I've seen your face,' Wyatt felt he had no other choice. To protect you kids, he took a life."

All the blood that had rushed to Carter's face drained away. He had been so certain that Wyatt had been the kind of hero and father anyone could aspire to be. If what his mom said was true, Carter's dad carried more guilt than Carter could imagine. He probably had until the day he died.

And if he was honest with himself, Carter had done questionable things, as well. Breaking into Wheaton's penthouse when he wasn't even sure of the CFO's guilt was among them. He excused it because he was trying to bring a killer to justice. Did that make it right? He doubted his father had asked the same question about murdering a man.

"Why are you telling me this?" he asked.

"Because people will do unimaginable things to protect their children. But because of grace, your father overcame his mistake and is remembered as a hero." Joanna rose and shuffled away. "Just remember that, baby."

* * *

Gideon sat on the couch in Wheaton's penthouse and waited. He could not be sure McCrory would show up that night, which made the wait more agonizing. From the pinched expression on the CFO's face, Gideon suspected Wheaton felt the same way. He might not be able to sense emotions as he once could, but that superpower had taught him to read people. Wheaton was terrified. Wheaton's wife, Courtney, stood nearby, cradling Nathaniel.

"Maybe you don't need to be here," Wheaton said. "Maybe it was a bluff. Or maybe—"

The penthouse lights died. Gideon reached into his belt and withdrew his truncheons. It was torrentially raining, and there had been a few flashes of lightning. A glance out the window confirmed that all the other buildings in the area still had power. Wheaton's apartment had been targeted intentionally. McCrory had arrived.

Gideon took a position between the door and the window. "Get them to safety."

"Courtney?" Wheaton looked at his wife. "Take Nathaniel to the panic room."

She nodded and rushed for the stairs to the penthouse's upper level. Gideon stood and walked toward the door. Wheaton, for his part, retreated into the kitchen, using the corner for cover, and trained his gun on the door. Two of his bodyguards followed his wife, while the third remained with him in the kitchen. Other than the pattering rain on the window and the occasional rumble of thunder, the room was silent.

Gideon's fingers tensed around his truncheons.

A flash of lightning illuminated the room, casting Gideon's shadow on the wall in front of him. A second bolt flashed, and another shadow joined his.

Gideon spun. The terrace door crashed inward, and a dark figure rolled into the room, extending its left hand. Gideon raised his truncheon to deflect a *shuriken*. Wheaton opened fire, and another *shuriken* spun across the room. The CFO grunted, dropped his gun, and stumbled back into the kitchen. A third star struck the bodyguard in the chest before he could fire. Gideon advanced on the figure, who drew a sword and rushed back toward him.

Gideon ducked under the swinging blade and jabbed his left-hand truncheon into the man's ribs. He spun as he delivered the blow, bringing his right truncheon toward his opponent's lower back. The aionium rod connected. McCrory lurched forward but used the fall to turn and swipe his blade upward toward Gideon's face.

Gideon pulled back and felt a light sting across his cheek. McCrory changed the angle of his attack, coming down toward Gideon's neck. Gideon stepped in and raised his arm, catching his opponent's sword hand under the wrist. McCrory drove his left fist into Gideon's solar plexus. The air left Gideon's lungs, and he stumbled back and took a gasping breath. McCrory advanced on him.

The sword descended. Gideon raised his truncheons in a scissor block. McCrory's blow landed with the force of a jackhammer, staggering Gideon. As McCrory brought his blade in for another strike,

Gideon dropped his truncheons and stepped in, grasping at McCrory's wrists. McCrory brought his foot up into Gideon's gut. Gideon gasped but refused to release his grip on McCrory's wrists.

Something heavy struck him in the back of the head. Gideon dropped to the floor and spun as he fell. Through hazy eyes, he saw two more men, clad identically to McCrory, save for their lack of silver sashes. Each of them held a pair of black metal truncheons.

"I'd hoped you would be more of a challenge," McCrory said. "The famed Seraph brought so low with barely a struggle."

"I'm not . . . done yet." Gideon gritted his teeth and forced himself to his feet. He blinked the fog from his vision. "You're not getting Wheaton."

"Mm, he has grit. Good." McCrory tilted his head toward his accomplices. "Finish him."

The two Sicarans lunged forward. The one to Gideon's left struck his shoulder with a truncheon. Pain shot down Gideon's arm. He threw himself into a forward roll as they swung at him. He came up in a crouch behind him and kicked one in the back. As the assassin stumbled forward, Gideon leaped over him and drove his fist into the face of the second. The assassin recoiled and lashed out blindly with one truncheon. The weapon struck Gideon in the ribs. He wrapped his arms around the extended weapon hand, turned so he was grasping the assassin in an armbar, and jerked the limb upward. The assassin cried out as his elbow popped.

Gideon had to break off the lock as the other assassin rose from the floor and swung one of his truncheons. Gideon jerked his head to the side to avoid the strike, snapped his foot up into the assassin's gut, and turned to the one he'd had in an armbar, slamming his fist into the assassin's face again. As he approached the first assassin, he received a truncheon strike across the jaw. Stars exploded in his head. He rubbed his face and staggered away from his opponent.

"Impressive," McCrory called. "But if you cannot defeat my apprentices, what hope do you have against me?"

The assassin in front of Gideon advanced, swinging his truncheons in tight arcs. Gideon stepped out of the way of the weapons, shoving one of the man's wrists away with the palm of his left hand, and stepped forward. He drove his elbow into the side of the man's head. The assassin collapsed.

A scream echoed from upstairs. Gideon spun to look up at the second-floor balcony. *Courtney!* He knelt and picked up his truncheons. McCrory stood in the middle of the living room, and Wheaton lay behind him, unmoved from where he had fallen earlier. Both of McCrory's apprentices were unconscious on the floor. *Who is upstairs with Courtney?*

"I'm impressed," McCrory said. "But you will not be as fortunate against me."

CHAPTER 45

Ty glanced at his watch. 11:45.

His mind threatened to cave beneath the weight of so many secrets and subterfuges. He was deceiving his sister-in-law, the one person he felt he could trust with anything. Instead of being honest with her, he was arranging for her to be arrested.

"Time to go, Lurk."

Joanie's voice was gentle, but it nearly caused him to jump from his skin. He swallowed and refocused on the task at hand.

G-Storm and Shock Jock stood in front of the federal reserve's front doors. Lurk looked up at the security cameras. If they were still on, they wouldn't see anything but a figure in a black ski mask and tinted goggles. In contrast, G-Storm's blue-and-tan jacket and Shock Jock's red one were practically signal flares in the dark, but they had masks on. Joanie had the cameras down, anyway, so there was nothing to worry about. And she was fifteen minutes away from being arrested.

Lurk reached down to the energy damper on his belt and flicked it on. They had run out of time to test it; and if the police believed his call, they were already on their way. He might never know for sure if the energy conductor worked as Liang said it would. A green light flickered to life on the small box. He willed his body to dematerialize, reached out, and phased through the door.

"He's in!" G-Storm said over comms.

"Get back here and let us in," Shank said. "We're standing out here like sitting ducks."

It occurred to Lurk that he could leave Shank and his crew outside to be picked up by the police, but that presented too much of a risk. If Shank and Joanie were both arrested, he could still get his hands on her. Lurk wasn't leaving anything to chance. He opened the doors for G-Storm and Shock Jock and walked inside.

"On our way," Shock Jock said.

While they let Shank inside, Lurk would move up to the computer room and insert the virus. The sooner it was in, the better. Motherboard would have more time to complete the hack. Once the clock struck midnight, her time was up. He bounded up the stairs two at a time.

"Why are we all here again?" Shock Jock's voice was tinny in Lurk's earbud.

"In case the swordsman shows up," Shank said. "Your toy guns from Sterling Labs are our best chance at beating him."

"Oh, yeah." Shock Jock sounded subdued. "Right."

Lurk raised his left hand and put it on the strap that encircled his body from left hip to right shoulder. The strap held a sheath containing the sword he had borrowed from Liang. Other than the four throwing knives on his belt, the sword was the only weapon Lurk carried.

He wove his way up several flights of stairs and exited onto the floor where the reserve's databases were stored. Lurk lowered his left hand to his pocket and drew out the flash drive Joanie had given him back at the house. All he had to do was plug it directly into the mainframe. The virus would do the rest.

Another glance at his watch showed that it was 11:51. Nine minutes to go. Lurk found the door Liang had highlighted on the blueprints and phased through it. The room was surprisingly small, and all four walls were lined with computers. Lurk stepped toward the nearest one and pulled open the glass panel that encased it.

"I'm in. Preparing to insert the virus."

"And no sign of the swordsman or the Kid Crusader," Shank said. "Heh. We may pull this off without a hitch."

Lurk found a receptacle and inserted the flash drive. A small light on the inside of the drive lit up, indicating it was active.

"Package delivered, Motherboard."

"Copy. Commencing hack."

"Good work." Lurk swallowed the lump in his throat. "See you soon."

* * *

Jolie crept toward the SUV. As Vickers's call indicated, it was a black Chevy. Either this was a trap, or he had been completely honest. Jolie still couldn't imagine why he had given up his own heist, so she would keep her guard up until he and his accomplices were in handcuffs. Keeping her gun trained on the SUV, Jolie circled the vehicle. Four of her fellow officers flanked the target with their rifles shouldered.

Jolie extended her left hand and tugged on the driver's door handle. A young woman sat in the front passenger seat, typing furiously at a tablet. She looked up at Jolie, yelped in surprise, and dropped her tablet.

"Hands up," Jolie said.

Officer Rojas opened the door and pulled the girl out of the SUV. She shrieked and slapped at the cop. Jolie circled the vehicle and examined the girl. From the file photos they had, she appeared to be Vickers' sister-in-law, Joanie. Jolie frowned. Why would Vickers give up one of his only remaining family members?

"Where's Vickers?" Jolie asked.

"Like I'd tell you!" Joanie slapped Rojas again. "How did you find me?"

"We got a tip." Jolie tapped her earbud. "Crusader, there's no sign of the rest of the crew. They must be inside already."

"Copy that," the Crusader replied. "I'm on my way in."

* * *

The Crusader entered the federal reserve through the rooftop access point. If Vickers and his team were inside, Jolie and the cops already had the ground entrances covered. But if the thieves tried running to the roof, the Crusader would be there to intercept them. He opened the stairwell access and entered the building.

"No sign of Vickers using his powers on our scanners," Jolie said. "But that doesn't mean he's not in there."

"Right. Anything on the security cameras?"

Jolie paused. "Joanie Sellers took them down. Looks like she' Vickers's computer whiz. We're working on getting the feed active."

"Loop me in when you do." The Crusader descended the stairs. "Otherwise, this is going to be a long game of hide and seek."

"From the look of Joanie's tablet, they were trying to hack the mainframe. Start there and work your way down."

"On it. Which floor?"

"Fifth. Hurry. If Vickers knew we were coming, he's probably on his way out. He didn't call us without an escape plan."

The Crusader bounded down the stairs to the fifth floor and pulled the door open. His feet left the ground as something lifted him into the air, leaving his stomach behind. A man in a blue-and-tan jacket stepped out from a doorway on the left side of the hall. The mag-gun that had been used to rob the armored car was cradled in his arms. The Crusader grimaced and tried to wiggle free of the magnetic field.

"Well, well." The man giggled. "Looks like I caught me a superhero."

* * *

Gideon's truncheons clanked against McCrory's blade. The assassin swept his sword horizontally, and Gideon blocked with both his batons. The swordsman swept his leg to trip Gideon, but he jumped over the sweep and transitioned into a kick, striking McCrory in the shoulder. As the assassin spun, he flicked his left wrist. Expecting what came next, Gideon threw himself behind the couch as a throwing star shot overhead and buried itself in the drywall.

He rolled aside as McCrory leaped over the couch, ramming his blade into the floor where Gideon had been lying. Pushing himself to his feet, Gideon rushed at his opponent, swinging his truncheons. The swordsman blocked the blows once, twice, three times. Gideon scissor-blocked a counterstrike with his batons.

Courtney and Nathaniel were still in danger. With Wheaton incapacitated in the kitchen, Gideon was their only hope. But McCrory was one of the best fighters Gideon had ever faced. For every blow Gideon attempted, McCrory had a block. For each time Gideon blocked, the assassin had an alternate move ready. It was like fighting someone with the fluidity of a river.

McCrory pulled back from the lock and spun, slashing at Gideon's right bicep. Gideon managed to turn and block, but McCrory kicked out, striking his knee. Gideon cried out as something popped. McCrory grabbed him by the collar, hoisted him, and hurled him over the couch. Gideon landed next to Wheaton in the kitchen. Grimacing, he pushed himself to his knees. Both of McCrory's apprentices were gone. Gideon turned his attention back to the swordsman, who approached with his weapon raised.

Wheaton's gun lay on the floor between them. Dropping his truncheons, Gideon lunged forward, grabbed the gun, and stood, pointing the barrel at McCrory's chest.

McCrory laughed. "You don't expect me to believe you'll actually shoot me, do you? You haven't killed anyone as long as you've been the Seraph, Gideon Turner."

"No, but I have killed before." Gideon racked the gun. "Besides, I'm a surgeon. I can pinpoint a nonlethal but very crippling, *very* painful shot."

McCrory held his sword casually at his side. "I'm faster than you think."

"Step aside. I'm going to help Wheaton's family."

"Hm. I don't think—" McCrory tilted his head. "Ah . . . it seems my target has been found. Goodbye, Turner."

Gideon squeezed the trigger. At the same time, McCrory flicked his wrist, sending a *shuriken* flying across the room. Gideon's bullet miraculously struck the throwing star—or maybe that had been intentional on McCrory's part. Either way, the assassin was already moving toward the balcony. Gideon rushed after him.

He froze when he remembered Courtney and Nathaniel. They were more important at the moment. He knelt next to Wheaton and checked his pulse. The man was still alive but unconscious. Gideon picked up the fallen truncheons and rushed for the stairs.

He bounded up the steps two at a time, rushing across the balcony and to the hallway. He rounded the corner to find four Sicarans standing in the hallway over the bodies of the other two bodyguards.

The two he had faced downstairs were armed with truncheons. The third and fourth each held a hatchet.

The two closest assassins lunged toward him. Gideon hurled his left truncheon, and it struck the closest man in the face. Gideon pushed off the hallway wall with his left foot, giving himself a height advantage, and descended toward the second assassin, bringing his truncheon down toward him in an overhead strike. As the assassin raised a truncheon to block, Gideon landed, bringing his knee up into the assassin's gut, followed by a blow to the back of his head with the truncheon.

The hatchet-wielders rushed Gideon with their bladed weapons drawn back. Gideon used his empty hand to shove aside the closer assassin's hatchet and crossed his right arm over to block the second attacker's weapon. He snapped a kick backward into the first hatchet-wielder's kneecap. The assassin screamed—judging by the pitch of the cry, it was a woman. The second ax-wielder slashed diagonally. Gideon slid his baton up under the edge of the ax, caught it, and twisted it aside.

As he delivered a punch to the ax-wielder's jaw, the unarmed assassin started to stand. Gideon's fist landed, and he jerked his arm backward, striking the crippled woman in the back of the head to render her unconscious. He swung his baton in a heavy overhand strike to the unarmed assassin's head.

The four Sicarans lay moaning and panting in the hallway. Gideon brandished his truncheon and marched to the open door at the end. A final assassin stood in the middle of Wheaton's bedroom, arm wrapped around Courtney's throat, a dagger pressed to her neck. Nathaniel wailed nearby. Gideon scanned the room and saw the boy lying in the middle of his parents' bed, seemingly unharmed.

"Drop the weapon!" the assassin said in a distinctly female voice.

"No chance." Gideon stepped forward. "Let her go. You're all out of backup, and your boss left you here alone. It's over."

"Mac Tíre is completing his mission. He trusted me to finish things here."

"You have no reason to hurt them. They were only pawns in McCrory's game. They're of no more use to him, so why kill them?"

"They have seen too much."

Gideon tensed, ready to move. He'd never reach her in time. She could open Courtney's throat before Gideon took two steps. If he still had his powers, he could blind her or blast her with a beam of light; or if he had a *shuriken* or a gun, he could take her out. But with only a truncheon in hand, he couldn't do anything for risk of hitting Courtney or—

Bang.

The assassin slumped, and Courtney screamed and backed away. Gideon spun. Wheaton stood in the bedroom door, his gun unwavering. He glanced over at Gideon and nodded. Gideon nodded back.

"Good shot."

"Thanks." Wheaton jerked his head toward the door. "Get the rest of them out of my house before I shoot them, too."

CHAPTER 46

The Crusader gritted his teeth as the guy with the mag-gun held him over the floor. Behind him, two men stepped out into the hallway—one wearing a red bomber jacket and armed with a shock rifle from Sterling Labs, and the other wearing a Red Dogs jacket and carrying a massive .50 caliber pistol. Judging from the look in the latter's eye, that gun was about to make a significant hole in the Crusader's body.

A .50 caliber bullet would punch through his less-armored arm or leg with ease, and he would bleed out very quickly. He had to get out of this. Fast. His gauntlet was still set on grappling mode; and inside the magnetic field, the cord wouldn't do any good. If he tried to reach for his gauntlet to switch it to shock beads, the Red Dog might shoot him.

A man in a black suit and ski mask appeared from one doorway. The thief glanced at the group for a moment. His gaze locked on the Crusader for a second longer.

"It's done!" Carter recognized Vickers' voice. "Come on; let's get out of here!"

The Red Dog glanced over his shoulder. "After I deal with—"

The Crusader reached over to his gauntlet, switched it to stun beads, and extended his wrist. He fired at the guy with the mag-gun. The bead exploded, and blue sparks arced over the man's body. He stumbled back and dropped his weapon. The Crusader fell to the ground, landing in a crouch. He picked his sword up off the floor and stood.

Vickers backed away. "Run!"

The Crusader stepped past the still-twitching body of the guy with the mag-gun. Bomber Jacket raised his shock rifle. The Crusader darted to the side and lashed out with his sword, striking the underside of the rifle and knocking it upward. The thug fired, but the bolt went high and struck the ceiling. The Crusader spun and rammed the pommel of his sword into the thief's gut. As the man doubled over, the Red Dog raised his pistol. The Crusader dropped to the floor as the huge gun fired, its ear-splitting crack echoing through the narrow hallway. The bullet struck the wall behind the Crusader.

"I said, 'Run!'" Vickers shouted.

The Crusader started to stand and fell back as a knife struck the floor in front of him. Vickers grabbed Bomber Jacket's shoulder and pulled him up, dragging him down the hallway. The Crusader jumped to his feet, and the Red Dog opened fire. The Crusader leaped into a side doorway to avoid the powerful gunfire.

"Backup, fifth floor!" the Red Dog ordered.

"Jolie, I could use a hand in here!"

"Officers on their way in," she replied. "Where are you?"

"Fifth floor, east side!" The Crusader glanced out the door and pulled his shield from its sling. "Vickers and his crew are headed for the west stairwell!"

He stepped into the hallway. Mag-gun was gone. One of his companions must've dragged him away. The Crusader rushed down the hall in the direction they had gone. There was no sign of them. They must have rounded a corner. He came to an intersection and turned right into an elevator bank.

Crack-crack-crack.

A bullet pinged off the Crusader's shoulder. He lifted his shield as automatic rifles peppered his position. *Right. Backup.* The other Red Dogs had been lying in ambush around the corner, which meant Vickers and his crew might already be on their way to the rooftop.

"Anytime, Jolie!"

"We're pinned in the lobby!" Muffled gunshots filled the comms. "There was a team of Red Dogs waiting for us!"

"Same thing up here." The Crusader grimaced as bullets pelted his shield. "All right. I'll have to improvise."

"Hang tight, Carter," Raina said. "Backup's on the way."

The Crusader frowned. "Huh?"

"Trust me. They won't see it coming."

The Crusader leaned toward the corner and pulled back again as bullets shredded the wall around him into dust. Whatever Raina's backup was, he hoped it showed up soon.

* * *

Lurk opened the door to the stairwell and held it as Shank and Shock Jock walked through, the latter helping G-Storm hobble along. He glanced over his shoulder. Rapid gunfire cracked in the distance, but he wasn't confident that the team of Red Dogs could hold the Crusader for long. He had seen the young vigilante fight. With his shield and his wits, the Crusader was more than capable of getting around a squad of thugs.

"Up the stairs," Shank said. "Go!"

"Why are we going up?" Lurk asked. "On the rooftop, we'll be trapped!"

"Relax." Shank patted his shoulder. "I've got a plan."

"Why does that not comfort me?"

Shank glared at him for another moment before following Shock Jock and G-Storm up the stairs. Lurk looked back down the hallway. The guns were still firing. The Crusader hadn't taken the Red Dogs out yet, but it also meant they hadn't killed him.

Lurk would do it Shank's way. The rooftop would be a more convenient place to kill him, anyway.

* * *

The Crusader's cover was quickly disappearing. Sooner or later, the gunmen would realize he wasn't going to advance. They would come after him. As more of the corner was blasted away, he had to retreat farther to keep safe. At least, he had his shield; but against multiple enemies, he could not risk closing in. As soon as he engaged one of the thugs, the others could shoot him in the back. He had to improvise. There was a doorway back to his left. If he ducked inside, he could wait for the Red Dogs to come after him and ambush them from the room.

"How many?" Raina asked.

"Five . . . maybe six?" The Crusader grabbed the doorknob. He took a shock bead from his utility belt and set it on the hallway floor. "Hard to say in the middle of a bullet storm."

He backed inside. It was a janitor's closet—small and cramped—but it suited his purposes. He hoped they hadn't heard the door opening. Seconds later, they stopped firing. The Crusader tensed, ready to move as soon as he heard them approaching.

"Where'd he go?" a voice whispered.

The Crusader put a hand on the door, ready to push it outward and hit them as fast as he could. Vickers and his crew could be down to the lobby, backing up the Red Dogs in their gunfight with the cops.

Or they might've located a different escape route altogether. At least, Vickers couldn't use his powers without the police picking it up.

"He's gone," another voice said.

The Crusader shoved the door open, its edge slamming into one of the Red Dogs. He kicked out, striking the same gangster and knocking him into the opposite wall. No sooner had the Crusader's foot returned to the ground than he knocked a second gangster's gun aside with the face of his shield. With a flick of his gauntlet, he activated the shock bead he had placed on the floor earlier. Two more Red Dogs convulsed and went down.

He brought his sword around to strike, and a Red Dog grabbed his wrist and pulled the Crusader in. The vigilante brought his left hand up to catch a thrown punch from the Red Dog's other hand. The Red Dog cried out as his fist struck the Crusader's aionium shield. Twisting his dominant hand, the Crusader pulled it back from his opponent. He angled low and rammed his shield into the Red Dog's leg. The gangster's knee buckled, and the Crusader punched him across the jaw, knocking him to the ground. A kick to the face rendered him unconscious. Three down.

The Crusader found himself staring down the barrel of another man's rifle.

The Red Dog grinned wickedly. "Lights out."

His finger pressed against the trigger—and he grunted and dropped to the ground. A man stood behind the Red Dog. He was clad in gunmetal gray armor with cobalt blue highlights on the shoulders and forearms. He wore a matching helmet, its design similar to a SWAT trooper's. His eyes were covered by blue-tinted goggles.

The Crusader fired a sonic bead. Sound pierced the narrow corridor, and the remaining Red Dogs screamed and clutched their ears. The

Crusader's helper pummeled one of them across the jaw. The Crusader downed the last two.

"Who are you?" the Crusader asked.

"Call me Stonewall."

The Crusader furrowed his brow. The nickname was unfamiliar, but the voice . . .

"Silas?"

"Codenames only in the field, Crusader." He kicked the Red Dog at his feet. "What if one of these guys heard you? Raina said you might need help."

"Since when are you a vigilante?"

Stonewall walked past him. "I took a page from Mercer's book—agent and vigilante. You needed help, and I was in a position to offer it."

Stonewall's gear didn't appear to be made of aionium, but it was heavier than the bulletproof weave of the rest of the Crusader's gear. Stonewall was unarmed, save for the gauntlets he wore. They looked like Sterling Labs concussion gauntlets, which could deliver a skull-splitting punch.

"Let's catch some bad guys," Stonewall said. "You're the expert here. I'll follow your lead."

"Thanks. Jolie, do you see Vickers or his crew?"

"No sign of them!" A gunshot. "These Dogs are trenched in. It's going to take a while to get past them. I'm afraid you're on your own."

"No, I'm not. Good luck down there." The Crusader smiled at Stonewall. "Maybe Vickers' team went up. Let's check the rooftop."

CHAPTER 47

Ty shivered as the freezing rain struck his body. They couldn't stay on the rooftop for long. He wondered what Shank had planned. The next closest building was dozens of yards away. Even if they could get a line across, it would be hard to break inside without leverage. Ty could phase in through a window, but the rest of them would have to dangle there until he could phase them in one at a time, which raised the risk of them being spotted.

There was nothing stopping Ty from leaving at that moment. He could cut and run. Joanie was safe. The police had her; he'd heard it over the comms. Shank couldn't hurt her. Ty could stab Shank in the back, phase back down inside the building, leave Richie and Ned behind, and disappear. He could go back to his godfather's house, demand help in retrieving Emi, and get out of town.

Ty reached for his sword and shuffled behind Shank.

"What are we doing?" Richie shouted over the rain.

"We're waiting," a new voice said.

Ty swiveled on his heel. Liang stood behind them, a cane in his right hand. He wore a long, gray trench coat that covered the rest of his clothes. Seeing his godfather present at the scene of the crime rocked Ty's confidence. There was no way he could kill Shank while Liang was watching.

"What . . . what are you doing here? Waiting for what?"

"For my old friend McCrory." Liang stepped forward. "He has been hurting my business for too long. It ends tonight."

"This was all a ploy?" Ty asked. "A trap for McCrory?"

"Indeed. Between your powers and the weapons that your friends stole from Sterling Labs, we should be sufficiently prepared for him. Oh, the money we'll get from the girl's hack will be welcome. We do have to rebuild. But stopping McCrory before he can cause further carnage is more important."

Ty clenched his jaw. Why had he ever trusted his godfather? Ty grabbed the sheath wrapped around his back, pulled it off, drew his sword, and threw the sheath to the ground. He could kill Liang and Shank. Neither one expected it. All he had to do was throw one of his knives into Shank's chest and attack his godfather. He was confident he could beat the old man in a fight.

He had been a fool, he realized. Even if they defeated McCrory and escaped, Liang would never help him. He held Emi over Ty's head as a bargaining chip, but he did not care about the girl—or about Ty. If Ty wanted to get Emi back, he would have to do it on his own, and Liang was in his way. He took a step forward.

A dark figure dropped onto the rooftop, sword drawn.

"Hello, old friend," Liang said. "Welcome."

McCrory. Ty could deal with Liang and Shank later. McCrory was the greater threat.

"It's time to face judgment," McCrory said.

Liang tilted his head. "All this time, and you still hold a grudge?"

"It's not a grudge. You betrayed your vows." McCrory flourished his blade. "Meet your end with honor, Ègùn. Tell your accomplices to stand aside and fight me."

Ègùn? Ty cast a glance at his godfather. It was a Chinese word, one Ty recognized from his years living with Liang. It meant rogue, scoundrel . . . villain. He wondered if it was an insult on McCrory's part or if it was Liang's Sicaran title.

Liang removed his trench coat and raised his cane, which he split in two, revealing a hidden sword. Beneath his coat, he wore a uniform identical to McCrory's, down to the silver sash. McCrory reached up and removed his mask. His hair and beard had strands of fiery red mixed with white, which were matted by the rain. Heavy wrinkles lined his cheeks and forehead. He was at least Liang's age, if not a few years older.

Is Liang really going to fight McCrory? He had brought Shank, Ty, Ned, and Richie there to defeat McCrory, but he seemed ready to engage in a duel. Ty took a step forward, his boot splashing down into a puddle. Freezing water seeped inside his shoe. The rain had slowed to a drizzle, but it was cold enough to raise gooseflesh. He forced himself to ignore the cold and focus on the confrontation in front of him.

"McCrory!" Ty bellowed.

"Stay out of this, boy." McCrory's hard gaze scrutinized Ty. "You are no match for me. I've had a lifetime to prepare. You are a novice."

"I don't care. You killed my parents!"

"I will correct Ègùn's lies shortly. Let me end him, and I'll explain the truth."

Before Ty could question him further, McCrory charged. Chaos erupted on the rooftop.

* * *

The Crusader burst out of the stairwell, moving to the left so Stonewall could flank him, and stared at the scene unfolding before him. The Red Dog with the .50 caliber pistol and the two thieves from downstairs were firing on Mac Tíre, who was dancing out of the way of bullets and stun blasts. The blue-and-tan jacketed man with the mag-gun was training his weapon on Mac Tíre, waiting for his opportunity to trap the assassin. Vickers and another man, who was wearing an outfit almost identical to Mac Tíre's, stood to the side, each man holding a sword.

"What is going on?" Stonewall said.

"I think McCrory picked the wrong time to find his target. Is that Liang next to Vickers?"

"I think so." Stonewall glanced at him. "Want to get in there?"

Crusader nodded. "I've got Vickers."

He twirled his sword and rushed toward the superhuman thief. Vickers looked up as he approached and raised his own sword. The Crusader leaped when he was five steps away, raising his weapon for an overhead strike. Vickers brought his sword up under the blow. Expecting the move, the Crusader lowered his shield at the last second, blocking the blade and pushing it aside as he landed. He danced around Vickers, spun to face him, and struck the small of his back. His sword phased cleanly through Vickers's body.

The Crusader extended his wrist and fired a stun bead. Vickers rolled aside, avoiding the projectile, and rushed in swinging. The Crusader blocked the blade and pushed it aside with his shield, bringing his sword around for a blow to Vickers' head. Again, the blade passed cleanly through Vickers without touching him.

The thief slashed at the Crusader's abdomen. The vigilante lowered his left arm, catching the blade with his shield. He stepped in and kicked out—and once again, the blow passed through the incorporeal man.

Vickers stabbed, driving his blade toward the Crusader's chest. The Crusader spun to the left and swung downward, aiming for Vickers's elbows. The thief pulled his weapon back quickly, and the aionium sword struck the edge of his blade. Vickers slipped his blade away and slashed inward. The Crusader stepped back, but the edge of Vickers' sword dragged along his midriff. His suit took the blow without a scratch.

"Nice gear," Vickers said. "You can't hit me, and I'm not going to kill you. Why not let me go?"

"I can't do that, Vickers. You've broken the law. You've endangered lives. You've evaded us for too long. It's time to surrender."

The men exchanged a flurry of blows, their swords clanging together over the sounds of the other combatants. Vickers lashed out at the Crusader's neck, and the vigilante ducked under the swipe and jabbed his shield at Vickers's gut. Partially distracted by his own attack, Vickers did not phase in time; and the electrified shield face struck him. He grunted and stepped back.

"Good hit." Vickers lowered his sword. "Come on. All I want is my kid back."

"You should've thought of that before you became a criminal."

"I did it for her!" Vickers shook his head. "It was wrong, but it seemed like the only choice I had at the time."

"There's always another choice."

A series of gunshots split the air. Mac Tíre was still dancing around his foes, trying to get in striking distance. Stonewall had gone for the

Red Dog with the big gun. That left Liang still standing on the sidelines, watching everyone else fight his battles for him.

A sword pommel slammed into the Crusader's forehead. He grimaced and sank to the ground, clutching the wound. Vickers stood over him, shaking his head.

"Sorry. There's too much at stake to stand around talking."

* * *

Shank was distracted.

Ty did not recognize the new vigilante that was drawing the Red Dog's attention, but it didn't matter. Disabling the Crusader gave him enough time to sneak around behind Shank while he fought the armored man. All Lurk had to do was wait for the right moment. He could bury his knife in Shank's back. With one blow, he could avenge Rachel's death and ensure Emi and Joanie's safety. He could focus on Kane McCrory afterward.

He slid a knife from its sheath with his left hand, sparing a glance over his shoulder at the Crusader. The kid was pushing himself to his feet, but the blow to his head had done its job—he was unsteady, wobbling as he struggled to stand.

Shock Jock and G-Storm were putting up a surprisingly effective fight against Mac Tíre. McCrory was quick, and none of Shock Jock's stun bolts had hit home yet. The assassin had to keep moving or risk falling into G-Storm's magnetic field. Liang was still standing where he had been before Mac Tíre had charged. He had lowered his sword and was watching the battle unfold, but his attention was on Mac Tíre, not on Ty.

One of Shank's bullets hit its mark. The armored vigilante grunted and stumbled back, clutching his abdomen. Shank leered at the vigilante.

"New guy on the scene," Shank said. "Bad night to be you."

He pointed his gun at the new vigilante's head. Lurk clutched his knife, ready to hurl it and end Shank's life. His hand spasmed, dropping the blade. He grunted and dropped to his knees. His whole body wracked with convulsions. He looked up to find the Crusader approaching, his arm held out in front of him, trained on Lurk. The vigilante swiveled to face Shank, and a marble-sized bead shot from his gauntlet and exploded around the Red Dog. Shank spasmed and collapsed. The vigilante must have used the same stun shot to disable Ty.

It wasn't over. In moments, the current would leave Lurk's body. He could rejoin the fight and finish off Shank. He pushed himself into a crouch, waiting for his chance.

Mac Tíre continued to weave around Shock Jock's attacks. G-Storm tried to follow him and trap him in a mag-field. Mac Tíre jumped and front-flipped between both men, causing Shock Jock to stop firing, lest he hit G-Storm. As the bolts of electricity stopped, Mac Tíre landed and rammed his sword into G-Storm's gut.

Ty pushed himself to his feet. *Oh, Ned.* His friend was a lot of things—greedy, short-sighted, corrupt—but he did not deserve to go out so brutally. Shock Jock stumbled back, horrified. Mac Tíre advanced on him. He raised his blade for a killing blow, and the Crusader stepped in, blocking the strike with his shield. The other vigilante in blue and gray rushed in behind Shock Jock. With a feral cry, Richie pulled on the concussion gauntlets from Sterling Labs and engaged the vigilante.

Lurk looked around. Shank was still kneeling on the ground, his body trembling from the effects of the shock blast the Crusader had delivered. Liang had backed away closer to the edge of the roof, moving out of the way of the conflict. Lurk staggered forward, looking back and forth between Ned's fallen form and Shank. He had an opportunity. He could strike.

His sword was too far away for him to reach, but he still had two knives left on his belt. Drawing one in each hand, Ty moved on his target.

Ty could end Shank's life and get out with Liang. But what of McCrory? Ty had seen McCrory in action, and he bore some kind of grudge that stretched from Liang to encompass Ty. If McCrory was not satisfied with ending Liang's life, he could come after Ty; and that would endanger Joanie and Emi, too. Shank was a gangster. He had influence in Sojourn City, but that was the extent of his reach. McCrory and the Sicarans were infinitely more dangerous.

Ty halted, frozen with indecision.

What's really best for me? And what's best for Emi?

CHAPTER 48

Jolie squeezed the trigger three times, and the last Red Dog in the lobby dropped. Lowering her gun, Jolie stepped inside. Four officers, led by Sergeant Pulaski, followed, while Paul remained outside with Joanie.

"Where to, Detective?" one officer asked.

Jolie tapped her earbud. "Raina?"

"Last I heard, they were on the rooftop. There's been a lot of chaotic sound, but no word from either Carter or Silas."

"We're on our way." Jolie pointed to the stairwell. "Rooftop."

Pulaski led the team toward the stairs. Jolie followed, her breath heavy as she advanced on the stairwell. *Why am I so winded?* She hadn't moved that much during the shooting, and she hadn't been hit. As she entered the stairwell, she grabbed the railing. Jolie kept one hand tightly around her gun and the other on the rail. She gathered her breath and rushed up the stairs toward the roof.

* * *

The Crusader grunted as he and Mac Tíre exchanged blows. It was the first time he had seen the man's face, and he thought he preferred the featureless mask. Beneath the black visage, Mac Tíre had the look of a cruel and merciless man. He reminded the Crusader of Luca Serban. It was no wonder Monahan had gravitated toward the crime lord. If this was the man who had trained her, Serban had probably reminded her of him, too.

The Crusader struck Mac Tíre's shoulder with the edge of his shield. The older man scowled and pulled back, swinging his sword in an upward diagonal arc. The Crusader jerked his head back, and the blade narrowly passed his chin. The Crusader had dropped his sword when Vickers struck him earlier. Without it, he was at a distinct disadvantage, but he had been too busy stopping Vickers from approaching Stonewall and the Red Dog to pick it up.

"I know why you want Liang, McCrory," the Crusader said. "Let us take him down. He'll get more justice in prison than if you kill him."

"American justice is not Sicaran justice." Mac Tíre shook his head. "Ègùn must die by my blade tonight."

"That's not going to happen. You're going to answer for all the people you've killed."

"Murderers, thieves, drug dealers—their lives are no loss." Mac Tíre shrugged. "Your streets are cleaner now. Had your father been so proactive, boy, perhaps your city would not be in the mess it is."

"They're still people." The Crusader blocked a blow from Mac Tíre's sword. "They have as much right to life and a second chance as you or I do. My father knew that."

"Your bravery is commendable, but you are out of your league. Stand aside so that I may finish my mission. Go home to your family. They are your concern. Liang is not."

Carter's stomach fell at the double confirmation that McCrory was aware of his true identity. He would ask the assassin how he had discovered it once he was behind bars.

The Crusader fired an adhesive bead. Mac Tíre spun aside, and the bead missed him and exploded, covering the still-collapsed Red Dog behind him with the blue-green goo. Mac Tíre lunged at the Crusader, aiming for his throat. The Crusader blocked, and his shield spun out of his grip. He took a step back and dodged as Mac Tíre swung again. For an instant, his body was gripped in panic. His limbs refused to respond, and sweat broke out on his neck, mingling with the frigid rain. Gideon's teachings steadied him. Whether armed or not, the Crusader could still fight.

Mac Tíre swung again; but as the Crusader prepared to move, Ty Vickers stepped in, blocking the sword with two knives. He unleashed a barrage of attacks on Mac Tíre, so fierce that the Crusader was taken aback for a moment. His eyes widened, and he watched as the thief stabbed and slashed with his blades, driving the assassin back on the defensive.

The Crusader scooped up his shield and searched for his sword. Once it was back-in hand, he felt his confidence returning.

"Heads up," Raina said. "Cops are on their way."

"Thank God." The Crusader rushed toward the fray. "I don't know how much longer I could've handled this."

* * *

Blind rage drove Ty, turning his vision red. Somewhere during the fighting, his mask had been torn off, the consequence of a blow that Ty had been too slow to phase through. For all his own skill, he had met his match in Kane McCrory. The assassin was the most skilled fighter Ty had ever faced, surpassing his own father. That he was not only holding his own but pressing back boggled Ty's mind and set him on edge.

His mind acknowledged those doubts, but his body did not respond to them. He lunged and slashed, dodged and blocked in a beautiful, deadly dance with McCrory. His knives set him at a significant disadvantage to McCrory's longer sword, but his superpowers made up for it. He was able to phase through McCrory's blade and get in close to jab and slash with his knives. But no sooner would he do so than McCrory would fall back out of Ty's reach and again unleash a furious attack. Ty was getting tired, but he was set on a single goal—killing McCrory.

There was no way he'd get to Liang or Shank. He had sacrificed that opportunity for the chance to fight McCrory instead. In doing so, he had chosen one vengeance over another. Yet perhaps, he had also given himself and his daughter the best chance for survival. Shank was in handcuffs. McCrory had influence and reach that Ty could not quantify.

Ty was committed, and he was determined to stop Mac Tíre from hurting anyone else. He wouldn't take anyone else's parents or friends.

"Your father taught you well, lad." McCrory sidestepped a stab from Ty. "But you've not been fully trained in the way of the Sicarans. You're angry. Distracted. Your powers should make you unbeatable; yet here you stand, unable to bring an old man down."

"Shut up!"

Ty surged in, cutting toward McCrory's throat; and something heavy slammed into the small of his back. He tucked himself into a somersault and came up in a crouch, spinning to see what had hit him. The Crusader stood between him and McCrory. For a moment, it looked like the vigilante was going to say something. But before he could get the words out, McCrory lunged. The Crusader fell back, barely blocking the onslaught with his shield.

Ty rose and stormed toward the dueling opponents, determined to take down one or both. The Crusader meant well, but he was getting in the way.

He leaped forward and phased through the Crusader, extending his right foot to plant his boot in McCrory's chest. He snapped the foot backward, gutting the Crusader. He rammed the pommel of his knife toward the Crusader's forehead. The vigilante reached up and caught Ty's wrist, shoving it back. Ty spun and nearly met McCrory's blade. He phased as the sword passed through where his arm would've been. He brought his knives up to push the sword aside as it came back. Sparing a quick glance over his shoulder, he phased as the Crusader attacked from behind. The vigilante passed through him and swung his sword at McCrory.

The assassin and the vigilante exchanged a flurry of blows, and the Crusader managed to land a few strikes on McCrory's body with the flat of his blade. Ty was impressed, but that kind of restrained assault wasn't going to be enough to finish the fight. The edge of the Crusader's sword was more than sharp enough to kill McCrory; but the vigilante refused to use it, opting for non-lethal strikes only.

Ty couldn't make the mistake of assuming the vigilante was an ally. But for a few moments, perhaps he could be an ally of convenience.

"Truce?"

The Crusader ground his jaw. "No one dies."

"No promises."

Ty descended on McCrory, his knives flashing forward rapidly. The swordsman parried, locked his blade against one of Ty's knives, and spun it. The knife flew free of Ty's grip. McCrory swung his sword back, aiming for Ty's neck. Ty ducked.

He needed to get the upper hand, and fast. The longer this fight went on, the less likely it would end in his favor.

* * *

The Crusader was relieved by Vickers' sudden choice to team up. Unfortunately, the thief was entirely too intent on murdering McCrory. Carter hoped they could take the assassin down and restrain Vickers before he took the Sicaran's life. That would be easier with police backup on the scene.

"Status on the cops?" he asked.

"Two floors down." That was Jolie's voice. She sounded winded. "Almost there."

Carter watched as Vickers and Mac Tíre exchanged another flurry of blows. Stonewall was grappling with Vickers' last-standing teammate. The man had dropped his shock rifle and now duked it out with a pair of concussion gauntlets that matched Stonewall's. The men's blows collided with powerful *booms*.

"Enough games." Liang swept in like a panther, his sword extended. "Finish him!"

The Crusader blocked Liang's sword. He struck with surprising force for such an old man. Vickers spun abruptly and rammed one of his knives at Liang's breastbone. The Crusader snapped up a kick, knocking Ty's blade aside. Without missing a beat, Vickers returned to his assault on McCrory.

Mac Tíre stepped in and slashed at the Crusader's neck, the blade bouncing off the aionium collar. The Crusader batted the sword aside and slashed at Mac Tíre again.

Vickers phased through the Crusader's body' and as he passed to the other side, the Crusader felt his sword leave his fingertips. He frowned. *What—?*

Vickers stood in front of Mac Tíre with the Crusader's own sword buried pommel-deep in the assassin's chest. Mac Tíre gasped and stumbled back. Vickers released his grip on the sword. Mac Tíre leaned forward, clutched Vickers's shoulders, and whispered something. Vickers shoved him to the ground.

"That's how you use a sword." Vickers faced Liang and twirled his knife. "You're next."

The Crusader stepped forward. "No, he's not. Vickers, that's enough. You have to come in—"

The door to the stairwell burst open, and police officers poured onto the roof. Liang's eyes widened, and he rushed to the stairwell on the opposite side of the building. The Crusader extended his wrist and fired an adhesive bead. The goo cemented Liang's feet to the rooftop.

"Stand down, Vickers." The Crusader took another step forward. "It's over. Make this easier on yourself . . . on your family."

"I want my daughter back!" Tears welled in Vickers' eyes. "I want another chance. I was trying to protect my family."

"Move in," Jolie said.

Liang did not struggle against the goo, but his eyes were locked on Vickers'. "Young fool. In betraying me, you lost your last chance to have her back."

Police officers went to cuff the Red Dog and Vickers's surviving companion, whom Stonewall had finally rendered unconscious. Pulaski circled around to Liang. The Crusader turned his gaze back to Vickers. The thief's eyes were on the Red Dog.

"Please, you have to watch Shank. He'll kill Joanie." Ty clenched his fists. "He should have died."

"Killing won't solve anything, Vickers." The Crusader stared at Mac Tíre's body. In its place, he pictured the man his father had killed. Wyatt had learned that lesson. Maybe Ty still could. "No one had to die here. No one should've died."

"He murdered her." Vickers' gaze was still on the Red Dog, Shank. "My wife. It's his fault. His and Liang's."

"Killing him wouldn't have changed that. Come on, Vickers. Turn yourself in. Make it easier on yourself."

"No. No. If I go to jail, what happens to Emi?"

"Vickers!"

"Protect them. You have to keep them safe!"

The thief vanished, phasing through the rooftop to the floor below. The Crusader clenched his jaw. Jolie rushed forward to his side.

"Where'd he go?" she asked.

Vickers could go anywhere. Despite that, Carter doubted he would immediately flee the city. Everything he knew about the man, everything that had happened on the rooftop, suggested one destination.

"I have a hunch." The Crusader retrieved his sword from McCrory's body and looked at Jolie. "Take care of the rest of them. I'll catch up with Vickers."

CHAPTER 49

The house that formerly belonged to Vickers sat empty. It had remained that way in the weeks since the criminal went on the run. For the first few days, the police had left a watch behind, hoping Vickers might return. When it became apparent that he wouldn't, they had given up on the venture to focus on tracking him.

The Crusader stopped on the street outside the house and watched it. He had no proof that Vickers would visit the house, but something—maybe instinct, maybe something more—told him that he would. It was the man's last connection to his daughter. If he went anywhere in Sojourn City before he fled, Carter suspected it would be the house. He had to be careful not to startle him. Vickers was likely to run as soon as he saw the Crusader. Carter did not want to fight again, but he would be ready for one.

He walked toward the house and reached for the screen door. It was unlocked. He pulled it aside and tested the doorknob. It, too, opened. Carter pushed his way gently inside. The living room was lit only by the streetlights outside the window, by which he could tell that there was no one there. He stepped further into the house. A soft light shone from the hallway to the left. Carter followed it, walking slowly on the shag carpet.

Stifled sobs became audible as Carter approached the door the light shone from. A pang of sympathy tore at his heart. Vickers was a man who had lost everything—his chance at a good career, his family, his wife, his daughter. That night, he had lost his friends, who had either been arrested or killed. He had nothing left.

The room was a nursery—sparsely decorated, fitting with Vickers's lack of income. The few furnishings in the nursery were more expensive than anything else in the house. Vickers stood next to the empty crib in the corner of the room, leaning against the bars and crying softly. Tears stung Carter's eyes. He took another step forward.

Vickers spun. "Really? Even here?"

"I'm so sorry." Carter knelt and placed his sword on the floor. "You've had a hard life. I can't fix that. I can't change the past, no matter how much I wish I could."

"No one can." Vickers clenched his jaw. "But I wasn't trying to. I wanted to make a better future. Until . . . until I heard Shank and my godfather talking, and I realized they killed her. They took my Rachel from me, took her from our daughter. They deserve to be punished for that. I could've done that."

"Killing them wouldn't have made you feel better. It would've destroyed you."

"Oh yeah?"

"You killed McCrory, didn't you? But you're here, crying into a crib. Killing him didn't fix anything, didn't make you stronger. It ripped you up inside."

Carter was more grateful every day that he had chosen the high road when he had dealt with Katrina Monahan. He could have killed the woman during their fight in Chicago. Instead, he had honored what his father eventually came to stand for. Monahan was serving consecutive life sentences in prison. They would be served in a CLOUD detention center going forward, rather than a penitentiary, but the justice of her sentence remained. Ty would never have that satisfaction with McCrory. But was he so different from Wyatt?

"What's done is done. I'm leaving. You can't stop me."

"Vickers, think about your daughter."

"I am thinking about her. If I come with you, I'm looking at hard time in prison. How am I supposed to look out for my baby girl from inside a prison cell, huh? I can't."

"You're not getting her back, man. You'll never find her; and eventually, you'll get caught, and things will be that much worse for you. Come with me, and we'll work out a deal. I've got friends. I can make sure your daughter gets put in a home that will love her and give her everything she deserves. And once you've served your time, maybe we can arrange for you to visit her."

"No! She's my kid. Mine. She needs me."

"What kind of a life are you going to give her? You robbed the federal reserve. The FBI will be on your tail. You really want to try building a life with Emi while you're running from them? *She doesn't deserve that.*"

Ty's eyes widened, and he backed toward the crib. Carter was as surprised by the fire in his own voice as Vickers was. He realized with a start how similarly his own life could have gone after his father's death but for a few changes. If not for his mother, Gideon, and the rest of the Vindicators, Carter could have followed a very similar path to Ty's.

He would do anything for his mom, Ellis, and Rhonda. But he had been set up for success. His dad's example had set him on that path, and Gideon's mentorship and Dean's generosity helped cement it. If Carter had been lonely and broken when his father died, it wouldn't have taken much for him to follow Ty's path. But for a few good people, Carter could have *been* Ty. So maybe this was his chance to pay that forward.

Carter remembered his conversations with Rhonda. She believed Vickers had good motives behind his crimes. He pictured Ty's tearful gaze on the rooftop. *You have to keep them safe!* Those were not the words of a hardened, murderous criminal. Ty was a man desperate for the safety of his family—just like Carter's father had been when he took a life.

So, maybe Vickers didn't need a hunter. Maybe he needed a shepherd.

"Stand down and come with me. If you do, I promise I'll call in every favor I can to make sure your daughter and Joanie are safe."

"How can I trust you?" Vickers asked.

The Crusader reached up and removed his mask. He softened his gaze and held out a hand to Vickers.

"Do you recognize me? I'm Carter—Rhonda's brother."

Vickers blinked but said nothing.

"I promise that Emi will be taken care of. I know what it takes to protect a family—the sacrifices and the challenges. I may not have your life experiences, but I've got my own people to look out for. Trust me, this is the best way." Carter stepped forward. "Come on. Stop running, man. Do the right thing."

Vickers let out a long breath and stared at Carter's hand. Reluctantly, he extended his own hand and clasped Carter's.

CHAPTER 50

Jolie stood in the parking lot outside the federal reserve and watched as the officers around her hauled the surviving Red Dogs, along with Liang and the remaining member of Vickers' crew, off to jail. A coroner was handling the body of Vickers' other friend as well as McCrory. Pulaski stuck close to McCrory's body, no doubt confirming his death so he could wrap up his case. Moments ago, Carter had called and said that he'd convinced Vickers to turn himself in. It was finally over.

An approaching car engine caught Jolie's attention. A familiar Mustang pulled into the parking lot. The vehicle stopped, and Gideon jumped out and rushed to meet her.

"I'm so glad you're okay," Gideon said.

"Same here." Jolie leaned back and smiled up at him. "Did everything go all right on your end?"

Gideon touched a cut on his cheek. "It got a little rough, but Wheaton and his family are safe."

"Good job. You see? Without your powers, you're still a pretty terrific hero."

"Thank you." Gideon kissed her on the top of her head, a gesture that always melted her heart. "What about here?"

"McCrory's dead. Vickers killed him. One of Vickers' teammates died, too, along with a bunch of Red Dogs who ambushed us in the lobby. We took a few hits, but none of the officers were fatally injured. We collared Liang, along with his right-hand man, who goes by Shank, as well as Vickers' surviving accomplices, including his sister-in-law, Joanie. Vickers got away, but the Crusader pursued and convinced him to turn himself in."

Gideon raised his eyebrows. "How'd he do that?"

"Convinced him that it was the best move for his daughter, I guess."

Jolie looked back over the parking lot. Silas, still dressed in his gunmetal-and-blue armor, stood back and watched while the police operated. The officers seemed content to let him remain there. Their attitude toward vigilantes had certainly shifted in the past year.

"Our tech guys found a virus in the reserve's computer system that would've allowed the Red Dogs to steal millions from people's accounts—not to mention their identities. It's a good thing Vickers called this in."

"Yeah." Gideon frowned. "Any idea why he did that?"

"According to what he told the Crusader on the way back here, he thought it was the only way to keep Joanie safe from Shank. It sounds like Shank was the one who killed Vickers' wife, but it was Liang who gave the order."

Gideon whistled. "How cold can you get? Ordering your own daughter-in-law's murder."

"Liang is stone cold, all right."

Jolie wrapped her arm around Gideon's waist. She wondered if she should tell him about the strange fatigue she'd felt as she climbed the stairs. It hadn't abated after they reached the rooftop. She still felt exhausted. But until she knew the cause, she didn't want to worry Gideon. It could wait.

"Why don't you head home?" Jolie asked. "It's going to be awhile—lots of reports and other little details to iron out. I'll be back as soon as I can."

"Okay." Gideon kissed her. "Take care of yourself. Love you."

"Love you, too."

* * *

Carter dropped face-first onto Raina's couch, groaning in exhaustion. He felt a tingling sensation on the back of his head as her fingers gently played with his hair. He smiled, comforted by the simple feeling. After tonight, he needed it. His body ached from the blows he had taken. A nice, long bath sounded like the best thing in the world.

"You did good," Raina said softly.

Carter rolled over to look up at her. "Thanks."

Raina was kneeling next to the couch, her left hand still on the back of his head. Carter thought she had never been more attractive. Maybe it was the tragedy of Rachel Vickers' death hitting him, but he had never been more grateful that Patrick had helped them find each other.

"So . . . Silas, huh?" he asked.

"I pulled him aside after our last meeting in the garage and asked him to support you out in the field. I knew he had the skills. I saw it when he saved my butt from those Red Dogs at the gym."

"The way Silas tells it, you did a pretty good job protecting yourself."

"Well, I helped, but he did most of the work. He told me he had some CLOUD gear he could use to help. I figured you could use it, considering how many guys you were probably going up against."

"I'm glad he was there." Carter grinned. "Stonewall?"

"I came up with it. I mean, his last name is Rockwell; change 'rock' to 'stone' and 'well' to 'wall,' and you've got a pretty epic superhero name, right?" Raina shrugged. "What can I say? I'm an *artiste.*"

Carter laughed. "I like it. Speaking of which, how's your poem coming?"

"It's . . . coming. I should have something readable within a few days."

"Can't wait." Carter sat up. "I should probably head home. I'm beat. But the team should meet in the garage tomorrow night, if possible. Debrief."

"I'll make sure they're all there."

"You're the best."

I love you. The words echoed in Carter's mind. He'd never said them to her before; but at that moment, they almost slipped out. He wanted to tell her at a special time. But knowing that he felt that way made butterflies rush through his gut. He smiled at her. It must have looked incredibly goofy, but he didn't care. He kissed her on the cheek.

"See you tomorrow," she said.

"Yes, you will."

CHAPTER 51

Carter squeezed between Raina and Silas and pushed himself up to sit on the table in the corner of the garage. Gideon and Jolie were there, too. Gideon had a few cuts and bruises on his face. He had told Carter earlier that day about his encounter with McCrory and his apprentices. After Wheaton shot the assassin holding his wife at knifepoint, they had gone into the hallway to deal with the other assassins, only to find that all four of them had vanished. They probably ran back to wherever the Sicarans called home. With McCrory dead, they were either gone for good or—Carter feared—they would be back for vengeance.

For the moment, things had been wrapped up. The Red Dogs' leadership had fallen apart. Liang had been their leader; and Shank, the Red Dog from the rooftop, had been his top lieutenant. Without them, the Red Dogs were floundering. Vickers and his companions were going to jail. Carter suspected the sister-in-law, Joanie, would get out. Apparently, Vickers planned to testify that she had been acting under duress.

"I wanted to thank you all," Carter said. "In my first year of being the Crusader without the Vindicators, this is the first real crisis I've faced. I couldn't have come through it without all of you there to back me up."

Gideon inclined his head. "Anytime. You made your father proud."

Carter nodded. No words would come in response to that. He still felt guilty that McCrory and Vickers' associate had both died, when he had been doing his best to ensure everyone survived the night. His father had always tried to keep everyone alive, but Carter understood that Wyatt had never been the perfect hero, either. What made him special was moving on from his mistakes and becoming better. Carter had saved the majority, and Emi still had her father and aunt, even if they were in jail.

"We all made him proud," Carter finally said. "He always knew you were a hero, Gideon. It wasn't your powers he appreciated. It was your heart. Like him, you saw a city that needed fixing, and you decided to do something about that."

"We're all doing the same thing." Gideon put a hand on Jolie's shoulder. "Together."

Carter glanced at him, at Jolie, at Raina. Finally, he looked at Silas. The older man kept his head down, looking at the tops of his boots. He still felt distant from them after revealing his secret, Carter knew. But as Stonewall, he had more than proven that he was really on their side.

"What do you have for us, Stonewall?"

"The virus Vickers planted in the reserve has been undone. No one's going to be stealing any information."

"And the Brooks is starting to settle down again," Jolie added. "Without the gang war between the Red Dogs and the Tyrants, the streets are a lot safer. The Tyrants are still out there. They'll have to be dealt with at some point." She shivered and pulled her brown leather jacket tighter around her. "Man, it's cold in here."

"Speaking of which," Carter said, "I've been thinking. If we're going to keep meeting like this, we need a more permanent location."

"A new base?" Silas half-smiled. "I think I can do something about that."

* * *

The power-dampening cuffs around his wrists made Ty feel like he was cut off from a part of himself. He had become so used to the sensation of phasing that being unable to feel it was disturbing. It was like having eyes but being unable to open them or having fingers but not feeling anything when they touched something. It was funny. Once, he had hated how his powers felt. Now, he longed for it.

He shuffled down the hallway, escorted by a guard in a gray uniform. He had a visitor—the first one since he had been imprisoned. As he walked, he passed Richie's cell. His old friend gave him a sober nod. Since Ned's death, Richie had been surprisingly reserved. Maybe Richie blamed himself for everything, but Ty didn't—not anymore. Richie was the one who had accrued a gambling debt to the Red Dogs, but it was Liang who was really to blame.

A few cells down, Ty passed Shank. Shank's death would've been far preferable to imprisonment. That way, he wouldn't have been a danger to Joanie or Emi ever again. But at least in prison, there was no way for Shank to get to them. And if he ever tried when he was released . . . Well, he would regret that. Ty would make sure of it.

Before they reached the visiting room, he passed Liang's cell. He wished he could stop and speak to his godfather—to tell him that it was Ty who had alerted the police to the reserve job. He wanted to see the look in Liang's eyes as he realized that Ty was responsible for him being in prison. He wanted the man to realize that Ty knew Liang had ordered Rachel's death and that justice had been served. He also wanted to ask about what McCrory had whispered before his death. *Liang betrayed your father.*

Liang didn't look up as Ty passed.

"Come on," the guard said.

He opened the door to the visiting room. Ty stepped through and approached the booth that the guard inside motioned to. On the other side of the glass sat Carter and Rhonda Jonson. Ty blinked in surprise. He hadn't expected his visitor to be the vigilante who'd brought him in. Carter was an enigma, that was for sure. For all his intensity, his determination, he had . . . grace. And Rhonda . . . *The poor kid must've been scared to death.*

Ty sat down across from them and picked up the phone. Carter smiled sympathetically and picked up his own phone.

"Hey," Carter said. "You doing all right in there? No one's bothering you? Your godfather? Shank?"

"No." Ty stared at the table in front of him and chuckled humorlessly. "If they did, they'd regret it. I may not have powers here, but I'm a better fighter than either one of them. And I already tried to stab Liang once. I think he'll give me a wide berth."

Carter paused. "Yeah."

"So, to what do I owe the pleasure of this visit?"

"I wanted to check in on you. You're a good man. You made some bad choices, but you can come back from that. Turning yourself in was a good start. I have something for you—a Bible. One of the guards is going to deliver it to your cell if you want it."

Ty had never been a man for religion. His father had been pseudo-religious back in Japan, but it had been more rote than anything. Liang held Buddhist beliefs, but Ty had never been invested. He knew little about Christian religion. But if that was the reason Carter could fight criminals and still extend a kind hand to Ty, maybe it was worth looking into.

"No promises I'll convert or anything," Ty said wryly. "But you can have them deliver it, yeah."

"Thanks."

"So, is that it?" He leaned forward. "I was kind of hoping for news about Emi."

Carter smiled at that, and Rhonda perked up, too. "We have good news about that," she said. "There's a family looking to foster her on a semi-permanent basis. They'll take care of her until your sentence is over and you're back on your feet."

"If Joanie is found not guilty, she'll be allowed to visit Emi whenever she wants," Carter added. "And the same goes for you, once you're out. When you have a job and can take care of her, they've agreed that custody will revert to you, provided it's what Emi wants."

Ty felt a lump forming in his throat and tears welling in his eyes. He wished he could raise her himself; but if he couldn't, he was glad to hear that she would be well taken care of and that he and Joanie could still be involved in her life.

"Who is it?" he asked. "Who's the family?"

Carter glanced over his shoulder. "Actually, her foster dad is here with me. I thought you might want to meet him."

A man with skin nearly as dark as Carter's stepped forward. Dressed in dark blue jeans, a plaid shirt, and a leather jacket, he was bald and clean-shaven; and he had a kind look about him, despite an impressive array of tattoos and scars poking out from underneath his clothes. Ty knew at a glance that he was a good man.

"My name's Silas Rockwell. Emi will be taken care of and loved with my family."

Ty swallowed the lump. "Thank you, Silas."

"And if Silas ever needs help taking care of Emi, he's got a babysitter all lined up," Rhonda added.

Ty nodded. "How could I ever repay all of you?"

"Start off by reading that Bible a little bit, okay?" Carter shrugged. "And who knows? Those powers of yours are pretty useful. Maybe one day, I'll have a problem and need a guy who can phase through walls to fix it."

"If you ever do, I'm there."

"Did you ever have a nickname?"

"Yeah." Ty smiled sheepishly. "Called myself Lurk."

"Lurk? Man, we've got to do better than that."

Ty laughed. "I'll think about it."

"We'd better get going. But I'll come back and visit you again, and we can talk about anything you've read in that Bible, if you want."

"I'd like that. Thank you all."

Carter, Silas, and Rhonda each raised a hand to wave goodbye. Ty waved back, watching them as they went. How had he been so lucky to meet such kind people? He certainly didn't deserve it. But he was thankful for it, all the same.

"Time to go, Vickers," the guard said.

The guard escorted Ty back to his cell. As he did, Ty did not spare a glance at his father nor at Shank. Whatever McCrory's cryptic words were about, their meaning would become plain in time.

He looked over at Richie's cell and gave his friend a nod of respect. He settled down in his cell to begin counting the days until he could see his daughter again.

* * *

Gideon whistled happily to himself as he bounded up the steps toward the apartment. In the last few days, he had made several important decisions. First, he quit his job at Sterling Labs. Jolie made enough as a detective that they could get by if he didn't get a job right away. Despite Jolie's urging, he didn't feel that CSI work was right for him. Being a CSI meant he would arrive after a crime had already been committed and lives lost. He had realized after saving Wheaton's family that saving lives was in his DNA, even if superpowers weren't anymore.

Instead, he had applied to be an EMT. It had been too long since he'd used his medical knowledge to save lives, and the emotional scars of killing guerrillas in Venezuela had healed. Provided the application was accepted, Gideon would soon be a first responder.

His last big decision was the one he had come home to surprise Jolie with. He'd taken some of his savings from his career as a surgeon and bought Jolie a new car to replace her junky, old Camry. A brand-new, cobalt blue Camaro sat on the curb next to his Mustang. He couldn't wait to see the look on her face when he brought her outside and handed her the key fob. He broke off his whistling as he unlocked the front door and stepped into the apartment. Jolie wasn't in the living room; but through the bedroom door, he could see that the light was on in the master bathroom.

"Babe!" he called.

"In here!" Jolie replied from the bathroom.

Gideon stepped toward the bedroom to meet her. As he did, she stepped out of the bathroom, meeting him in the middle of the bedroom floor.

"I've got a surprise for you," he said.

"I've, uh, got one for you, too."

"Really?" Gideon furrowed his brow. "Well, come on. Mine's really big. You've got to see!"

"Oh, I bet mine's bigger."

"You think so, huh?" Gideon smirked. "You're on."

Jolie held up her hands. In them, she held a pregnancy test. Gideon's stomach flipped. He blinked rapidly, struggling to process. Was she joking? She hadn't actually *said* the words.

"I'm pregnant."

There they were.

He swallowed. "You win."

* * *

"Heading out early today, sir?" Carter asked.

It was nearly quitting time, but Wheaton usually stayed in his office well after the rest of his employees had gone home for the night. Carter was surprised to see him crossing the lobby at an hour when the sun still hadn't fully set. There was less of a limp in his step. He was, however, favoring his shoulder where Gideon said McCrory had hit him with the throwing star.

"Yes," Wheaton said. "I think it's past time I set aside my work for my family."

Carter smiled. "Sounds good, sir. Is your shoulder okay?"

"It's fine." Wheaton forced a smile. "Strained it . . . "

"Exercising? Say no more, sir."

Wheaton's smile turned genuine, and he nodded to Carter and exited the lobby. Maybe he wasn't as bad as Carter had initially thought. Still a little stuck up, sure, but Dean had chosen him for a reason. Dean had an eye for people. Perhaps with Wehaton, he had made the right call.

Carter clocked out in the security office and made his way down the halls to the back door. Raina said she had something she wanted to show him once he got off. Silas had also called him and said he had a surprise for him. Assuming they were different surprises, he wondered what they could be. He suspected Silas' had something to do with finding a base for Team Crusader. But Raina's . . . Carter wasn't sure. All he knew was he wanted to find a special way to tell her he loved her.

Since she hadn't specified where he had to be for her to show him her surprise, he had asked if she could meet at the walking bridge that ran beneath the main bridge leading from the rest of Sojourn City to the Platform. The walking bridge looked out over the lake; and on an early spring day, it would be the perfect romantic spot to tell her.

He checked his watch. *Right on time.* Raina should be parking on her side of the walking bridge as Carter was pulling up to the Platform-side parking lot. They could meet in the middle; Raina could show him whatever it was; and he could tell her that he loved her. It was a perfect setup.

He crossed the street to the parking garage, found his car, and weaved through the dense traffic of the Platform. The bridge was always congested during rush hour since it was the only route off the Platform. Many people had become so tired of it that they took the maglev to work instead, leaving their cars parked back in the city proper. Carter didn't blame them. He'd done the same more than once. He wished he'd done it today; traffic seemed especially stalled. He drummed his fingers on the steering wheel and tried not to get impatient with the cars in front of him. It wasn't their fault they couldn't go anywhere.

Finally, traffic parted enough for him to make it to the parking lot outside the walking bridge. It was almost completely deserted. Carter wasn't surprised. It was a two-mile walk to the other side of the bridge.

At the halfway point, he glimpsed Raina approaching in the distance. Her face split into a grin when she saw him. Carter picked up his pace and wrapped her in a hug.

"Are you nuts?" Raina asked, chuckling. "My feet are killing me."

"Sorry." Carter smiled ruefully. "I don't know what I was thinking."

"It's all right." Raina reached into her pocket and withdrew a folded piece of paper. "Here. This is what I wanted to show you."

A breeze tugged at the paper, so Carter clutched it tightly as he took it from her. Carefully, deliberately, he unfolded it. Every line of the notebook paper was filled, front and back, with written lines that were uneven and almost random. He realized it was a poem.

"You finished it?"

Raina nodded. "Go ahead. Read it."

Carter held the paper in both hands and read what she had written.

> *He rose amidst our darkest night,*
> *Knowing what we'd need—A hero good and true and strong*
> *Doing a good deed.*
> *He made a choice to fight back fear,*
> *To guard and protect the weak.*
> *He stepped into the darkness of night,*
> *A battle against evil he did seek.*
>
> *Before him stood a sneering devil,*
> *But he stood against it through sheer force.*
> *All the land's mightiest who took oaths to defend their fellow man*
> *Saw the devil, feared him, and turned their course.*

But our shining knight,
Our hero dressed in black,
Took up the cause, rushed the devil,
And went on the attack.

The devil laughed and ran right back,
Gathering all his might,
Prepared to meet this lonesome hero
And crush him in a fight.

But our hero soon discovered
That he was not alone;
For as the devil descended,
From the darkness, a new light shone.

Beside the mighty hero was
An angel, wreathed in white,
Who came to aid the hero
And shielded him in light.

Now the hero and the angel,
Joined as comrades in arms,
Ran together at the devil,
And sounded the alarm.

From across the land, the people saw
The hero and angel's valor;
They took up arms and joined the fight
In the city's darkest hour.

Now the devil met the comrades
In darkest combat fierce.
And as the blows began to fall,
The hero's heart the devil pierced.

The angel cried in horror.
And with a blaze of light,
he destroyed the devil and his imps,
Sent them back into the night.

But for our hero,
The victory came too late;
The blow the devil dealt him
Had already sealed his fate.

But as his light began to fade,
He opened his mouth to speak.
A bold declaration he had to make
As his heartbeat grew too weak.

"My Son," the hero said,
"Can now take up my banner."
For his son was like him in every way,
Down to his very manner.

As the hero's life slipped away,
The son, with tears in his eyes,
Knelt to take the hero's mantle
And beside the angel did rise.

Now, though the hero has fallen,
The son has taken his place.
And when the devil tries to return,
A new hero he must face.

And as this hero stands in the gap
To beat back every invader,
The people of the land look to him and say,
"There is our Crusader."

Carter blinked back tears as he finished the poem, afraid that one of them would drip down onto the sheet and ruin it. He looked up at Raina and smiled behind a sob. This was the most beautiful tribute to his father he could've ever asked for. He had no idea she had been working on something like it. He stepped forward and pulled her into a fierce hug, letting the tears stream down his face, since the precious poem was safely tucked behind her back.

"It's beautiful," he whispered. "I love you, Raina."

She sobbed, too. "I love you, Carter."

* * *

The emotional rollercoaster of the bridge encounter still working its way through Carter's mind, he struggled to keep a straight face as he stepped into Pop's Gym. Raina walked in beside him, and he saw the same glow on her face that he felt on his.

Silas appeared from a doorway across the room, dressed in tan pants and a light blue Henley shirt—not the look of a man who'd been working out in the heat. He motioned for Carter and Raina to join him. Carter circled around the boxing ring in the center of the room and approached Silas.

"You said you had a surprise?" Carter asked.

"I do." Silas grinned. "But we've got to wait for the others to get here."

"The others?"

Silas nodded. "We're all part of Team Crusader."

The swinging doors to the gym opened, and Gideon and Jolie entered. Carter grinned as they approached. Gideon wrapped an arm around Carter's shoulder and hugged him. Carter hugged him back and stepped over to hug Jolie while Raina took his place hugging Gideon.

"How are you guys?" Carter asked.

"We're good. Really, really good. But today isn't about us." Gideon grinned. "Silas, what do you have for us?"

Silas gestured to the doorway behind him. The group filed through into a stairwell that descended below the gym. They took the stairs one at a time, Silas leading and Carter following closely behind him. The stairs led into complete darkness, it seemed. Carter could barely see the back of Silas' head in front of him.

"Pop's Gym was going out of business," Silas said. "I didn't want to see it die, so I arranged for CLOUD to buy it. I own the gym, although I'll be keeping the name. It has a certain ring to it. Since it's my property, I'm free to do whatever renovations I want. For example, to upgrade a basement that's never been used except for storage."

They reached the bottom of the stairs. Raina bumped into Carter's back and murmured an apology. Silas disappeared for a moment, ducking into the shadows. The basement's lights flickered on.

Carter gasped.

The center of the room was occupied by a wide training mat, larger than the one he and Gideon sparred on in the garage. To one side of the mat was a desk with a computer and a police scanner and to the other, a pair of mannequins—one dressed in the Crusader suit and the other in Silas' Stonewall suit. Set slightly behind them and encased in a glass box was a third mannequin, this one dressed in Gideon's original Seraph suit. Next to the mannequin was a rack containing Carter's sword, shield, and staff, along with practice swords, a few truncheons, and a variety of other hand-to-hand weapons. On the far side of the room was a ramp leading up to a garage door. Next to the garage door sat a pair of sleek, black motorcycles.

"Silas . . ." Carter stammered.

"This is incredible!" Raina exclaimed.

Gideon let out a low whistle. "I thought my lair was nice when I was Seraph, but *this* is a headquarters."

"It also has a kitchen." Silas pointed to his right, on the opposite side of the room from the crime-fighting equipment. "Long nights fighting crime can make anyone hungry. And in case of emergency, there's also a cot that can be used as either a bed or a surgical table. And we're fully stocked with medical equipment."

"Dean would be jealous," Gideon said. "This is almost as top-grade as the Vindicators' tower base."

"Yeah, it is." Carter grinned. "Silas . . . thanks."

"Anything for the team. From here, Team Crusader can make a real difference."

Carter looked up at the ceiling and imagined Wyatt watching them from Heaven. His dad would be overwhelmed by everything his legacy had become.

Carter walked toward his suit. "All right, team. Let's do it."

EPILOGUE

Failure was seldom tolerated among the Sicarans. Failure was a teacher—perhaps the best teacher. But it was a teacher only for novices and apprentices. By the time one had become a full member of the order, they were expected to have learned all the lessons failure could teach. If they had not, they were clearly below average.

Thankfully, Mac Tíre's failure had been repaid by his own death. Had he survived, the other Sicarans surely would've ended his life, regardless. Despite that, his failure had revealed their existence to a number of people. However small that number might be, it was outrageous.

Roland Demirci, Mac Tíre's chief apprentice, knelt before the Elite of the order. They would decide whether the mission's failure was the fault of Roland or his master. Either way, he was prepared to accept his lot.

"Rise, Keskin," said one of the Elite.

Roland stood at the sound of his Sicaran name.

Another leaned toward him. "Although Ègùn lives, that failure resides with Mac Tíre. His zeal for eliminating his old friend clouded his judgment. Still, Ègùn sits in prison. He can no longer be a tool for Charybdis."

"Because of this, you are absolved of failure," the first Elite said. "In fact, it is impressive that you managed to stand against Gideon

Turner in combat at all. We believe you are ready to take the next step in becoming a member of the Sicarans. You have proven yourself."

Roland felt his pulse pounding in his throat. *Finally.*

"The son of Swift Star, the boy with the ability to walk through walls," one of the female Elite said. "Recruiting him should have been Mac Tíre's true mission. It has long been foretold that one of the Watanabe family would be the key to ending Charybdis. This is why Ègùn betrayed and murdered his longtime friend and stole away with Taro."

"Yes." The leader of the Elite, sashed in red, leaned forward. "Swift Star's son showed how to blend superpowers with our teachings. The world is changing. Superhumans are on the rise, as it was foretold. Charybdis will use this."

"Your task," the second Elite said, "is to find us a superhuman. One we can mold in our ways. If the Sicarans are to continue our mandate in this new world, we must have a champion. If the legends were wrong and Taro Watanabe is not to be that champion, we must find a replacement."

Roland nodded. "I understand."

"Seek out untrained superhumans. Recruit them. Train them to become members of our order."

"It will be done."

"Then go." The original speaker waved his hand. "You have your task. Do not disappoint us as your master did, Keskin."

"I will not."

Roland marched from the chamber with a new confidence. He would pursue this mission with every ounce of his being. He would prove his worth to the Elite. And one day, he prayed his mission would bring him back in contact with Gideon Turner. And when it did, he would not fail.

SPEEDSTER'S SPARK PREVIEW

It was strange that the most freedom Ty Vickers had known in his life was found behind prison bars.

Since childhood, Ty's life had been in turmoil. When his parents died and he was adopted by his godfather, Chin Liang, Ty had felt like a prisoner. Liang was a cruel taskmaster determined to turn Ty into a warrior. Although Ty's real father, Shiro Watanabe, had trained him with a disciplined regiment, he had been a kinder teacher . . . gentler.

When he had turned eighteen, Ty—under the adopted name Tao Liang—could not get out from under his godfather's roof quickly enough. He had set out on his own, met a girl named Rachel Sellers, and applied to the police academy, using his birth name, Taro Watanabe. After he and Rachel married, they'd had a daughter named Emi.

But things had turned sour when Ty's godfather was outed as a criminal. Ty had left the police academy in shame and changed his name from Taro Watanabe to Ty Vickers. Shortly thereafter, his godfather was believed dead in Luca Serban's Uprising.

For a while, Ty's life had been difficult but happy—until Rachel died. Devastated and unable to care for his precious Emi alone, Ty had turned to a life of crime. Joined by Rachel's sister Joanie and his friends Ned and Richie, Ty had become a criminal mastermind, using the superpowers granted to him in a monster attack earlier that year.

The string of events that followed led to Ned's death, Liang's reemergence into the public eye, and a battle with an assassin called Mac Tíre—The Wolf. Liang insisted that Mac Tíre had killed Ty's birth parents, but Ty had learned that Liang was responsible for Rachel's death. Mac Tíre had claimed with his dying breath that it was Liang who had betrayed Ty's parents.

Ty had been determined to kill his godfather but was forced to flee the scene, thanks to the vigilantes known as the Crusader and Stonewall. It was the Crusader who had convinced Ty to turn himself over to the authorities in the hope that he could be released one day and eventually have a relationship with Emi. In a last act of kindness, the Crusader left Ty a Bible that he should read while in his cell.

Although there was much about the Bible Ty did not understand, he was doing his best to read it. The Crusader—Carter Jonson—had done all right by him. He had ensured that Emi was put in a good home with a man named Silas Rockwell, and he had delivered word to Ty that Joanie was not facing prison time. The least Ty could do was skim the small, leather book.

The words offered comfort. But Ty's sense of freedom came not just from the Bible but from knowing that his godfather was in prison and could not lay a finger on Emi. Ty was not bound to secret identities or hiding from the police anymore. And though that meant he faced years in prison, he was willing to accept that. When he finally got out, he would be truly free.

Free of everything except Mac Tíre's ominous words: *Let me end Liang, boy, and then I'll explain the truth.*

What truth had Kane McCrory wished to impart on Ty? Was it merely about Liang's involvement in the Watanabes' death, or was there something more? Ty would never know now. He had killed McCrory to avenge Ned's death. That action would stay with him for the rest of his life, he knew, but those haunting words would stick with him even more closely. What was the truth about this mysterious organization, the Sicarans, and their bitter rivals, Charybdis, that the assassin felt compelled to share with Ty?

It would be just as well if he never knew. Once he served his time in prison, got out, and had his daughter back, he would be content.

The outer wall of Ty's cell exploded inward. Ty cried out as he slammed into the unforgiving steel bars and slumped to the floor. A sharp ringing filled his ears. Dust and debris were everywhere. He coughed and struggled to sit up. His head spun, filled with static, as he struggled to figure out what was happening. He caught sight of a small, black shape on the floor and reached instinctively for it. He snagged the Bible from the floor and tucked it beneath his prison uniform.

A quartet of dark-clad men stormed into his cell with automatic rifles at their shoulders. The leader of the group stepped up to Ty and knelt next to him.

"Taro Watanabe?"

Ty furrowed his brow. "I'm Ty Vickers."

"We know who you are." The leader gestured, and two of his men grabbed Ty by the shoulders. "You're coming with us."

"What? No." Ty struggled against their grip. "I'm not—"

A fist cannoned into his face; and then, Ty's world went black.

For more information about
Jake Tyson
&
Phantom's Blade

please visit:

www.creatingforcreator.wordpress.com
www.facebook.com/jaketysonauthor96

For more information about
AMBASSADOR INTERNATIONAL
please visit:

www.ambassador-international.com
@AmbassadorIntl
www.facebook.com/AmbassadorIntl

*If you enjoyed this book, please consider leaving us a review on
Amazon, Goodreads, or our website.*

Elaine Smith is content with her life as a widow in the small, coastal town of Sabal Palms. She enjoys her time with friends, and she enjoys writing stories and devotionals, despite the advice of her friends. When a southern squall hits the coast, Elaine's abandoned writings start showing up in the most mysterious places. Can God actually use Elaine's trash to become someone else's treasure? Is there more to her writings than she even realizes?

After Catherine Reed's husband dies, she moves back home in order to accept a new position as the teacher for the town's one-room schoolhouse. Samuel Harris has suffered his own loss and guilt has burdened him ever since. When his old flame comes back to town, he wonders if they can find healing together . . .

King Solomon is well-known as a wise man and the wealthiest king to have ever lived. But with great power often comes great corruption, and Solomon was no exception—including his collection of wives and concubines. But who were these women? What was life like for them in Solomon's harem? S.A. Jewell dives into a deeper part of Solomon's kingdom and shows how God is always faithful, even when we may doubt His plan.